# FORTY THIEVES

## Also by Thomas Perry

# FORTY THIEVES

## Thomas Perry

The Mysterious Press
*New York*

First Grove Atlantic hardcover edition: January 2016

First Grove Atlantic paperback edition: January 2017

*Published simultaneously in Canada*
*Printed in the United States of America*

FIRST EDITION

ISBN 978-0-8021-2638-2
eISBN 978-0-8021-9064-2

The Mysterious Press
an imprint of Grove Atlantic
154 West 14th Street
New York, NY 10011

groveatlantic.com

17  18  19  20    10  9  8  7  6  5  4  3  2  1

For my wife, Jo

# 1

The man floated in darkness, the water buoying him and washing him along the concrete channel, slowly at first, but then steadily increasing his speed as hours passed and the heavy spring rain splashed on the pavement a few feet above and flowed into the storm drains to augment the current. From time to time the growing torrent of water bumped him against the concrete side of the channel, or scraped him along it for a moment. But the force of the tons of water flowing downstream was too strong to let him remain anywhere for long. And then it wasn't.

It was after midnight when Bill Carmody stopped his white DPW truck two hundred feet from the corner and stared through his rain-streaked windshield at the small lake that was forming in the intersection ahead. The pavements around here were all crowned so the rainwater ran off to the curbside and flowed along the gutters to the storm drains.

It had been raining relentlessly for two days, and now the third was beginning the same way. The quantity of rainwater that was streaming down into the valleys was unusual. Southern California didn't often get this kind of storm. It had been a wet winter for once, and this storm was the biggest of the season. He tugged his cap down on his head, put the collar of his yellow slicker up, and stepped out of the truck. He sloshed to the back of the truck bed, opened the built-in tool chest, and took out a rake and a wire basket. This wasn't, strictly speaking, a supervisor's job, but if they had wanted a man who would stand around when he saw a problem he could solve, then they wouldn't have hired Carmody.

He splashed along the street into deeper and deeper water toward the intersection. There was the glare of a set of headlights, and then he saw an SUV barreling along on the cross street. Its tires threw spray fifteen feet to either side like a speedboat, and formed little rooster tails behind them. The water was up to the hubcaps, so he could tell the depth was at least ten inches in the middle of the street. He waved at the driver to make him slow down a little, but either the driver didn't see him or didn't care.

It was too late to avoid the splash, so Carmody turned his back and let the water hit the back of his slicker and run off him.

The wind was a steady fifteen miles an hour, and so as he reached the corner the raindrops angled into his face. He tugged the brim of his hat farther down and used his rake to pull the debris from the grating that was set into the side of the curb. He could feel that it wasn't working. He had expected to feel a current. He felt leaves and twigs, but the water was as still as soup. He walked to the one across the street, and then to the next and the next. He went back to the truck and got his crowbar and flashlight, then returned to the first drain and stepped up on the concrete slab set into the lawn above it. He pried up the manhole cover. The debris trap was full of water. He dragged his rake along the inner grill, and found nothing blocking it. Instead, the water was welling up out of the manhole cover and running into the street.

He carried his basket, rake, and crowbar back to the truck, got inside, took out his cell phone, and pressed the call button.

"Department of Public Works."

"This is Carmody. There's a complete storm sewer blockage at the intersection of Interlaken and Grimes in North Hollywood. The water is only about a foot deep now, but it's rising. Water is welling out of the upstream drains."

"How do you want to handle it, Bill?"

"I checked the debris traps, so all we can do is open up the street and see what's blocking the main sewer. We'll need a jackhammer and a backhoe to start with."

"Starting when?"

"We can either do it now, or we can wait until the water gets high enough to flow into somebody's house."

An hour later, the backhoe lifted its latest load of dripping mud and broken chunks of concrete from the narrow trench it had dug, turned, and dumped it on the pile it had built a few feet away. As the operator turned the machine to swing its arm back to sink its scoop again, Carmody gave a shrill whistle and waved both arms over his head.

"Hold it a minute," he called. "Let us take a look."

He and two of his men waded close to the spot where the backhoe had opened the pavement, and used their shovels to scrape away a few chunks to expose a mound of weeds, twigs, and leaves. They pried and tugged some of the foliage out of the hole, lifted armloads of it, waded to the truck, and threw it into the bed.

The growling engine of the backhoe stopped, and there was a sudden silence. Carmody turned to look. The equipment operator stood in front of his seat and stared down the cantilever arm of his backhoe into the hole. He pointed. "Jesus, a body! It's a man!"

Officer Stearns stepped closer to the human form lying on the wet pavement. He was always affected. It was hardly ever a hundred-year-old guy who had been happy and prosperous and had his spirit depart gently, and not unexpectedly. Instead, there was always a story of loss and tragedy waiting to have the actual details filled in later, but clear enough from the start. He looked more closely. This one was an African American male who appeared to be in his early forties, wearing a sport coat and a nice pair of pants. His shoes weren't with him, but that didn't mean anything because they often came off dead men who were violently set into motion.

The motion was the odd part. The Department of Public Works had just pulled the man out of a blocked storm sewer in the center of a pile of leaves, branches, and weeds about the size of a bale of hay. According to them there was no telling how he had gotten in there, or how far he might have traveled in the stream of storm runoff before he'd come to this snag.

Stearns stayed just inside the yellow police tape and watched the medical examiner's people and the crime scene people as dawn approached. The curious pedestrians would not show up until the rain stopped. Stearns thought about the victim. The man's skin was a medium brown, and smooth. He was a healthy weight and had a good haircut. If there were marks on him, they weren't visible to Stearns right now, but that meant nothing either. The medical examiner would be all over him in a few hours, looking at every centimeter of him, including his internal organs. Stearns watched as the coroner's crew bagged the body and then lifted it onto the gurney and loaded it into the coroner's ambulance.

It was not easy to tell what had happened to this man, but Stearns was willing to make a couple of guesses. He was not a suicide. Somebody might overdose or take poison, but he wouldn't then put himself into a storm sewer to float downstream under the street until he became a blockage. But that was all Stearns could guess with any confidence. Unless this turned out to be one of those cases where the guy's enemy had sworn in front of the crowd at Dodger Stadium that he was going to kill this man, or his wife had taken out a five-million-dollar insurance policy on him last week, the homicide detectives would have to do some work and get lucky to find out how he had ended up here.

When the coroner's people closed the rear door of their van Stearns was relieved. He didn't like standing around in the presence of a body. He supposed that what he really hated were the waste and the sadness—the obvious disparity between a living, thinking man and the forlorn remnant in the pile of brush the workmen had dragged out of the drain.

The forensics people worked to untangle the mound of plants and trash that had been trapped with the man. As each piece was freed, they examined it and then set it on a tarp under an awning they'd set up a few feet off. Now and then a technician would produce a plastic bag and put something inside. Stearns saw no moments of excitement, certainly no elation, no signal that anybody thought anything was worth showing to a colleague. Maybe they were picking up vegetation because they wanted typical examples of the plants along this man's route. Maybe they were just as lost as he was and it was the only thing they could do.

A year and one day later, Professor Daniel Millikan glanced out the tall window of the lecture hall to verify that the rain still had not stopped, and then looked out over his class of serious-faced first-year graduate students. He was coming to the end of his lecture, and he decided that he was in no hurry to go out there into the wet world.

He had been visiting professor at the Luskin School of Public Affairs at UCLA for three years now—a long visit. The other members of the criminal justice group—there were only five of them in a large department—were academics. Dan Millikan was an old cop. In appearance he wasn't very different from the other male professors. He was not large, a trim, erect five foot nine and in his fifties with short, graying hair. He habitually wore gray or dark blue sport coats and light blue shirts with a subdued necktie.

He had done his share of research and written enough papers to get him invited to speak at conferences regularly, but his university work was a footnote. His real career had been the twenty-five years he had spent with mean drunks, small-time thieves, drug dealers, and gang shooters. He had learned how quickly a man's mind could focus when he was forced to wrestle a violent suspect to the ground. He had learned to see a lie coming before his suspect had phrased it—sometimes before the suspect had even seen the need to make something up to fill that part of his story. Millikan had learned about forensics as each step of the science was invented, perfected, and became police practice. He had spent his final ten years in homicide, where he became expert in the terrible things people did to each other. After twenty-five years he applied for his pension and began his application to graduate school on the same day.

Millikan was at the front of the room, standing straight, no longer behind the podium, because the final few minutes of his class didn't require notes or references. He had already covered the lecture on the origins and evolution of the search and seizure laws. Now was the moment when he let his students ask questions about anything they wished. He nodded at a male student in the second row. The name came back to him. "Mr. Terrano?"

"When you're searching a home of a homicide victim who is lying on the floor, what is the first thing you're looking for?"

"A place to step."

There was a small wave of laughter, but Millikan rolled over it.

"There's often blood and other organic matter, of course. Your first concern is to be sure you don't contaminate the scene. You have a single chance to protect it and be sure nothing there is lost or damaged, and nothing new is introduced. We live on a planet where it's not possible to move through a space without bringing with us a trail of particles and compounds. The killer has left something of himself here, and taken with him particles that he got here. But you have to be aware that you'll do the same."

"And the second thing to look for?"

"Nothing."

A dozen hands thrust up, but he ignored them for the moment. "You don't look for anything. For a few minutes, you just stand still and look. You don't start sorting through your theories about the scene, or the case, or anything else. You make your eyes move to the floors, the walls, the ceiling, the windows, and everything else you can see. You pay attention to what you can hear and smell. Now, I'm assuming this isn't a case in which there are twenty witnesses around who have already said, 'We saw her husband shoot her.'"

"No, sir. I was thinking of the other kind of case."

"Right. Well, once you've given yourself time to look at every inch of the place, you move, cautiously and sparingly, focusing on details. Your attention will be drawn to the body of the victim and the area around it, and you'll find that your mind notices things that start to tell a story."

A woman to his left said, "Cause of death?"

"That sort of thing, of course. But here's a tip. Most murders are first murders. Amateurs never seem to have any trouble getting to the point where the victim is lying dead on the floor. The crime is called 'premeditated' because he came to the house to kill the victim. But the crime doesn't fit the commonsense meaning of the word. Not much meditation went into it ahead of time. Most murderers seem to be able to think ahead only to the point when they've killed their enemy, but they often seem to have been incapable of thinking past that."

Another young man near the front said, "Why not?"

"They killed out of hatred, jealousy, greed, fear, envy. Then, suddenly, they're standing in a room with a body. Half the time they haven't decided what they were going to do with it. So here they stand, and they have to act quickly.

Some try to stage the scene to look like a suicide or a robbery. Others try to wrap the body up in a tarp, a blanket, or a bag, and move it to a car, and then come back and clean up. Anything they do will show, and it will expose them to additional chances of being seen, to contaminate their own clothes, cars, and so on."

"What's different about a professional?"

"He's killed people before. He knows a body contains about five quarts of blood, and that it doesn't clean up well, so he doesn't try. He knows in advance that he'll need an alibi, a way of getting out unseen, a place to get rid of the weapon, a way to get far away before the body is found. And he's left nothing at the scene that can lead to him—objects, fingerprints, or DNA."

"How do you catch a person like that?"

"Follow the leads you have, and hope your luck is better than his. If he never gets unlucky, then you don't catch him."

Far off, the bells of Powell Library chimed. "Remember to read chapters seventeen through twenty in Rosenberg and work on your paper topics. See you on Friday." He stepped past the podium, picked up the file folder that held notes for his lecture, and kept going out the door.

Millikan walked down the crowded hallway, turning his shoulders to the side now and then to step between streams of young people coming out of their last classrooms or heading toward the next. When he got into his office, he inserted his file into the cabinet drawer in front of the last lecture and pushed it closed just as he heard the knock.

His office hours didn't start for an hour and a half, and the times were on his printed syllabus, on its online version, and posted beside the office door. Whoever this was probably didn't have much of a future as a detective. He stepped to the door and opened it.

The man standing in the hallway was about six foot three and slim. He wore a dark gray suit that fit him perfectly, and a tie with a dark blue pattern with small round designs that Millikan couldn't identify without his reading glasses. The man smiled and held out his hand. "Professor Millikan, I'm David Hemphill."

Millikan shook the hand. There was nothing about Hemphill's grip that revealed flaws. It was firm and friendly, a single shake and release.

Hemphill said, "I'm sorry to show up unannounced. I just wondered if you could spare a moment for a question."

"Come in." Millikan pointed to one of the three leather chairs facing his desk.

"Thank you," Hemphill said, and sat. "I saw that you have office hours in a while. You're probably hoping to get to lunch, so I'll be quick. I need a referral from an expert, and I've been told by three sources that you're the one to ask."

"Go on."

"This is about a murder. It's been just over a year since it happened. The police investigated immediately and for a long time afterward. But now they've frankly admitted that their progress has stalled. They haven't found a new lead in several months. They have no open avenues left to pursue."

"I'm sorry," said Millikan. "I'm not the one to help you. I've been retired from the police force for years. I teach now, and my academic responsibilities keep me very busy."

"I understand," said Hemphill. "I've been warned that you wouldn't consider getting involved in a case. But I wonder if you could do me the favor of giving me the name of someone else."

Millikan didn't permit his face to reveal anything, but he felt the urge to know more. "Was the victim a friend of yours?"

"No," Hemphill said. "I never met him. We both worked for the same company, Intercelleron, but in different capacities. His name was James Ballantine. This is not personal. I'm acting on the orders of the board of directors. Because he was one of our own, they've taken an interest from the beginning. Now they'd like to continue the investigation."

"Ballantine. The name is familiar, but I can't quite place—"

"He was the man who was found in a storm drain during the big rainstorm last spring."

"Of course," said Millikan. He remembered the case from the newspaper accounts. "I read about it at the time." He paused, but asked the question anyway. "Where does the victim's family stand?"

"The board decided that it should act on the wife's behalf, but confidentially and without involving her at this stage. She has two children, whom she's raising alone. The company didn't think it was fair to involve her in this."

Millikan nodded. "You're doing the right thing, sort of."

"Sort of?"

"In not getting her involved in an expensive investigation or giving her false hopes."

"I don't know if they are false. Are they?"

"The Los Angeles Police Department has more than its share of murders, which is why it also has some of the best homicide detectives in the world. An independent murder investigation is fine. But ultimately, the case belongs to

LAPD homicide. They're the only ones who can compel witnesses, or make an arrest. They have sole possession of any physical evidence that exists, any crime scene photographs and notes, and so on. To be honest, they're good at everything except sharing."

"I can see why you feel a private investigation is an unlikely solution."

"And I can see you're still intending to try it," said Millikan.

"It's not my choice," said Hemphill. "The board has decided, and set aside the funding, and so on."

"What am I missing? You said it's not personal. Are they expecting a lawsuit? Is there something he was responsible for that's disappeared?"

"I honestly don't know," Hemphill said. "And I wouldn't be too surprised if they didn't know either. I think they're trying to do the right thing, but none of them really knows how. I think that the only thing they're sure of is that they shouldn't just let it go." Millikan was silent for a moment.

Hemphill said, "I know I've used up more of your time than I should have. If you could just give me a recommendation— a name will do—I promise not to bother you further."

"All right," said Millikan. "I'll tell you what the other people you consulted should have. There are about a dozen honest agencies with competent staffs, experienced and well trained. They'll do the footwork, and so on. For your money you'll get a very slick, attractively printed report that proves they've done their job and looked under all the rocks. Or you can skip that and go to the final step."

"The final step?"

"Hire the agency where cases like this sometimes get solved—the cases where the trail is cold and time has passed and none of the evidence has ever added up to anything. Those cases are their specialty. They're a last chance— sometimes to find out what happened to a victim, and sometimes to set somebody free. They're a couple of old cops like me."

"What's this agency called?"

"Abels. If you're going to do this, that's the kind of help you want."

Hemphill took a small black notebook out of his coat pocket, and a silver pen. He wrote "Abel's."

Millikan saw it. "Without the apostrophe. The name means more than one Abel."

# 2

The prime moment of a night at the Galaxy Club was a sweet stretch that began after 1:00 a.m., but before the bartender started taking last-call orders. This bartender was an attractive woman about fifty years old, with sharp, alert blue eyes, and hair that looked as though it might be something lighter and wilder than platinum blond. It was actually natural gray. She was wearing a pullover top and jeans that made her look much younger from a distance. She had a strong, athletic body but graceful hands with manicured nails. Her gray hair hung behind her in a long, low ponytail, so it swung a little when she moved.

At one o'clock people were still arriving from late suppers, shows, and other bars where they shouldn't have wasted their time. As they arrived, the bartender glided along the bar listening to orders, taking money, bestowing garnished glasses, wiping the mirror-shiny wooden surface, and focusing her piercing blue eyes on the next customer. "What can I get for you?"

The wise customer would reply quickly, knowing from the energy of the place that there would be a brief chance to order, and a long wait before the next chance. The bartender would listen and then nod and begin to make the drink, or she would wait then say, "I'll be back." As she stepped away along the bar, the customer would have to resign himself to waiting for her next circuit.

At the far end of the bar was a broad-shouldered man wearing a gray sport coat and a crisp white shirt. He seemed to be in his fifties, out alone, watching the stream of people coming and going at the Galaxy, but without a great deal of interest in any one of them. He drank steadily from a narrow chilled glass with a slice of lime and clear bubbly liquid.

Now and then customers might speculate about him as they waited for a turn at the bar. He was only about six feet tall, but he gave the impression that there was much more to him than that—something solid and heavy. Some professional football players had that quality, but a person could stare at this man all evening without recognizing his face. He couldn't be working at the Galaxy, because he was drinking continually, and that meant he couldn't be a cop either. He was about the age and description of the sort of man who came to the Galaxy to look for much younger women who liked money. But there were plenty of those women here tonight, and he barely glanced at any of them. He wasn't friendly or hostile or shy or drunk. He was just there, not a permanent fixture but in no hurry.

At one thirty, his eyes flicked to the bartender and stayed there until she happened to see him in the mirror behind the bar when she turned to reach for a vodka bottle.

She didn't hesitate or change her expression, but as she pivoted toward the bar to get the glass and pour, she let her eyes pass across the man at the end of the bar. After a half second she looked in the direction of the person he was looking at and then gave her customer his drink and took his money.

The man who had just entered the bar was about thirty-five to forty years old. He wore a pair of yellow-brown glasses with lenses just dark enough to keep his eyes half-hidden from view, and a black sport coat and jeans. When he had come three steps inside, two younger men came in after him and remained behind his shoulders, scanning the crowd intently. He looked across a stretch of floor at a table where there were four young women. These four could be seen at the Galaxy most nights waiting to find somebody who could do something for their careers.

They had seen him, probably, before he had pushed open the door. They all stood and hurried over to him, impersonating four naïve girls who were honestly smitten by his fortuitous arrival, because it let them strike poses and utter noises that would make people notice them. He gave them each a quick hug and walked with them to their table. Their smiles were sincere, because he was Alex Rinosa, the music producer. He had money, drugs, and the ability to walk up to doors that were closed to most people, enter, and bring anyone in with him.

The two bodyguards took extra chairs from a couple of nearby tables, and the group launched into an overlapping stream of banter, forced laughter, and nervous chatter. After a minute, Rinosa turned toward the bar wondering why the waiter hadn't come, but he didn't see one. He told his two bodyguards to go up and get three bottles of Cristal and some glasses.

The pair walked to the bar, stood there, and pulled from their pockets some hundred-dollar bills to make it clear that they should receive prompt attention. They had to wait their turn while the bartender worked her way to them.

When she reached their section of the bar, one of them said, "Bring us three bottles of Cristal and seven glasses. Open a tab."

"Can't open a tab after one thirty, Cristal is seven hundred a bottle here, and there's no waiter right now. You'll have to carry it yourselves."

"For twenty-one hundred? Are you a—"

"Careful," she said. Her eyes were metallic and steady. "If I think you're drunk I can't serve you."

The other man smiled. "Yes, ma'am." He counted the hundred-dollar bills out on the bar. She took them to the cash register, set up a tray of seven champagne flutes, and knelt to take three bottles out of a small refrigerator under the bar.

The two men walked off with their drinks, and she resumed her rounds, starting with the man at the end of the bar.

"Sounded good," he said.

"Thank you," she replied. "I like to set a mood." She put a new glass of ice on the bar in front of him, held it under a spigot to fill it with tonic, quickly lifted a gin bottle over it, but kept the nail of her thin, graceful finger over the end of the pour spout.

He said, "Just keep your eye on which glass belongs to Rinosa, and we'll be out of here for good."

"I'm on it," she said, pushed a fresh slice of lime onto his glass, set it before him, and moved on.

At ten minutes to two, the bartender hit a kill switch by the register to silence the music, and said into a microphone, "Last call. Last call for drink orders." She let the music start again.

There was a last group of customers who made their way to the bar for a final drink, and among them was one of the bodyguards. He counted out seven more hundred-dollar bills, got another bottle, and walked back to the table with it.

At two o'clock, the manager of the Galaxy, a tall thin man with gray hair, appeared from his office at the back of the building with two burly men in black Windbreakers with the white letters SECURITY printed on them.

The security men stood flanking him while he hit the kill switch again and announced, "Good evening, ladies and gentlemen. It is now closing time. The Galaxy is closed. I'll have to ask everyone to finish up now and head toward the front doors. If any of our patrons needs a taxi tonight, we will be happy to call one for you. Otherwise, thank you for coming, and we hope you'll be back soon. Good night."

The bartender removed the cash drawer from her register and the manager and one security guard took it with them. The other security guard stayed to help oversee the stream of people leaving the building. Two others, one inside the door and a second outside it, looked on.

The bartender took a large tray and made her way among the tables, clearing glasses. When she reached the table where Rinosa, the girls, and the bodyguards were, they were just standing up to leave. She took a couple of glasses, and then reached for the one Rinosa had used.

A hand shot out and snatched her wrist. It was Rinosa.

The bartender said, "You're going to want to let go of me."

"Sorry," he said. "But I'm taking my glass with me."

"What?" She looked at him as though he were insane, and she had no sympathy for the insane.

"My glass. I want it. For twenty-eight hundred, I deserve a souvenir, don't I?"

"No. I get charged for those. And by the way, thanks for the tip."

"It was an oversight." He smiled.

As he spoke, the quiet man from the end of the bar seemed to be passing the table on his way to the men's room. Unexpectedly, he bumped one of the two bodyguards, his foot somehow getting between the bodyguard and Rinosa.

The man fell against Rinosa just as the bartender swung her arm in a circle to free her wrist. When it broke free, it completed the arc to deliver a chop to Rinosa's throat.

The two bodyguards didn't notice because they were preoccupied with the man who had bumped into them. They launched themselves at him from both sides. The man clutched the head of the one in front of him and pushed it downward as he brought his knee up, then propelled him facedown onto the floor. Instantly he brought his elbow back into the face of the second attacker, rocking him backward, and then completed his turn and punched the man twice as he fell.

He turned to Rinosa, who was holding his throat with both hands, shocked by the bartender's blow. The man delivered a single left jab to Rinosa's nose, and it began to stream with blood. He said, "Oh, sorry. I thought you were with those guys." He produced a clean white handkerchief and roughly dabbed at the blood streaming from Rinosa's nose while Rinosa tried to turn away, shouting hoarsely, "Get away from me! Get away!"

The bartender shouted, "Security!" She pointed at the two men on the floor and Rinosa. "These three!"

The security men in black jackets rumbled in across the floor like a storm front, and dragged the three battered men out the front door. The victims had revived enough to begin struggling and shouting, but made no headway at all against the broad, heavy shapes of the security men.

Three minutes later, the bartender stepped out past the steel door at the rear of the building and got into a waiting car. The car pulled away from the building and accelerated.

The bartender turned in her seat and looked down the street behind the rear window. "Looks all clear back there," she said. "Are you okay?"

The man at the wheel said, "Me? Nobody grabbed me by the wrist. I just figured if I had to distract them while you got the glass with Rinosa's DNA, we might as well get a blood sample too."

"I hope you didn't get it all over yourself, Sid," she said. "I love that sport coat. It took me hours to pick that out."

"I didn't get any on me. I put the handkerchief in the plastic bag right away, and cleaned my hands with antibacterial wipes."

She opened her purse and lifted her own plastic bag where she had put the champagne glass. "Here's my trophy. Tomorrow morning the lab will be open and we can get the DNA tested. Before long Manny Escobar will be declared innocent and let out of jail. Maybe the end of next week."

"Maybe the end of next month," he said. "Even with the rush on the lab work."

"Anyway, we did it," she said. "And Rinosa's DNA, legally obtained when he attacked two private detectives in a bar, will be a match for the DNA the police found on the body." She edged closer and kissed his cheek. "You really are a tough old bastard, aren't you?"

"Why thank you, Veronica," he said. "I didn't think you noticed."

"Of course I did. If I hadn't been so busy collecting evidence, I'd have shouted, 'Don't shoot him. He's got some life in him yet.'"

"I was proud of you too," said Sid. "That's no lie. I do have to say the drinks were a little weak."

"When we get home you can make us both a real one while I'm soaking my feet." She sighed. "God, I love winning. We won't make any actual money after the lab costs, but victory is sweet."

"Victory is sweet," he agreed.

The morning sun was streaming in the windows as Sid Abel drank his coffee. The phone across the room rang. It rang again. Sid looked up over the top of his newspaper at it, and then over at Ronnie, who was at her desk staring at her computer.

"Whose turn is it?" she said.

"I guess that means it's mine," he said as he stood up and walked to the work desk to pick up the phone.

"You should be a detective."

He said, "Abels Detective Agency, this is Sid Abel."

The man on the other end said, "Mr. Abel, my name is David Hemphill."

"What can we do for you, Mr. Hemphill?" he said as he wrote the name on the pad beside the phone.

"I work for Intercelleron Corporation in Woodland Hills. One of our employees was murdered just over a year ago. I'd like to discuss the possibility of hiring your agency to look into it."

"All right," said Sid. "Are you free for an hour or so today?"

"I can make time for this. If you'd like to come to Intercelleron—"

"Not just yet," said Sid. "If we need to look around there later, it would be better if we aren't familiar faces. Can you meet us today for lunch at Merinal restaurant on Grand Avenue at twelve thirty?"

"Yes," said Hemphill. "I'll be there."

"How do I recognize you?"

"I'm wearing a navy blue suit and red tie. I'm six foot three."

"See you at twelve thirty."


"Eyes open," Sid said. "Keep your eyes open. Don't blink when you punch."

"They're open when I hit you," Ronnie said. "I blink when *you* hit *me*. Ow."

"Don't wince, either." He walked in on her, throwing a combination of punches that were fast, but had little force behind them. "Think about your next chance to get me. This is not about me hitting you."

"It is when you hit me."

She sidestepped a punch, jabbed her left hard to his chest, and brought the right toward his face, but he deflected the blow with his forearm.

"Good," he said. "That was about you hitting me."

She jabbed again, this time bouncing her fist off his shoulder. "Again, good."

"Good because I missed your ugly dumb face?"

"Because you're looking, turning this into a fight. Dodge, weave, keep my punches from connecting the way you've been doing, but always keep looking for your chance to hurt me."

She saw his next jab coming, moved her head to the side slightly so his fist went over her shoulder, and brought her left into his face just as she pushed off with her right foot. The blow went to his cheekbone, and he moved his head to her right to evade it, straight into her right hook. He dodged the next punch.

"Great," he said, and hit her with a few quick taps. "Your eyes were wide open all the way, and those shots were good."

"Thanks, you patronizing jerk."

"If you don't like it, do something."

She launched a quick attack, her arms moving as she advanced, jabbing at his eyeline with her left to blind him, and launching body blows with her right.

He defended against her attack without counterpunching, letting her feel her blows landing, watching her work out the ways to press her advantage.

The bell on the timer rang, and she let her arms hang limp, stepped into him, and leaned on him.

"That was a great job," he said.

"My arms are so tired. I don't think I could lift them again if I had to."

"That's good too," he said. "When you're fighting, use everything you have. Don't save anything. There's not going to be a better use for your energy later."

She smiled and looked up at him. "Remember you said that later."

"No need for intimidation tactics." He took off his practice boxing gloves and then untied and pulled off her right one so she could untie the other.

She said, "That was a pretty good fight, though."

"I never fight with my wife. That was a workout."

"Let's go up and get a shower. We've got to meet Mr. Hemphill." She popped up and kissed his cheek.

They stepped off the thick gym mat, hung up their gloves, and put their shoes into the cubbyholes along the wall, then went to the stairs.

As they climbed, she said, "Thanks for being my practice dummy."

"I prefer the term 'sparring partner.'"

"I suppose you would."

David Hemphill arrived at the parking structure, found a space on the roof, and got out of the Lincoln Town Car the company leased for him. He noticed that two aisles away, both front doors of another car opened and a couple emerged. Hemphill didn't look straight at them, but he kept them in the corner of his eye as he leaned into the backseat to retrieve his suit coat and then put it on. They were both dressed in business attire, but from here he couldn't tell more than that. They seemed to be looking at him, but it didn't make him self-conscious about his appearance. His appearance was his best quality.

David Hemphill looked like an ambassador to some important country. He wore conservative suits in blue, gray, or black, perfectly pressed shirts, and ties held fast by subtle clasps. He seldom used slang or rough speech. Because of the way he presented himself, the company often used him as its representative in meetings that required discretion and tact but no technical knowledge or strategic expertise. In reality he was only a bureaucrat raised a little above the middle range because of long tenure. He was in charge of personnel administration for a single section. That was the title in his personnel file—Human Resources Director, Research Section. Not mentioned in his file was his keen ability to sense when things around him were not as he had expected, and the coincidental arrival of two people had made him watchful.

He stood by the open door of this car and pretended to be checking the seat for some lost object while he waited for the man and woman to reveal which way they were going. They were walking toward him. It occurred to him that getting involved in a murder investigation might not be entirely safe. Then he wondered what he would do if this were some kind of unfriendly approach.

"Mr. Hemphill?" said the woman.

"Yes," he said.

"I'm Veronica Abel." She smiled fleetingly and gave his hand a shake. "This is Sid Abel."

Another shake from Sid, this one a much larger, stronger hand, but the same duration and intensity. The couple looked like a pair of high school teachers, the sort who had seen everything at least five times, and hadn't been particularly disturbed by it the first time.

The woman, Veronica, was talking again. "We noticed that the restaurant was a little crowded and noisy, so we picked another one on the next street over."

The man, Sid, said, "This stairwell over here." Hemphill went with them. He had not really been given a choice, but he wasn't sure whether he should mind.

The alternative restaurant was a revelation. It was called Anthony's, and it was old, with dark wood panels and a bar that ran the length of the eighty-foot dining room. There was a lunch crowd, but it looked to Hemphill to be about half composed of men who talked in guarded voices and raised their eyes frequently to be sure nobody was close enough to overhear, and couples who behaved the same way. A large man with a shaved head saw them enter and said, "Ronnie, Sid. I'll put you over here," and led them to a booth by the back wall.

They sat, and Hemphill suspected that the Abels had never intended to meet him at the Merinal restaurant. The last-minute change had simply prevented anyone at his office from knowing in advance where this meeting would be. Were there suspects already? A waiter came a few seconds later and gave them menus. When he had gone, Ronnie Abel said, "So. Would you like to explain your problem to us?"

"It's about a colleague of mine at the Intercelleron Corporation. Or really, about his murder."

"You said he was murdered a year ago?" said Sid.

"Just over a year ago. The body was found on March sixth during a rainstorm. It was the last big rain of the year. There was a great deal of water in a short time. I don't know if you remember. There was a pond forming in North Hollywood at Interlaken and Grimes, and they couldn't clear the drains. They had to open the sewer and remove a clog of foliage and trash that had caught there. In that mess was the body of James Ballantine."

"What was the official cause of death?"

"The medical examiner who did the autopsy found two bullets in Mr. Ballantine's head. I don't expect you to take all this information from my memory. I have a very thick file in my car. It's got all the details the police detectives would give the company, as well as copies of the newspaper articles, insurance reports, and so on." He reached into his inner coat pocket. "I brought a few things here with me. Here's a copy of a *Los Angeles Times* article that gives a pretty good overview. It was printed about two days later."

He set it on the table. The Abels glanced down at the photograph of James Ballantine at the top and then at each other. Ronnie picked it up and scanned it.

Sid said, "I assume that the reason you're here is that a year has gone by and the police don't seem to be making progress."

"It's not just our impression," said Hemphill. "After a few months of work, the detective on the case—his name was Kapp—died in a car accident. Other detectives had the case added to their workload, but no real progress has been made. A police lieutenant spoke with one of the company's directors recently and confided that the police have run out of things to check. They seem to have done everything they could think of over the past year, and now all they can do is wait for something to change."

"What division was Detective Kapp?" asked Sid. "North Hollywood?"

"Yes."

Sid looked at Ronnie, but she didn't say anything. Instead she turned to Hemphill. "Who's on the case now?"

"The detective's name is Fuentes. Miguel Fuentes."

"I worked with him for a while," Ronnie said. "He's very good. Did he tell you nothing was happening?"

"I haven't spoken with him. What I've told you came to me from the board of directors."

"What's your job at Intercelleron?" asked Ronnie.

"I'm the personnel director for the research section."

"Does your company do research for the government?" asked Sid.

"Some, but it's not the sort of thing that—"

"Do people have security clearances?" Sid asked.

"Some do, but not everyone. I don't, for instance."

Ronnie said, "Right after the murder, were there any investigators from the federal government? FBI or military?"

"Early on, there were two agents who came to look around and talk to a few people. I wasn't one of them, and the agents were gone in about a day. I believe they didn't find any indication that Mr. Ballantine's death had anything to do with his work."

"What can you tell us about his work?"

"He was a research scientist. He had a PhD in chemistry from the University of California at Berkeley. He had been a professor at Indiana for a few years before he came to Intercelleron. He was with the company for about four and a half years. I don't know much about his projects, because I'm not a scientist. I was told that he had been trying to synthesize compounds that would result in additives to make food more nutritious. There was nothing directly connected to the military."

"Why does your board of directors want to hire outside investigators now?" asked Ronnie.

"That's interesting," said Hemphill. "Professor Millikan, the man who recommended you, asked the same thing."

"And what did you tell him?"

"That I think they're not entirely sure themselves. They feel it would be wrong to let the murder of one of our people go unsolved. Since he asked, I've thought more about it. I think that people don't want to believe that events are random, that a person is born and raised to adulthood, then educated at great expense and effort, only to die for no reason. And I think that people who are highly educated and successful are probably more susceptible to this fear than the rest of us." He smiled. "That's not the kind of answer you're looking for, but it's true. People like the board members don't want to think that their lives are vulnerable to a chance encounter with some lunatic or petty thief, or that their own high place in the world might be due to luck. They want the answers to make sense—a certain kind of sense that they'll find palatable."

Ronnie said, "We're capable of doing a competent homicide investigation, even on a cold case. But we can't guarantee you or them that a murder will make sense. Most of them don't accomplish anything that couldn't have been done in an easier way."

"I imagine so," said Hemphill. "What the board would like is everything—the identity of the murderer, his methods, motives, and proof of his guilt. But what they'll take is whatever it's possible for you to find out."

Sid said, "We also like to make clear that the services we offer have limits. If we find the killer, we won't administer some kind of justice. I hope you can find a tactful way to let the board know that."

"That should be assumed," said Hemphill.

"You'd be surprised at how seldom it is," Ronnie said. "We collect and provide information only. If it's information the police should know, we give it to them too."

"The board will want me to discuss the fee for your services."

Sid took a set of folded papers out of the inner pocket of his jacket and handed it across the table to Hemphill. "Here's the standard contract. We charge a daily fee seven days a week, plus itemized expenses. We work one case at a time. If we need to travel or hire outside experts, there will be additional charges."

"I'll take this to the board," said Hemphill. "But I'm sure they'll agree. Once they decide to act, they're pretty impatient. I'll let you know very soon."

Ronnie gave an indulgent, motherly smile. "No rush. We'll use the time to decide whether we want to work for them."

# 3

Sid and Ronnie Abel liked to shoot at a small range in an industrial area down near the airport. It wasn't usually very crowded, and there was plenty of parking on the street because it was the sort of the neighborhood where it wasn't a good idea to leave a car parked after dark. Ronnie parked the car while Sid pocketed his phone.

Ronnie said, "What have you found out about them?"

"Not a lot," Sid said. "The company is about forty years old, which seems good."

"Right," she said. "If they haven't been caught at illegal or morally repulsive acts in that time, then there's some chance they might not be doing any."

"They also haven't gone bankrupt, so their checks probably won't bounce," said Sid.

"That's a nice change."

Ronnie led the way into the building. They stopped at the counter in the anteroom to pay the tall, spectacled young man with long, curly black hair for admission and two boxes of ammunition and give him their identification. They placed their Glock 17 pistols on the tray inside the small door so the range master could examine them and give them back once they were inside. When they reached the steel entrance door Ronnie leaned into it to open it with her shoulder. "Anything else?"

"That last call was Winters over at UBS. I asked him about them, and he advised us to invest."

"Good enough," she said. They took their pistols and stepped to the big workbench for their earphones and safety glasses. Ronnie took two fresh paper targets to an empty stall on the range, clipped them to the overhead wires, and pressed the buttons on the pulley mechanisms to make them skitter down to the seven-yard mark.

As cops they'd both been habitual bonus shooters, taking advantage of the department's policy of giving police officers who requalified once a month at Marksman level and above a slight bump in pay.

In order to requalify with the Glock 17 each month the standard test was forty rounds, all in timed-fire sequences at 7, 10, 15, and 25 yards. The highest possible score was 400, which required placing all rounds inside the 10 circle. Expert was a score of 380, Sharpshooter 340, and Marksman 300. The Glock 17 was light, simple, reliable, and accurate at those distances, but it wasn't designed for competition. It was a fighting weapon, the one they had both trained on and carried for many years. They put loaded magazines into their pistols, charged them, and each set two more loaded magazines out on the counter at the firing line.

Ronnie went to her spot on the firing line, set the clock, and said, "Ready?"

They fired their first four-shot sequence in three seconds. They ran through the rest of the qualifying session without speaking—firing, changing the targets and distances, reloading and firing the next sets, down to the seventh at 25 yards. At the end of forty rounds, they left their pistols on the counter with the breeches open, and pushed their earphones down around their necks. They examined their targets.

"How did you do?" Sid asked.

"Looks like three eighty," Ronnie said. "You?"

"Three sixty."

"Pretty fair," she said. "If I were a man I would be embarrassed if my wife was that much better than I was, but marksmanship's probably not that important."

"A cynical use of my own presumed sexism against me? Assuming I'm sexist would be sexist itself, and not at all like you."

She gave him a smile. "If you're satisfied that your shooting will be good enough to save us in a fight, then I'm satisfied too."

"You know that as long as every round is inside the body outline on the target, the guy goes down."

"A shot in the ten ring means he didn't survive to fire again at your lovely wife, or to get up and sue us for pain and suffering."

"Very humane of you to say so," he said.

She shrugged and put her pistol in the holster under her jacket. "I'm only interested in your happiness. It's up to you. It's not my manhood that's at stake." She stepped toward the steel door.

"Where are you going?"

"Down the block to that coffee shop. I'll save you a seat. I assume you'll want to hang around here long enough to fire a box of ammo for practice and then try to get a better score. See you there."

As soon as the door closed behind her, Sid returned to the firing line. He reloaded three magazines with a total of forty rounds, set the clock, and ran the requalifying sequence again. This time he scored 383. He loaded another magazine and put his pistol into the holster covered by his jacket, folded up his target, and brought it with him.

When he arrived at the coffee shop he could see Ronnie at the table by the window typing something on her cell phone, then moving it around with her finger. He saw she had bought two cups of coffee and one of them was by an empty seat. He sat down beside her and sipped the full cup.

"What are you doing?" he asked.

"Hemphill called to say they've signed the contract. It's in the mail."

"And that?" He pointed at the display on her screen.

"I'm playing with an ad. I thought we might like to offer a reward for information leading to the arrest and conviction in this case."

Sid shrugged. "What the hell. It's been a year and nobody's said anything so far."

"You mean it's a waste of time?"

"No, I mean it's a great idea," Sid said. "We'll never have to pay off."

"What do you think—ten thousand?"

"Make it twenty-five," he said. "It's more eye-catching, and we can easily afford to not pay a much larger amount."

She typed a line on her phone, and then pressed something that made an electronic whoosh. She said, "There. It's done. It will be published tomorrow." She put her phone into her purse. "How did you do in your remedial shooting?"

He handed her his paper target, and she examined it carefully. "Not so bad. I make it about three eighty." She set it aside.

"Three eighty-three."

"Right," she said. "About three eighty."

"No, that's what you got. I got three eighty-three."

She looked at him, her eyes amused. "Very good, Sid. Let's hope if we get into a gunfight, it's long enough so you get to warm up."

# 4

"This is the neighborhood where they found him," said Ronnie. "It's nice. Look at all those big old trees. Sycamore, camphor, sweetgum, Aleppo pine."

"It's pretty much what I expected," said Sid. "The twigs and leaves and needles are probably what caused the storm drain to get blocked."

"The report Hemphill gave us seems to support your theory. The first cop on the scene was a guy named Stearns. He said the body was entangled in vegetation when the DPW found it."

Sid parked the black BMW at the curb. "Where's the drain where they found him?"

"The map indicates they opened the one right by the corner, on the northwest side." They walked to the corner and looked down at the storm drain opening. It was set sideways into the curb, with a metal grate covering it. From the curb nearly to the sidewalk was a concrete slab with a manhole cover set into the middle.

"I don't think I ever looked at these things closely before," Sid said.

Ronnie looked at the printed sheet she carried. "It says here that each year these drains keep eight hundred forty thousand pounds of trash from entering the LA River. There are twelve thousand of these things, called 'connector pipe screens, or CPS.' The fancy ones like this one have 'automatic retractable screens, or ARS.'"

"Why do they always have to do that?"

"Give initials?"

"Yeah. As though you couldn't figure out what the first letter of each word is, and as though the initials mattered."

"It's a government publication, or GP."

"Thank you," he said.

"It's a pretty impressive system, though." She read. "'Even on the driest day, there are enough millions of gallons of runoff from sprinklers to fill the Rose Bowl. On a rainy day, the flow can be ten billion gallons.' The storm drains are completely separate from the sewage system. This water all goes straight into the ocean."

"When was the system built?"

"The nineteen thirties and forties, like most things in the east Valley. These screens and things are much more recent."

Sid stopped and looked up and down the street. "I'm starting to get a feeling this can't be the crime scene. He wasn't killed here and dumped into the drain. People would see the killing or hear the gunshots. And the screens, retractable or not, would keep anything as big as a man from getting into the main drainpipe."

"Maybe he was put into the system somewhere upstream from here, and he got washed along until he hit a snag."

"It's possible they hoped he would make it into the river channel and get washed all the way to the ocean," Sid said.

"We'll have to find out where he could have gone in. Where did he live?"

Ronnie leafed through her printed sheets. "Twelve thousand eight sixty Cambridge in Woodland Hills, number six."

"Something like eleven miles west of here. I guess that's out."

As they walked along the street toward their car, Ronnie said, "He must have been dumped at some access point somewhere upstream. He could even have been murdered a day or two before the big rain. When the storm came, he would suddenly be in a high-pressure bath, cleaned of every bit of external blood, hairs, and fibers, and as he went along, he'd have an unknown quantity of meaningless stuff attach to him."

"I'm starting to see why the homicide people got nowhere." Sid stepped onto the concrete slab above the curb, knelt and took a large screwdriver out of his coat, then put the end of it into one of the holes on top of a manhole cover and pried.

"What are you doing?"

"Getting a feel for the structure of these things." With difficulty he lifted the edge of the cover and slid it onto the concrete.

"I read that these covers weigh a hundred and fifty pounds, which is why scrap scavengers sometimes steal them—that's a lot of iron."

"It's not light, but one man can get one open." He looked down, with Ronnie at his shoulder staring down into the space beneath the concrete. She took a small LED flashlight out of her purse and shone it into the manhole. The space was a concrete box about six feet square, and then a screened-off opening to the underground conduit.

She said, "There's another screen down there before water gets to the storm drain. Even if you pushed a body through the manhole, it wouldn't go into the drainage system. It would just stay here. I guess that's what it's for—not bodies, but keeping things from plugging the main drain."

"So where did James Ballantine get into the system?" he said.

"Time to take a trip downtown to the Department of Public Works."

Two hours later, they were in the main office of the DPW, talking to a supervisor named Alan Weiss. He took a large notebook off a shelf in his office and said, "I remember the case very well. We helped the police try to figure out the same thing. There was a detective from the North Hollywood division. Detective Kapp. We looked up the information for him. We have lots of breaks in the water supply system—three or four a day. Not many in the storm sewers. I can show you what we found."

The Abels followed him to a small office, and watched him set the notebook down. He leafed through the notebook, took out a map, and unfolded it. "Here. Here's what we found. Nothing in the existing system had been opened for months before then. With the catch basins and the grates over the openings, there's hardly ever a reason. And the drains themselves have held up for about eighty years."

Ronnie pointed. "What are these red marks on the edges for?"

"Progress. Each of those dots is a place where a developer was building a new subdivision. Up there in the north edge of the Valley in the foothills is the only place where there's room."

"New streets, new storm drains," said Sid. "So they were adding new ones at that time?"

"Right," Weiss said. "They weren't all going in at once, but when we went through the records for Detective Kapp, we found out that during the week of the murder, there were three places where new streets were going in. And under them, drain sections were being added to the system."

"And if somebody dragged the body into an open section of storm sewer—far enough in so that the workers wouldn't see it—do you think they might pave over that section before anybody noticed?" said Sid.

"That's what I think is most likely," said Weiss. "When you add a section to a drain, you dig up the last few feet of it to make a connection, but no more than that."

"Do you have a theory about which drain it was?" asked Ronnie.

"I don't," he said. "But Detective Kapp did. This one, the farthest south."

"Did he say why?"

"Because this site was the closest to where Mr. Ballantine ended up, and closest to populated areas. He said the killer would be more likely to have driven by and noticed the construction. Whether Mr. Ballantine was lured to the spot or carried there, the process would be easier if the place was closer. And if his body was liable to get caught up in a snag somewhere—which is what happened—then the theory that it traveled from one of the longer distances starts to seem less likely."

"It sounds logical," said Ronnie. "But if you were going to commit a murder, particularly with a firearm, wouldn't you look for the most remote spot you could find?"

Weiss smiled. "That's not really my field, but I would think so."

Sid finished writing down the addresses of the drains that had been open a year ago. "Well, thank you very much, Mr. Weiss. You've been terrific." In two more minutes, the Abels were out of the building and walking to their car.

Ronnie said, "What do you think?"

"The killer found a place where there was an opening in the storm sewer system a year ago," said Sid. "Which one he found is pure chance. He wouldn't have had any way of knowing about all three of them and picking one. He must have seen one and used it."

"We probably ought to take a look at all three and see if there's anything about one of them that connects to James Ballantine."

"We'll need to know more about Ballantine before we can do that," said Sid. "Right now I'd like to go home and spend some time going over the information that Hemphill gave us."

They drove home and sat down at the pair of desks they used in what used to be a recreation room, and Sid untied the thick package that Hemphill had given them. There were a number of file folders, most of them full of papers that had been made on copying machines. They split the pile of files and went to work.

There were folders of newspaper clippings, a copy of James Ballantine's personnel file, files of correspondence.

They read through a few files, and Ronnie held one sheet up. "I'm surprised they have these on a case that's still open. It quotes the autopsy report."

"Somebody at the company must be pretty persuasive. What does it say?"

"Cause of death was two shots to the back of the skull, both .22 Long Rifle, 36 grain, copper plated. Unable to determine a manufacturer. They bounced around inside the skull doing damage, but didn't go through."

"Interesting. The cheapest, most common round for sale, and probably the quietest. Fired in semiauto pistols, revolvers, rifles of every configuration. He was dead before he hit the water, right?"

"Yes. No water in the lungs. And they didn't determine a time of death, because he was in the water so long. He could have been dead for days before he got washed away." She paused. "What does this sound like to you?"

Sid shrugged. "If they'd shot him once, I'd say it might have started as an accident. If they'd beaten him up first, I'd say it was a robbery. Not this—two to the head. What they wanted was to kill him efficiently and make him disappear."

"So maybe a personal enemy, maybe a pro."

"Have you found anything in the files you looked at that might suggest any enemies?"

"There's a memo here that the company president wrote recording what Detective Kapp told him about his interviews." She pushed papers aside until she found it. "Here it is. The memo is dated June eighth, a couple of months into the investigation. Everybody the police interviewed said Ballantine was a quiet, decent man who got along well with everyone at work, but didn't socialize much with his colleagues, except at official events—company conferences, the Christmas party, and so on. No evidence of drugs, drinking, gambling. Took very few sick days." Ronnie shrugged. "Of course, saying nice things about a murdered man helps keep you off the suspect list."

"Let's keep at it," Sid said. "All this is information we don't have to work for. There's got to be something that the homicide people have missed."

They kept at it until they had each read every bit of paper that Hemphill had given them. At eleven o'clock they went into the kitchen, where Sid poured them each a glass of scotch on ice, and then to the living room. Ronnie switched on the television and they watched the local news at a low volume while they talked. "Did you hear from Mitch or Janice today?" said Sid.

"Mitch texted me. He wanted to know what to get Nancy for their anniversary."

"A new husband who knows what she wants."

"Nice, Sid. That's our son. And Janice wants to know if we can fly to Chicago for Thanksgiving."

"Who the hell knows what he'll be doing in eight months? What kind of life would that be?"

"Never been my problem," said Ronnie. "For the past thirty years I've been looking forward to being bored. I'm just not sure I want to go fifteen hundred miles for that and a dry turkey."

"Nice, Veronica. That's our daughter. "

They both knew they would go, and that Sid would make the plane reservations the next day, before prices began their inexorable rise month by month until holiday season. If he forgot, she would remind him. He stood, holding his glass, and took a step toward the bar.

"Better not drink too much if you still want to fool around," she said.

He set the glass down on its coaster and sat down on the couch beside her. "I just don't want to rush you."

"The hell you don't." She kissed his cheek, stood, and walked off toward the hallway to the bedroom.

It was afternoon the next day when they drove north on the 170 Freeway toward the northern part of the San Fernando Valley. Away from the city center past the hillside houses that belonged to the rich or the optimistic were pockets of poverty that hadn't gotten much better than they'd been before World War II, only more crowded. Beyond them were the old places that were not small ranches anymore, but still had enough land to pasture and stable horses. More and more of the land had been broken up into communities that had no reason to be built except that the population never stopped spreading outward to cover any empty space. Ronnie kept looking at the picture of the storm drain map she had taken with her cell phone in the DPW office, and then switching to the GPS map for their present location.

"One of these streets ahead is Cobblestone Way," she said. "Keep your eyes open for the sign, and don't drive so fast."

"There's traffic building up behind me," he said.

She spun around in her seat to glance at the empty road behind him. "There is exactly one car, and it's half a mile back."

"Sure," he said. "Because he doesn't want to crowd me. Here's Cobblestone already. Good thing I drove fast." Sid turned and they moved slowly up the side street. The houses were all new, all two-story buildings on lots they filled almost completely. There was a miniature Tuscan villa, a Cape Cod with clapboards, a Spanish-style house, a Tudor. It didn't take the eye long to notice that they were all made from a single set of plans, with variations in roof material, siding, and windows to imply a variety of styles. The next series had the same selection of styles, but used a mirror image of the sequence, so the garage was on the left and the entrance door on the right.

"This is the first possibility," Ronnie said. "Nothing that's here existed a year ago. The storm drains got closed in on March fifteenth, and the final stage of paving happened on April second. When James Ballantine turned up in the storm drain in North Hollywood, this was one place where he could have started. He was at work on March fourth, and was found March sixth. It would have been on or just before March fifth."

"Okay," said Sid. "So I'm picturing this block on March fifth. It was raining hard, and had been, on and off, for a couple of days. If these houses hadn't been framed and closed in yet, there wouldn't be any carpenters working on those days—too wet."

Ronnie studied the storm drain map. "Right. This place is Detective Kapp's candidate for crime scene."

"But there are quite a few older houses on the next block that were certainly here a year ago. If he was put in the drain here, he was probably dead already so nobody would hear the shots, and they'd have to do it at night, so nobody saw it."

They visited another site in the northern part of the Valley in the foothills below the wall of mountains. It looked similar to the first neighborhood, with a few variations.

"This is a little bit newer," said Ronnie. "If you picture the place a year ago, it's a possibility. There wouldn't have been people living close by who would hear a small-caliber gun-shot, and probably nobody would pass by to see the body being dragged into the pipe. But this place isn't on the way to anything, and it would be hard to discover by accident."

They reached the third development as it began to get dark. This was the farthest north, a bit higher elevation than the others, but still not high enough to notice unless the observer happened to be thinking about water flows. There were two streets that looked like the others, with many of the homes already occupied and only a few that still had the realtors' signs on their lawns. But there were also three more streets with houses in varying stages of construction, and one that was only a gravel track through an empty field. On one side there was a single row of foundations dug and poured, with the wooden forms still installed. Far down at the end there were two houses that had been partially framed, like skeletal remains of something that had been started and abandoned. There were no streetlamps in yet. The street was dark.

"Now we're getting somewhere," said Sid. "This would be a good place to kill somebody."

"Or dump a body, anyway."

Sid stopped the car. "There aren't any cameras or fences like they sometimes have on construction sites. I guess there's nothing here to protect yet. Nothing to steal."

"At least without prying apart the lumber they've nailed together," said Ronnie.

"Too much work for thieves, I guess. Okay. Let's try to work this out while we can see it. So this guy decides to kill James Ballantine."

"Or gets hired to kill him."

"He figures a good place to do it would be in a sparsely populated area north of the city, a place where he can discharge a firearm without waking the neighborhood, because nobody lives in the houses yet. He drives Ballantine up here to look at the lots for sale, or brings him here, maybe drugged or tied up. At some point he shoots him twice in the back of the head with a .22 pistol. The street has an open trench dug in the middle, with a big concrete pipe being laid in as the main channel for storm runoff. The pipe is big enough to drag a body in, and the start of it is already connected to the existing part of the storm drain system. So he drags the victim as far as he can into the completed part of the storm sewer. Right now is the rainy season, and he hopes that as soon as there's a storm, the body will be swept downstream, maybe all the way to the ocean. Or he might have done this after the rain had already begun. He saw the water running into the drain and realized he had a solution to his body problem."

"This doesn't seem like a crime of opportunity to me," said Ronnie. "There's too much that's ideal—no lights, nobody who lives nearby, a way to wash the body of all trace evidence and transport it far away at the same time. You don't usually find all of those things by happy accident."

"Okay," said Sid. "He knew that this development was all new streets, so they'd have to put in pipes to connect with the main storm sewer system. He could have come to the construction site any night and looked closely at the place. With online weather forecasts, he could know in advance when there would be a good day for putting a body in a storm drain. A big rainstorm would also wash away things like footprints and tire tracks and the marks where he'd dragged the body. So it was probably planned."

Ronnie said, "Right. The .22 rounds would indicate that he met the victim knowing what he was going to do. A pro might use a .22 because it's relatively quiet, but the victim is just as dead, if you shoot him in the head or heart. But nobody would bring a .22 to a gunfight. He had to know in advance what to bring."

"Yes," said Sid. "Is 'he' a woman?"

"Maybe," Ronnie said. "A .22 would be much easier to hide than a bigger pistol on a small body. And a woman could find a way to get in very close."

"Other possibilities?"

"Dozens," she said. "Maybe he or she posed as a realtor, an architect, or contractor, and said, 'I'll drive you around to look at the lots.' That way there's no extra car left here to raise questions. Maybe the shooting took place at an even more remote spot, and he just dumped the body at a construction site on his way home. And there's still the possibility that this was a psycho out plinking at bottles who saw a lone man in a remote place and wondered what it would be like to kill somebody."

"And we can't ignore the fact that Ballantine was black," said Sid. "It might be too early to rule out racial hatred as a motive."

"I guess the only things we can rule out right now are suicide and accident. Neither involves two shots to the back of the head," Ronnie said.

She noticed that Sid was staring into the rearview mirror. "What do you see?"

"I'm not sure. Do you remember about two stops back, there was a car behind us at a distance?"

"You mean when you were speeding?"

"Yeah. Just now, a car came by that intersection back there, and stopped. Whoever was in it seemed to be watching us. Then it pulled forward to where I couldn't see it, but slowly. It looked like the same car. It's a fairly small sedan, colored somewhere between dark gray and a dusty black."

"At the entrance to this street?"

"Yes. They could have been parking up there just out of sight."

"Why would anybody come down here in the dark?"

"That's what I'm wondering." After a moment, he said, "Maybe they've been following us all afternoon waiting for a chance to corner us."

She looked around. "This doesn't look like a place I want to be cornered." She released her seat belt.

Sid said. "How do you want to do this?"

"Let's get out of here, but cautiously. Turn around and head out. Keep our windows open and guns ready, but try to look like a normal couple who were just out looking at a new housing development." She took out her pistol, released the magazine to verify that it was loaded, reinserted it, and pulled back the pistol's slide to put a round in the chamber.

Sid swung the car to the side of the road, backed up, and turned around. He drove back along the unpaved road toward the intersection at a slow speed, as though he had not seen anything that made him suspicious. Ronnie rested her pistol on her knee with her finger straight along the side of the trigger guard.

Ronnie said, "I'm trying to spot them, but I don't see anybody yet."

"Good."

"Do you think they could be guards of some kind?"

"There's not much here to guard yet," said Sid. "If they are, they'll be satisfied to see us leave, and not bother us. Of course, it could be somebody from an old case, just waiting to get us into a place like this. It could even be Alex Rinosa."

"Even if he's been arrested by now, he wouldn't know who we are yet."

"Not usually, but it could happen."

"Thanks for not saying it's because I took out the ad about a reward for the Ballantine murder," she said. "Even though it is."

Sid drove along the gravel road, staying in the center while they both watched the side windows. When he reached the end of the road he turned to the right, the direction the car had gone. A quarter mile ahead of them was the dark-colored car, sitting beside the road. "That looks like the one," Sid said.

He accelerated toward the car, but the driver pulled out and drove off quickly. As Sid sped up, so did the dark car, moving off now at a high speed.

"Interesting," said Ronnie. "I guess he isn't in a mood to chat."

Sid kept accelerating. "I am now."

"Me too," said Ronnie. "But if that's not possible, I'd be satisfied to get a picture of their license plate." She took out her cell phone and prepared it to take a picture.

They were slowly gaining on the car ahead of them. Ronnie steadied her phone on the dashboard, and then decided that she could hold it steadier in her hands at this speed.

Ronnie said, "Get closer. I want to get a license number when he goes under a streetlamp."

They were gaining. Far ahead, Ronnie saw the shape of a human torso extend itself out the passenger window of the car. "Wait a minute, Sid. That looks like a—"

They saw and heard it at once, a flash from the car far ahead of them, a bang and a sound like a hammer hitting their car, an explosion of glass into the front seat that sprayed Sid's neck and chest and stung his face. There was now a big spiderweb crack in the windshield above his head with a bullet hole in the center.

Sid took his foot off the gas pedal and let the car coast while he feathered the brake pedal to slow it without losing control.

The dark car's tires squealed as it spun around the next corner, leaving a small gray cloud from the burning rubber.

Sid stepped on the gas pedal again, heading for the place where the car had disappeared. Ronnie said, "Sid!"

"I know. But now we really want that picture."

The air was so still that the cloud from the burned rubber hung over the intersection long enough for the Abels to drive through it into the turn.

No car was visible. Sid slowed down and they coasted onto the new street. It was a deserted street ending in a cul-de-sac. "What the hell?"

"I don't know," Ronnie said. "I'm looking."

"Most garage door openers have a lightbulb that stays on for a time after they've been used. Look for a glow at the edge of a garage door."

They drifted along the street looking for any sign that a car had been driven into a garage, but they saw no lights and no motion. When they reached the end of the street, Sid stopped the car and they got out.

Ronnie said, "He knew we were going to catch up. How did he manage to disappear?"

"I'm beginning to think he does this for a living," Sid said. "I'll take this side and you take the other."

"Be extra careful," she said. "I'm not quite done with you yet."

"You too. If you see anything at all, signal me and wait."

They took their positions and began to advance back up the silent, deserted street. There were SOLD signs on most of the lawns, and the few houses that didn't have one seemed not to be completed. None looked occupied. Sid and Ronnie walked across front lawns with their guns drawn, each of them keeping one shoulder close to the front of each house, stopping at the end to look around the corner, then crossing the driveway or the lawn to the next one. If a garage had a window they aimed a flashlight into it. They directed their flashlight beams down the spaces between houses, trying to detect a place where a driver might have hidden a car.

They were on opposite sides of the street, about three houses from the corner, when Ronnie signaled Sid with her light, and he ran to join her. "What have you got?" he whispered.

"This." She aimed her flashlight beam between two houses. In the beam Sid could see that a car's tires had flattened the side lawn in two ruts. She said, "Some of the others have fences or trees between them. He found one where he could drive all the way through to the next street over. He's long gone."

Ronnie and Sid watched the helicopter making its passes high overhead, completing larger and larger circles in its search for the dark car, its rotors beating the air with a deep throbbing noise. Now and then its spotlight would sweep across a promising sight on a nearby street, go back and stay on it, and then move on.

Sid looked at his watch. "It's been hours. They could be in Palm Springs or Santa Barbara or Victorville by now, having their third drink."

Ronnie sighed. "It's after closing time. But maybe there's a minibar in their hotel room."

Sid said, "I wish there were one here."

They watched the line of five cops walking the straight road away from them, their flashlights sweeping back and forth on the pavement, the gutters, and the weedy margins as they went.

The radio in a nearby cop's hand said, "Hold up." There was a brief silence and the voice said, "I've got something."

Two sergeants and a detective hurried down to the spot to join the cop who had spoken. Sid and Ronnie listened to the radio traffic and watched the cops. In a few minutes the officer in charge of the scene, a plump, red-faced detective named Hebert, returned holding a plastic evidence bag with a brass casing. He announced to nobody in particular, "It's a .308 Winchester. It must have been a hell of a shot from a fast-moving car. About three hundred yards."

"I was impressed at the time," said Sid.

Hebert said, "Have either of you thought of a good reason why the two men would shoot at you?"

"Not a *good* reason," said Sid. "We were trying to come close enough to see who they were, or get a picture of their plate."

"We told you about the case we came here to investigate," said Ronnie. "We were trying to figure out where a victim could have been dumped in a storm drain a year ago during the storms and end up in North Hollywood. We're just getting started."

"What do you mean?"

"It's not as though we knew too much, so somebody would want to kill us. We don't know anything yet. The original homicide detective in North Hollywood, Detective Kapp, had been trying to figure out where the victim was dumped, and we were just here to see if we could sort out which of the leads he had was the right one."

"I'd say the shooter may have just told you," said Detective Hebert. "Well, it's after two a.m. I think we've got about all the information you can give us for the moment. If you two want to go home, you can."

"Thanks," Sid said.

"We'll call if we need anything else."

Sid and Ronnie walked back to their car. Sid got in behind the wheel and looked up at the hole in the windshield and the milky, pulverized safety glass around it.

"I'm alert enough to drive," Ronnie said. "If you're about to doze off and kill us both, I'd be delighted to take over."

"No, thanks," he said. "I'm feeling alert. That big shot of adrenaline just after night fell got me going, and then standing around for hours didn't make me tired, just frustrated." He drove to the end of the road and then south away from the development. The roads at the northern edge of the San Fernando Valley were dark and sparsely traveled at this time of night. It was too late for the bar crowd to come home and too early for the early risers to go to work.

"Did you buy Hebert's theory that the shooting told us that was where James Ballantine was killed?"

"No. The only thing this told me is that I have to get the windshield replaced. And I feel stupid. It never occurred to me that somebody would decide to follow us today."

"Well no," said Ronnie. "We're supposed to be following them. A fox doesn't look over his shoulder to see if he's being stalked by chickens."

# 5

Nicole Hoyt picked up the .308 bolt-action rifle, her five-foot-three frame and her small, thin fingers making the rifle look huge. She released the magazine from the rifle, then pulled the bolt up and back to keep the chamber open. She verified that the chamber was empty, as she had known it was, but she checked because that was what a pro did. It didn't matter how many kills you had if the last one was you. This had been a long night, and she didn't want to leave anything to chance when she was tired.

She set the rifle on the work table with the bolt still back so Ed would see it that way when he was ready to clean it. The Hoyts were an old-fashioned couple in most ways. They had both grown up in parts of the country where men and women generally kept their places. There was no more mystery to it than knowing whether you were looking at a cow or a bull.

Nicole could strip, clean, and oil a weapon better than Ed could, with her smaller, nimbler, uncalloused fingers, but the man cleaned the guns. She shopped and cooked, and God knew she did most of the housecleaning. Ed did the outdoor stuff, took care of the cars, and lifted anything that weighed more than forty pounds.

She heard him come into the mud room from the garage, and she went to join him. "Did you call to say what happened?"

"Yeah," he said. "He's fine with it."

She watched as he stepped out of his running shoes, let his jeans and shorts drop, and pulled one leg out and shook the other leg out of them. As he pulled the long-sleeved T-shirt up over his head and the shirt came off and joined the rest of his clothes on the floor, she pretended she hadn't been looking. She stepped forward. "Give me those clothes, and I'll wash everything right now."

Ed bent to snatch up the clothes from the floor and held them out in a bunch with his left hand so she had to step close to take them. As she reached for them he spun her around and gave her a sharp smack on the ass with his free hand before she could get away.

"Jesus, Ed!"

"Couldn't resist," he said. "I'm only human."

"Barely." She stepped into the laundry room, tossed his clothes into the washing machine, turned it on to fill it while she added detergent, and then stripped off her own clothes and tossed them in too. There probably wasn't anything much on his, but there would be traces of powder and heavy metals on hers, because she had fired the rifle.

Nicole padded through the house bare, not concerned about anybody seeing her. They had neighbor-proofed the house before they moved in. There were blackout curtains on all the windows.

When Nicole reached the master bedroom she could hear the shower already running. She glanced in and watched

Ed for a second. She had read in a women's magazine a few days ago that the type most American women preferred was a tall man without much body fat who drove a black pickup truck. In other words, American women lusted after Ed Hoyt. She had laughed, and thought about telling him, but after a few seconds the impulse faded. He was hers, and she hadn't wanted to add to his temptations.

She might have considered getting him to put a tattoo on him that said her name, but their profession made that a stupid idea, and Nicole was not stupid. People like them could not afford to have unnecessary identifying marks on their bodies. There were other ways to make sure he stayed.

She walked up to the glass door of the shower, opened it, and said, "Got room in there for me?"

He pulled her into the shower and let her get wet, and then held her in his arms and kissed her. After a few minutes she felt warm and clean. Then she wriggled herself free of his arms, sank to her knees, and did one of the things that made her pretty sure he wasn't going to go looking for women who liked him more than she did.

After that, Ed took her to the bedroom and made all of the choices and decisions for a while. His attention made her feel very desirable. Ed Hoyt was not a romantic, but he had an intensity of interest and focus that left a woman feeling no doubts about herself.

He got up and walked into the bathroom while she lay there feeling limp and catching her breath. Then he came back. "I'd better go clean that rifle and put it away. I forgot about it."

"Oh hell, Ed. Don't bother with that. Stay here with me."

He gave a small exhale, almost a laugh. "It won't take long." He stepped into a pair of sweat pants and a fresh T-shirt.

"I'll go get us something to help us sleep." She crawled to the end of the bed and got up, then put on some pajamas and walked back into the kitchen. When she got there he already had the bolt out, and the cleaning brush reaming out the barrel to the muzzle. He was smiling to himself as he worked.

She almost asked him what he was smiling about, but then realized she shouldn't. She preferred to believe he was remembering some part of what they had just done—what he had just done to her, really—something that made him feel happy just to picture now. If it was something else, that would be okay, but she hoped it wasn't. Sex was a very big deal to Ed Hoyt.

Nicole went to the counter, opened a cabinet, and took out a bottle of cognac. She set it on the counter and then went to the cupboard to get some glasses.

She turned to look back at Ed. He still looked the same way he had nine years ago when she had spotted him at the Training Command summer camp in Tennessee. Men didn't age the same as women. Women started to go soft, to sag a little here and there. Men seemed to dry out and harden, to look more and more like they had been carved out of wood. She gave herself a sidewise appraisal, looking at her reflection in the glass front of the cabinet beside her. Not yet. Still pretty good.

She set down the glasses and poured Ed about two fingers of the deep amber cognac, took it to him, and set it on the table.

"Thanks, babe." He took a cautious sip.

"It'll relax you," she said. She went back and poured about half as much into the second glass and carried it back to the table.

He said, "You got in a good shot tonight—wham, and he comes to a full stop."

She shrugged. "I just hope the customer isn't unhappy about it."

"We kind of can't miss. If they'd caught up, we'd have had to kill them. This way, nobody knows anything."

"I was thinking that maybe we should have taken them out," she said.

"We may regret not going ahead sometime down the line. But for the moment, I don't want to do things the customer hasn't asked for. It doesn't make them think you're being intelligent and strategic. They just think you're crazy and dangerous, and that can turn into a big problem."

"I guess you're right," she said.

"Even if we're wrong, then making things right might earn us some more money."

He finished the cleaning and they were deep asleep in twenty minutes. They were still asleep when the job phone rang. Nicole jumped out of bed and snatched the phone up before the second ring. When she touched the screen the time appeared—7:00 a.m. The job phone was a cell phone that was assigned to this client only, so she had no question in her mind who was going to be on the other end. "Hello," she said.

"Good morning." The voice was his, all right. "I'm calling early because I know you'll want time to plan your day. Can you meet me at nine?"

"Where?"

"The same place."

"All right. We'll see you at nine." She pressed the button to end the call, and then switched off the power. She didn't want to wonder whether the call hadn't disconnected and the client was still picking up her next conversation.

Beside her Ed rolled onto his back, his forearm covering his eyes. "Did I hear you say nine? Nine a.m.?"

"Yes," she said. "That's two whole hours. He wants to meet in the same place."

Ed slowly sat up, swung his legs off the bed, and sat there staring at his feet. "Does he know we were up nearly all night?"

"I won't tell him what we were doing if you don't."

Ed said, "Seriously."

She headed for the door. "I'll start the coffee. Don't go back to sleep."

An hour and a half later they were dressed and ready to leave. Ed was wearing a pair of jeans and a Hawaiian shirt that hung down to cover the gun he was carrying. Nicole tried on a couple of outfits, and in the end decided to wear her new light blue shorts, flip-flops, a tank top with her oversize Ray-Ban sunglasses, and to carry her compact .380 Beretta Pico in a small shoulder bag. It was important to look the right way for the place where they were going. While Ed was waiting for her she stood between the two mirrors and approved the way her body looked in the shorts and the tank top. Once in a while it didn't hurt to have Ed see another man's eyes linger on her for a little too long.

On the way out, Ed set the alarm system. They had signs in the yard and decals on the windows that gave the name of a fictitious security company, but the alarm was real. It sent a silent phone signal to their cell phones to let them know a breach had occurred. What would happen after that was up to them.

They got into what Nicole called the invisible car, a Toyota Camry with windows tinted as dark as they could be without having the police pull the car over. It was impossible for an observer to see the Hoyts inside unless he was a few feet in front of the grille. The car was a dark gray that was close to the dusty asphalt color of a California highway. The car had a V-6 3.5 liter engine instead of the standard 4-cylinder model, so it was nearly as fast as Ed's black pickup.

Ed drove to the parking lot at the end of the long entry road at South Weddington Park near Universal Studios. The park was a big L-shaped stretch of grass in a flat valley below the parking lot for the subway station on Lankershim Boulevard. Around the largest section of grass was an oval track ringed by tall old trees, and beyond the parking lot was a fenced baseball field. Ed pulled into a space between a tall SUV that made their car hard to see, and a couple of small Japanese cars that made it hard to remember.

Ed and Nicole sat for a moment looking ahead at the baseball field. It was a Wednesday, so the field would be empty for at least six hours, until the Little Leaguers would arrive for evening practice. Vincent Boylan had chosen the park as a meeting place, and the Hoyts had agreed because it had the right combination of open space and steady traffic that included pedestrians. Sometimes cab and limo drivers parked in this lot in the shade while they waited for their next pickups. The entry road would be lined with food trucks catering to the studio workers in a couple of hours, but for the moment, there were only a few people walking dogs or jogging.

"There he is," said Ed. "That's him in the bleachers. Third base side."

"I see him. Let's go."

They got out of their car and walked around behind the backstop to the bleachers on the other side. Boylan was sitting on a bench about halfway up the bleachers, so his body wasn't high enough to present a silhouette. Behind him was a stretch of grass and then the twelve-foot brick sound wall that separated the park from the Ventura Freeway. The wall was screened by a long line of trees so it didn't look like what it was. Boylan wore a hooded sweatshirt, jeans, and a baseball cap, so he didn't look like what he was either. He was gazing out over the infield as though he were watching remembered players running the bases and fielding balls. Ed and Nicole climbed up and sat on either side of him.

He turned to Nicole. "Is there room in that little purse for this?" He produced a thick envelope from the marsupial pocket in his sweatshirt.

"I'll make room." The envelope disappeared into her bag. "Do we need to count it?"

"No. It's fifty thousand."

Ed said, "What's it for?"

"It's a down payment on a new part of the job. I want you to be sure when we leave here that you'll always get your pay."

"I already was sure," said Ed. "A person would have to be brain-dead not to pay us."

"Don't be rude, Ed," said Nicole. "Just say thanks."

"Thanks," Ed said.

Ed Hoyt's expression gave Boylan a chill. It was the eyes, he decided. They were wide open, unblinking, watchful, but they didn't change the way human eyes did. They revealed nothing. "It's okay. Ed's right to be puzzled. I don't usually give you a pile of cash we haven't talked about. But I wanted to ask you to do something right away, and I didn't want you to think I was trying to put it on a tab."

"What do you want done?" asked Nicole.

"The man and woman you were following last night. The Abels. They need to be taken out."

"It would have been easy to do then. Now, it's not so easy," said Ed.

"We just got the go-ahead a couple of hours ago," Boylan said. "I called you as soon as I knew."

"Do you know anything about them that we can use?" asked Nicole.

"Pretty much what you already know. They're both former LA cops, working as a two-person detective agency. They're very well known. As soon as the client found out who they were, the Abels got added to their list."

"The price of being very well known," Ed said.

"This needs to be quick before they find out anything."

"What's there to find out?"

"If I knew that, there would probably be somebody else here hiring you to kill me," Boylan said. "I've got to assume it's this thing the Abels offered the reward on. This guy that got killed a year ago."

"It's all right," said Ed. "We'll manage." He stood up and began to make his way down the bleachers.

Nicole got up too. "We'll let you know when it's done."

When they got home, Ed said, "I don't think their post office box is going to be a good enough address after last night." He went into the den to call his contact at the boiler room sales service. The operation consisted of a big room over a furniture store with long tables where men and women sat and cold-called people, then read scripts trying to persuade them to buy things. Their biggest customer was a contractor who got people to sign contracts for kitchen remodeling, took a deposit, and never came back. The contractor's business name changed about once a month, but he paid the phone sales service without fail.

The phone sales service worked with a computer program that they would set for an area code and a three-digit prefix indicating a smaller area, and it dialed the last four numbers in sequence, one after another. When the computer dialed the number and the call connected, its screen would display the name and address, so the script reader could ask to speak with that person.

Ed turned on his phone browser and looked up the numbers the Abels supplied for their reward then dialed the number of the sales service manager. "Hi, Ron," he said. "This is Ed Hoyt. I've got a phone number for you." He read it from the Abels' ad.

After a moment, the manager said, "That's a cell phone."

"Can you get me the billing address?"

"Sure. Give me ten minutes, and I'll call you back."

"Good enough." He hung up. Ed was tempted to use the landline to call a contact he had at the DPW while he was waiting. He had another one at the gas company. If he had taken the license number of the Abels' car last night he could have cooked up some nonsense about a hit-and-run accident to put on the DMV form to get the address of the car's owner. He had lots of ways to get an address, and some that he hadn't even used yet.

# 6

The Abels went out to their garage, where one space was empty, a reminder that the BMW was in the dealer's shop having its windshield replaced. They got into the black Volvo that was left and drove out of the gate at the end of their driveway. They had bought this house in Van Nuys while they were still police officers.

Ronnie had noticed the house while she was patrolling the old, quiet neighborhood. She had driven past it many times, until one night shift she saw a newly posted sign that the house was for sale. She had always been curious about the house because it had a bit more than a triple lot. There was nothing else special about the house or the neighborhood. The house itself was a white ranch-style bungalow that sprawled on its plot without apparent planning because rooms seemed to have been added whenever the place grew too small for its occupants. The trees on the block were old, but they were mostly the low, bumpy magnolias that infested this part of the Valley. They provided little shade and dropped their thick, leathery half-brown leaves twelve months a year and their oversized white flowers for one week, leaving cone-like seed carriers the size and shape of grenades. Ronnie had simply been ready for her own house, and she liked this one.

On the first break of her shift she had called Sid, who was working homicide from the Metro Division at the time, and told him there was a house he had to see. They had not been able to meet at the address until after 8:00 a.m., when they were both off the clock.

They had walked the perimeter, gone off to breakfast together, then called the realtor and returned with him to look at the inside. Sid had been largely silent, because he knew by then that Ronnie was already determined, and the walk-through was a formality, a concession to his need to persuade himself that he wasn't participating in a purely emotional decision. Ronnie did not believe that emotion was a bad basis for a decision about where and how a person lived—certainly better than numbers—but she let him look and pretended to listen when he spoke.

Over the years, the house had changed little. It still looked like thousands of other houses in the center of the San Fernando Valley—a small and undistinguished old house that had a two-story addition in the back. The house had a bit more land around it than some. Most of the first ones on their street had been orange groves or apricot orchards two generations ago. This had been out in the country then.

After many years and raising two children here, they had needed to replace the cracked and uneven asphalt driveway, and so Ronnie had picked out a style made of artificial paving stones, and Sid had decided they may as well add a new gate that didn't require him to get out of the car to shut it. As they drove out of their driveway in the Volvo, they could hear the automatic gate roll along its track and then give a satisfying clank.

"You know," said Sid, "I sometimes forget how much I like this car. I get used to driving that BMW, but this thing is like an old friend."

"It ought to get us up to Osborne Street if you can keep from chasing down any more shooters."

They were on their way north to the Foothill station to meet with Detective Hebert, the officer in charge of the investigation of the shooting. When they arrived, Hebert came out to the lobby to meet them. "Come on in," he said. "Let's go into an interview room so we can talk."

Sid and Ronnie exchanged a glance so furtive that he didn't see it. Ronnie said, "All right."

"Here," he said, and opened the door of an interrogation room. "You can wait in there while I get us some coffee."

Sid and Ronnie entered and sat down in the two seats normally reserved for the two officers conducting the interview. The video cameras were aimed downward from above and behind them at the empty chair. They shared an understanding that Detective Hebert had gone to turn on the cameras and microphones to record what they said to each other, so they did not speak.

Hebert returned with a uniformed cop who carried two paper coffee cups. Hebert carried his own and opened the door. "Thanks," he said, and the cop set down the two cups and went away. "I brought you cream and sugar." He reached into his coat pocket and then placed some thimble-sized creamers and small envelopes in front of them on the table.

"Thank you," said Ronnie.

Hebert hesitated for a few seconds, then sat down in the only empty chair and pulled it closer to the table. "Well, let's talk about this shooting incident last night," he said. "I'd like to go over some of the impressions I got last night, to be sure we've got all the information we need. What were you doing up there on Clovermeadow Lane last night after nightfall?"

Sid said, "The reason we were up there was that we had visited the Department of Public Works office, where we got a list of the construction sites where there might have been an open storm drain on March fifth of last year. That site was number three, the last one of the day."

"And that was part of the investigation you're on?"

"Right," said Ronnie. "The body of a man named James Ballantine was found stuck in a storm sewer under a street in North Hollywood around then. There was no easy way for him to have gotten there, because the drains along the streets are designed not to let anything big, like a body, get into the system. So it had to be an open drain somewhere upstream."

"And of course, you're both former LAPD officers." He paused. "I assume you both left the department without any issues?"

"You didn't check?" said Sid.

Ronnie said, "No issues. I left after ten years and Sid left after twelve because we wanted to work together on our own."

"Is that working out pretty well?" asked Hebert. "I think I've heard your names a few times."

"It's okay," said Sid.

"Good, good," said Hebert. "And you just said you were looking into the death of James Ballantine last March."

"Yes," said Ronnie. "We did."

"A homicide. Who hired you to do that?"

"Mr. Ballantine's employer, Intercelleron Corporation. The contact person is named David Hemphill."

"Hemphill," said Hebert, and wrote the name on his note pad. "And what does Mr. Hemphill say his company wants?"

"Two new pairs of eyes looking at the case. He says the directors of the company are concerned because one of their employees was murdered, and they're willing to pay to keep someone working actively on the case. It seemed to us that reaching the anniversary of the crime was the trigger."

"I've seen that before," said Hebert.

"We see it often," Ronnie said. "The survivors get a lot of information at first, but then the flow slows down and they tell themselves they'll give the police until some particular time. If the case isn't solved when that time comes, they'll hire their own investigators."

"You ever get any results on that kind of case?"

"Sometimes," said Sid.

"Really? Ever apprehend any perpetrators and get them convicted in a court?"

"Some," Sid said.

"How many?" Hebert said. "One?"

"Sid doesn't like to keep score," Ronnie said.

Hebert leaned back in his chair and his lips began to curl upward into a smile.

But Ronnie wasn't finished. "But I do. Since we left the LAPD we've had twenty-one homicide convictions, about half of them murder one and the others bargained down to second degree or voluntary manslaughter. There were also four who were guilty but got themselves killed while officers were trying to make the arrests. I think a couple of those were suicide by cop." She paused. "Of course, we don't usually take on murder cases. When we do, we usually work for defense attorneys."

Hebert was silent for several seconds. "Ever think of coming back to work?"

"No," said Ronnie. "Not once."

"Why not?"

"We still have a lot of friends on the force, but—"

"I'll bet you do, with all those convictions."

Ronnie ignored the interruption. "We like to work together. No department in the country would let us do that."

"I see," said Hebert. "But I guess it's safe to assume we can count on you to cooperate with the official investigation of the shooting."

"We always do," Sid said. "At the moment we haven't got much to share. We've just started to look at the Ballantine case."

"That case belongs to somebody in North Hollywood homicide. I'd be satisfied to get the person who shot out your windshield. That's my case. What's your theory?"

Ronnie said, "We put out ads online and in print offering twenty-five thousand dollars for the Ballantine case. We were followed, so we decided maybe we should go after the other car and see who was following us. We got too close, and they fired."

"You're sure that it wasn't because you found the place where they'd put the body?"

"We don't think we'd found anything," said Ronnie. "We were there because one of the streets was at the stage of construction when a storm drain might still have been open, not paved over, and we wanted to see what it looked like. When Ballantine was murdered, that street was probably still empty field. The street where it could have happened would be one or two streets west of there."

"You're pretty sure that your going out there was what caused the shooting?"

Ronnie said, "Has anybody else been shot at out there?"

"Not that we know of," said Hebert. "We'll have to look into it. Any other thoughts on what happened out there last night?"

"Not right now," said Sid. "We hope to later."

"Well, then, thanks for coming," said Hebert. He stood and held out his hand. "It's been interesting. Don't hesitate to get in touch."

"Thank you," Sid said. He shook Hebert's hand.

Sid walked out of the small room. As they moved down the hallway toward the foyer, they heard the door open and close again. When they reached the front of the building and were out in the open air again, Ronnie said quietly, "I'm not going to hold my breath waiting for him to share anything."

"I'm not going to hold my breath waiting for him to have anything."

Sid Abel walked up the sidewalk toward the Figueroa Club at eleven o'clock that evening. There were the usual three men watching the door from outside the club. One looked like a valet parking attendant standing behind a black podium of the sort that contained a pegboard with car keys on it. Sid knew that this pegboard held a lot of car keys that didn't go to any car, and that the board was on hinges, just the door to a hidden cabinet containing a steel plate to make the podium bulletproof and a short-barreled semiautomatic shotgun. The attendant switched off about once an hour with one or the other of the two men sitting in a car along the curb. They were there to pull ahead at high speed and make any unfriendly intruders unhappy in proportion to their sins.

The setup had not changed in at least three decades, since about the time when the club had moved here from Figueroa Street. This was a bad neighborhood, and the club was one of the principal things that made it that way.

"Hi," Sid said to the attendant. "Is Jimmy Pascal around tonight?"

"I can ask," said the attendant. "Who can I say wants him?"

"Sid Abel."

"You look like a cop."

"I'm not. You look like a parking attendant."

"I'm not."

Sid took out a fifty-dollar bill and handed it to the attendant. The attendant pocketed it. "This isn't much money."

"Jimmy's not much of a guy." He stepped past the attendant. "Sit tight. I'll go find him myself."

The Figueroa was a private club, founded many years ago by a group of people who had shared a belief in after-hours drinking, and free enterprise that often included the exchange of goods and services that were not supposed to be for sale. It had retained that character long after many of those activities had gone out of style and been replaced by something worse, or become legal.

He walked in and could see the club had not changed since his last visit years ago. There was a long polished bar with stools and shelves of bottles backed by a big mirror. The rest of the front room was filled with round tables, where men and a few women played cards or just drank and talked. Beyond a broad arch was a room with three pool tables and long benches along the walls.

Sid spotted Jimmy near the end of the bar talking with two men. Jimmy Pascal was a short black man who weighed about three hundred pounds. He habitually wore a voluminous pair of khaki shorts, a billowing Hawaiian shirt, and a pair of size nine and a half quadruple-E sneakers. He was in his sixties, and made his living now in indirect ways—brokering agreements, selling items of mysterious provenance, introducing people—but when Sid met him twenty-five years ago, he had been a killer.

Sid went to the bar and sat on a stool where he could use the big mirror as a way to watch his back. The bartender, a young, strong-looking man with a beard, said, "Are you a member, sir?"

Sid took out his wallet and produced a tattered card.

The bartender was shocked. "That's really an old one. I haven't seen you before."

Sid shrugged. "I haven't come much since you were born. Can you get me a beer?"

"Yes, sir." He turned toward the draft beer taps. "On tap we have—"

"Miller's fine."

The bartender turned away and picked up a glass, and Sid felt the heat of a large body close to his shoulder.

"Hey, Sidward."

He raised his eyes to the mirror and saw Jimmy. "Hi, Jimmy. How have you been?"

"So-so. You like getting old? Me neither."

"I'll take it," said Sid. "You got a couple of minutes?" His glass of beer appeared in front of him and he put a ten on the bar.

"Bring your beer. There are always people in here who will put stuff in it."

"I know," said Sid. "I didn't plan to drink it."

They walked to the back of the room past the pool tables where men who seemed to be waiting for something played listlessly. They went past the open door of the kitchen, and then out to a small parking lot in the rear of the building where Jimmy leaned against the hood of a car. "So?"

"We were out working on a case last night up in the northern part of the Valley. I noticed that a car had been behind us for way too long. They were waiting for us while we made our last stop, so I drove toward them to see who they were. The car took off, and I chased it. I started to gain on them, but I was still at least three hundred yards back. And then a passenger stuck a .308 rifle out the window and put a bullet through my windshield just above my head."

"From a moving car?"

"At least ninety miles an hour on that stretch. And from the passenger side, it's a left-handed shot." He paused. "I'm wondering if you've heard anything that might give me some insight into my future."

"You're probably right that it's a pro," said Jimmy. "But I don't know who. Nobody has been shopping a hit on you that I know of. Of course, LA is a big place, and the only times I've been in the North Valley I was on the freeway driving past it to somewhere else. A lot of people hated you in the old days, but they don't usually wait ten years to let you know. Are you working on something now that would worry that kind of people?"

"A week or two ago we helped get a guy named Alex Rinosa arrested for murder."

"The music guy? That was you? I'll ask around and see if he's been trying to hire anybody, but I don't think so. He's got to have too much attention on him to try that, and nobody I know would even talk to him now. What else you been up to?"

"We're trying to find out who killed a man a year ago and put his body in a storm sewer up there," said Sid. "We're not close to finding out."

"I haven't heard anything about that either. What was the guy's name?"

"James Ballantine. He was a chemist working for Intercelleron in Woodland Hills. A black guy."

"A chemist, huh?"

"Not that kind."

"They're all that kind if they want to be."

"No sign that he wanted to, though."

"I'll listen for you. I'm always listening. If I hear anything about you or him, I'll tell you."

Sid said, "I know you don't owe me a favor."

"No, but if I get you something, you will."

"Thanks, Jimmy." He stepped to the alley beside the lot and poured the beer out on the ground. "Good night." Then he walked off down the alley, and turned toward the street where his car was parked. He had other people to see.

\* \* \*

Ronnie watched the back door of the halfway house swing open to let a young Hispanic woman with a scrollwork tattoo on her neck step outside. Ronnie lunged forward, caught the door before it closed, and went inside.

Coming up the hallway was a stern-looking middle-aged woman with no makeup and her hair pulled back tight. Her eyes narrowed when she saw Ronnie, but during the five steps before they reached each other, their eyes met and stayed locked, and a change took place in the woman. "I'm sorry. I have to ask," she said.

Ronnie said, "I'm Tiffany's mom." As she flashed a driver's license, her shoulder holster with the Glock in it was just visible under her tailored jacket.

"There hasn't been a Tiffany in two months."

"Then I'm Maria's mom."

The woman passed by, on her way somewhere. Ronnie kept going. Whenever she passed one of the small residential rooms, she glanced inside. She went up one corridor and then turned to walk along the next.

"Ronnie?"

She turned. There was a small bedroom, outfitted to look something like a cell and something like a room in a bad motel. A small, too-thin woman with dyed red hair, a pointed jaw, and protruding cheekbones came to the doorway.

"Hi, hon," said Ronnie. "I thought you might be getting out just about now, so I made a couple of phone calls."

"You came to see me?"

"No big deal," said Ronnie. "I was working on something and it happened to bring me by here. So I thought, 'I think I'll stop in and see how Elaine is doing.'"

Elaine shrugged. "You can come in if you'd like."

There it was, Ronnie thought. After a stint in prison, having a room you could invite people into or throw them out of seemed to be a great luxury. "Well, just for a minute." Ronnie entered the small room. She looked around at the sparse furnishings, and then lifted a chair that was in front of a small, plain table. She spun it around and sat down. "So tell me, honey. Is everything all right?"

Elaine shrugged again, and Ronnie could see her collarbones protruding. "While I was gone my boyfriend sold all my stuff and went off with a woman who wasn't nearly as good-looking as me."

Ronnie nodded. "They can be like that," she said. "They don't say no a lot to the one who's right there in front of them."

Elaine gave a little laugh. "Like I needed another reason to stay out of jail."

"Any reason will do. Have you got any money?"

"When he took off, I lost my apartment, of course. That was where I'd stashed my money. But they give us food and clothes, and this time they're going to get me a job."

"Wow, that's great," said Ronnie. She patted Elaine's thin arm with her left hand, reached into her jeans pocket with her right, and pulled out a pair of hundred-dollar bills. She held on to Elaine's arm and put the bills in her hand. "Here's a little bit to hold you over until you get your first paycheck." She looked at her watch, stood, and put the chair back by the table.

Elaine looked confused. "What do you want for this? I haven't told you anything. I just got out."

"It's okay," said Ronnie. She took a business card out of her purse and handed it to her. "In case you've forgotten my phone number. If anything comes up that you think I'd like to know, you won't forget me."

"I won't forget you," she said. "You said you're working on something tonight. What is it?"

"A man got shot and shoved in a storm sewer almost exactly a year ago. Nobody knows why. He was a scientist, a black guy named Ballantine. Well, got to go, hon."

Ronnie made six more stops in different parts of the city during the night, talking to women she had met before. They were business contacts made in the course of a long career. Two were escorts who went on outcalls together because it was safer than working alone. They had stopped in a coffee shop for a late dinner, and when Ronnie called, they invited her to meet them. Another was a woman bartender in a restaurant where men had been known to be offered jobs that could be done quickly but paid very well. Ronnie drove up Sepulveda Boulevard very late and spotted two women on the street in spots they had worked when Ronnie was still a cop in the Valley. At each stop, Ronnie gave someone a business card and a hundred-dollar bill as a present, and asked for nothing specific except that the recipient call her if anything that might interest her came up.

She got home at three thirty, in time to see Sid arrive in the rental car he'd gotten to replace the BMW. He had made ten stops, making the rounds of his own informants.

"Anybody know anything?" she asked.

"Nothing so far. They're all going to listen."

"Maybe we don't know the right offenders."

"I guess that's not entirely bad. Let's go get some sleep."

The next day they were up and out of their driveway in their black Volvo by noon. After an hour, a white van with magnetic signs and seals on the doors that said LOS ANGELES DEPARTMENT OF WATER AND POWER pulled up in front of the gate and a man in hard hat and coveralls got out and unloaded a few tools. The van pulled ahead a few feet and parked.

Nicole Hoyt sat in the van and watched Ed in the rearview mirror until he had gotten the electric gate at the Abels' house open and gone in to work on their driveway. She had studied the place on aerial photographic maps she found online. Ed had been happy when he found that the driveway was made of paving stones all fitted together like puzzle pieces. Now he was prying up pavers and digging.

Nicole had set out orange traffic cones in front of the van and behind it. Anybody willing to buy a few cones could get away with just about any nonsense he wanted. The van was a good place to be while she served as Ed's lookout. She watched for cars and for dog walkers and delivery people, but there were very few on this quiet block today. As she sat there she thought about Ed, and pictured him working. He was prying up the stones as quickly as he could, then digging a trench in the dirt, putting the dirt into buckets, and dumping it in the flower beds. Next he would place a thin layer of plywood over the trench and cover that with pavers so it looked the same as the rest of the driveway.

Ed was strong and had machinelike stamina, but he was racing against an unknown deadline. The people who lived in that house might come home at any time, and Nicole was the only one who could warn him. If they arrived too soon, Nicole was determined to start the van and back it into their car. If she and Ed had to finish this contract the simple, direct way in daylight, then they would, and just hope they could get away without leaving too many eyewitnesses.

Nicole looked down at the digital clock on the dashboard. As each second passed, she hoped Ed was getting closer to finishing. She tried not to look at the clock again to see if it had changed to the next minute yet. At times like this she was always worried that she would lose him, and the clock watching made her anxiety worse.

Meeting Ed had solved a lot of problems. She had been alone for a long time, and had never liked it. She had grown up in a small, hot town in southern Arizona, the sort of place illegal immigrants hurried through because it was neither big enough to hide them nor nice enough to make them want to stay. When she was younger she went through men like a woman trying on shoes at a sale, hoping each one would fit, but never finding one that did. The right man never appeared, and nothing seemed to take her mind off her loneliness.

She had tried drugs in most of their common forms while she was still a teenager, and accomplished a lot of throwing up, a heart that raced enough to make her think her blood was about to burst out of her ears, and some very ugly scabs where she had clumsily injected drugs into her veins. She had liked drugs. They seemed to combine her two favorite feelings, being uncontrollable and then being unconscious, but they had begun to weaken her in preparation for killing her, like a friend who was really a sly and patient enemy. There were only two ways for a girl like her to afford drugs, and her parents caught her at one of them—stealing cash and credit cards from their wallets—and threw her out. Fortunately, she had already stolen enough to get to Phoenix.

Once there, she decided she needed to recover her health. While she was working to repair herself, her narcissism emerged and made her obsessed with the way she looked. She wanted desperately to be pretty. She enrolled in cosmetology school so she would be an expert. The instructors taught her to cut, style, and color hair, gave her enough of a basic understanding of aesthetics to take care of her skin, and taught her to do nails. She became a model of her own skills and a showcase for the beauty supplies she pilfered from the school. When she graduated, her appearance got her a job, mostly dying hair and doing makeup for proms and weddings. She lasted three months. The constant exposure to formaldehyde, dibutyl phthalate, ammonia, and other chemicals had already made her sick.

She had never lost her interest in men, only lost men's interest in her during the final phases of her drug period when she got too skinny and lizard-like for most of them. Once she looked better she'd resumed her effort to try to sort out the available men and end up with a good one. All she got was a growing memory of men she didn't like very much, and a familiarity with disappointment.

Men were astoundingly simple. They were motivated by sex and greed. The greedy ones were always trying to manipulate her into paying for things that they should have bought—dinners, tickets, airline reservations, hotels. They were always calculating and straining for advantage over everybody, and she was nearest and easiest.

The ones who were primarily motivated by sex were better, because she could withhold or grant it to manipulate them, and be in charge most of the time. The one drawback was that they liked sex, but they weren't always particular about whom they had it with. Ed was one of those men, but she had so far been able to keep him where she could see him and make sure he was happy she was around.

She met Ed only after she had come down to her last idea. She had not found a man she could tolerate who would be willing or able to support her, so she needed a career. She had tried many different jobs and failed at each of them. She had enrolled in four schools of various kinds, joined three churches, gone online in a hundred guises. All that was left was military service. That would not only provide her with necessities and a little spending money, but would surround her with men.

She didn't want to simply commit herself to a branch of the military before she had some idea of what she would be doing. The solution was to skip out on her lease and use the savings to attend a camp in Tennessee called Training Command. They claimed to have marine veterans as instructors in combat techniques, survival, martial arts, and use of the M4 rifle, Beretta M9 pistol, and M249 Squad Automatic Weapon. After giving it more thought she sold her car and signed up for the eight-week course.

Nicole was put into a class with twenty-six men and three women. She was terribly intimidated at first, but since her drug days she had taken great care of her body. She ran pretty well, and could do a few push-ups. When the physical training began, her confidence collapsed. She strained and suffered to stay ahead of the two old men who were in their sixties and the three women. As she ran she would feel the air searing her lungs and her legs giving out, and watch the main group of men disappearing far ahead up the road between tall pines. When the class did pull-ups the men did them endlessly. She could do three, but only because by then she had lost a lot of weight.

Then one day she discovered she had a talent. She could shoot. There had been no reason whatever to expect this. She was not athletic. The only indications of good command over her muscles had been pretty penmanship and the ability to dance, and her style of dancing relied more on an ability to move her hips than her feet.

Nicole was good. She instinctively did the things a person had to do to line up the sights of a weapon on the bull's-eye. In spite of her small size, the grips and forestocks seemed to have been made to rest in her hands and the rifle butts to nestle into her right shoulder. She had perfect vision, but it had never seemed to her to be a big advantage before. She often wore contact lenses anyway, to make her eyes the color she wanted that day. But she could put a hole in a bull's-eye just about any time she wanted to.

At the beginning of her second week on the range, her name started going around the camp. After two more days, students from other classes started to appear behind the firing line to watch her shoot. Soon there were instructors among them.

Eventually Ed Hoyt turned up. He was tall and muscular but not freakishly big. He had dark brown hair, and at that time he had a mustache. Nicole had always thought of a mustache as a declaration that a man was celibate, or at least not interested in women, because so many gay men and cops had them, but that turned out not to be accurate in Ed's case, and within a week she had gotten him to shave it off.

She was, by the end of the eight-week course, well prepared to become a marine. She could perform all of the
rudimentary martial arts moves they would teach her in
boot camp. She could break down and reassemble all of the
standard-issue firearms blindfolded, and she was the best
sharpshooter in the school. She was good, but not quite
as spectacular, on the combat pistol course. Still, her small
size and guile made her unbeatable at the hide-and-seek,
run-and-gun kinds of games the school set up in the forest.

Then the camp ended. Instead of taking the bus to the
nearest recruiting office, she carried her backpack out of
the cramped women's cabin and got into the passenger seat
of Ed Hoyt's Dodge Bighorn pickup and waited while Ed
loaded her gear into the cargo box in the bed with his and
locked it. He drove her south to his apartment in Tampa.

When they reached his place, they unloaded their packs
into his spare room, then locked the door, turned on the air
conditioner, and stayed indoors for six days. It was less like a
honeymoon than a contest. They broke each other the way
trainers broke wild horses. They exhausted each other and
then came together again, wrestled and fought, overcoming
every sense of reserve or separateness. If one of them was awake
and wanted, the other had no right to refuse or to hold back.
Because he was the man he always began as the aggressor, but
her knowledge that she could wait him out and demand more
would arouse her to ask. And hearing her ask would tease him
into the next encounter. The only time she wore anything,
it was an old camouflage army shirt that had HOYT embroi-
dered over the left pocket and had a black scroll that said 75
RANGER RGT. It went down nearly to her knees, and protected
her skin from being spattered with grease when she cooked.

At the end of the week they were through. Nicole had lost more weight, and she could see he had too. The bed linen desperately needed washing, and the recycling bin was filled with empty liquor bottles. The trash was overflowing with cans, because after they'd used up the fresh food, they had opened most of the canned food in the apartment, heated it hurriedly, and eaten it together from the pot.

They went out for breakfast at a restaurant on Tampa Bay. When they had ordered their food he leaned forward with his elbows on the table. He said, "Are you tired of me yet?"

She said, "No. Are you tired of me?"

"No. I never met a woman like you. I think we should get married."

"Why? Do you think I've been holding something back for my future husband?"

"All this week I kept wondering what next week would be like. I want to find out."

"I don't want to marry somebody who will cheat on me."

"You ruined me. Another woman would have a hard time holding my attention. And if I cheat, you're welcome to cut off my ring finger to take the ring back."

She remembered him looking straight into her eyes across the table when he said that, and she remembered reminding herself that all liars stared into a person's eyes, but still being swayed by his disgusting offer.

The buzz of Nicole's cell phone startled her, and she reached into her pocket, pulled it out, and pressed it to her ear as she stared into the rearview mirror. "I'm still here," she said.

"I'm done," Ed said. "Bring the van to pick me up."

Nicole jumped down from the van, put the orange cones into a stack and tossed them into the back, then got in and swung the van around to pull up beside the driveway of the Abels' house.

Ed was standing by the entrance in his orange and yellow DPW vest with his pickaxe, chisel, hammer, and spade. He opened the back door, set everything on the floor and went around to the driver's seat while Nicole crawled to the passenger seat. He drove off.

After a couple of turns he glanced at her. "Have you got something to tell me?"

She shrugged and said, "I was just thinking that I like to see you all sweaty like that."

"How long can you hold that thought?"

"Why? Where are we going now?"

"We still have to get rid of the van and get ready for the Abels."

"Oh yeah," she said. "You might want to park the van in some isolated place for a little while first. We can put the sun shade over the windshield so nobody can see in."

# 7

It was after midnight when Sid guided the Volvo up the street toward home. Ronnie said, "The thing that keeps bothering me is why those two in the car had a .308 rifle with them in the first place."

"I don't know. I assume they knew we were investigating the Ballantine murder. Maybe they killed Ballantine and were watching us to be sure we didn't find anything."

"And they just happened to have the rifle with them, knew we'd spotted them, and didn't have an explanation for the rifle that the cops would buy?" she said.

"That doesn't feel right," Sid said. "More likely they'd been following us since we left in the morning, waiting for a good place to kill us."

"What if this has something to do with the place itself, that housing development? Maybe they killed Ballantine there because there's something they didn't want anybody to see."

"You don't kill somebody and then watch the place where you dumped the body for a year just in case somebody looks there."

"I guess I'm giving them too much credit. The only reason they'd open up on us from their car is if they got surprised when we went after them, and panicked."

"Right," said Sid. "I think tomorrow morning we should back up and start over again. This is still a regular homicide. Solving it is going to be done the same way it was when we were cops—footwork and asking the right people the right questions. We should start with the people who knew the victim best."

"At least when we were cops, the suspects didn't generally shoot at us until we were closer."

They reached their gate and Sid pressed the remote control to turn on the electric motor to open the gate. He pulled forward into the driveway and pressed the button again to close the gate behind them. He began to drive up the long driveway toward the house.

"We've got a lot to look at," Ronnie said. "We need to talk to—"

The car gave a sudden violent lurch and dropped abruptly. The undercarriage hit the pavement with a spine-jarring jolt and a loud bang. The front of the car was angled downward into the ground, caught there.

Sid said, "It's a deadfall. Stay low and get ready to run for the house." He freed himself of his seat belt, took out his pistol, and switched off the dome light. Then he flung his door open and slipped out.

Ronnie had started to open her door when the first shot came. The round pounded the door and Ronnie pulled the door shut again. She slithered over the console between the two front seats and into the backseat while bullets smashed through the side windows above her head, spraying her with glittering bits of glass. She pushed out through the opposite door onto the driveway beside Sid.

Sid aimed his pistol over the hood of the car at the two spots where he had seen muzzle flashes, fired four rounds, and then ducked down. "It's coming from the yard over by the porch."

During a bad case three years ago the Abels had equipped their new Volvo with half-inch steel plates inside the door panels to protect them from small arms rounds piercing the doors. Now they could hear bullets punching through the outer sheets of painted metal and ricocheting off the steel plates to rattle in the space between.

Ronnie hit 9-1-1 on her phone and said, "This is Veronica Abel at 13551 Vista Matilija in Van Nuys. We're under fire in our driveway from unknown attackers." She ended the call, and then lay across the driver's seat to reach the remote control, and pressed the button to reopen the gate to the street.

Sid said, "Is that to let the shooters leave or the cops come in?"

"I'm not particular."

The firing began again. Three shots came from the right side by the garden, and then two more from twenty feet to the left of it, punching through the rear window and spraying glass into the backseat.

Sid fired at the flashes, aiming by resting his arm on the car door. Ronnie crawled along the side of the car to the trunk, and lay on her belly to look for targets from beneath the car.

The next time the shooting began, the muzzle flashes came from different places. One shooter had moved up the lawn toward the house, and the other was firing while trying to make a run along the hedge. Ronnie fired six rounds at the darker spot in the dark yard that she judged to be one of the shooters, and then two more into what she hoped was the other, then scrambled to hide behind the armored door.

Both shooters fired now, their rounds punching through the far side of the car, across the inside of the trunk, and then pounding against the inner wall, by then mushroomed or fragmented so they didn't penetrate. Other rounds punctured both rear tires, so the car sat down hard and closed most of the space Ronnie had used as a window for her line of fire.

Ronnie sat with her back to the rear wheel and saw that lights had come on in the upper windows of nearby houses. "It looks like we woke the neighbors."

"It's about time." Sid glanced at the lighted windows across the street as he reached to his shoulder holster pouch and took out a loaded magazine. "Do you have a spare magazine?"

"Three of them." She reached to the passenger seat and pulled out her purse by the strap. "Want one?"

"No. Just be ready to reload."

"Are you thinking we should make a run for the house?"

"I think that's what they're hoping we'll do," he said.

"Me too. So let's not."

"I think that as soon as they hear sirens they'll make their last, best attempt to kill us."

"I'm ready. Are you?"

Sid reloaded. "Yes."

"Aren't you grateful that I shamed you into taking more target practice yesterday? Admit it. I'm a good wife."

"You are. If you light up one of these bastards, you'll be a great wife, and mother of the year."

"I think I hear sirens. Ready?"

In the distance there was the *whoop* of a police siren, then another, and then the sirens blended into a single steady noise, getting louder as the cars moved closer.

The firing had stopped. Sid crawled to the front of the car where he was protected by the engine block and peered across the yard. "I don't see them."

They both became aware of a new sound that was overwhelming and drowning out the others—the deep throbbing of a helicopter's engine. "That explains it," she said. "They heard it coming and knew they were out of time."

Sid remained on his belly at the front of the car, his pistol in his hand aimed in the direction where he'd last seen muzzle flashes. The sirens stopped and the road outside the gate was suddenly bright, the canopy of tree limbs and leaves above the street lit by alternating flashes of red and blue.

The helicopter arrived overhead, circling, as three police cars sped past the others and bumped up over the gate's track into the driveway. An amplified voice said, "Place your weapons on the ground and move away from the car."

Sid and Ronnie obeyed. They kept their hands up with their fingers spread and their palms visible. The world brightened as the light from the helicopter shone down on them and the spotlights mounted on the police cars swept the yard.

In the lights they could see the reflected golden glow of brass casings that had been ejected from the attackers' guns on the far side of the yard. There were also casings from their own Glocks scattered at their feet on the driveway.

Police officers rushed to Ronnie and Sid while others fanned out all over the property with guns drawn and flashlights dissolving the pockets of darkness along the hedges and near the fountain. There were sounds of more police cars that arrived and never stopped. They continued up the street and then turned in various directions to search for the shooters.

The four police officers who stood by the Abels kept close watch on them while a sergeant spoke to them.

"What happened here?"

Sid said, "They dug a trench across our driveway and covered it, so when we drove in tonight the car got caught in the trap. Then they started firing."

"Who are they and why did they want to kill you?"

"We're private investigators, and we're on a case that seems to be worrying someone. Last night, two men shot out the windshield of our BMW up in the North Valley, and now this."

"Did you get a look?"

"Not really," said Ronnie. "There were definitely two of them both times. We opened the gate, thinking we'd see them when they ran off, but they didn't go that way. They were firing at us, and then when we heard the sirens and the chopper, the shooting stopped."

The sergeant surveyed the driveway and gestured at the brass. "I see you returned fire. Is there any chance you hit one of them?"

"I doubt it," Sid said. "They would fire and then move in the dark. We were always firing at the place where they'd been. And they kept us pinned down pretty well. I think they were using compact semiauto rifles—Uzis, Tec-9s, or something like that."

The sergeant spoke into his radio. "We're looking for a minimum of two shooters. Possibly on foot. Any pedestrian you meet could be one of them, so proceed with caution."

A cop hurried up to the sergeant, and handed him a brass casing.

The sergeant looked at the end of it, and spoke into the radio. "We've got lots of brass from the shooters at the scene, 9mm. Could be a compact tactical weapon, like an Uzi or Tec-9." He didn't need to say the rest, because the other police officers knew the implications—that the weapon might be hidden under a coat, or that the suspects might be at a distance aiming at them right now.

The sergeant's radio squawked a rapid series of short messages, units in the search conveying their locations and directions. After a few seconds there were some overriding instructions from an unseen supervisor to redirect a couple of units. The sergeant turned to the Abels. "Is there a chance they got into your house?"

"It's possible," Sid said. "We didn't see them leave. We reopened the front gate so they might leave if we returned fire, but they didn't go that way."

"All right," said the sergeant. "Can you lend me the keys?"

"They're on the keychain in the car ignition."

"Sit tight." He took the keys from the car, assembled six men, and sent them to take positions around the house. An assault group of another six appeared, three of them carrying shotguns.

In a moment they were in the front door, and as they cleared each room they turned the lights on and moved to the next. The sergeant kept silent as the team reported their progress.

Five minutes later the team declared all the rooms cleared, and began to leave the house. The sergeant said to the Abels, "They didn't get into your house."

"Cops!" said Sid.

"What do you mean?" the sergeant said.

"The only people we've seen are cops. That's how the shooters got off the property," he said. "They must have been dressed as cops."

"Sid's right," said Ronnie. "They knew that if they fired rifles in the middle of a residential neighborhood, police would be arriving in serious numbers in a few minutes. After a couple more, there would be officers going in every direction. All they had to do was wait until then and walk out after them."

The sergeant said into his radio, "The shooters may have left the yard dressed as police officers. Look at faces. Look at badges and equipment. Ask yourself all the questions when you approach another team. I repeat. The suspects might be wearing police uniforms."

Three miles away, Ed and Nicole Hoyt sat in the alley behind a row of closed restaurants and stores on Nordham Street in Northridge. Nicole pulled a gray sweatshirt down over her black, short-sleeved police uniform shirt and handed Ed his plaid flannel shirt. He pulled it over his head, and then buttoned the top two buttons. Nicole adjusted the radio scanner beside her to 506.975. It clicked and then a male voice said, "One zebra twenty-six. We went on a burglary at the Springfield Cleaners yesterday morning. They thought a few uniforms might have been part of the missing property."

"Copy," said another voice. "Any security video?"

"Negative," the cop said. "The detectives were planning to check the cameras on other businesses that might have picked something up."

"We know they won't find any pictures of us," Nicole said. "It was as dark as the inside of your pocket that night, and we had ski masks on."

Ed started the engine and the car crawled down the alley toward the next street. "Even if they don't catch us, tonight was crap."

"I know," said Nicole. "I still don't know why they're alive. I'll bet we put sixty rounds each into that car."

"We broke a lot of glass, but the shots didn't go through the doors."

"Why not?"

"I'm guessing Abel put steel plates in the door panels. That's when they should have died—right away, when they were still strapped in their seats and ducking their heads."

"But are you sure there were steel plates?"

"Pretty sure. They should have tried to run. Instead they stayed behind the car, because they knew the doors were armored. We should have learned more about them, and we'd have known they'd pull something like that."

She knew better than to press him about what they should do to kill these people now. When he was in a bad mood, Ed Hoyt had a tendency to go nonverbal.

# 8

The police questioned the Abels separately. Because they had both done this kind of interview themselves, they were not surprised that the process lasted most of the day. Detectives took turns talking to them in shifts while other cops analyzed the scene, canvassed the neighborhood, and studied surveillance footage. There were long delays while officers verified the Abels' histories, checked with the divisions that were investigating the Ballantine murder and the shooting incident in the North Valley, and talked with the people at Intercelleron.

Other officers checked on the Alex Rinosa case, but ruled him out as a suspect. He had been denied bail as a flight risk, and so far he'd spoken only with his attorney, a former federal judge who had no prior connection with Rinosa and would never have agreed to serve as a go-between.

It was evening again when the officers drove the Abels back to their house, where the doors were locked but every light was still burning. Their ruined car was still there, waiting to be towed to a police lot to be reexamined by technicians, who would certainly find nothing that wasn't immediately visible. The police lot was only a stop on the way to the wrecking yard.

Sid closed the front gate and they walked up the driveway and in the front door. They relocked the door and then went from room to room to be sure nobody had entered since the police had searched. When they had cleared the house, Ronnie stopped.

"I know this sounds stupid, but would you mind sleeping downstairs in the basement tonight?"

"Is it something I said?"

"No, silly. Both of us. We can drag a mattress down there. Then we can lock the steel doors."

"The cops said they were going to keep an eye on our house for the next few days."

"You know what that means," she said. "They don't have enough officers on duty to do more than drive by a couple of times tonight, and come quickly if there's a call with our address in it."

"You know, we're probably safe upstairs, with the doors locked and the alarm turned on."

"'Probably,'" she said. "That says it all."

"I don't mind being down there for a night, if it'll make you feel better."

"Thanks, Sid."

"Let's get the place set up," Sid said. "We've been up all night and day, and pretty soon I'm not going to want to drag mattresses around."

"Okay." She took his arm and they went to the guest room that had been Janice's bedroom when she was a child. Ronnie got pillows and blankets and carried some into the kitchen near the doorway to the basement stairs. Then they both dragged the mattress from Janice's bed through the doorway and down the steps.

Within a few minutes they had set up their bed for the night. Ronnie stared down at it for a couple of seconds, and then looked around the basement. Across the basement there was a concrete stairway that led up to a sloped set of doors at ground level. The owner before them had installed a steel door at the bottom of the steps to make the basement burglar proof, so all she saw was that. The rest of the basement was dimly lighted concrete walls interrupted by a hot-water heater, a few pipes, a sump pump, a workbench.

"Pretty dismal, isn't it?" she asked. "Like a dungeon."

"Old-world charm. As long as we sleep with our eyes closed it will look fine."

"Let's go change into something comfortable. And let's not forget guns and ammo."

"Do I need to be armed when I'm asleep?"

"Of course you do. A team of killers narrowly failed to get us last night. Even if you're too thick-skinned to die you should want your wife to feel safe. Humor me."

He sighed. "All right."

They went upstairs, changed into jeans, T-shirts, and sneakers, and brought their pistols, holsters, and reloaded spare magazines. They walked the house one more time to be sure nothing had been left unlocked, and then went back to the basement.

Ronnie set their two pistols on the floor at the head of their improvised bed and lay down beside her husband.

"This is actually pretty comfy," she said.

He didn't reply. They had been busy all day with their investigation, then lived through an ambush and firefight, and finally spent the rest of the night and part of the day at the police station. Now they were home, underground, behind a steel door designed to protect commercial buildings. The night was silent.

Ronnie moved closer on the mattress and held her body against Sid's. "Thanks for putting up with this," she said. "It just makes me feel good to be barricaded down here where nobody can get at us for one night."

"Yep," Sid said. "Tomorrow we'll talk about remodeling the basement. If we're going to sleep here more than once we might want to decorate. Or at least dust."

They were silent for a few seconds, and then she said, "Sid?"

He sighed. "I'll go check." He got up and walked across the basement to the steel door in the concrete wall. He unbolted the door, and then climbed the narrow concrete steps up to ground level. Above him was the sloping wooden door. He unlatched the door, lifted it about six inches, and looked out to scan the moonlit yard for a few seconds, then lowered it again. He bolted it, descended the stairway, closed and bolted the inner door, and walked back to the bed he and Ronnie had made.

Ronnie's eyes were shut and her chest rose and fell in the deep, slow rhythm of sleep. Sid looked down at her for a few seconds, and then went to the wall switch, switched off the lights to throw them into darkness, and slid onto the bed beside her.

He kept thinking about what had happened last night, going over all of it in his mind. The shooters must have planned many hours earlier to kill them and to escape by impersonating cops. Thinking about the police uniforms stolen from a dry cleaner's shop disturbed him, but also brought back a memory of the day he had met Ronnie.

They had been married over thirty years now. At first he was not quite able to believe in her affection. He had wondered if she was one of those career-oriented people who went into relationships assuming they would end pretty quickly anyway, so there wasn't much of an emotional investment. His mother's sister Amelia had been married about five times and she had never seemed especially elated to begin a relationship or sad to end it. Men were just one of many commodities, and she paused to sample a few of them as she passed by on her way to something else that interested her.

Ronnie had not been that way. They had met on a task force that was assembled to break up a Los Angeles group that was moving prescription drugs they'd obtained in a series of hijackings and burglaries in eastern states. He had been attracted to Sergeant Veronica Hall instantly—the gleaming brown hair, big, intelligent blue eyes, and incredibly smooth skin made it hard to keep his eyes from returning to her whenever she wasn't looking. He was at the meeting with another detective who was called out unexpectedly and took their car, so Ronnie had offered to drive him back to Metro.

On the way they talked easily and found things to laugh about, and he caught the moment when she was stopped at a light, and in midsentence flicked her eyes downward from his and double-checked his left hand for a ring. His pulse quickened. She must be interested. But maybe she wasn't, because what she said next was, "Would you mind if I made a very quick stop on the way? I have a couple of uniforms at the tailor's."

"At the tailor's?" he said. "You have uniforms tailor-made? Not that you don't look great, but are you taking money from the evidence room or something?"

"It's just alterations," she said. "They're a necessary expense. Women's uniforms have to be taken in at some places and let out at others or they don't fit right."

"You mean everybody still does that in this day and age?"

"Only people who aren't shaped like men. Meaning women. Female officers."

"But that's not fair. You should complain."

She laughed. "Don't cry for me. The world's nearly perfect. There's body armor made to fit women, sort of. If you and I were the same rank I'd have the same title and be getting the same pay as you. And if you were to put your hands on me without my permission, I could get you suspended and probably fired. That's enough progress for one lifetime."

"I'll remember to keep my distance," he said.

"Very prudent," she said. She pulled to a stop in front of a small shop. "I'll be right back."

He watched her run inside, hand a woman at the counter a credit card, sign a slip, and take a couple of uniforms on hangers, then hurry back. She put the uniforms in the trunk, resumed the driver's seat, and pulled back out into traffic, heading toward the police headquarters building. "I apologize for that," she said. "Of course, your wife probably picks up your uniforms from the cleaners on the rare occasions when a detective needs one." So maybe she was interested, but she wasn't sure if he was married. Plenty of married cops didn't wear a ring on duty.

"Interesting thought," he said. "I'll add it to my collection of fantasies about my future wife." He felt a moment of pride for the way he had slipped that into the conversation.

"I hope the rest of them are better than that," she said.

"They are, but they can't all be about the same subject or I'll seem shallow."

"You'll have to tell me the others another time," she said. "Here's your stop."

He thanked her, got out, and went into the building. As soon as he was inside where he could watch her pull away, he regretted not asking her to go for coffee sometime, or asking for her phone number, or giving her some absolutely clear signal that he wanted to see her again.

That part solved itself a few days later, at the next meeting of the task force. He came into the conference room and sat down, and she came in a moment later and sat down beside him. All through the meeting he wondered how to broach the idea of seeing her alone. When the meeting ended, they both took an exceptional amount of time packing papers into file folders and briefcases, while others left the room. When it was safe he said, "I'd like to talk to you for a moment," but she replied by placing a business card in his hand. She said, "Then call me."

He nodded and walked out, and took a few paces to think it over. She'd had the card ready in her hand before he had spoken. As he took it he had seen the standard police business card, but he had also seen a personal number written in a fine, tight script.

He dialed the handwritten number about an hour after the shift ended. She said, "This sounds like the police force's most eligible bachelor."

"Right. I'm sick of that," he said. "I called to see if you would marry me."

"I think we should start with something less risky. How about dinner and a movie? If we don't like each other during dinner we can skip the movie."

He said, "That sounds safe. What kind of movies do you like?"

"I don't care. I'll sit through anything that doesn't have cops in it, or lovable thieves. I don't care if it's got British actors whacking each other with swords, just so it's not like work."

"And for dinner, is there anything you don't eat?"

"Surprise me. If I hate it, I'll have something to complain about and I won't have to strain my brain for stupid small talk."

"I'll pick a place from the Health Department warning lists."

"There should be a lot of tables on short notice."

"Cheap too. Want to give me your home address so I can pick you up?"

"Okay. It's 5-9-9-5 Montevideo in Sherman Oaks, apartment B as in Bravo."

"I know the building. Adobe brown stucco on top and wood brown below. I got a homicide in the apartment on the left in the back once."

"That's apartment D," she said. "It's kept the rent low. If it hadn't happened I'd have had to kill somebody here myself."

"Maybe it's good that we didn't solve it. See you at six thirty."

They went to dinner and got so deeply engaged in conversation that they forgot about the movie and went to her apartment. They talked from the moment they arrived at her door until he left at 2:00 a.m. When she let him out the door she said, "Thanks, Sid. That was the best first date I ever had." She watched him nod, but he said nothing, so she added, "I thought I was pretty fun. Aren't you even going to kiss me?"

"I figured you'd find a way to let me know if you thought that was a good idea. You brought up the permission issue the first time we met."

"We've been talking ourselves hoarse all night. You couldn't find four words to ask?"

He took her into his arms and gave her a long, gentle kiss. When he pulled back, she was still standing in the doorway with her eyes closed and her head tilted up toward him. After a second she opened her eyes. "I guess you'd better get going."

"Didn't like it?" he said.

"Liked it too much," she said. "See you." She shut the door.

Tonight, as Sid lay on the mattress beside her, he spent a few seconds thinking how glad he was that his captain had put him on that task force years ago. Then his mind returned to the events of last night.

In spite of his exhaustion it was hard to get his mind to stop going over and over the situation they were in. He and Ronnie had made no progress yet on the murder of James Ballantine. They had barely caught up with the information the police compiled right after the crime. Yet there were two potential killers out there at this moment who wanted Sid and Ronnie dead, and their last attempt would have killed them if it hadn't been for sheer luck. The Abels hardly ever drove the Volvo with the steel in it for work anymore. They'd only done it last night because the BMW had taken a rifle bullet through its windshield. He still hadn't seen the shooters, or heard their voices, or even identified the make of their car. He kept reminding himself that lying here awake was getting him nowhere. He needed to sleep. The only way to get rid of the killers was to solve the murder. But solving the murder required going out and interviewing people, and going out would expose them to the killers. Only after he had followed the circle enough times did he slip into sleep.

# 9

Nicole Hoyt hoped this would be the success that she and Ed had coming. She looked up and down the quiet night street, where the streetlamps every hundred feet or so made small pools of light on the sidewalks and a little portion of the street. Nobody was visible, and the only cars were parked along the curb. All the houses had gone dark hours ago. She watched Ed kneeling on the strip of grass by the curb. He reached into the small concrete opening in the lawn and turned the wrench clockwise to shut off the water supply to the house. Then he replaced the cover and stood.

Together they moved to the high hedge at the front of the yard. Ed lifted her into it so she could reach the chain link fence hidden inside the hedge's foliage. She pulled herself over, and then lowered herself through the hedge with a whisper of leaves and the soft crackling of twigs. She pictured herself as a ghost going through a wall.

She waited, and Ed reached over the fence to hand her the five-gallon can he had brought, and then climbed over to join her. His transit through the hedge was louder than hers, but it was over in a moment. They crouched by the hedge for thirty seconds to see if anyone had heard, and then walked up the driveway to the front of the house. Ed had spotted the antique leaded-glass window when he came to dig the car trap a couple of days ago. Most of the house had replacement windows that were double-pane safety glass that you couldn't break with a hammer. But the Abels must have had a soft-headed view of the antique glass, and left it in when they updated the place. Ed used his knife to bend the lead frame, pried out a pane of the glass, then another, and another, until there was a space large enough for Nicole to fit through. He boosted her up and in, and then handed the five-gallon can in after her.

Nicole waited for a few minutes to let her eyes adjust to the deeper darkness while any sounds she'd made faded into the past. Then she walked lightly to the middle of the house, where she reached the stairs up to the two-story addition. Upstairs there was a long central hallway with bedrooms on both sides. The darkness here was relieved a bit by a long skylight that let moonlight in to reflect on the polished hardwood floor. She advanced about twenty feet, looking into rooms as she went, and then stopped. This was as far as she dared to go. If she went on trying to find the room where the Abels slept, she would risk waking them. This spot would serve her purpose. She unscrewed the top of the can and poured a pool of gasoline on the hardwood, and then watched it spread along the hall in the grooves of the floor as she backed down the stairs to the living room.

She soaked the carpet in the living room because that was the way a person awakened at night would try to get out. Next she went from room to room on the ground floor pouring a stream of gasoline along the outer walls. When she finished the walls she had some left, so she poured a pool under the gas stove, another one in front of the back door, and the last on the floor at the front door. Since the cause of the fire was going to be impossible to miss, she left the top off the empty gas can and set it on the living room coffee table.

She stood on a chair to climb out the leaded-glass window again, gave Ed a thumbs-up signal, and kept going down the lawn. As she passed the punctured husk of the Abels' Volvo she stopped to look inside. She silently conceded that Ed had been right. There were dozens of bullet holes in the outer side of each door, but none of the bullets seemed to have made a single hole coming through the inner side.

Nicole kept going down the driveway to the gate and looked up and down the street. The neighborhood was still quiet. The windows of the houses were dark and the air was still, so all she could hear was the occasional distant *swish* of a car a block away on the boulevard.

When Nicole was satisfied she turned toward the house and saw Ed standing at the front of the leaded-glass window, watching her and waiting. She waved to him, and then saw him step to the side of the window, strike a match, and toss it toward the open gap in the glass. His match didn't quite make it into the house, because the gasoline fumes from inside ignited before it reached the opening. There was a sound like *whooomp* and a bright orange flame tinged with blue shot outward a few feet and then subsided.

Immediately the house began to burn. The flames streaked around the rooms and across the floors and slithered up the walls to the ceiling. Each instant made the interior brighter.

Ed ran toward Nicole along the driveway, and behind him she could see the fire growing, flames rising to light up the windows. She knew that the flames were mostly just gasoline at the moment, but the wood and fabric would be fully involved in a minute or two, and while these flames were turning the living room floor into a lake of fire, others were marching along the unseen hallway to the bedrooms in the back.

Ed reached her and they sat down just inside the fence in the deep shadow of the tall hedge. They took their MP5 assault rifles out from under their jackets, extended the stocks, pulled back the cocking levers, slid the selectors to auto, and studied the doors and windows of the house. A few seconds later all the alarms and smoke detectors seemed to go off at once.

Like a shriek in the dark, the loud, high-pitched beeping of the fire alarms woke Sid, and he sat up and reached out to touch Ronnie and reassure himself that she was still there. She clutched his arm once then let go.

Sid stood, stepped to the wall, felt for the light switch, turned on the lights, and then climbed the stairs and gingerly touched the doorknob. "The metal's hot. The house must be on fire."

"Are you sure? I don't smell smoke."

"Smoke rises, so it's not down here yet."

"We'd better get dressed," she said, and reached for the clothes she had folded and left on the workbench. She tossed his clothes to him.

He stepped into his jeans and put on his running shoes and T-shirt, then stuck the pistol into his belt and the spare magazines in his pockets. He handed Ronnie her pistol and spare magazines.

She pocketed the ammunition. "You know, we probably won't need these. It could be something normal. A short circuit. I was exhausted, and I could have left the coffeepot plugged in."

He said, "It's time to get out of here."

She looked up the stairs. "We can't go that way," she said. "I guess it's got to be the other way into the yard."

They made it to the steel door across the basement just as the light went out. The fire alarms had gone off with the light, and the quiet was a relief. Sid unbolted the door and they went through and closed it behind them. They climbed the concrete steps to the cellar door. Ronnie tugged on the bolt.

Nicole Hoyt watched the doors and windows while the fire burned, but nobody came out. The fire alarms had melted into silence as the fire grew, but they had apparently been loud enough to raise some of the neighbors. Lights came on in houses along the street, and Nicole knew people would be calling the fire department. She waited for Ed to notice, and then realized that he already had. In the light from the fire she could see the muscles in his jaw working. They had wanted to stay long enough to shoot the Abels as they tried to escape from the fire, but time was passing. He looked up the street at the houses again.

"That's it," he muttered. "Time to go." He stood.

They both moved to the hedge a few feet apart, put their MP5 rifles against their bellies and zipped their jackets over them, then pushed the foliage aside, reached in to grasp the fence, and pulled themselves up and over.

They both trotted around the corner of the street to their car. They got in and Ed drove them out of the residential streets onto the boulevard and then to the parking spot in the alley near the office building they had chosen. They got out and stepped to the back of the building.

Ed had already prepared the way into the building hours earlier. He had used a crowbar to pry the shield away from the lock and a flexible shim to pop the door open, and then taped the latch bolt down so the door would be ready when they arrived. He opened the door and they were in. He pulled the tape off the lock, and they ran to the first-floor elevator, rode it to the top floor, and then climbed the stairs to the roof access door.

They stood on the roof and stared down at the quiet street, which was now lit up with a waving, flickering light from the flames. They both took out their rifles, found firing positions, and studied the Abels' house. After a few seconds Nicole said, "I can see the house and some of the yard pretty well because of the fire, but I still can't see anybody coming out."

"I can't either," Ed said. "A lot of times when you try to burn somebody out at night, the smoke kills them before they wake up." He kept watching in silence for a full minute before he added, "There's also the fact that all houses burn different. Sometimes the space in the center for the open-beam living room channels the heat up into the peak and it burns like instant hell. They could be crispy critters by now."

"Should we test?"

"Yeah. Get ready." Ed shouldered his MP5 and aimed at the shadow of a big tree in the Abels' yard.

The silence was shattered by a shot, and Sid saw dirt kick up twenty feet from either of them. They both crouched. "Don't fire back!" he called to Ronnie.

"I can't. I don't see them."

"They don't see us, either. They're trying to draw fire so they'll spot a muzzle flash."

They waited for a few seconds, and there was another shot. This one hit in the shadow of a tree on the left side of the yard.

"That time I saw the flash," Ronnie called out. "They're on the roof of that office building over on the boulevard."

"Okay," Sid said. "Do you have your phone?"

"Yes. I'll call it in."

While Ronnie called 9-1-1, Sid plotted a route to the office building. In this part of the city the zoning prohibited office buildings over four stories tall, so the shooters were only about sixty feet up. Their view was probably hampered by the upper boughs of the tall trees in the neighborhood, and even by some of the newer houses, all of them two-story mini-mansions built to nearly cover their lots, and shouldering right up to each other.

Ronnie's voice came to Sid. "I called it in."

Sid said, "I think once we're out of this yard we can make it to that office building without giving them a shot at us."

"I'll meet you at the far side of the Fogels' house."

Sid moved into a spot where he was out of the shooters' view behind the hedge on the right side of the yard. He saw Ronnie emerge from the shadows, run along the side of their burning house, then into the hedge. It looked as though she had merged with it, but he knew she had reached in among the leafy branches to clutch the chain link fence and pull herself up and over it.

There was another shot, and bark sprayed from the tree that Ronnie had just left. Sid backed into the area along the front fence, sidestepping to keep from separating from the foliage or presenting a human shape to the shooters on the office building rooftop. He knew he would be visible for a second or two when he reached the bare iron gate.

Sid reached the end of the gate and crouched beside the electric motor. He heard the distant sirens of the fire trucks and police cars and knew that this was the moment. The shooters would be distracted for a few seconds, looking for the emergency vehicles. He flipped the manual switch to engage the motor's battery power, and as the gate rolled along its track to the side, he ducked low and slipped out.

He ran eight steps along the sidewalk before the shots began. There was automatic rifle fire, a burst of it chipping the sidewalk behind him at first and then adjusting to hit the pavement ahead of him, but always to his left. Apparently the shooter had only had a glimpse of him as he cleared the gate, but the tops of the magnolia trees along the street had given him cover the rest of the way.

The fire engines were not far off now, and their sirens were making dogs all along their route answer them with howls. Sid and Ronnie ran along the dark space between two houses onto the next street. A hundred feet beyond it was the boulevard.

Sid and Ronnie turned toward the office building and made their way along the lighted boulevard, past closed stores and coffee shops. They put their guns in the backs of their waistbands under their shirts and hurried along. Sid said, "Keep your eyes open for anybody coming this way carrying anything, and look at every car. They could be hoping to shoot us out here."

"I am," Ronnie said.

They reached the front door of the office building, found it locked, and kept going to the side. At the rear of the building was an alley with an entrance to the parking lot that took up the ground level. The entrance was covered by a steel cage for the night, but around the rest of the lot, there was only a four-foot concrete wall.

The Abels went over the wall into the lot and ducked down immediately to keep from being seen. They crouched, ran to the wall of the building, and found the door to the stairwell. Sid ran his hand along the edge of the protective plate over the lock. "It's been jimmied," he said. "The plate's bent outward."

Ronnie said, "This looks like the only way in. I hate doors that are the only way in."

"Me too," he said. He tugged on the door, but it didn't open, so he reached into his pocket, opened the pocketknife on his key chain, pushed it into the crack between the door and the jamb where the plate had once protected it, depressed the spring, and tugged the door open.

They stepped inside and closed the door without letting it make a noise, then climbed the staircase as they had been trained to do, one of them aiming a weapon upward between the railings of the staircase while the other climbed up one flight and then waited on the landing to cover the other, making little noise and listening for more sounds from above them in the building.

Sid and Ronnie climbed the next flight quickly, turned at the landing, and then saw the door to the roof at the top of the next flight. The door was propped open, so they could see the starlit sky. They moved upward and stepped out onto the roof, looking over the sights of the pistols they gripped in both hands ready to fire.

The roof was deserted. Sid ran along the roof to a raised section that shielded a second door. Sid flung the door open and took the stairs downward, then came back up. "There's another staircase that goes to the back of the building. They must have left this door open to draw everybody's attention away from that one. They're gone."

Ronnie moved to the edge of the roof near the waist-high wall and looked over it at the pavement below. As Sid approached he could see that a few feet to her right there was a scattering of brass casings. He picked one up. "Nine millimeter. Same as the last time, except this time they used full auto."

"Oh my God." Ronnie looked over her shoulder at him, and then pointed.

The fire at their house was visible through gaps in the trees. The flames were steadily devouring bare, blackened studs and piles of half-combusted rubble. Fire trucks and police cars had arrived and firefighters had run hoses through the front gate, but all they were doing was wetting down glowing spots on charred lumber. Police cars blocked the road to protect them.

"My house," she said. "I can hardly believe it. I loved that house."

Sid said, "It's hard to figure out what these people are trying to accomplish."

"Other than killing us? Nothing comes to mind."

# 10

Sid and Ronnie rented a car at the Burbank airport, then drove it to the office of their insurance agent on Riverside in Burbank to break the news about their house and their car. Their third stop was at a gun store a few blocks east on Magnolia, where the owner knew them. They bought a supply of 9mm ammunition for their Glock 17 pistols, a new cleaning kit, and six spare magazines. Just down the street they bought two new laptop computers.

As they drove west, Sid said, "You're thinking about the house, aren't you?"

"Aren't you?"

"You want to drive by there and look?"

She looked at him in mild irritation. "It's gone, Sid."

"Houses can be replaced."

"I was happy there for over twenty-five years. We picked it out together, and worked together there. We raised our kids there. They brought the grandchildren there to see us, so it's the place they'll remember us in. The place wasn't fancy or even very pretty, but I would have liked to die there."

"You had your chance last night."

"You couldn't resist that?"

"Sorry. Look, the only way either of us is going to feel better about it is if we get the people who did it. First we find a comfortable hotel, so we have a place to sleep for now. Then we get started."

They checked into a hotel in the western part of the Valley in Calabasas using a credit card in Ronnie's maiden name, pulled their car around to the rear of the building, and backed into a parking space near the center of the lot so it was unlikely that they would be blocked in. They didn't like being right next to the building. In an emergency they could push another car out of their way, but they couldn't batter down a wall of the hotel. They went into their room and began the process of searching the Internet for a rental house.

It took three days to find and rent the right one. The house was a small two-story building with white clapboards on a street that ended in a cul-de-sac. The house was furnished, and the yard was small and dominated by a rose garden, but it was shaded by trees and looked pleasant to Ronnie. As soon as they signed the rental agreement in the real estate office, they drove to another electronics store and bought two more sets of devices. One was a six-camera all-weather surveillance system that could be monitored and controlled from a computer based anywhere. The other was an array of tiny pinhole cameras, each with its own battery-operated transmitter.

When they reached the house they installed the internal cameras first. They trained one on the front entryway, one on the kitchen door at the back of the house, and one on the upstairs hallway that led to the two bedrooms. Next they installed three cameras outside—one on a tree limb aimed at the back of the house, one under the eaves of the garage to cover the driveway and the side of the house, and one on the roof aimed down toward the front walkway and the lawn. The cameras were not large or obtrusive, but the Abels made an effort to make them difficult to notice.

When they finished with the outdoor cameras, they spent much more time and effort installing the pinhole cameras. Sid removed a strip of crown molding in the living room, drilled holes near each end, aimed the lens out one, fitted the transmitter into a space he cut in the underlying wall, and put the molding back up. He and Ronnie placed other pinhole cameras in other spots in various rooms. There was one in a box of cereal on a shelf in the kitchen, and one had its transmitter inside a sound system speaker with the camera lens looking like part of the manufacturer's logo. Others sat in glass-fronted cabinets, bookcases, or under pieces of furniture. One was inside the keypad for the alarm system. Sid opened their computer, signed into the monitoring site for the larger cameras, looked at each image one more time, and then repeated the procedure for each of the pinhole cameras. They made a few adjustments to the angles of the cameras to provide the best coverage of the interior of the house.

When they finished, Ronnie and Sid walked the house again. She said, "Not bad. They'll probably see the security cameras, and do something to disable them. While they're doing that, the pinhole cameras will get plenty of footage of them. Even if they find all of the pinhole cameras, some of them will have recorded them tearing the place apart."

"Let's hope it works that way," said Sid. "It shouldn't take a pro more than a few days to find out we've rented a house, and then we'll see."

"We should put more stuff in here so it looks as though we've moved in," Ronnie said. "Of course we don't have anything, because it all got burned up, and they know it."

"Just the same, we'd better do some shopping and leave some new clothes and things here tonight." Sid said. "Just don't buy anything that you want to keep."

They drove to a few stores where they could pick up clothing and furnishings. Everything had to be new, but it didn't have to be expensive. They bought supplies at a grocery store, and returned to the rented house in Burbank. They hung some clothes in the closets, put the clothes they'd been wearing in a laundry basket, spread some magazines around in the living room, and put food in the refrigerator. Then they made a stop at the phone company store so Sid could replace the cell phone he'd lost in the fire, and went back to their hotel.

Late in the evening Sid looked over at Ronnie, who was lying on the bed and staring at the ceiling. He said, "I know you still feel rotten about the house, but you've been doing a good job, as always. You're a pro."

She said, "What else can I do? But I'll feel rotten about this forever. I had things at home that I can barely even think about. Our wedding pictures. The pictures from the hospital when Mitch and Janice were born. Things like that."

He went over to the bed where she was lying and lay down next to her. "Remember when the kids had that party for our thirtieth anniversary? Janice made all those place cards and table decorations and things from the old pictures? There must have been a couple hundred different ones, including our wedding. And there were baby pictures. She did it with a computer. I'm sure she's still got the file with the original photographs she scanned."

Ronnie sat up, her eyes wide. She leaned over and kissed Sid. "You sentimental old bastard. All this time you've been thinking about it too."

"I remembered those pictures because the other night I just happened to be thinking about when we first got together. Somehow they were connected."

"I'm going to call Janice right now." She got up and went to the table to pick up her phone.

A few minutes later she ended her call. "She's got them."

"I thought she would."

Ronnie looked at him from the corner of her eye. "Just which parts of when we first got together?"


The next morning they changed rental cars again at the Burbank airport and drove to the Intercelleron Corporation complex in the West Valley. As they approached the address, Ronnie dialed her phone.

"Hi, Mr. Hemphill. This is Veronica Abel. We're almost to your company. Can you meet us outside the front gate?" There was a pause. "Good. See you in a minute." She hung up.

Moments later, they approached the main building of Intercelleron Corporation. The building was a long and low self-consciously modern structure. It was set into a grassy hillside so it looked as though it were a taller building that had nearly completed the process of sinking into the earth. There was only one sign, an unobtrusive tan brick rectangle with script that said the single word, and it was also set into the hillside as though about to be submerged. Hemphill appeared at the glass doors in the front of the building and walked out to meet them as Sid drove to the curb in front. When he reached the sidewalk, Ronnie said, "Get in."

Hemphill looked confused, but opened the door and got into the backseat. "Where are we going?"

"Just for a little ride while we talk," said Ronnie.

As soon as Sid pulled away from the curb Hemphill said, "I'm glad to see you. I've been worried about you. The police have been here at least three times. A Detective Hebert came, and then another detective from the North Hollywood station named Fuentes, and then another from Van Nuys. One said you had been attacked, and the next said your house had been burned down."

"We're fine," said Sid. "But there seems to be somebody who is very interested in this case. How are things here? Have you or any of your colleagues noticed anything unusual since you retained us?"

"I don't think so. What sort of thing do you mean?"

Ronnie said, "Anyone watching the facility or following you. Anybody showing up from the power company or the phone company to check the wiring in your office. Somebody from your insurance company, or fire marshals who need to do an inspection."

"Oh, I see," said Hemphill. "You think someone might have bugged my office or phone or something. That's why we're out here driving around instead of sitting in my office."

"It's a precaution," said Sid. "Some precautions take a lot of work and expense, and some are simple. We're wondering if there might be a leak, because the attempts to kill us started the day after we met with you."

"I see," said Hemphill. "I'll check with the people at reception, and also the security people, and see if anyone has been doing repairs or anything. But I think if they had done something in my office, I or my assistant would have known."

"That brings up another issue," said Ronnie. "Are the company's security people in-house employees, or do you have a contract with a security company that provides guards and surveillance?"

"They come from an outside service, but it's Quimby's. It's hardly an unknown company. They used to guard stagecoaches."

Sid said, "Quimby's is a famous name, about as old as Brinks or Pinkerton's. But any company can hire the wrong job candidate."

Ronnie said, "Do you know the guards?"

Hemphill said, "Know them? You mean personally? No. But they're all in uniform, with ID badges. And they're bonded. They carry guns, so I assume they've been trained and had background checks. Are you thinking a bogus security employee killed James Ballantine?"

"We don't have any idea who killed Mr. Ballantine," Ronnie said. "Right now we're just trying to figure out how a pair of shooters turned up behind us the first day after you hired us. Knowing that might tell us more. We'd like you to be observant, and see if there's anything that's not normal."

"This is getting terrifying," said Hemphill. "I don't know where to look."

"Wherever you can," said Ronnie. "Think about your office and your house, and search them thoroughly. Look for anything that's plugged into an electrical outlet that you didn't put there, anything new that you see in the phone junction box on the outside wall of your house. Look around the neighborhood for people who just moved in and have a view of your house, or any parked vehicle that could be used to watch you."

"We don't want to scare you," said Sid. "But maybe somebody isn't happy about the company's decision to pursue this. If you find a suspicious device or notice somebody following you or paying too much attention, call us, and we'll come right away."

"All right. What else can I do?" said Hemphill.

"One thing we missed in the packet you gave us is a list of employees," Ronnie said. "We need their names, phone numbers, and addresses. Maybe you could get us a copy of the company directory."

Hemphill frowned. "I don't know. It's against company policy, and they're very touchy about the directories. If I were caught carrying one off the premises—"

"All right. Don't try. Lay it out on your desk, open it, and take pictures of it with your phone, two pages at a time. Send them to my phone." She handed him a business card.

"Anything else?"

"Don't tell anybody what you're doing. Observe the people around you, and let us know anything that catches your attention."

"What should I be looking at?"

"Everything that isn't the same as it was a month ago."

# 11

Ronnie came out of the shower in their hotel room, and put on a pair of sweat pants and a T-shirt. She saw Sid sitting at the table near the windows looking at the screen of the computer. "What are you looking at?"

Sid said, "I'm just going over the images from the surveillance cameras we installed in the decoy house." He turned it so she could see the screen was divided into six images. He clicked on the fast-forward arrow and the images stayed almost exactly the same, but the lighting on the six scenes changed simultaneously and rapidly, the shadows moving across each scene, melting into darkness, and then brightening again when the sun came up and the light shone through the windows. The play of lights and shadows went through another cycle to night.

The camera mounted on the tree caught a set of headlights that stopped in front of the house, and a second later, backed out of the frame.

"Hold it!" said Ronnie.

Sid stopped the video, backed it up slowly, and froze it. "They stopped and then backed up to get out of sight. Do you think they saw the camera?"

"In the dark? They'd have to be pretty good."

"They *are* pretty good."

He tapped the brightness adjustment on the computer a few times and then reversed the video and brought the car to its farthest point forward, where it stopped. There were the two headlights and the front bumper and the hood, but the windshield carried only the reflection of the streetlamp across the street. Sid brought the car forward and back a couple of times.

Ronnie said, "Maybe somebody can clean it up and get an image of the driver through the glass."

"I see a Toyota symbol on the hood, the thing that looks like a T with turned-up arms in a circle. I can't read the plate, though. Can you?"

"No. The glare from the headlights washes it out."

"If it's them, it's probably a stolen plate anyway," he said.

He let the recording go forward. For a few minutes, there was no change in any of the six images, so Sid sped up the video again. Then the image from the tree camera went black.

Ronnie said, "They found that one."

"That was the delay. They must have walked around behind it to unplug the camera, so they wouldn't be recorded while they did it."

One by one, the other two exterior images went black. No image of a person had appeared on any screen. Then in a single stroke, the three interior cameras went black. "They must have turned off the power to the house."

Sid sighed. "It's okay, that's what we expected, remember? We put that set of cameras in so they'd have something to find and think they'd gotten everything."

"I didn't actually think they'd do it without ever showing up on a screen."

"Let's see how we did with the pinhole cameras." He closed the link to the first camera system, and then went into the computer's memory and selected the pinhole camera he had designated pinhole 1. The image on the screen was a plain gray with a couple of horizontal white lines.

"Oh, crap," said Ronnie.

"Wait. That's the one I put inside the alarm system keypad housing."

"Fast-forward and see if anybody opens it."

Sid sped up the recording. After a while, the horizontal white lines became bright. "There," he said. "Somebody is in the house at this point. They turned on a light." The light remained on for a while, and then went out again. It stayed out until the recording slowed when it reached the present. "Okay. They didn't open the keypad."

Ronnie said, "They didn't have to, since they already fooled the alarm system. But I'm thinking we may still get them. We just saw that the pinhole cameras were transmitting. Even if these people found them all, they'd have to go back in time to keep their images from being recorded while they were dismantling them. Now that we know they were in the house and turned on the lights, we know we've got something."

Sid switched to pinhole 2, which was in the kitchen. It provided a clear, bright, well-defined shot of the back door, a few feet of counter, and a Viking stove. The image was dark, and then it lightened, with a square of sunshine appearing through the east window on the floor, showing the shadow of wooden divisions between panes. The shadow moved across the floor and disappeared again, and then reappeared, but no human figure ever came across the screen.

The third pinhole was the camera hidden behind the crown molding, and it showed a clear image of the living room. Sid rushed through the sequence from the first night and day until evening. The room got dimmer and dimmer, until most of the light came from a table lamp in the corner of the room. The table light went off, and then they saw the front door open. Sid returned the recording to normal speed.

A large, muscular man stepped into the room. He wore a black jacket, blue jeans, and tight leather gloves. Over his head was a knitted ski mask with holes for his eyes and mouth.

"A ski mask," said Ronnie. "I guess we should have expected this. They had seen the cameras outside, so they expected there would be cameras inside too."

"Wait," said Sid. "He's studying the cameras we expected him to see. As soon as he's sure he's disabled them, maybe he'll take the mask off."

They watched the man move a chair, stand on it, and unplug the camera in the corner of the room.

While he was doing it, a second person came in the front door wearing a ski mask. This one was shorter than the first. He set down what looked like a black canvas tool bag, and then stepped into the dining room and stood on a chair to unplug the second camera.

Ronnie and Sid both leaned forward and stared hard at the image on the computer screen. When the two intruders got down off their chairs and walked toward the stairs, they both realized the same thing.

Ronnie got it out first. "That's a woman!"

Sid said, "It is."

They kept their eyes on the screen. The man moved quickly through the house looking for more cameras, found the one that had been trained on the back door of the house, and unplugged it. He kept moving, but didn't seem to find any of the pinhole cameras. He went out the back door, and a minute later the power in the house came on. The digital clock above the stove blinked, and when the man came back in he saw it, looked at his watch, and reset the clock.

The Abels switched back to the living room camera to stay on him. The table lamp that had been off was on again.

The woman picked up the small canvas bag she had left in the living room and followed the man up the stairs toward the second floor.

"Can we pick them up on the cameras upstairs?"

Sid clicked from camera to camera until he found the one that showed the upstairs hallway. A moment later the intruders appeared. They walked down the hallway quietly, the woman carrying the canvas bag while the man went ahead. He looked into each room he passed.

"They're looking for the master bedroom," said Ronnie.

Sid spoke to the screen. "How can you stand those masks? They're hot and itchy. Come on! Take them off!"

But the two kept the masks on. They went all the way to the room on the end, which was the master, and stepped inside.

Sid was still staring at the screen, not moving.

"Well?" said Ronnie. "Switch to the next one."

"There's no camera in there." He stopped the playback.

"What?" She looked at him, astonished. "You didn't put a camera in the bedroom?"

"I only had a few pinhole cameras. They're in the entry, living room, kitchen, upstairs hallway, dining room, and alarm pad. We'll have to wait for them to come out."

She punched his arm just below the shoulder.

"Ow! Why would you hit me?"

"Because I'm speechless."

Sid started the recording again and sat rubbing his arm while they watched. After only about two minutes, the intruders emerged into the hallway. Sid adjusted the sound until the faint squeaks of the intruders' rubber-soled shoes could be heard, but there was no sound of speech. The two passed close to the camera. "No question that's a woman," Sid said.

"No question," Ronnie said. "Let's pick them up on the living room camera."

"Okay," Sid said. "The time on it says nineteen thirty-two oh one." He switched to the living room camera and clicked on the fast-forward button and watched, then paused at the matching time. "Nineteen thirty-two and one second." He started the tape again.

The man descended the stairs first. His gun was now in his hand. While the woman came down the stairs he stepped to the front window to look out.

"Stop it again," said Ronnie.

Sid stopped it.

"Where's her tool bag?"

"She hasn't got it," said Sid. "Let's see if she had it when she left the bedroom." He switched back to the hallway camera.

When the two came out of the bedroom there was little light. The woman's head was bent down slightly, and her hands seemed to be doing something. "She seems to be folding it up." The woman stuck the folded canvas bag into the pocket of her jacket.

Sid said, "Whatever she brought with her is in that room."


Ed and Nicole Hoyt sat in Ed's big black pickup truck on the hillside above Forest Lawn cemetery. They found a spot that was perfectly aligned with the street in Burbank where the Abels had rented a house. Ed had a sixty-power spotting scope propped on the dashboard of his truck with a short-legged tripod to keep it stable.

He kept watch, leaning forward and resting his chin on the steering wheel to keep his eye to the scope. He could see the front of the house clearly, and the street leading up to it and away from it. The place was nice—a few big trees, a deep green front lawn that wasn't so big it would be a chore to keep cut, and a neighborhood that had looked deserted for much of the day. The image through a high-powered scope was silent, but he could imagine the sounds of birds. He leaned back a little and looked at the clock on the dashboard. He sighed and returned his eye to the scope.

Nicole looked up from the game she was playing on her phone. "We should have got out of bed earlier. They could have gone out and come back five times by now."

"Probably," he said. "But I was just thinking I was glad we didn't."

Nicole smiled. "Thank you, Ed."

"Yeah," he said. "We would have just been sitting up here for, like, two extra hours."

"God. You really are a dope."

He turned his head and grinned at her, and then returned his eye to the scope.

Nicole felt better. Ed could hardly ever resist acting like a big, stupid guy who could barely be bothered to put his shoes on the right feet. It seemed to be a lot of fun for him. But she had been watching him for too long to buy it. She had seen him use exceptional, not intelligence, exactly—because that implied an ability to think about things that were abstract, and he apparently never tried—but mental acuteness. He was keenly observant. His eye was focused to pick up the subtlest changes in the visible, substantial world that might tell him something he could use—a weakness, a vulnerability, a tell. Whatever tigers had, he had.

"Something's happening," he said.

"At the house?"

"Yeah," he said. "I hope you've got it wired right."

"I always do," she said. "That one time when it didn't work was because it was there so long the phone battery got weak. This time I looked everything over before we left. The phone battery is new and fully charged. It'll work. So what do you see?"

"A guy just drove up and got out. I'm pretty sure it's Abel. Different car, of course. The last one had a lot of holes in it."

"Is he going in?"

"No. He's standing by his car. He seems to be waiting for somebody."

"Can I see?"

Ed lifted the scope on its tripod and moved it to her side of the dashboard. She adjusted it and then stared into the eyepiece and adjusted it some more. "That's Sid Abel all right. But this doesn't look good."

"It looks pretty good to me," Ed said.

"There's a truck coming up. Looks like a big UPS delivery truck. It's pulling up in front of the house. We can't do anything until that guy's made his delivery and left. Wait. Something else coming up behind it—oh, shit—a cop car. Two of them. One's going around the truck to this end of the block, and the other is staying back on the other end. Abel's talking to somebody in the truck. It's not a delivery truck. A guy's getting out the back. He's carrying one of those protective suits. Bomb squad."

"Damn," said Ed. He was uncharacteristically quiet.

"How do they know?"

"We must have missed one of the cameras the other night."

"You want to look?" she asked.

"Okay." He took the spotting scope back, readjusted it, and watched.

Thirty seconds passed, and then Nicole said, "What's going on now?"

"It looks like they're getting one of the guys ready to go into the house. They're getting him into the bomb suit. This will take a few minutes. The thing weighs, like, eighty pounds. They also have to do something to clear the area of people in case he screws up. It looks like the cops at both ends of the street are out of their cars and knocking on doors."

"What do you think we should do?" Nicole asked.

"See if Abel goes into the house to show the guy where to look. Dial the first part of the phone number. All but the last digit, and get ready. I'll spot for you."

She put in the area code and the first six numbers and waited.

\* \* \*

Ronnie sat in the back of a police car with a sergeant from the police department bomb squad. They were a full block from the rented house. The sergeant said, "This is a nice neighborhood. Did you have a hard time finding a house?"

Ronnie said, "We used a realtor, but even so, we were pretty lucky. We wanted it to be a long distance from where our own house is—was. This one was for rent furnished, and it was available right away."

"Not bad. If it weren't for this little problem you have right now, I wouldn't mind living around here."

"It could be a big problem," said Ronnie.

"Well, don't worry too much. The bomb squad gets a lot of calls—about four a day, but on the average only one-fifth of those calls are anything that would blow—"

The police radio interrupted. "Squad one. Officer Rylands is out again. There's a device upstairs in the bedroom."

The sergeant said, "Can you describe it?"

"The device is a pipe bomb. It's attached to the back of the mirror on the female dresser about four feet above the floor. The pipe is about eighteen inches long and three inches in diameter, capped on both ends with regular threaded plumbing caps, one of them drilled for wire. There's duct tape wrapped around the side to hold ball bearings. The device appears to be correctly wired to be triggered by a cell phone, and the double wire coming out looks to Rylands like the lead to a blasting cap."

"Give your present location."

"We're back in the van and we're preparing to move it back to a safe distance as soon as Andros is deployed."

"Roger." He switched frequencies to normal police band and said, "This is Bomb Squad Unit One. We have a Code Five Edward at the location 3-1-3-2 Bluff Street."

"Copy, Unit Three."

The sergeant switched back to the bomb squad frequency. Ronnie knew that Code Five Edward meant they were going to try to render a bomb harmless in an open area. Other units, and especially aircraft, were to stay far away.

She took out her phone and hit a preprogrammed number. "Sid, will you please get in the car and get out of there?"

"On my way," said Sid's voice.

The sergeant put his microphone back in its holder. "Now all we can do is wait while the guys do their job."

Ronnie said, "I heard the name Andros. They're using the robot?"

"Yep," said the sergeant. "Pipe bombs aren't usually too complicated, but there are some awful exceptions. This one is wired to a cell phone, so it can get tricky."

Sid Abel's car drove by the police car and parked fifty feet past it. Far down the street they saw the robot roll down the ramp at the back of the bomb squad truck on its tank treads and wheels. The van pulled back about five hundred feet. A man inside the truck was guiding the robot using its onboard video camera, but the man in the bomb suit walked with it. The robot whirred steadily along the street, up the driveway to the front steps, and then ground its way up the three low concrete steps onto the porch. The man opened the front door and straightened the robot so it could ascend the last step into the living room. He closed the door and took a step.

In an instant, the morning air seemed to harden into something solid, and a shock hit the ears, the stomach, the skin. The bomb technician was blown off the steps to the ground, and all the windows of the house shattered outward at once. The car where Ronnie and the sergeant sat jumped a few inches and bounced. Instantly there was debris in the air, a mixture of glass, dust, and bits of wood, some of it flying upward, so for a few seconds it rained onto lawns and sidewalks. Before the last pieces had come down, there were two police officers sprinting toward the fallen man in the bomb suit.

The sergeant had the microphone in his hand. "Squad One, give me your status."

There was a slight delay, and then someone said, "No injuries. Repeat, no injuries."

"Copy, Squad One." He turned to Ronnie Abel. "Your suspects aren't giving up. You must be getting close."

# 12

Sid and Ronnie spent the rest of the morning and most of the afternoon at the North Hollywood station being interviewed by a team of federal investigators from Alcohol, Tobacco, Firearms and Explosives and the FBI. After they were satisfied that the Abels knew nothing they hadn't learned from the police bomb squad, they left, one by one. The last one to leave was an FBI agent who said to Sid and Ronnie, "I don't know what to advise you except to watch where you step, what you eat, and change cars a lot. I can't think of a good way to convince these people you're giving up."

"That's okay. We're not giving up," said Ronnie. "But thanks."

A few minutes later the Abels were down the hall at Homicide. They sat in front of Detective Miguel Fuentes's desk while he looked at the video they had just watched over and over with the federal agents. "This is definitely a break," Fuentes said. "There are very few women in that business. But there are so few that I don't know offhand what to do with the information."

"What do you mean?" asked Ronnie.

"About ten percent of killings are done by women. About three percent of all murders are done for hire. So how many women around here are in the business of doing wet jobs for money? I don't know of any right now. Are there five? Ten?"

"At the moment we're only interested in the one," said Sid. "These people have managed to keep us so busy defending ourselves that we haven't been able to do any investigative work on the case. We're leaving to go out of town to do an interview. While we're gone, if you can find any women in the system anywhere in the country who have a history of murder for hire, we'd obviously be interested."

"Since the Ballantine murder is now one of my cases, I'll do my best to help you help me. But this is the same problem we've always got with killers," said Fuentes. "You both know that. It's hard to find repeat offenders. If we know they've done it before, they're probably in jail."

"It might also be a good idea to give us any violent male offenders who have been known to work with a female," Ronnie said. "And the pinhole camera footage shows that she was the one carrying the black bag with the bomb in it. So you might want to pull the active list of women who have used explosives."

Fuentes said. "Okay. Of course, carrying it doesn't prove she was the maker."

"I think there's a pretty good chance she was, though," Sid said. "It was a big black powder pipe bomb wrapped with ball bearings and set off electronically. I can't see a bomb maker letting somebody else carry that bomb, when he was going to be in the same room with that thing."

"All right. I'll put in a separate inquiry with ATF. They may have some female candidates. Any other signifiers we should try?"

Ronnie said, "The night they shot at us from a car out at the housing development, it was the passenger firing a rifle from some distance—one shot, no misses. A few seconds earlier we had seen what we're pretty sure was a man in the driver's seat."

"So the woman was the sniper?"

"That's what we think," said Sid. "The other two times, both fired at us. But when it was only one shooter, she was the one. Maybe there's a woman in the system who's a great shot."

"It's possible. How about weapons? Anything distinctive?"

"At the construction site what they used was a .308 rifle. The casing got ejected and the officers found it on the road. There are a million of those around. The night they burned us out of our house, they had full auto rifles, 9mm. Something like an Uzi, Tec-9, or MP5."

"I don't have much hope for that one either," said Fuentes. "I'll get a look at the list of legal compact assault weapons that people grandfathered in when the California ban took effect, but killers are not likely to have registered any guns. Maybe we'll do better with the list of people who've been caught bringing assault rifles into the state or restoring them to full auto."

"That can't hurt," said Ronnie.

"What should I put down for a description of the female?"

"Small and thin," said Ronnie. "Five two to five four, a hundred to a hundred twenty."

"Her hair was hidden under her ski mask, and she wasn't close enough to the camera to pick up her eye color," Sid said.

"In other words, just some young woman," Fuentes said. "I'll call you if one turns up. In the meantime, let's hope you don't get a closer look. Stay safe."

Nicole and Ed Hoyt sat in the bleachers beside the baseball field in the park. They were at least a hundred yards from the nearest person. The only one Nicole could see right now was a young woman in shorts and a tank top walking the path with a big black Labrador retriever.

She glanced at Ed. He was watching the woman too. She knew that Ed's thoughts were different from hers, but she didn't blame him for that any more than she blamed the Lab for his thoughts, which were probably more lofty than Ed's. She had listened to a lot of women complaining about the way men looked at them, but she had said nothing. She had only laughed to herself. What the hell did these women think made a man give them all his money and attention—somebody to sit next to them at church?

She glanced at Ed again. He was staring still, but she wasn't bothered. Ed couldn't see the girl any better than she could at this distance. She looked in the other direction, along the trees by the wall along the freeway near the end of the park. There was Boylan, walking along in his hooded sweatshirt. He must have approached on the path beside the concrete bed of the Tujunga Wash, and then slipped through a gap in the fence.

"So that's how he does it," she said.

Ed turned his head to watch Boylan approach. "He's a weasel. I suppose if he comes and goes that way, he's hard to spot and harder to follow. There are about eight ways he can go once he's out of the park, and his car could be waiting just about anywhere."

"From here he could even take the subway," she said. "The Red Line station is right over there past the parking lot."

"Or a bus. There's a bus station above the subway."

Nicole said, "We should be glad he's that careful I guess, but I don't really feel glad."

Ed shrugged. "He's no harder to kill than anybody else."

Nicole patted his knee. Words would have added nothing.

Boylan walked along inside the line of trees until he reached the bleachers. He stopped at the foot below the Hoyts and looked up at them.

"Aren't you going to say anything?" asked Nicole.

"Bear with me. I'm a little bit upset."

Ed said, "Did we call you? I'm pretty sure you called us."

Boylan said, "You don't seem to understand what's happened. You set off a bomb in a house in Burbank. A bomb. Think about it."

"It worked pretty well," said Ed. "They said on the news that the only reason the bomb guy spotted it was that the back of the mirror was dusty so the tape on one of the wires didn't stick right. Otherwise, they would have been scraping Abels off the walls with putty knives."

"You set off a bomb and think everything's going to be the same?" said Boylan. "The federal government is interested in bombs. LA has one of the best bomb squads in the world, and they catch people. Bombs make the TV news."

"I just said that. We had to detonate it because they were sending a robot in there to disarm it. We didn't want to leave them anything to trace."

"And you think you succeeded at that?"

"Pretty sure. The blasting cap was from a tool shed on a road-building project in Montana eight years ago. The pipe and end caps were from a going-out-of-business sale for a plumbing supply store at least five years ago. The cell phone was a prepaid one I lifted from a shopping cart in a parking lot. Nothing has any connection to us."

"Do you know that dynamite has identifying tags mixed in when they manufacture it?"

"Yes, we do," said Ed. "Black powder doesn't."

"You used gunpowder?"

"Yeah," said Nicole. "We wanted to take out two people in a bedroom, not strip-mine a mountain. We keep a supply around."

Boylan was fuming, his mouth a thin horizontal line and his eyes bulging as his breaths came through his nose in snorts. After a few seconds, he seemed to contain himself. He said, "The Abels are both alive and unhurt, after you've made three tries. And I wish you hadn't used explosives. You've got everybody looking for you."

"We'll just have to watch out for those folks," said Ed. "It's going to be part of this job, I guess. But we won't charge for the extra risk."

Nicole raised her hand to cover her mouth so her laugh wouldn't be too big, and she tapped Ed's thigh with her other hand.

Ed took the hint. "We didn't intend to put you or your clients in danger, and we'll be sure not to. The rest is our problem." He stood. "We'll let this settle down a bit, and then finish the job. We'll get in touch with you afterward."

Ed and Nicole climbed down from the bleachers and walked past the backstop of the baseball field to the parking lot. Nicole said, "I can't help wondering about Boylan. We've done three jobs for him this year, and all we know about him is a cell phone number, and a name he probably made up."

Ed said, "We can follow him home if you want."

"What could we say if he saw us?"

"We saw a suspicious, weaselly-looking man and followed him. Glad it was only you, Boylan."

She laughed. "It's stupid, but I feel like it." They approached their small gray car.

"Get in."

They drove up the long road from the lot out to Lankershim Boulevard and turned left, and then turned left again. Ed pulled into the parking lot behind a small restaurant and sat still.

"What's here?" she asked.

"If he came by car, he will have parked it in the lot on this side of the wash, by the rec center and the other baseball fields. This is the way out of there. If he didn't bring a car, we'll know that too."

They waited. Nicole tapped her feet, listening to a tune that her memory was playing in her head. She looked at the back windows of the restaurant, which had been reinforced with plywood and bars so that nobody could break in. She wondered if the windows had been dirty before they had been boarded, or dust had somehow gotten in a grain or so at a time over the years. If people spent time behind restaurants, nobody would ever go out to eat. "He's taking a long time," she said.

"He is. But he's afraid we're bringing the wrath of God down on him, so he'll want to be sure we weren't caught leaving the park before he comes this way."

"How do you figure this stuff out?"

"Hunting wild turkeys. You have to sit still and wait them out, because they don't trust anything that moves. Everything is their enemy, because they're delicious. I guess Boylan must think he is too."

She smiled, but she knew Ed was partly serious. He had grown up moving around in the Appalachians. He wasn't a hillbilly—nothing as natural and dignified as that. His people seemed to have evolved straight from apes to thieves. They had not settled anywhere, exactly, just stopped until each county got used up. They lived in places that sounded to her like dens—ramshackle structures they moved into on the edges of civilization, most of them abandoned after somebody went broke trying to farm land that was too rocky, steep, or tangled with stubborn woody plants. They made claims and settled in until something made them move on.

He told her he'd killed his first man in Kentucky when he was about eighteen. He started hunting as a young boy, and by that time he had killed just about every species in the region that could be eaten or exchanged for money except one. The client was a preacher who was in the habit of fooling around with a few of the wives in his congregation. One woman's husband had found out and already placed his name on the agenda to speak at the next meeting of the elders. It was pretty clear that what he intended was to call the preacher out and disgrace him publicly. So Ed got his first job. He waited in the pasture for the man to go out to bring his dairy cows in for the evening milking, killed him, carried him far back into the forest, and buried him there.

Ed's talent for stalking made him good at deception too. He knew it was time to leave the little town, but leaving right after his first victim vanished would have made him the major suspect. So he circulated the word that he was thinking of enlisting in the army. He took a bus to Louisville, went into a recruiting office and got brochures and applications and the business cards of the recruiting sergeants. Then he hung around the local bar that served underage boys and discussed his plan with his friends. He showed them the brochures, and asked the advice of a couple of older men who had been in wars. He even went to a medical clinic in the next little town to get a physical checkup. He asked the physician's assistant to be sure to check him for problems that might keep him out of the army. By the time he left town there was nobody in the area who wasn't familiar with the idea that Ed Hoyt was going to serve his country. On his last Sunday in town he went to church, and the preacher who had hired him to do the killing asked God to bless the brave Ed Hoyt.

As soon as Boylan drove past the restaurant, Ed Hoyt started the car, but he did nothing for a few seconds, just waited for Boylan to turn onto Lankershim Boulevard in one direction or the other. The way Boylan chose was left, and Ed and Nicole saw his car swing into the far lane and head north.

Ed waited. Then he pulled out behind a truck and went up Lankershim after Boylan. He kept behind the truck so Boylan couldn't look back and see his car, but Ed could see a strip of open road to the left of the truck and a strip to the right. If Boylan's brown SUV kept going straight, Ed didn't need to see it. If it turned, Ed would know.

Boylan didn't turn until he reached Oxnard Street. This time Ed saw him turn from two hundred yards behind. Ed went past Oxnard instead of following him. Ed saw Nicole's surprise, and said, "This is where he'll look behind him." He spoke with perfect confidence and authority, so Nicole didn't question why this was where Boylan would look. It just was.

Ed turned left at the next street and drove west parallel to Boylan but invisible to him. After a few blocks, Ed turned left again, and then right, and came out far behind Boylan. Ed said, "If he sees us now we'll seem to be totally new to him. It's just one of the stupid things about the human mind. Like when people are looking for somebody waiting to jump them, they look everywhere but up."

"Thank the Lord for stupid things about the human mind. They pay the bills."

"Amen."

Ed merged into a line of cars, most of them wider and taller than their Camry, and stayed there for a time. When Boylan turned to the left and headed south again Ed followed. He was going to a lot of trouble to keep from being followed, but he wasn't very good. When he crossed Ventura Boulevard into a zone of big houses built on low hills, they followed, but Ed slowed the car considerably. "Here's where it starts to get hairy."

Nicole could see what he meant. There were fewer places to turn now, and each turn led into a smaller road. Many of them wound into others, some stopped dead, and some of them even circled back. These roads were entirely residential, and had very few cars on them in the middle of the day.

Ed kept Boylan's car far enough ahead of him so he could just catch a glimpse of it as it went around a curve, and then speed up to the curve and catch a taillight before the car disappeared again. After a few minutes Ed said, "Get out your phone and get it ready to take pictures."

Nicole took out her cell phone. Just before the next curve, Ed slowed, opened his window, and listened. He let the car coast almost to the curve and stopped, then got out, but didn't shut his door completely so it didn't make a noise. He held out his hand, and Nicole handed him the phone through the open window.

A few minutes later Ed walked back around the curve, then got in and handed her the phone. He performed a three-point turn on the narrow road and started back the way they had come.

Nicole looked at the photo album in her phone. Ed had taken six pictures from different angles. All the shots showed a tall two-story white house on the top of a small rise in the land surrounded by a jungle of trees, overgrowth, and vine-choked brush. Boylan's brown SUV was parked at the top of the steep driveway in the open garage. "That's his house?"

"He went up to the door and opened it with a key," Ed said. "He put his car in the garage."

"I would have liked to take a closer look."

"The way things are going we may have to sometime."

"Is that why you took pictures?"

"Yeah. If we need to come back here, it'll probably be after dark. It's good to know the layout so we don't trip over something and get ourselves killed."

# 13

Sid and Ronnie Abel took an evening flight to Houston and endured the hour-long cab ride from the airport to the city. They checked into their hotel and stayed in their room to review the information they had brought for the interview they'd scheduled for the morning.

The next morning shortly before ten they sat side by side at a table facing the wall of windows in the coffee shop on the bottom floor of their hotel. Houston was hot and humid today, as it had been every time they had been here. The sky was always a milky gray that somehow allowed a glare without showing any sun. After a few minutes, Sid said, "She doesn't seem to be coming."

"She'll come."

The window looked out on a paved area about a quarter mile across. There was a dry fountain at the near end of it, and there were several places on the flat concrete square with small roofs over them, but no shady places to sit. On each of the square's sides was a huge building, broader than it was tall, with rows of identical windows that had been designed to let light into interior spaces, but to show nothing to the outside. The buildings were designed to face outward toward the surrounding streets, so there were no broad entrances, only a few man-size doors a few hundred feet apart leading onto the parched and empty square.

Sid said, "I've been looking out there for twenty minutes. I've seen exactly two people come out of any of those buildings."

"I know," Ronnie said. "They both came here to get something to drink. I don't think I've ever seen a less hospitable landscape. At least deserts have plants and animals."

"I still think she's going to stand us up."

"She won't."

"Want to bet?"

"Sure."

"Then let's bet something that will make it interesting."

Ronnie sat in silence, still staring out across the plaza.

"Well?" said Sid.

"I'm thinking about what you would consider interesting. I don't want to bet that." After a pause she said, "This place is something. It reminds me of one of those artificial cities that some tyrannical government built in the middle of the wilderness, and nobody ever moved in."

"There are people in there, all right. I don't blame them for not coming out in that heat," Sid said. "But right now we're probably looking at a lot of the people who operate the world's oil industry. We just can't see them behind that glass."

"This could be her."

Far across the vast, empty plaza, a tall, slim black woman in a dark blue suit walked along the center of the plaza toward the hotel. She made no attempt to skirt the plaza to place herself in the thin strip of shade from one of the buildings, just headed in a straight line directly toward them.

"You win," Sid said. "I thought she'd stand us up."

"Not when she can get rid of us with a ten-minute chat over a cup of coffee."

"And maybe she figures there's some slim chance that we'll actually solve her husband's murder."

"I wouldn't think that's part of her calculations," Ronnie said. "You read the stuff that Hemphill gave us. Remember what she said when they told her he was dead? 'Too bad.'"

The woman's strides were long and quick. When she reached the coffee shop door, the Abels both stood and went to greet her. "Mrs. Ballantine. This is Veronica Abel, and I'm Sid."

The woman shook Ronnie's hand, and then Sid's. "Selena Stubbs," she said. "I don't use Ballantine anymore." Her expression was not unfriendly, but she didn't smile.

Ronnie said, "We've got a table over here. What can we get you to drink?"

Selena Stubbs's eyes swept the room in a movement that most people would not have noticed. She was clearly gauging the potential of the coffee shop as a place for a quiet conversation. She rejected it. "Are you staying at the hotel?"

"Yes," said Ronnie.

"Then let's get some iced coffee and take it up to your room."

Ronnie and Sid exchanged a quick glance, but all Selena Stubbs saw was Ronnie's smile. "Of course," Ronnie said, and Sid stepped to the counter where the barista was waiting.

Sid ordered the coffee, and then joined the women while they waited. He said, "We really appreciate your willingness to meet with us. We know you must be very busy."

She looked at Sid, her eyes holding his. "If I had refused, would you have taken that as final and flown back to LA?"

Ronnie said, "Probably not."

"That's why I'm here."

Sid returned to the counter, where the barista was putting the three plastic cups into an egg-carton tray. He paid and carried the tray. Selena Stubbs walked with the Abels to the elevators, and then rode one of them up with them. She kept her eyes in front of her, and not on their faces as a signal that she had no intention of chatting until they were upstairs. She followed Ronnie to the room, and waited while Sid unlocked the door and held it open.

They stepped inside and Sid let the door swing shut. The room was spacious. There was a couch, where Selena Stubbs and Ronnie sat. Ronnie took the coffee tray from Sid, who moved the coffee table a little closer to the couch, and then took the chair from the desk, turned it around, and sat.

Selena Stubbs said, "I was wondering how long it would take them to send detectives to talk to me here in Houston."

"Nobody sent us," Ronnie said. "If we gave you the impression that we're police officers, then we've—"

"No, don't worry," said Selena Stubbs, holding up her hand. "But we should be open with each other, or this is a waste of time. I'm sure you learned what you could about me, and I looked you up too, and made a few inquiries. It's true—you're not cops. You're not exactly not cops, either. You have an agency. You do what you always did. Only you don't have to take orders anymore. Isn't that right?"

Sid said, "Nobody pays for something he's already getting for free, so we tend to get hired to do things the cops aren't doing. Your husband's employer hired us to take a second look at his murder."

"Ex-husband," Selena Stubbs said. "And I agreed to meet you because otherwise you would try to reach me at home. I have two kids—girls—aged six and eight. I wanted to spare them this kind of conversation."

"We have no intention of upsetting anyone," Ronnie said. "We just want to ask a few questions about your ex-husband, and try to understand what happened to him."

"Now I'm shocked," said Selena Stubbs. "Even you? Is there really any mystery about what happened to him? A black man shot execution style and his body stuffed into a sewer? Come on."

"Some kind of racial motivation is a possibility, but we can't make assumptions," Sid said. "We'd like to find out who did it. If we knew more about Mr. Ballantine, maybe we could."

"Okay. I'll pretend the world is different than it is. Ask what you want."

Sid said, "We've been piecing together the early stages of the police investigation. Detective Kapp, the officer who spoke to you at the time, died in an accident after a few months on the case. A very good detective named Miguel Fuentes has taken over. But nothing new has come up in months. And nobody seems to have been able to tell the police much about Mr. Ballantine."

"Maybe that should tell you something," said Selena.

"That's why we thought we had better start over with you," Sid said. "You would know the most."

"All right. Ask."

Ronnie said, "How did you meet?"

"In grad school at Berkeley. We both enrolled in the PhD program in chemistry," Selena said. "The day the university got our applications we were destined to be thrown together constantly—two black chemistry grad students the same age, et cetera. I'm sure you can imagine. You want to get along with everybody, but the minute you walk into the lab that first Monday, you see the person who looks like you, and he's looking at you the same way."

"You were attracted to him right away?" said Sid.

"Not at all. Seeing him there was a disappointment. Having him around seemed limiting, as though we had to be connected. It was more that way than usual, because we were the only black students in that class," she said. "It wasn't that I didn't like him. Have you seen his picture?"

"Yes," said Ronnie. "He was very handsome."

"Yes, he was," said Selena. "And he was very bright and very nice. At the time I resisted that information. He seemed too good. I had come straight from the University of Texas. I was in a new town where I knew nobody, and I wasn't sure I trusted my own judgment. I kept thinking this must be what an arranged marriage would feel like. The other person is shoved right in your face, and there's a little part of you that says, 'Hold on. I didn't get asked about this.' So I was cordial, but I kept him at a distance. When other men asked me out, I dated them."

"How did he react to that?" asked Ronnie. "Did it make him more interested?"

"I don't think so. He went out with other people too. When we finally got together, it was unexpected. We had been colleagues for a while, and we enjoyed being together, but always with other friends. One afternoon all the other regulars were either busy or went home early, and by default, the evening turned into a date. After that it was always a date."

"And when did you get married?" Ronnie asked.

"Just over two years into graduate school. We had both finished our course work, and passed the qualifying exams. We had already begun our own research for our doctoral dissertations. We knew we'd be working long hours in different labs for years, but we had more control over which hours those would be, so marriage started to make more sense."

Sid said, "I assume the marriage seemed good at first?"

Selena Stubbs shrugged. "It was a good marriage. We were about as happy as you can be, given the nerves and the exhaustion, and the uncertainty. We were not only in competition with the other graduate students for the grades, the grants, the jobs, but we were in competition with each other, too. But we both got through that phase of it, still loving each other. We defended our dissertations in the spring of the fifth year, and graduated together in June."

"Wow," said Ronnie. "You must have felt like the smartest people in the world that day."

"I'm afraid not even the smartest in town. Everybody was smart, and in a university town, you're never likely to be the smartest. But we were pretty pleased with ourselves."

"You had a problem, though, right?" Sid said. "You both needed jobs in the same field at the same time."

"It was more complicated than that. Our specialties were very different. James had studied complex compounds that affected the metabolisms of muscle cells. Pharmaceutical companies were after him, but he loved universities, and wanted to teach and continue his research in the academic world, so he applied for assistant professorships."

"And you?" said Sid.

"That was what made things complicated." She looked out the window at the giant oil company buildings bordering the square. "My field was oil. My interest was in petrochemicals, and I'd published research on the molecular signifiers in upper strata that indicate the presence of oil below. Companies were flying recruiters to me as soon as my dissertation was filed."

Ronnie and Sid had both noticed that Selena tended to keep her eyes on Ronnie, and to address her answers to her. Ronnie was capable of projecting a soft, motherly sympathy when she wanted to set a witness at ease. They exchanged a glance, and then Sid leaned back and turned his body slightly away from Selena Stubbs. Ronnie leaned toward her to look straight into her eyes.

"What happened?" Ronnie's big blue eyes were wide with interest.

"He got job offers, and I got job offers. The difference was I was pregnant and he wasn't. We decided it would be best to let him take his best offer, and move to Bloomington, Indiana, together. He would be a professor, and I would have the baby and keep my name out in the world by working a little bit as a consultant, mostly from home."

"Did you resent that?" asked Ronnie.

"No. I wanted kids, and I loved them. We were happy for about five years, before it ended badly."

"What went wrong?" Now Ronnie's eyes were filled with concern.

"Just about everything," said Selena. "First James got his official fifth-year notice that he was not going to be granted tenure."

"I thought that was seven years," said Ronnie.

"Legally, if they let you teach for seven years, they've given you de facto tenure. So they make decisions early and give notice. At the end of five years you get an evaluation. They tell you either that you'll be getting tenure, or that while you're teaching for your sixth year, you'd better also be looking for a job."

"And that's the notice James was given?"

"Yes. It was devastating, and not just to James. I had stepped out of the career track for five years. I had been satisfied that I'd done the right thing. I had two beautiful children to show for my decision. But if I was going to sacrifice my career, I at least wanted it to buy him the career he loved so much."

"What did you do?" asked Ronnie.

"I did nothing for a few days, just kept my feelings to myself while he grieved. Then I sat him down and we talked about what to do next. Academic life was effectively closed to him once he had been denied tenure. So we made a list of companies for him to write for jobs. I helped. I wrote to contacts, friends, and colleagues all over the country. He got quite a few interviews."

"Quite a few interviews doesn't sound like good news," Ronnie said. "It means he didn't find a job right away."

"Very perceptive," said Selena. "The job search took most of his sixth year at Indiana. He would finish his last class of the week, pack up the papers for grading, and get on a plane to another city for an interview. He would be back the morning of his first class. He was tired all the time. When he finally got a good offer at Intercelleron in California, I was so relieved I could hardly contain myself. That lasted awhile."

"Only awhile?" Now Ronnie's expression was sad.

"We made a plan. In June he was to go out to California, start work at Intercelleron, and find a house. That way he would have no lapse in paychecks, and start getting the bigger income the company was paying. I would stay in Indiana with the kids, sell the house we had in Bloomington, and then wrap up our affairs, pack up, and join him."

"That's a lot to do."

"It was," said Selena. "But people do it. The first problem was that our house didn't sell. I listed it as soon as we knew we were leaving, but it was a buyer's market. We had to put off everything—buying the new house, and moving out to join him. James was out there in Los Angeles working, and he found plenty of houses, but we needed to sell the old one to get the down payment for the new one. It dragged on, and then the summer was gone and fall started. I would go to the market and see people we knew from the university, and it would make me feel sick. I had promised myself I'd never see these people again, but there I was. 'What's James doing these days?' It was awful."

"It must have been."

"He would fly home to see us every two or three weeks, but while he was there he wasn't much use in selling the house. He liked visiting with the kids, but they were small, and they were getting a little too used to his being away all the time. So was he. When he was there, it was like he was babysitting. One weekend was particularly bad, and when he left, I made a new plan. Over the next week, I packed everything up and had it moved to a storage facility so the house could be scrubbed and painted and put on the market empty. The kids and I got on a plane and flew out to join Daddy at his apartment." She paused and shook her head slowly, and Ronnie and Sid could tell it was an involuntary response to a bad memory.

The Abels waited. They had each interrogated thousands of people. They both recognized that they had reached a delicate moment. If they pressed too hard, she might decide to resist and say nothing more specific or personal. But she had told most of this incident, and she would be feeling the need to get the rest out. After a minute she started again.

"We went to the apartment he had rented, but he wasn't there. It was already late, and I didn't want to call another cab to take us to a hotel, so I went to the manager's apartment and asked her to let me in. I had my ID, and no burglar brings a four-year-old and a two-year-old. So we got in. He didn't come home that night. He came in at seven a.m. to shower and dress for work. He was in a big hurry, and said he'd been at a get-together for a retiring colleague and had too much to drink, so he'd stayed overnight instead of driving. It was true and it wasn't. He had been drinking. I could smell it. But the party was between him and one woman, who wasn't nearly old enough to retire. When I looked at him I knew it."

"I'm sorry," Ronnie said.

"He had changed. I think what happened was that he had the nice beaten out of him. He had sacrificed all his life to become a certain kind of man, but it didn't work. He was fired—not from a job, but from a life. Right after he heard he wasn't going to get tenure I watched him secretly for signs that he was going to commit suicide. I needn't have bothered. The man I had married wasn't there anymore. The new James was different."

"How was he different?" asked Ronnie.

"He had decided that his whole life had been a mistake. The way to live was to deny himself nothing. He didn't just make some drunken slipup or get tempted when he was lonely. He had at least four other regular women. He was spending a lot of money on them, but mostly on himself. New clothes, new car, new friends. When I watched him, I realized he had lost interest in the kids. He went through the motions, but he really didn't want to spend any time around them."

"What about you?" Ronnie asked. "Was he still interested in saving the relationship?"

"By then there was nothing much to save. I put up with the new James for about three months, and then filed for divorce, took the kids, and came here to Houston to start looking for a job. He didn't try to stop me, and didn't try to bring me back afterward. When I had to fly to Los Angeles over the next few months for meetings with the lawyers and trial dates, we barely spoke. The lawyers did most of it."

"And after that?" asked Ronnie. "What about more recently?"

"I've been working here for about four years. James visited the kids a few times during the first year, but after each visit the kids were less interested in the next one, and so was James. After that there were some excuses, and then even the excuses stopped. When the Los Angeles police told me he had died, I hadn't seen him in three years. All I could say was, 'Too bad.'"

Ronnie placed her hand on Selena's, and Selena didn't pull away. She sat staring at the carpet for a moment, then seemed to straighten and looked at Ronnie again.

"But I did mean what I said—too bad. James had started living a different way. He was out very late at night, sometimes alone, and sometimes not. He ran into the sort of people you meet that way, and one or more of them killed him." Selena Stubbs stood up. "I wish you luck in your investigation. Now I'd better get back to my office."

"Thank you for your help," said Ronnie. "I know talking about this is painful. But just one last question. Do you happen to know the names of any of the women he was seeing?"

"Yes," she said. "Thanks for thinking of that. I made a list of the names and addresses for you, and I would have been disappointed later if I hadn't remembered to give it to you." She reached into her purse and took out a plain sheet of white paper from a computer printer with a dozen lines of print and handed it to Ronnie. "Maybe one of them knows more than I do."

# 14

The Abels flew from Houston to the Long Beach airport instead of LAX or Burbank, and rented their next car at the airport lot. They drove into Los Angeles on the Long Beach Freeway and then took a series of surface streets to make their way to a new hotel they'd reserved from Houston. They parked in the lower floor of the underground lot, checked in, and took the elevator to their floor.

When they entered their room and locked the door, Ronnie said, "When we come home from a trip it makes me sad not to be able to go into my own house and my own bedroom and flop on my own bed."

Sid put his arms around her and held her while she rested her head on his shoulder. "I'm sorry," Sid said. "We'll have them again. I promise."

"Will we?" Ronnie said. "I'm worried that having a house makes us too easy to kill."

"We can make it much harder from now on."

"I suppose," she said. "But that house meant a lot to me. Not the things, or the money, or whatever. It was a feeling. In a way the place was me, or at least my memory. A big part of our lives happened there. I could sit in a room and remember things—sights and sounds from some particular day twenty-five years ago. It feels as though I've lost that."

"Houses don't matter. We matter, and we're still okay. At some point this case will be over, and then we'll either build again on that lot, or find a nicer house and buy that one. The old memories will come back, and we'll have new ones."

She stood on her tiptoes and kissed him. "Don't forget. You promised."

"I did."

She said, "Okay. For now, we live in hotels. If we get to work, we may be able to correct that. We've got to start catching up. There are a lot more things to know about James Ballantine."

Sid said, "You know what this reminds me of? Those cases where some ordinary law-abiding schmuck gets hit on the head, and suddenly his whole personality changes."

"I know," said Ronnie. "Getting fired from the university seems to have had a traumatic effect on his brain. And come to think of it, we don't know he didn't also get literally hit on the head. He was away by himself for weeks at a time, and then he was single. Nobody would know."

"We've got to take a new look at everything about him," Sid said. "All this time we've been looking over our shoulders and trying to stay alive, so we haven't even had a chance to figure out who Ballantine really was. Nobody seemed to know anything."

"And now we've got a list of four women who knew him really well."

\* \* \*

At 5:00 a.m. the streets of Los Angeles were already filling up. There was never a time when the roads were empty, but a change of people occurred before dawn, with the last of the night people giving up and going indoors to sleep until their next chance occurred at sundown, and the day people charging out to take their turn. Sid and Ronnie had worked both day shifts and night shifts as police officers, so they were good at recognizing which group a person belonged to. They drove through Griffith Park and up into the hills of Los Feliz, then took a winding road higher until they found the right house. It was modern, tall and narrow, built into a hillside right at the edge of the street. "Nice house, nice neighborhood," said Sid. "She's got some money."

They continued down the street a few hundred feet and then pulled over to the curb, leaned back comfortably against the headrests of their car seats, and adjusted the rearview mirrors so they could watch the house without being noticed from a distance.

"Well, here I am again," said Ronnie. "Sitting in the car and looking at somebody's darkened windows while they get the sleep I want and richly deserve."

"There," Sid said. "A light just came on upstairs."

"An early bird. Maybe I'll like her."

They watched the house while Kirsten Tilson got up, turned on a light in a textured window near the back of the house that had to be a bathroom, and prepared for her day. At six twenty the upstairs lights went off and others went on downstairs. At seven they all went off. The garage door slid open.

"Watch for her," Sid said.

The front door opened and a woman came out and walked toward the garage. She could not have looked more different from Selena Stubbs Ballantine. She was short, with long red hair and very pale skin. She wore high heels, but she walked in them without tottering or taking short steps as some women did. Her knee-length skirt was subdued and stylish. Ronnie watched her walk to the car. "Well, she's sort of a surprise." She waited, but Sid said nothing. "Isn't she?"

"I'm withholding opinions."

"When we blow this case you'll have a great career in diplomacy."

The woman got into her black Audi, performed an expert sweep of her left hand to bring her skirt in with her, and shut the car door. The car backed out of the short driveway into the street and then moved forward.

The Abels followed her at a distance, watched her go up an entrance to the Hollywood Freeway and merge into the stream of cars before they entered too.

They followed her to the Intercelleron lot, watched her enter, went past the gate, and kept going. "It looks like we've got a woman who also works for Intercelleron."

"An office romance. How sweet," Ronnie said, her voice even and unenthusiastic. "Just like us."

"We never worked in the same station, let alone the same office," Sid said.

"I don't mean as cops. I mean now. Of course, we no longer have an office."

"That's just temporary." Sid stopped the car, turned around, and pulled to the curb where they could see the front of the building.

Ronnie took the binoculars from the glove compartment and watched as Kirsten Tilson got out of her car, tossed her head to make her hair hang the way she wanted it to, and strode in the front entrance of the building, past the uniformed guard at the counter.

"Did you see that?" said Ronnie.

"What?"

"That guard looked at her and bowed, practically. She must be important."

"That could be a problem. She might have underlings we have to get through to talk to her."

"I'll look her up in the directory and see what we're up against." Ronnie took out her phone, found the e-mail from Hemphill, and scrolled down through the names.

"Here come the *t*'s," said Ronnie. "And here she is. Damn. She's not a regular employee."

"Then what is she?"

"A member of the board of directors."

Sid took out his cell phone. "Read me her office number."

Ronnie read the phone number from the picture of the directory while Sid punched in the digits. He put the phone on speaker.

"Intercelleron, Miss Tilson's office, Ellen Ryder speaking."

"Hello, this is Sid Abel. May I please speak with Miss Tilson?"

"Can you tell me what this is in reference to?"

"She'll know my name. *A-B-E-L*. I'm a partner in a company the board is dealing with."

"Please hold." There was a sudden lack of sound.

While the assistant was gone, Sid covered his phone. "How did I sound?"

"Dumb," said Ronnie. "You ended your sentence with a preposition."

"She asked me what this was in reference to. I was just trying not to embarrass her. I want her to like me."

"You're a master of subtlety."

There was a return of ambient sound, and then another female voice. "Hello, Mr. Abel. This is Kirsten Tilson. How can I help you?"

"I'm calling as part of our investigation of James Ballantine's death. We would like to meet with you briefly as soon as possible. It won't take more than an hour of your time."

"To tell you the truth, I'm surprised by your call. I'm not really the right member of the board—not the one who's handling this. We asked the CEO to take care of the Ballantine issue, and I think that he assigned Mr. Hemphill to serve as the company's contact person. Would you like his number?"

"No, thank you," said Sid. "We need to speak with you personally. We just have a few questions about Mr. Ballantine, and it's best to do these things in person."

"Well, I had met Mr. Ballantine, but—"

Sid interrupted. "Yes, I know. We'll be talking to everyone who knew him or worked with him. If you'd like to do it now, we can be at your office in ten minutes."

There was a moment of silence. "My schedule is very full when I'm here. I think I'd prefer to meet sometime away from the office, where we won't disrupt the schedule and distract the office staff."

"If you'd prefer it, we could meet at your home this evening."

She was taken aback. "This evening?" She thought for a moment, and then conceded. "I can be available at eight."

"We'll be there."

"Would you like the address?"

"We have it," Sid said. "See you at eight." He ended the call.

Ronnie looked at him. "You certainly didn't give her much space."

"I didn't mean to," said Sid. "We can't let this investigation get delayed and sidetracked any longer. Every day, we're putting ourselves in front of people who want to kill us, and seem to have a lot of ways of doing it."

"Let's hope that after we're through interviewing her, she doesn't become one of them."

At eight Sid and Ronnie walked up to the front door of Kirsten Tilson's house. They had arrived just after nightfall and parked near the end of the block so they would see anyone driving along the street from either direction. They watched the house for a half hour before they got out of their car and rang her doorbell.

When she came to the door to let them in, she was wearing a dress in a blue-and-white print that accentuated her red hair and blue eyes, and made her look softer and more feminine than her business clothes had.

The interior of the house was modern and spare, and everything in it looked expensive. There were white stone pedestals of different heights in the foyer, each holding a single object—a celadon vase that was beautiful in its simplicity, a small bronze statue of a Thai dancer in a pointed headdress, a stone mortar and pestle. The bookshelves held antique leather-bound volumes, interspersed with a few eye-catching curiosities—a clear orange glass ball, a framed daguerreotype miniature of a young girl in a bonnet and dress with pantaloons, a cameo brooch in a velvet box.

She led them through the living room, but didn't stop at any of the conversation areas with couches and matching chairs. Instead she went up a half story to a room beside a huge window that looked out on a garden with a vine-covered stone wall. There was an asymmetrical polished burl table of some dark alien-looking hardwood. She sat at one end and gestured toward the other chairs beside it. She said, "Thank you for coming all the way here. Can I get you something to drink?"

"No, thank you," said Ronnie.

"Then maybe we should just get right to it," Miss Tilson said. "What would you like to know?"

Sid said, "Anything you can tell us about James Ballantine will help. There doesn't seem to be much in the records of his case that's useful."

Kirsten Tilson tossed her head, as though to get her hair out of her eyes so she could move forward. "I don't know very much about him, really. I believe we recruited him away from Indiana University. It was about five years ago, give or take. He seemed to be a nice man, but he was a scientist."

"I don't understand," said Ronnie.

"Since Intercelleron deals in research, we hire lots of them, and they usually tend to be a little shy and nerdy. They don't open up much, so I don't really know a lot about his life outside the office."

Sid looked at Ronnie and she gave a slight nod. Sid said, "One reason we're here is that we interviewed Mr. Ballantine's ex-wife. She gave us a list of women she referred to as her ex-husband's girlfriends."

"Really. That's a surprise. He didn't seem to be the type." Her mouth had suddenly become dry, so when she said it, there was a slight click of the tongue.

"I have to tell you that you were on the list."

Kirsten Tilson's body went rigid, but her face moved. As she tried out various responses, her facial muscles tentatively assumed the appropriate expressions, each in turn—shock, anger, amusement, confusion. That one seemed to suit her best, so her face held it. If she'd had better warning, she might have remembered she was in the presence of two people who had watched many people lie. But she didn't appear to be aware that her facial muscles had already told them she was constructing a story in front of them. "I don't know how that could be. I never met the woman. And I sincerely doubt that her husband told her I was his girlfriend. I certainly wasn't."

Ronnie said, "I doubt that he did tell her. When the police were through examining his apartment for evidence, they would have released his belongings to his family."

"I had understood he was divorced from his wife." She realized she'd revealed too much. "I don't even remember who told me that. Maybe he wasn't."

"He was. His only remaining heirs were his children. Since their mother had sole custody of the heirs, she also had responsibility for everything he had, whether she wanted it or not—his address book, any photos that were on his phone. Any videos."

Ronnie watched the reaction to the final word. Kirsten Tilson looked as though she had been punched. She turned paler for a few seconds, and then her cheeks reddened. She looked distracted, staring at the table. "I really should send someone to talk to her and let her know that this is just a misunderstanding." She looked up at the Abels. "Perhaps you could explain it to her."

Sid had also seen her react to the word "videos." He said, "If you'd like us to, we could pass it on. But I don't think our telling her would have any effect. She was adamant."

"Well, she's wrong. You said she gave you a list of names?"

"Yes," said Ronnie.

Kirsten Tilson extended her hand. "Let me see the list. I can help you eliminate any other misunderstandings and save you some time."

"We can't do that," said Sid. "We've got to respect the privacy of the women on the list, just as we're respecting yours."

She glared at him. "The board of directors hired you. You work for us."

"I'm sorry," said Sid. "We have responsibilities to other people too. Those women probably wouldn't want to have that information shared. And as you said, it might not even be accurate."

"The directors of the company are paying you. All information I pay you to find belongs to me."

"No it doesn't," Sid said. "The board of directors of Intercelleron is a client of Abels, an independent contractor. That entitles the board to a written report when we're finished. The report won't include rumors, preliminary leads, or notes from interviews."

Ronnie said, "Maybe we should get back to you. We'll pursue other avenues while you decide what you'd like to tell us." She reached into her purse and took out a card. "This has our numbers."

Sid stood. "Good night, Miss Tilson. Thanks for your time." He turned and walked toward the door, then waited there for Ronnie to catch up.

They had nearly reached the door before Kirsten called out, "Wait. Come back."

As Sid and Ronnie walked back toward the table she said, "I want to find out what happened to James Ballantine as much as anyone does. I was the one who kept pushing the board to hire investigators after the police ran out of ideas."

"Why?" asked Ronnie.

She looked at them for a moment. "I have to be sure this is absolutely confidential. That means you make no record of it, and you don't tell anyone else."

Ronnie said, "We don't violate people's privacy. Why did you push the board?"

"Because it was the right thing to do, and I didn't want it on my conscience that I just shrugged off his death. I wasn't James's girlfriend. I was nothing of the kind. But I suppose that Selena had the right to call me that. I did know him well. We had reasons to keep that secret."

"What reasons?" asked Ronnie.

"I was a member of the board of directors, and he was an employee of the company. We have guidelines to keep the company out of sexual harassment suits. Technically, I was far above him at the top of the hierarchy. Anyone in the company who figured out we were seeing each other could make terrible trouble—claim I had caused a hostile work environment, or discriminated against the people who weren't sleeping with me. Or anything else their lawyers could dream up. The board would protect itself by throwing me out."

"Did you think at the time that's what would happen if people knew?" Sid asked.

"At first, I don't think I cared. Later on, I had second thoughts. Right now I have no doubt at all. The reason I have a seat on the board is that my father was one of the founders. The stock he left me gives me a seat. But there's a big advantage to getting rid of a member of the board. You get more power, and you can always find ways to convert power into money. I would have been insane not to keep James a secret."

"How did you meet Mr. Ballantine?"

"The company threw a party to welcome James and a few other new hires. We held it at the Graysford Estate in Montecito. Do you know the place?"

"We've seen it," said Sid.

"The company uses it a few times a year for important conferences, and once in a while for a reception like that one. It's a beautiful place, and it's about ninety minutes from here, so people aren't likely to come for a few minutes and duck out, and it's too far to drive home late at night. People are expected to stay over."

"Who introduced you?" asked Ronnie.

"Nobody. I just noticed him. He was easy to notice. He was handsome, tall, very well built. He had extremely knowing and intelligent eyes. And of course, he was black."

Sid said, "'And of course?'"

"I'm sorry." She frowned. "His race was the first thing I noticed, the first thing that I knew about him. And his blackness made me curious. I'll admit it. Curiosity is, above all, an attraction. And there were other things about him that made him strange and different. He had been described to me as a brilliant chemist who had grown bored with academic life. But there was a sadness to his expression, and that made me feel for him. As I watched him, I thought that, in this odd crowd that had been assembled, he knew nobody."

"Odd crowd?" said Ronnie.

"When you assemble a group of scientists, you get a diverse group—lots of Indians and East Asians, a few Europeans, black people, or Latin Americans. But the upper management, the people serving as hosts at these gatherings, are white Anglo-Saxon Protestants, and if it's possible for one group of those people to be whiter than white, these are. I had been told that he'd been offered a job, but hadn't decided to take it yet. I thought about how isolated we must be making him feel. So I decided I'd pick up a fresh drink and go make him feel wanted."

"Just him?" asked Ronnie.

"Him first. Him above all, because he seemed not to be mixing with the others. Most of them were very young—right out of grad school, and most of these were the sort who got PhDs in a couple of years, so they were even younger. James had been a professor for six years. He had a gravity, a reserve that made him seem mysterious, and he had that sadness. He was, by far, the most interesting one. And he wasn't a boy genius; he was an adult. A prodigy is not very interesting. The only thing about him that's remarkable you can't see—his brain processes certain kinds of information very quickly. It doesn't make him fun."

"I assume you managed to make him comfortable," Ronnie said. "He took the job."

"He did," Kirsten said. "Maybe because I overdid the welcome."

"How?"

"I don't know how much it's necessary to say—how specific this has to be."

Ronnie said, "We're a pair of old cops. There is hardly anything that a person can put into words that we haven't seen with our own eyes. We need information badly. Any detail that you remember regarding James Ballantine might be important without any of us knowing it right now. So what did you mean, you overdid the welcome?"

"I can't characterize this simply, in abstract terms. I smiled as I approached. I introduced myself. You have to realize that when you're a Southern California company, your biggest recruiting tool is the weather in the rest of the world. On the best day of summer Bloomington, Indiana, probably looks about as good as Southern California. Only here it's *always* summer. And the Graysford Estate is like a dream of beautiful colors and luxurious self-indulgence mitigated by good taste. So I asked him what he thought of what he saw. And he told me that the most beautiful sight he could see was me."

"What did you say?"

"I laughed at him, but I couldn't forget the words. When he looked at me, I could feel him thinking. He asked me to show him around the estate, so I did. I showed him the gardens, and he guided me along the path by putting his hand on the small of my back. Feeling that was like an electric shock, and the feeling didn't stop—it was presumptuous, and yet so natural, so unforced. I showed him the public parts of Graysford House—the long dining room with the huge table and chandeliers, the library, and then I took him up the narrow back stairs to the third floor where the servants used to live. On the way back down those dim stairs, something came over me. There's a kind of exhilaration you feel when you're with somebody you never expected to be comfortable with, but are. It's a victory—that you've won them over, I suppose. But it's really a feeling of power. And power never affects people well. As we passed my suite, which was originally the suite of the oldest Graysford daughter, I offered to show him how big and luxurious it was. I unlocked the door, and when we were inside I turned around to close the door just as he stepped toward me. It was an awkward moment, but instead of disengaging, we kissed. And in about a minute he was taking my clothes off, and I wasn't stopping him."

"And that grew into a relationship?" Sid asked.

"That was the start. I don't want you to think I was naïve, or that I didn't know exactly what I was doing. I was the seducer, if anyone was."

"Did anybody see you going in, or learn about it afterward?"

"No," she said. "I'm sure they didn't."

"Was there anybody present at the event who would have been jealous or feel betrayed if they'd known?"

"No. I wasn't dating anyone at the time, and James didn't know anybody. There were the other science hires, all of them practically teenagers, and a few members of the board, all of them from my father's generation. People saw us talking during the cocktail party, but nothing else. Later in the evening I made a point of talking to the new kids, and I'm sure the other directors noted how good I was. They've always admired the way I handle these recruiting situations."

Ronnie said, "And what were your plans with James? Were you heading toward marriage, or did you think of it as a temporary fling? Was it exclusive?"

"That's a lot to think about, so I didn't, at first," Kirsten said. "But the next day, when we all went home, the doubts began to set in. I realized I had made myself vulnerable to disaster, and I began to worry. For a month I tortured myself. I stayed away from the company offices, because I dreaded running into him. I was afraid he had told someone, so whenever I spoke to any of the directors on the phone, I was mostly listening for some veiled reference to him, or some change in tone that would tell me they knew. I decided I had to talk to James and reassure myself that there was no danger. If he was a decent man, he would keep quiet and let the incident be over forever. So I waited until about eleven thirty one night and called his house."

"How did that work?"

She shrugged. "He wasn't a decent man. No, that's wrong. He was far too bright and sophisticated not to know exactly what I was feeling and to see the rightness of it. He just wasn't in the mood to behave decently. He said he wasn't willing to talk about it on the telephone. He made me go to his house."

"Right then?" Ronnie said.

"Right then. I won't say I wasn't fully aware of what he wanted, or that I was naïve. I knew. When I called him, I had been sitting around the house in a sweatshirt and pajama pants. When I hung up I ran upstairs and put on makeup, a cocktail dress, and heels. I drove over there at midnight, speeding all the way so I wouldn't keep him waiting. That was the relationship."

"What do you mean?" said Ronnie.

"I mean I wasn't his girlfriend, or any kind of friend. We wouldn't see each other for weeks. Once in a while one of us would call the other and we would arrange to meet somewhere—his apartment, a hotel—and have sex. We treated each other pretty badly."

"How did the relationship end?"

"The attraction ebbed and flowed," she said. "But it never ended. I talked to him on the day he disappeared. We agreed to meet sometime that week, but there had been a couple of big rainstorms, so we postponed the meeting."

"Do you remember who called it off?"

"I think I did. I remember I was afraid the intersections near his apartment would get flooded and I'd be stuck there, maybe get noticed. I thought there would always be another day, but this time there wasn't."

"I'm sure you've thought often about what happened to him," said Ronnie. "Do you have any theories about the murder?"

"Some. Do I think I know who did it? No. I don't. I'm sure that what everybody told the police was what I told Detective Kapp—that James was a wonderful, nice person, and I couldn't imagine how such a thing could have happened. That wasn't exactly a lie. He could be nice. He could also be inconsiderate and selfish. He wanted what he wanted, and he wasn't willing to be patient. He wasn't especially interested in the other person at all." She paused. "In me. I'll admit that at times that suited me fine. Not having the responsibility of maintaining a connection with the other person—remembering his birthday, listening to his opinions, being polite when I didn't feel like it—was liberating. But it didn't make us close, didn't make me like him. And it didn't make me proud of myself, either."

"You were surprised to hear that there were other women in his life, weren't you?"

"I didn't know about them for sure, but it doesn't surprise me. James was very good at compartmentalizing his life. This does widen the number of people who might have wanted him dead. I think he could have died by fucking people he had no business fucking—a woman being married or having a boyfriend wouldn't have mattered to him at all. And since he wasn't always very nice, the one who pulled the trigger could just as easily have been the woman."

# 15

Nicole Hoyt woke up in the dark. She had an odd feeling that she couldn't quite identify, because her memory went back only as far as the moment when she had opened her eyes. Before that there was a dream—not a nightmare, just the usual nightly amalgam of frustration and unease. In her dream she had been working somewhere and unable to understand the job, and had to try to hide her inability by performing tasks randomly and appearing busy.

Something else must have caused her to wake. She kept her eyes open and waited for whatever had awakened her to be repeated. Then the memory of the sound came back to her. She had heard a car pull into the driveway and then sit there for a long period of time. She remembered the engine vibrating and the fan making a ticking noise. Finally the car had backed out of the driveway.

Nicole analyzed what was bothering her. People often pulled into driveways to turn around. But this one had sat there for too long. She refined her impression. The driver must have just been pretending he needed to turn around. This was like those times when she had been on the street and seen a stranger turn his head too slowly. He was pretending to have his eyes merely slide across her on the way to somewhere else, but she knew when she saw him that he had been checking her out and she had caught him. The car that had been outside had come here to study the house.

"Ed," she whispered.

"Huh?"

"There was a car in the driveway just now."

She spoke very quietly, but Ed was the kind of person who came to instantly, ready to talk rationally or defend himself. She felt the mattress shift as his muscles contracted and his body became tense. He was here, ready. "Is he there now?"

"I think he pulled out, but he was there too long."

Ed didn't need further explanation. He skipped ahead to the realization that he was going to investigate. He rose in the dark, silently as a snake uncoiling. She could tell he had already grasped the .45 with the silencer attached that he kept by the bed. He drifted out of the bedroom in the dark, the only sound the faint creak of a floorboard.

Nicole sat up too. She swung her legs off the bed and walked to the wall, where she reached up and took the second silenced .45 pistol off the shelf. She held it diagonally across her body and followed Ed into the living room. Ed had bought the pistols and had their barrels threaded for silencers because they were the perfect weapons for home defense. He had said that if they were bothered by intruders, it would be at night. He wanted to be able to handle the problem without waking any neighbors, and a silencer was a good flash suppressor, so they'd have another advantage. They also had a loaded Benelli semiauto shotgun under the bed, but she decided to leave that where it was.

She could see Ed standing at the window that overlooked the driveway, just closing the curtain. He moved to the other side of the living room to look out the corner of that window too. He saw Nicole waiting at the hallway entrance and moved close to her. "I don't see anybody, but I've got a feeling about this, so I'm going out."

"Give me a minute to get something on," she said. "You might want to get dressed too."

They went back to the bedroom and put on jeans, shirts, and sneakers. Ed went through the kitchen to the back door and out to the yard. Nicole kept twenty-five feet behind him. If their footsteps were far apart, the adversary would be less likely to hear them coming. She also knew that most shooters couldn't shoot two people that far apart before she could return fire.

They made their way across the dark yard, staying behind the row of bushes at the back fence because it was the best cover their yard afforded. Carrying the pistol with the extra eight inches of silencer attached was awkward for her, but she was glad Ed had insisted on keeping a pair of guns that way. In the dark there was no better advantage than silence.

The possibility that worried her most was that the car might have belonged to the Abels. There was nobody else that she and Ed had attacked or threatened lately, so even if it wasn't the Abels, it was likely to be someone after the Hoyts because of the Abels—the police, probably. How they could have found out where she and Ed lived was difficult to guess. In any case, somebody had come here tonight at 3:00 a.m. to do some reconnaissance.

Nicole thought about the implications. She and Ed might have to run away. The simple inconvenience of abandoning their house and leaving was intimidating. She and Ed had always kept large sums of cash hidden in various places—safe deposit boxes in other American cities, mostly. They also maintained bank accounts in a few different names—mostly female names. Nicole wasn't the type who inspired fear or suspicion among bank tellers, but Ed was kind of scary in person. But it could be hard to put her hands on the money and get out if the Abels knew who they were. The Abels were former cops, and they undoubtedly had some agency on speed dial that could close the borders to a pair of fugitives.

Nicole walked slowly, letting Ed get a bit farther ahead of her. She hung back because the distance made them harder to shoot. But she knew that if the enemy were the police, distance wouldn't do her much good. Trained and experienced combat shooters would know how to stay out of a cross fire, and there would be too many of them to fight.

As Nicole advanced she planned her moves. Keeping Ed about forty feet ahead of her made concealment easier for both of them. If there was a shot or a target appeared, Nicole would assume a two-handed grip and fire. She only had the seven-round magazine and one round in the chamber, so she would have to exert some discipline and not just blast away. She would have to make every shot a good one, hoping the suppressed sound and the diminished muzzle flash would give her extra time before they got her in their sights.

She moved forward from bush to bush, and then to the edge of the yard. Ed was already forty feet into the next lot, a big strip of land that had held an old bungalow from the 1930s when she and Ed moved here. A few months ago the owner died. The owner's son had planned to sell the land to a developer, but Ed had persuaded him to let him buy it. Ed had hired a crew to drive a bulldozer through the house and cart away the wood, brick, and concrete, so now the lot had been cleared to give the Hoyts another open, flat expanse of land that would give an intruder no place to hide. Ed had not yet gotten around to making the uneven, weedy lot into an extension of their lawn. Maybe he never would now.

Nicole thought again about leaving her house behind, and an inventory of important belongings entered her mind. She had thousands of dollars' worth of Lladro statues. She had the Wedding figures, Ballerina Waiting Backstage, Timid Japanese Girl, the Attorney. That one alone had cost over seven hundred dollars new. And the classic ones—Don Quixote, Cinderella, and the others—were famous. Porcelain statues were simply not things she could take with her on the run. And there were the guns. She and Ed must have fifty thousand dollars' worth of guns around the house. Guns were heavy, but leaving them would be dangerous. Police ballistics experts wouldn't have a lot of difficulty matching the guns to various bullets that had been fired into people over the past few years. If she and Ed had to bug out, they would have to do something with all of these belongings.

Nicole entered the empty lot, ducking lower and moving along the opposite side of the field from her husband. She could barely see him, and now and then he would stop and stay perfectly still. If her eyes didn't happen to be on him at that instant, she sometimes lost him until he moved again. When they went to bed there had been a sliver of moon, but it must have gone low behind a cloud or something, because there was no moonlight to help her now. She crouched and waited, letting the darkness and the stillness hide her while she watched and listened.

After a few more seconds Ed began to move again, and she sensed that something was different. He glided forward, stepping along at a walk, lifting his foot above the weeds at each step. Then he began to run. He reached the sidewalk, went to one knee, and aimed his pistol to the right.

Nicole kept her eyes on him as she began to run. Her place was up there where she could see the street and add covering fire for Ed.

A flashlight beam suddenly bathed Ed in white light. Ed fired two rapid shots in that direction with his silenced pistol, and then fired once more. At the training camp where they had met, they had been taught to fire two to the chest and then one to the head. The flashlight beam disappeared, and she knew before she reached the street that somebody was dead.

She looked up the street and saw a lighted flashlight lying on the sidewalk. In the aura around the beam of light, she saw the body of a man lying beside it.

Ed stepped to the prone figure, knelt, and scowled at the man's face. He felt the man's neck for a pulse, but abandoned that idea after a second or two. He turned the man over and patted the pockets. He dug his hand into one of them, came up with the man's key chain, and stood.

Nicole arrived beside him and saw it all in the light that still spilled from the flashlight on the pavement. And she noticed that in the light she could make out the color of the SUV that was parked ten feet away. Brown. She bent to look down at the dead man's face, and then looked up at Ed.

"Yep," he whispered. "It's Vincent Boylan. I don't know what the hell he thought he was doing." Ed bent and picked up the flashlight, turned it off, and then removed the pistol from Boylan's hand. "You'd better bring the car while I load him into his. Then follow me."

Nicole turned and ran along the sidewalk to their house, and then around to the back door. She hurried to the bedroom and retrieved her purse, and then dug out her keys on the way to the garage. She backed the gray Camry out of the garage, closed the garage door with the remote control, and drove up behind the brown SUV with her headlights off. She could see a big wet spot where Ed must have dragged out the hose and sprayed down the sidewalk.

Boylan's body was already gone, and she could see Ed must be in the driver's seat of the brown SUV, because he wasn't visible anywhere else. The SUV's engine started and the vehicle began to move.

Ed drove for a hundred yards to the first intersection, turned left, and drove a few yards past it before he switched on the headlights. Nicole turned on her lights, and Ed sped up. She wished he had his cell phone, so she could talk to him about what had happened and what they were going to do now. She supposed it was her fault that he didn't have it. She could have brought his phone with her when she'd gone to get her purse, and given it to him.

She followed the brown SUV as Ed drove out of their neighborhood and down the road to the freeway entrance. He got on the eastbound side and sped up. She hoped he wasn't going to lead her to some remote spot far out in the desert and make this night a worse nightmare. She was in no mood to drag Boylan's body around and help dig a grave, and then try to race home before the sun came up.

Just as she was beginning to feel fretful, Ed took the exit off the freeway at Coldwater Canyon and went south to Valley Vista Boulevard. He turned a couple of times on narrow roads before she was sure she realized where he was going. He stopped and idled just at the curve where he had stopped earlier in the day. They were almost to Boylan's house. He got out, walked back to their car, and gestured to Nicole to roll down her window.

Nicole said, "Aren't we going to bury him?"

"Not unless you want to bury his SUV too."

"I don't get it," she said.

"We don't have time to do anything with him that would make much difference, and this is our only chance to satisfy our curiosity about him. Come on. We'll park his car in his garage and see what we can find out in his house."

"But what about his body?"

"We'll just cover it and leave it in the back of his car. Nobody will find it for a day or two."

"What if he's married? Or he has a girlfriend?"

"If he had a woman in his bed then he shouldn't have gone out to bother us. Come on." He walked to Boylan's SUV.

*That's Ed all right,* she thought. She shook her head and got out of the Camry, then trotted to the passenger door of the SUV and sat beside Ed. He drove them ahead to Boylan's house, turned up the driveway, and pulled into the attached garage. Ed closed the garage door with the remote control, and they got out. He switched on Boylan's flashlight and opened the back of the SUV, where Boylan's body lay. He patted Boylan's pockets until he found a cell phone, and handed it to Nicole. "Put this in your purse. It's probably got our number in the memory."

Nicole put the phone in her purse and looked at Boylan in the dim, moving light. "What do you think he was doing? Why would he come and case our house?"

"I don't know yet," Ed said. "What I'm guessing is that he saw us following him here this morning and thought he'd kill us before we killed him."

"Jesus," she said. "He'd have to be an idiot."

Ed went to the back of the garage, found what looked like the canvas of an old awning, and brought it back and covered Boylan with it, then closed the hatch. He took a red shop rag from the workbench and wiped down the steering wheel, the door handles, the glove compartment, and the hatch.

"Come on. Let's go in." He stepped to the door that led into the house and aimed the flashlight in through the window, and then turned it off. "No sign of a Rottweiler, and the alarm system isn't armed. I guess you're right about him being an idiot."

He used Boylan's key to open the kitchen door. When they were both inside he locked it again. They walked through the room to the hallway that led beside the staircase to the front entry. When they reached the staircase Ed faced Nicole, put his index finger over his mouth, and then pointed upstairs.

Nicole nodded and screwed the silencer on her gun again, and then began to climb the stairs. She was much better than Ed was at moving quietly, since she weighed about forty percent less than he did. She placed her foot on each step right beside the wall, where the wood would be nailed tightly to the vertical board beneath, and not bend or creak. She reached the top in a few seconds and found herself in a carpeted hallway. She walked along the padded surface, moving nimbly and rapidly with her gun low in front of her. She glanced into each room to be sure it wasn't occupied, and then moved on.

After a few doorways she was beginning to feel relieved, because the place seemed to be empty. But as she approached the far end of the hall, she heard a female voice. "Vince?" it said. Nicole froze, her shallow breaths sounding loud to her and the back of her neck suddenly sweaty. "Vince? What are you doing?" The voice was sleepy and querulous, a young woman's voice. "Vince?"

Nicole called out in her softest, most motherly voice, "Don't be afraid, honey. They're putting the fire out now, but you'd better get dressed." She kept moving down the hall toward the woman's voice.

The woman stood in the doorway, just closing the button at the waist of a pair of tight jeans. She was tall and thin in a tank top with an open man's shirt thrown over it and her feet bare. When she saw Nicole she reached to the top of a dresser just inside the room and turned toward her with a pistol in her right hand.

Nicole's gun flashed, and in that half second she saw the long blond hair, the peach tank top, and the hole being punched into it at the sternum. Nicole fired twice more, each flash revealing the woman's look of utter surprise. The woman fell forward onto the floor and lay still. Nicole fired another round into the woman's head and then walked around her body toward the bedroom.

The stairway resonated with Ed's heavy footsteps pounding upward, and Nicole turned to see him arrive with his pistol in a two-handed grip.

"I'm fine," Nicole said. "Thanks for asking."

Ed switched on the flashlight and held its beam on the woman. "She's not. Who is she?"

Nicole looked down at her. "She's got a wedding ring on, so I assume she's his wife. I'll see if I can find her purse and check."

She took his flashlight, went inside the bedroom, surveyed the room, and saw a purse hanging on the doorknob of the closet. She looked inside, found a small wallet, and opened it. "License says she's Leslie Ann Kuyper, DOB June sixteenth, nineteen eighty-six. Her voice sounded a lot younger. I guess she used her maiden name."

"I don't like that," Ed said.

"I know," Nicole said. "This credit card says she's Leslie Boylan. Like her better now?"

"No. Let's start looking."

"Any idea what we're looking for?"

He said, "Anything that will tell us who his client was. An address book, other cell phones, a computer. And anything that has our name on it, or our address."

She handed Ed the flashlight, returned the wallet to the purse, and let it swing back on its strap. "I'll look around up here. Why don't you start searching the first floor?"

"All right." Ed left the room and she heard him going down the stairs. She reached into the large walk-in closet and found the light switch, then closed the door behind her before she turned it on so the light wouldn't show through the bedroom window.

She had read somewhere that people who hid things in their houses usually hid them close to where they slept. She wasn't sure if that applied to the whole population, but the kind of people she and Ed had been hired to kill seemed to do things that way. They tended to be people who wanted to protect their valuables themselves, and they wanted to be able to snatch them up quickly and get out of the house before whatever they'd done caught up with them.

Nicole opened the drawers of the built-in dressers. She found a very thin pair of leather gloves that belonged to the dead woman, and put them on to search. She started with the bottom drawers and worked her way up. She looked for papers, notebooks, flash drives, disks. About halfway up in the dresser across the room she found a drawer with a false bottom. She pried it up and found the money. It was all in neat, banded stacks of hundreds, laid in evenly to form a foundation for the false drawer bottom. The cash wasn't actually hidden, just stored as though Boylan wanted to keep the money separate and out of the way. She loaded the stacks of bills into a pillowcase and set it by the door so she would remember to take it. After that she found a gun in an upper drawer, but nothing else that was of any interest.

She saw that the woman had some pretty good jewelry, but taking it to a jewelry store to have it melted and reset would make the jeweler call the insurance companies to see if it was stolen.

She moved out to the rest of the bedroom, working with only the light from inside the closet. There was another gun in the nightstand on Boylan's side. There was nothing that told her anything she didn't already know. She moved to the next bedroom, the next, and the next. They were all spare rooms that had not been in use, and there wasn't anything hidden in, behind, or under any of the furniture.

Ed looked up when he heard her coming down the stairs, and saw the pillowcase. "What did you find?"

"A drawer full of cash and a couple of guns. I left the guns."

"Were you careful about prints and things?"

She held up her gloved hand. "Yeah. Were you?"

He held up his hand and showed her a bright yellow rubber glove. "I found these in the kitchen."

"Find anything besides rubber gloves?"

"Just a laptop computer. We'll never get into that. Nothing about the client. I think we're in trouble," he said. "Don't leave anything here. We aren't going to be able to come back."

# 16

Sid and Ronnie Abel rode the back elevator down to the lower level of their hotel's underground garage and got into their latest rental car. Sid drove up the ramp to the ground level and out into the side street that opened onto Calabasas Road. It was a bright, hot morning and the sun was already high in the sky. As they waited at the traffic signal, Sid said, "That was a really good bluff you hit on yesterday with Kirsten Tilson."

"Do you mean the video?"

"That's what I mean," Sid said.

"Think about it. We knew before we called her that she'd had an affair with Ballantine. When we called her, she claimed she barely knew him, and yet she was willing to meet with us privately to talk about it. Something had to be motivating that."

"Sure. She didn't want to be embarrassed."

"She's a bundle of contradictions," Ronnie said. "She's a bit of a racist, but Ballantine's race gave being with him a titillating edge for her. She says they didn't like each other, but they were still seeing each other three years later."

"She's an ordinary liar, but you made up the imaginary sex tape," Sid said. "You're the champ."

"It's not imaginary," said Ronnie.

"It's not?"

"If a video doesn't exist, then something like it does. Ballantine was a very secretive man. Why would he tell his ex-wife about the women he was seeing? Hardly. Would she even listen? Doubtful. She had divorced him, taken the kids, and moved to another city. She made a point of saying that they hadn't spoken in three years. She must have found something among his belongings after he was dead."

"Whatever the evidence was, Kirsten Tilson didn't know about the other women. She really wanted to know who else was on the list."

"Maybe she sees herself as the wronged party," said Ronnie. "Maybe because she saw him first."

"Interesting woman."

"She'd be pleased to hear you say that," Ronnie said. "She thinks so too. Just remember you're the same age as the other directors. And her father."

"He's dead."

"Yes." Ronnie smiled. "Probably old age."

"I'm flattered that you're so possessive."

"Let's go see the next girlfriend."

They had arranged to meet the next woman on the list in a shaded park in Burbank near St. Joseph Medical Center on Bob Hope Drive. They drove up the street scanning for her, but didn't see a lone woman sitting in a car, and this morning the park appeared to be nearly empty. A few young women—mothers or nannies—watched small children playing, and a couple of women in hospital scrubs walked briskly along a path together. The Abels stopped and remained in their rental car, studying the surrounding area.

After a few minutes Ronnie said, "You're looking at the roofs of the buildings on Alameda."

"I'm looking at everything, and so are you."

"I'm looking for Linda Bourget. You're looking for the people who've been trying to kill us. You think Linda Bourget is setting us up for them?"

"No, or we wouldn't be sitting here. But she did choose this as the place to meet with us, and she is late."

Ronnie looked to the right into the park, craning her neck to look over her shoulder. "Besides the rooftops, there's a lot of traffic along the street, and there are a few ways of getting in and out of here on foot."

"I think that might be her coming across the park from the hospital."

They watched as a slim woman in her thirties walked toward them. She had long dark hair and an olive complexion, and she was wearing a pair of designer jeans and low sandals, with a white top with a V neck and short sleeves. She wore a pair of sunglasses that were large enough to keep much of her face from being seen, and she seemed to be looking down most of the time, studying the path her feet were following.

Ronnie focused her attention on the woman, who was closer now, walking directly toward them. She spoke softly to Sid. "Expensive clothes. Those jeans are hard to find, let alone buy. The purse cost a few thousand."

"Let's get out and happen to run into her so this looks social."

They got out of their car and walked into the park, following the marked path of fine gravel, so their trajectory met hers. "Miss Bourget?" said Ronnie.

The woman didn't speak, but she pivoted on her heel and walked with them. After a few steps she said, "You're the Abels?"

"Yes," said Ronnie. "Thank you for taking the time to see us. I'm Ronnie, and this is Sid."

"I didn't really have a choice," said Linda Bourget. "I've expected this day to come, and so I've been preparing myself for a long time. If we can make our talk brief, I would appreciate it. I'm supposed to be at lunch with my sister. A sister is the only one you can really trust to lie for you. Anyone else might decide she's not such a good friend after all. A sister is stuck with you."

Ronnie began. "As I told you on the phone, we've been hired to investigate James Ballantine's murder. We didn't know very much about him, so we're asking people who knew him to tell us what they know."

"Okay. I'll try to be as honest as I can," said Linda Bourget.

"Let's start with the basics," said Sid. "When did you begin dating Mr. Ballantine?"

"That's not as simple a question as you make it sound," she said.

"I don't understand," said Ronnie. "When I called and told you why we wanted to talk to you, I thought you said we'd come to the right person."

"You have," Linda said. "I've waited for a year to have somebody come and talk to me about him. I thought the police would come in the first few days, but they didn't.

Then it was weeks, and then months. I kept thinking that they had already figured out who killed James and decided I didn't matter, but they hadn't."

"No, they hadn't," said Sid. "We're trying, and we need your help."

"To begin with, we weren't dating," Linda said. "We didn't have a regular, ordinary relationship."

Sid's and Ronnie's eyes flicked toward each other and Ronnie said, "How was it different?"

"I was married. If I had been caught with James, I would have lost my husband and my two children. James and I met in secret."

Ronnie said, "How did you first get to know him?"

"James and I were seated next to each other on an airplane, a red-eye from Chicago to Los Angeles. I was flying home from New York. He was flying from Bloomington, Indiana, where he was a professor. We had to stop in Chicago to change flights, but the weather was bad, so our planes arrived late, and our flight took off without us. We both ended up at the airline desk and they put us on the next flight, which left at ten thirty in the evening. The time went on and the airport started to empty out a bit. We sat and talked a little. Then he asked me if I'd like to have a drink with him. I did, we talked some more, and then our flight was announced. We said good-bye and went to the gate. When I got to my seat, I couldn't believe it. We were both right at the back of the plane—the last seats to go—and together."

"It must have seemed as though it was fated," said Ronnie.

"I dismissed that thought, because I had already picked the fate I wanted," Linda said. "It sounds crazy, but I loved my husband. We had two beautiful children, a boy and a girl.

I had a great life—exactly the life I had grown up wanting—and I didn't want to lose it. But just this one time, I got tempted."

"If you loved your husband, why do this?"

"It just sort of happened. The circumstances were perfect. I had already called my husband when my flight came in too late to get to Los Angeles, and said I'd be staying in a Chicago hotel and take a flight out in the morning. The replacement flight just opened up because another couple hadn't made it to take their seats," she said. "And James and I had been talking and we liked each other. He had that quality. He could make a woman know, without any doubt, but without anything embarrassing, that he liked her. When he looked at you, there was no way not to see yourself as he saw you—beautiful."

"You are beautiful," Ronnie said. "That can't have been a surprise to you."

"Thank you. But there was more than saying I was pretty. He made me feel fascinating. Exciting. Those are not things that I felt at home very often in those days. I was a mother with two young children and a husband who was always at work. He was a unit production manager on a television show. He made good money and had a great future, but his daily life didn't have much to do with mine. James Ballantine made me feel like a different person. And the way we were thrown together, the universe seemed to be telling me giving in was okay. So I acted like that different person."

"And you risked everything on a whim?" said Ronnie.

"Not on a whim," Linda said. "Before James ever touched me I thought about what I would say and do if it happened. That was something else I learned along the way. We're natural sinners. Nobody had to tell me how to go about any of this. I just knew. I checked to see when the next morning flight from Chicago would arrive at LAX and planned to get a shuttle to take me home from the hotel at the right time. I planned everything I was going to do and say to get away with this before I agreed to it. And then I went with James to the hotel he'd booked for his interview visit. He went to the desk, checked in and got his room key, and I met him there."

Sid said, "Were you ever discovered?"

"No," she said. "Never. I did everything I could to make sure there was no way I'd get caught. James didn't have risks like mine. He was getting rid of the people who would have blamed him. He had given notice that he was leaving the university where he worked, and had begun to let his communications with friends and relatives in the East gradually die out. He wasn't divorced yet, but he knew he was going to be."

"Did his doing all of that at once strike you as odd at the time?" asked Ronnie. "Maybe self-destructive?"

"I didn't think that way," she said. "While all of that was going on, I was thinking that it was making me safer. Nobody from his world would discover us, and blow things up. I still wanted to keep the life I had."

Ronnie said, "I understand. There were fewer people to notice anything, so it was easier to keep things a secret."

"I didn't really understand it," Linda said. "Maybe I don't even now. He was reinventing himself, and I didn't know why. When we met, we were both people who had lives and relationships to protect, but were just taking an exciting and brief peek into another life—not the life we should have had, or anything like that. It was just a secret world that didn't bring any responsibilities or failures or boredom. In it we were wild and sexy and glamorous. It was fun to visit that world once in a while, and then go back to reality. I was pretending to go to a therapist once a week, but I was seeing James instead."

"What changed?"

"He did, and I did, but slowly. Things started going better for me at home. A year made my kids that much older, and keeping up with them wasn't as grueling. My husband was working on a different show that was shot entirely on studio soundstages instead of two thousand miles away, and he spent more time with me. One morning I woke up and I didn't want to go see James that day. Then I realized I didn't want to go again, ever. I was ashamed, and I was afraid, and I knew I had to tell James it was over before I lost everything."

"And that's when you learned he had changed?"

"Yes. Or maybe what had changed wasn't him. Maybe he was always the same, and this was just when I understood. I told him that I wasn't happy with what I'd done to my life. I wouldn't be seeing him anymore."

"I take it he didn't like that?" Sid said.

"No."

"Did he get angry? Hurt?"

"No. He just refused to allow it to happen."

"What do you mean?" asked Sid.

"I told him it was over, and he said that it wasn't up to me. I was committed, had made my decision, and I belonged to him now. If I ended the relationship, he would make sure that my husband saw some videos he'd taken. All he had to do was send one to my husband's e-mail address. He also said he'd send one to each of my husband's co-workers, and one to each of the friends I'd ever mentioned to him. He seemed to remember all of their names. Later I realized he must have gotten the names off my phone one day while I was at his house."

"Was he bluffing?" asked Sid.

She took a deep breath and let it out. "I didn't know anything about any videos, so I assumed he was. I had been seeing him on Thursday afternoons at four, and that Thursday, I didn't show up. He called my cell phone, but when I saw his number on the screen, I didn't answer. He called again five minutes later. Then I heard the little signal that I was getting an e-mail. I opened it, and there we were—James and me—on his bed, in a video. It wasn't as though I were unrecognizable, some woman in a pornographic movie or something. You could see my face clearly, even on the tiny cell phone screen."

"What did you do?" asked Ronnie.

"I erased the video from my phone and called him."

"What did you say?"

"I told him he was disgusting and evil. I said I hated him, and hung up."

"How did he react?"

"He called me back. What he said was that he still expected me that afternoon as always. Then he hung up."

"What did you do?" asked Ronnie.

"I was shocked. I sat there paralyzed. I had only bad choices. He had already shown me everything that he could show me about my predicament. He had the graphic proof, and he had demonstrated that he had the capability and the malevolence to send the video everywhere—to ruin my life. So I went."

Ronnie said, "Linda, did you have anything to do with Ballantine's death?"

She shook her head. "No. I didn't. I'm not the kind of person who can kill someone. I spent a lot of nights wishing that I were."

"What did you do?"

"I cried. But I resigned myself to tolerating him for the time being, because I could think of nothing else to do. I went there every Thursday, and did whatever he wanted. Afterwards, I went home to my children and my husband. But for those hours, I was his property."

"I'm sorry," said Ronnie. "It must have been awful. Do you think it's possible that someone else found out what was going on and decided to kill him? Did you tell anyone?"

She shook her head. "I went along with everything. Sometimes he would tell me that I would get over feeling bad about it. This was just the way the world worked, and I had to find out sometime. Everyone was trying to get an advantage over everyone else, to take what the other person had. When he got into that mood it was awful."

Ronnie said, "If you didn't tell anyone about it, do you think it's possible that he did? That he might have tried to blackmail your husband or bragged to someone who decided on his own to put a stop to it?"

Linda shook her head again. "That's not what happened."

"Then how did it end?" asked Ronnie.

"One night, after I had put the kids to bed, I was waiting for my husband to come home. I was thinking about him, and how what I was doing to keep my secret was worth it. He came home, and sat down. He sat across from me and put his head in his hands. And he told me some news."

"What news?"

"He had decided to end the marriage. He had found somebody else. She was a twenty-four-year-old PA on the show where he'd been working, and eventually he got around to admitting that he had been sleeping with her for a year. The times when he had not been able to come home, he'd been with her. I said, 'It's all right. We can get through this. I'll forgive you, and we'll start all over again.' He said he couldn't. He wanted a divorce, and he planned to file right away. He wouldn't be a jerk about the property settlement in the divorce, because he wanted to take care of me. And if I wanted full custody of the kids, he would understand. Angela—that was her name—wanted to build her career, and having kids around wasn't part of her plan. But the one thing that was off the table was staying with me."

"Wow," said Ronnie. "That's tough."

"Out of curiosity, I asked him if he remembered the time about a year before, when I was in New York for my aunt's funeral, and my plane got delayed in Chicago. He didn't remember."

"Did that make him suspect something had gone on?"

"No. He was consumed by his own guilt. He thought I was asking whether my being away that night caused his cheating. After the divorce papers were filed, I told James Ballantine that the reason for the divorce was that I had finally told my husband the truth. I never heard from him after that."

"Do you remember the date when this happened?" Sid asked.

"May fifteenth, two years ago."

Ronnie said, "We really appreciate that you had the courage to tell us what happened. I wish you could have been spared all of that."

Linda said, "I was sure the police would find whatever he had kept about me, and they'd come to ask me about him."

"They didn't know what you've just told us, or they would have," Sid said. "A lot of people have been killed for a lot less than he did."

"At the time, I did think about killing myself. Not him," she said. "After that, when I wasn't in his power anymore, I felt nothing. Whoever killed him, it was for some other reason. I agreed to talk to you because when he died, I heard and read all this stuff about what a great guy he was. I thought somebody would tell the truth, or find the videos, and the police would come. They never came."

"There was no traceable connection between him and you," said Ronnie. "Nobody the police talked to even knew you existed."

"If it's possible, I'd really like it if you could keep what I've told you quiet—that I was the one. I remarried about a year ago, and—"

"We'll do everything we can to protect your privacy," said Ronnie. She touched her arm gently, and gave a comforting smile. "Thank you again."

A few minutes later, as they were walking to their car, Sid said, "You didn't tell her where all the videos went."

"Neither did you."

"Not my job. I was letting you take the lead on the interviews with the women. They always seem to trust you."

"They all see me and think they're talking to their mother. They're not."

# 17

Nicole's fear was like a whip. It woke her at dawn with an awareness of things she was going to have to force herself to accomplish, and the list seemed to have no end. She had already spent the past two days evicting herself from her house. Bugging out was incredibly hard work. First she had gathered items that were incriminating or might lead a pursuer to find her and Ed. Next she had gone through the whole house retrieving small but valuable possessions— money, her jewelry, a few garments that she knew made her look thinner or younger and that she could never hope to find in a store again.

In the first load she included a few well-disguised guns and the ammunition that went with them, thinking less of the cost of high-end firearms than of which ones were most likely to be useful in their current predicament, and which should be stored.

Nicole wanted to take the things out of the house that were dangerous to them, not empty it completely. She didn't remove any big items like appliances or furniture, or cheap items like framed prints or bedclothes or pots and pans or towels. She left enough of her clothes and Ed's so a person who didn't know them well would think the Hoyts had never left.

She was careful to remove every photograph. Most were pictures of her or of Ed, but she didn't leave any of the others either. She didn't want an enemy to have pictures of her friends and relatives, or of the places where she and Ed had been. In her time working with Ed they had been hired a number of times to hunt some person down and kill him. She had learned that people on the run tended to favor pleasant places they had visited on vacations or at school or in the military. Some of them were foolish enough to think they could seek shelter with their families, and some chasers were mean enough to start butchering the families to bring a fugitive out into the open. Photographs would show a hunter what she and Ed looked like, where they had been, what their relatives looked like, and maybe even where they lived. Sometimes she felt tempted to leave false leads for the pursuers, but she had learned that it was best to leave no information at all.

She left all of the things necessary to make the house look occupied. If it took a pursuer three days to be sure that the Hoyts were gone, then those were three whole days that Nicole and Ed could use. In three days, a person could go around the world and back. She even decided to sacrifice her Lladro figurines, because they were too pretty and expensive for anybody to believe she'd leave them. She moved them into the antique china cabinet that she and Ed had been using as a wine case, and stuck the wine bottles in a cheap wine rack she'd always refused to have in her way in the kitchen. The process gave her a chance to wipe the fingerprints off those smooth, perfect glass surfaces.

Nicole washed all the sheets, blankets, towels, and clothes that weren't already clean, vacuumed all the floors, and had Ed replace the vacuum bags. She put them in trash bags along with all of the shredded receipts, bills, and other financial paper, and drove them to a dumpster behind a store five miles away. She collected the credit cards and licenses and other identification cards and replaced them with the cards in false names that she and Ed had kept for an occasion like this.

She put everything she and Ed wanted to keep in a storage space they rented in a storage facility on Vineland Avenue in North Hollywood. It was a single building with a high fence around it, and all the spaces were inside, so there was no likelihood of casual theft. The company was having a long-term rental sale, so she rented the space for three years in advance. She took the batteries out of their cell phones and left them in storage, and then bought new prepaid phones.

Nicole left a little of the money she had found in Boylan's house in the rented storage space, and put the rest in their bugout kit. The bugout kit took quite a bit of planning, and that was where Ed concentrated his efforts now. The kit was in two medium-sized ballistic nylon travel duffels. Inside each duffel Ed placed a layer of stacked hundred-dollar bills in sealed plastic bags. Above that was a 9mm Heckler & Koch MP5 rifle configured for full automatic fire with a retractable stock and four loaded thirty-round magazines. In a pocket just under the zipper were a Sig Sauer P250 compact .45 semiauto pistol with a silencer and three full magazines. The rest of the duffel he filled in with clothes they would need.

Ed spent more time with their cars, particularly the gray Toyota Camry that Nicole called the invisible car. He changed the oil, filled the gas tank, adjusted the tire inflation, and loaded the bugout kits into the trunk. He had already decided that he would leave his big black pickup truck in the driveway if they ever had to disappear. That was a worthwhile sacrifice for several reasons. People would assume that he would never leave it, because anyone could look at that truck and know he loved it. The truck was clean, unscratched, and waxed by a detailer, and its deep, shiny finish was like a dare. The truck was capable of hauling heavy weights—its frame, engine, and wheels were big and strong—but it was not a work truck. Parking that truck in the driveway in front of the closed garage door was like placing a sign there that said the man who owned it was inside the house waiting for you to try something.

If Ed and Nicole had to go on the run, a vehicle like that would be far too memorable. And besides, leaving it would prevent Nicole from being tempted to bitch about the things she had to abandon.

When all of the cleaning and storage had been done, Ed and Nicole waited. Sooner or later somebody was going to find Vincent Boylan and his wife, and then the Hoyts would learn whether someone else—maybe the clients who'd dealt with Boylan—knew about them and wanted to kill them. Boylan had sworn he would never tell anyone, but that sort of assurance was worthless.

While Ed and Nicole waited, they continued their preparations. They plugged timers into most of the sockets in the house. The bedroom lamps came on at 6:39 a.m. and went off at 7:27, and then came on again at 8:22 p.m. and off at 12:17. A radio in the kitchen came on at 7:20, off at 8:33, and came on again for a time after lunch. The big television set in the den went on at 8:00 in the evening and went off at 11:30. Ed had the air-conditioning thermostat set to seventy-two so it would run whenever an observer expected it to. When Nicole had finished washing virtually every piece of cloth in the house, Ed set the washer and the dryer on timers so they would run once in proper sequence on the day after the Hoyts left. Every room had its own schedule, so something that made light or noise would turn on as it would if the home were occupied.

At the end of the fifth day Ed and Nicole learned that someone had found Boylan and his wife. The Hoyts had assumed that they would first read about it online or in the local paper, or see a story about it on television. Instead they saw the reaction.

Each night after midnight they opened the blackout curtains on the windows, went out, and sat on a pair of lawn chaises in the big yard behind their property to watch their house from a distance. Their gray Camry was parked on a street two blocks away, and the house was locked. Each of them held one of the silenced .45 pistols under a light jacket. The first couple of nights they had simply fallen asleep and awakened at dawn then gone to a hotel for the rest of their night's sleep.

But the fifth night felt different almost immediately. Their house was near the end of a road, and there were only three houses past the corner, but twice during the late evening a car passed, moving very slowly as though the driver were studying their house minutely. Then the street was quiet for a time.

Ed and Nicole watched for a couple of hours, and then fell asleep. But then the car came back, and Nicole awoke. She saw a dark SUV moving along the road toward their house. It was going so slowly that she couldn't think of a practical reason to drive that way except to keep the engine noise to an absolute minimum.

The SUV stopped at the curb in front of their house, but nobody got out. Then a second SUV came along the same route and stopped behind the first. Nicole reached out and touched Ed. He leaned forward with the stillness of a big pointer hound, his eyes focused on the part of the road he could see between the houses.

The lights of the two vehicles went out. Doors opened and shut. In a moment, shadowy shapes were moving along both sides of their house. She could see there were guns. Their weapons were short and stubby like Uzis or Mac-10s. Their movements were reminiscent of a police raid, but the cars and the equipment didn't look official. A couple of the men were silhouetted briefly in the light of a bulb over the Hoyts' garage. After a minute the light went out as though the bulb had been unscrewed. Each man took a position under one of the house's windows. A silent signal passed from man to man, beginning at the rear of the house at the kitchen door and moving to the front.

Nicole watched the kitchen window and saw a dim light at the end of the hall as the front door swung open, and then the shapes of men rushing inside—one, two, three, and then the front door closed and they were invisible. Ed placed his silenced pistol on his lap but stayed where he was, so Nicole imitated him.

Inside the house, flashlights came on as the men moved through the living room. Two of the lights went out and then reappeared in the back bedroom, dancing along the walls and the ceiling, and then moved on. The men were clearing the rooms, making sure nobody was inside waiting to ambush them, or hiding in a closet. Nicole could follow their progress by watching the men stationed at the windows, because they stepped up to the glass with weapons raised as the penetration team reached their areas.

After a few minutes a wave went from man to man along the outside of the house, and they all moved off in single file the way they had come. The men piled into the second SUV, and it backed up, turned around, and moved slowly up the street away from the house.

But the three men searching the house stayed. Their flashlights came on and they moved from room to room, this time not looking for the Hoyts, but conducting a search of the contents of the house.

Nicole leaned so close to Ed that her lips brushed his ear. "I'd like to get out of this yard."

He whispered back, "I'd like to get out of this state. But I'd better take a picture of that car's plates so we can figure out who these guys are. Meet me at the car."

Ed climbed over the fence to the next yard, and then moved forward to the road, staying as low as he could. He stopped and looked toward his house. The SUV was sitting driverless in front. The three men inside the house were still busy ransacking the place, but he knew that probably wouldn't go on for long. He and Nicole had taken everything out that was worth stealing, and anything that could be used to find out where they had gone.

Ed moved closer, trying to get a picture of the SUV on his phone, then looking at the image and seeing it was too dark to read the plate number. This part of the road had no streetlamps, the houses nearby were dark, and the moon seemed to be obscured by clouds. He moved onto the sidewalk and began to trot. As long as the men were busy they wouldn't see him.

He kept glancing at the front door of his house to be sure the men weren't coming out. Then he was close enough to read the plate number. He switched to the note function and a keyboard appeared, so he punched in the license number. He knew the plate might be stolen, so he stepped to the windshield of the SUV and used the faint glow of the phone's screen to illuminate the vehicle identification plate and punched the long number into the phone's memory.

The front door of the house swung open, and a man stood on the front steps, saw Ed, and raised his short-barreled machine pistol.

In an instant Ed read the man's reluctance to open up on the vehicle that was his way home, rested his silenced pistol on the hood just below the windshield, and shot him in the chest. He didn't wait for the fall. Instead, he ducked and ran to take advantage of the two seconds of confusion in the minds of the other two men.

When Ed made it to the rear of the SUV he kept running past instead of stopping to fire on them.

The second man had already trained his silenced subma-chine gun on the spot where he expected Ed to be, a foot behind the SUV, so when he fired, his bullet passed through the space Ed had just left.

Ed made it to the corner of his house near the driveway, but instead of sprinting past as the men now expected him to do, Ed stopped, dropped to his belly, brought his gun around the corner, and managed to shoot the second man as he jumped from the front steps to go after Ed. The bullet hit the man's torso just below the sternum, so when his feet hit the ground his legs buckled and he sprawled on the front lawn.

The third man was a quick thinker who saw instantly that there was nothing he could gain by staying. He sprang from the top step and dashed for the SUV.

Ed fired, but he was distracted by the quick series of muzzle flashes from the other corner of his house. The man looked from Ed's vantage as though he were running into the ground, his legs bending so they seemed shorter until his face hit the lawn. Nicole stepped out from the corner of the house and stopped to fire a round into the head of each of the three men, then approached Ed. "You okay?"

"So far," he said. "You?"

"So far. We'd better get these guys off the lawn."

They loaded the three bodies into the SUV, and then Nicole relocked the front door of the house and turned on the sprinkler system to cycle once and wash the blood into the lawn. Ed drove the SUV and dropped Nicole two blocks away at their gray Camry.

They drove a few miles to a neighborhood in Van Nuys where there were streets full of large old apartment buildings. Ed looked for one with big signs advertising vacancies, drove the SUV up the driveway to the parking area in the back, and found that four of the carports had no cars parked

in them at this hour of the night. Those must be for the ten-
ants of the vacant apartments. He pulled the SUV into one
of them, spent a minute taking the wallets and cell phones
from the three bodies, and then walked out the driveway to
the street, where Nicole waited in the Camry. Ed got into
the passenger seat of the Camry, and let Nicole drive off.

Ed began to look through the wallets he had taken from the
three dead men. "This one has a license from Kern County."

"Has he got a name?" she asked.

"Volkonsky."

"With an i?"

"No. A y."

"A Russian," she muttered. "What about the others?"

"Gregorin. Malikov. No Polacks. All Russians, I think.
Now we don't know if Boylan was working as a go-between
for Russian gangsters, or if whoever he was working for just
happened to know some Russians. Or if these guys were
members of a gang."

"Well they weren't a bunch of wedding planners."

"You know what I mean. Connected guys, not just guys
with Russian names."

"I don't think it matters a whole lot who they were. The
guy we have to worry about is the one who hired them. He
probably thinks Boylan told us who he is, and he's afraid of
us. He's got a lot of money and he can just keep hiring people
until one of them kills us."

Ed sat still for a few seconds, staring out the windshield.
"You're right. But we've got their cell phones. Those phones
will show the numbers of the calls they got, where they've
been, all kinds of things. The phones are our link to the guy
who hired us all—Boylan, us, and these Russians."

# 18

The Abels sat at the table in their hotel room with the curtain open, waiting for the coffee they'd made in the little machine the hotel supplied. The sky outside was still dark. In a half hour the upper floors of the building would be painted in the orange light of dawn while the lower floors would still be in shadow. There was a steamy, spluttering noise, and Ronnie got up, walked to the coffeemaker, and filled two cups.

She sipped her coffee, carried the cups back to the table, and sat down beside Sid. She kissed his cheek. "I guess we should start getting ready so we can go see what Ballantine's next girlfriend can tell us. She's got an appointment at nine, so she wants to see us before she has to leave."

Sid looked down at the file on the table. "Emily Prosser." He sipped his coffee and set it back down. He didn't look happy to have it.

"Is something bothering you?" Ronnie asked.

"Not really," said Sid. "I was just thinking."

"You're not eager to interview another one, are you? I would have thought you'd be interested in hearing all these women tell you about their sex lives."

"They all should have been interviewed a year ago, when their memories were fresh. If Kapp had asked Ballantine's wife right away, she might have told him about them."

"I met Kapp in the old days, when I worked North Hollywood. You ever run into him?"

"I don't think so," Sid said.

"It wouldn't have done any good if he had interviewed those women. They never would have told him anything."

"Really?"

She nodded. "He was okay, but he wasn't a woman, and he didn't have the right personality to make women open up. He was a tough, all-business cop, and no genius. They would have known at the start that they didn't have to tell him anything personal, just wait him out. And he didn't exude enough bogus sympathy to make them forget to protect themselves."

"I'm glad I married you instead of him," said Sid.

"I can believe it," she said. "I look better than Kapp even now. And with me around, you don't have to be sensitive, or even smart."


As Ronnie stood in the shower she thought about Sid. In his career as a cop he had worked with all kinds of people in rough situations. Each time he'd moved on, just about everyone had been sorry to see him go. He was tough—a lot tougher than Kapp had been. But he had gone into police work believing that people were worth risking his life for. He had walked away from the department twelve years later with approximately the same belief, just a century older and with lower expectations.

Hers were probably even lower. Seeing the things people did to each other had been a shock to her. And Sid had missed out on Ronnie's personal vulnerability on the police force, her sex. Every woman had to prove over and over again that while she couldn't be as big or as strong as a male cop, she could be good at the job. She learned to be an expert at talking desperate people out of doing things that were sure to cause them pain and sorrow. She trained herself to be one of the best at using the tools—the laws, the gun, the handcuffs, the baton—to keep the peace. Later, when she was a detective, she acquired encyclopedic knowledge of techniques of detection and the psychology of suspects, witnesses, and victims.

She'd also made sure that no cop who worked with her had ever needed to wonder how she would behave in a fight. She had gone first through a lot more broken-in doors than she should have, just to keep that question from entering anybody's mind. When she and Sid had both gotten about as good as they could get, built reputations as among the finest of the finest, they had given notice and then left.

They had wanted to work together, after years of see-ing each other for only a couple of hours between the end of his shift and the beginning of hers. They had been happy enough since then, and they'd managed to raise two children to adulthood. The kids were hardly images of their parents, and not even people she and Sid agreed with very often, but they were okay. And she and Sid had solved a lot of cases, in spite of the fact that most of them had come to their attention after they were essentially over—already worked to their limits and abandoned for lack of progress.

The murder of James Ballantine was another one. The case had turned dangerous as soon as they started looking into it, but the danger had revealed nothing. Now, at last, Ronnie was beginning to see some progress. Ballantine had been a difficult victim at first—impeccable history, no vices, no vulnerabilities, no enemies, no friends. But now she and Sid had found an opening, a way in. The way in was the women.

Emily Prosser opened the door of her apartment as soon as Sid's knuckle touched it. She was a tall, slim woman with pronounced Asian features and long, straight black hair. "Hi," she said. "You must be Mr. and Mrs. Abel."

"Yes," Sid said. "And you're Miss"—his eye caught the rings on her left hand—"Mrs. Prosser?"

"Mrs. Emily Lin Prosser," she said. She raised her left hand so they could both see the rings, and smiled. "I guess you're detectives, all right."

"We're just getting started this morning," Ronnie said. "We'll be quicker later in the day. Thanks very much for making time to meet with us."

"Yes," said Sid. "Thank you."

"Come on in. There's coffee. Want some?"

"That would be terrific," said Ronnie. "Can I help serve it?"

"Follow me."

Ronnie and Emily Prosser walked off into the kitchen, and while Sid stayed in the living room he used the time to look around. The room was dominated by high bookshelves that contained the sorts of books that weren't decorations. There were oversize textbooks in various areas of science and engineering, a number of shelves full of books in various languages, a few shelves holding great novels, mostly of the nineteenth and early twentieth centuries.

Part of one bookcase held perfectly aligned, identical issues of art periodicals, and another held jewel boxes of computer disks. Everything in the big apartment had an unpretentious, utilitarian quality. It was all used, all intended to function in service of crowded, active minds. There was a shiny baby grand piano in a corner, and it had a score open above the keyboard with pencil notations on it.

The women returned to the room with the coffee, and he and they sat around a large coffee table. Emily Prosser said, "So you'd like to talk about Jim Ballantine."

"Yes," said Ronnie. "This has been a tough case for the police, and now the Intercelleron Corporation has hired us to take a second look. The police officer who had been lead investigator, Detective Kapp, died a few months after the investigation began. We've looked through some of his notes and the records and reports in the case, and now we're trying to fill in some of the blanks."

"I'm one of the blanks?"

Sid said, "Detective Kapp followed standard procedures. When anyone is murdered, the police have to begin with the crime itself—the physical evidence, the crime scene, the body. In this case, the physical evidence was very slight. The victim was in the water so long, the crime scene was never located, and anything that went into the water with the victim could have been washed away. The second source of information comes from witnesses. There were none. The third source is the people who knew the victim—his friends, relatives, and co-workers usually know things that help. That's the phase where we are right now."

"We've examined the notes from the interviews that Detective Kapp conducted," said Ronnie. "Frankly, he didn't find them much help, and neither did we. Everybody seems to have said Mr. Ballantine was a smart chemist, a nice man, and a reliable employee. So we're going around asking a few questions, to get an idea why somebody wanted to murder a man like that."

Emily Prosser frowned. "What those people said was true, as far as it goes. Jim really was smart and personable and pleasant. And he did do his job the way he was supposed to."

"I wonder, though," Sid said. "Everybody has some people who like him and some who don't. There are strong human emotions—envy, anger, and in this case, maybe racism. And he was a single man in a business that included women, married and unmarried. Do you think he might have raised some jealousy?"

Emily Prosser shrugged and gave her head a shake. "He never mentioned anything like that."

Ronnie said, "May I ask how well you knew him?"

"I was probably closer to him than anyone," Emily Prosser said. "He had been at Intercelleron for about three years before I met him. He didn't have what I would call close male friends, but he said everybody was cordial and easy to get along with. And he had no relationships with women until I came along."

Ronnie's face didn't betray anything, but she spoke again quickly to signal Sid that she wanted to skip past that assertion. "What about relatives? Did he have any family nearby?"

"No," she said. "He was from the Midwest. If you listened to Jim, you'd think that people could never be pried away from there."

"Had he ever been married?"

"Yes. He was married briefly, when he was in grad school. He said it was one of those marriages that happen before either person is mature enough to be ready, and it ended almost automatically when they grew up and became different people."

"Any children?"

"No, thank God. They would be so sad now."

"Do you know the wife's name?"

"I don't think he ever mentioned her by name," Emily said. "If he did, it was in passing, and I forgot."

"How long did you date him?"

"Just after I met him at Intercelleron, until he died. That made it about two years. But we were much closer than that sounds."

"What did you do at Intercelleron?" asked Sid. "Did you work closely with him?"

"Oh, no," she said. "I'm an architect and interior designer. I was hired to redesign the offices, the labs, the public spaces. I started out by spending a few days looking at the facility and making drawings, and right away, Jim came to see me. He was in the process of designing his own ideal living space. He knew that he needed to learn something about design. That was what he was like. Nothing—including his own limitations—was a permanent obstacle. If he found out he needed to learn a new language or a special fabrication process or modify a dozen computer programs to get to the next step, he would."

"He was redecorating his apartment?" asked Ronnie.

"No," she said. "He was thinking about his house."

"He had a house?"

"He was planning to build one. He was looking for the right property to build on. I approved of that. People often come to me and ask me to transform what they've got into something completely different. They want their perfectly simple, respectable California bungalow recast as a French chateau or a Spanish adobe. They don't see that you have to respect the natural setting. He did. He knew he had to begin with the right piece of land and build what the land called out for, to complete it. Otherwise you have to use bulldozers to destroy the character of the land and every living thing on it, move and distort the ground to make room for something that doesn't belong."

"Did you ever go out with him to look at lots?" Sid asked.

"A few times, when he thought he might have found the right property. I remember one at the beach, and one on a hill above Echo Park."

"How long had he been searching for the right piece of land?"

"Maybe all his life. He had never had a house before."

"Interesting," said Ronnie. "You were dating him for about two years, and he never found the right spot in that time." As though it were an afterthought she asked, "Was he dating any other women during that time?"

"No. He said that since he'd arrived at Intercelleron he hadn't dated anyone, and we became serious about each other pretty quickly."

"Was marriage a possibility?"

"I don't know," she said. "If he had asked, I would have accepted his decision. He was very wise, and I would have trusted his judgment."

"Really?"

"Yes. It's fairly common for people to say somebody has an old soul. I don't believe in the idea literally, but I can see why people use that image. He was like that. He seemed too wise to have developed in fewer than forty years."

Ronnie said, "I don't know how else to ask this, but were you—"

"Sleeping with him? Of course. We were in love. When he died, I probably would have too, except that I knew he would have been disappointed in me for thinking that way. He believed in taking everything as it comes and getting the most out of each day."

Sid said, "Did you and he ever discuss finances?"

"Money?" she said. "No. It wasn't a very interesting topic for either of us. He worked for a good company, and I like to think my company is a good one too, since I'm the only employee. I suppose we would have had that conversation if we had decided to get married, but otherwise, why bother?"

"How about in reverse? Did he ever ask you about your business?"

"Nothing more than 'How was your day?' I probably gave him a longer answer than he really wanted, because I talk about things like that too much. I told him all about whatever project I had been working on. But he was sweet about it."

Ronnie looked at her watch. "I guess we'd better let you go in a minute. You've gotten married. I assume that was since he died?"

"Yes. The wedding was only about two months ago. Life brought a suitable husband. I wasn't looking for him or expecting him, but there he was. So I accepted him. Maybe Jim taught me that."

"You seem pretty happy."

"Very happy. A person has to move on when it's time."
"Yes," said Ronnie.
"Well," said Emily. She looked at her watch and stood up. "I hope I've told you what you need. If not, feel free to call me, and we can talk some more. Right now I'm afraid I have to get to the meeting with my client."

Sid and Ronnie stood up. Ronnie said, "That's just fine. We may take you up on your offer, but we're good for now. Thanks very much."

On their way down the hill to their car Ronnie said, "Ballantine certainly rolled out the bullshit machine for her."

"He was grooming her for something," Sid said. "He probably got killed just in time to save her."

"Since he studiously avoided talking about money, that's probably what he wanted," Ronnie said.

# 19

Ronnie could hear the occasional rustle on the other end of the phone line as Selena Stubbs moved papers from one pile into another. Occasionally she heard her pick up a pile in both hands and shuffle it vertically so it hit the desk surface three times to make all the loose sheets neat. She said, "When James was fired from his job at the University of Indiana, his pay went to zero. When he got the job in California it went up again."

"May I ask how much?"

"I think it doubled, approximately. I remember hearing him say something about how he was making twice as much, and so on, but it was a rough figure. We're not talking about a whole lot of money here. Assistant professors don't make much. But the money from the new job made a difference. We had to maintain the house in Bloomington, where the kids and I lived, and James's apartment in LA, and cars and insurance in both places. And we had to spend a lot of money for James to travel back and forth across the country every week or two. We were already in serious debt from our eight years of student loans, the mortgage, and all the expense of his year of flying around for job interviews."

"We need to get a sense of his situation after the divorce, when he was employed and living in Los Angeles. Do you think he could have been saving money at that point?"

"I don't have to think about it," said Selena Stubbs. "I know. I was still keeping track of our money until the divorce was final. At the end of the first year we had spent more than he made. The debts had grown, and a lot was on credit cards. We were paying plenty of interest."

"How about the second year?"

"I wasn't doing his bookkeeping at that point," she said. "But I would have to guess it wasn't a fast transformation. He was making progress, catching up on missed payments from some of the student loans, and trying to pay off credit cards. That didn't leave much room for savings. And James was paying off the divorce lawyers and trying to pay the child support ordered by the court. We still hadn't sold the house in Bloomington, so when the deficit got to be big enough he just signed the place over to me so I'd be stuck with selling it, and insisted that it took him off the hook."

"You accepted that?"

"Yes. By then he was the new James. He had already realized that nobody was going to do anything to him if he stopped paying child support, so he was about to stop."

"There are people whose job it is to—"

"It was an Indiana divorce decree, and the plaintiff had moved to Texas and the defendant to California. If I took him to court, he was ready to make a case that he couldn't afford that much. There really wasn't a lot of money to fight over. He still hadn't paid off the debts. He had bought himself a nice car, but he was paying for it on time. By then I was here in Houston making good money in the oil business. It felt better to me to be free of any dependence or even expectations. That was what he wanted, so I gave it to him."

"Is it possible that he was hiding money?"

"He lived in Los Angeles for three years after I last saw him. If he made a lot of money in secret, I don't know what he did with it. When he died there was a bit over seventeen thousand dollars in his bank accounts, and that was about what I had expected."

"How about the debts?"

"They were smaller than they had been, but by no means gone. I used all of his money and a bit of my own to pay the last of them off. I imagine between that and all the women, he didn't have much left of his paychecks."

"Would you know why he would be out searching for a house to buy?"

"With seventeen thousand dollars in Los Angeles? I don't see any way that a bank would have approved him for a mortgage unless he came up with a big down payment. Maybe one of his lady friends was going to pay for it."

"You mentioned his new car," said Ronnie. "Do you happen to have any information about it? An old registration or anything?"

"I know I have that. I had to sell the car, so I've got the paperwork. I'll scan it and send it on to you after we hang up."

"Thanks," Ronnie said. "And you just reminded me of another thing I wanted to ask you about. How did you go about compiling the list of women he dated? Did James tell you, or was there an address book or something?"

"I'm afraid that's not a question I'm going to answer."

"Would it be possible to tell me why?"

"I'm not going to talk about the subject at all."

"All right," said Ronnie.

"Here. I've found the papers for the car. It was a Lexus. And there's a photograph of it too. I posted that online when I put it up for sale. Do you want the picture too?"

"That would be great, thank you."

"You're welcome. It'll be in your e-mail. Anything else?"

"No. And thanks," Ronnie said. "We'll try not to bother you again."

"To tell you the truth, I'm not so worried about that anymore," said Selena. "I really hope that you do find out what happened to him and make whoever did it sorry."

Ronnie hung up and turned to Sid. "It's definitely videos. Probably like the one he showed to Linda Bourget."

"You could tell that?"

"Yes," she said. "I could tell she watched at least some of them to be sure, and probably felt like killing herself, then and for a while after. She won't say anything about it. And by the way, there was no money."

"What about his car?"

"She sold it, but she had to pay off the loan he'd taken to buy it. Still no money." She thought for a moment. "We should see if the police know anything about where the car has been."

Detective Miguel Fuentes watched the image appear on his computer screen. "There it is," he said. "Here are all the LPR hits on Ballantine's Lexus's license plate in the year before his murder."

"How many hits?" Sid said.

"Twenty-six. The database now has an average of twenty-two hits for every one of the seven million cars registered in Los Angeles County. Of course the information is still random. The readers on the patrol cars are on all the time, recording new plates while they scan for plates on the hot list, but there are plates that get lots of sightings, and some that get none."

"His ex-wife says she sold his car after he died," said Ronnie. "Do you know what sort of examination Detective Kapp gave it before he released it?"

"I haven't seen a record of the search," said Fuentes. "It wasn't found at a crime scene or anything, and if something had turned up we'd know, but Kapp wasn't a beginner. I'm sure he had the forensics people go to work on it before he let her sell it."

Sid and Ronnie exchanged a glance. "Do you know who owns it now?"

"I'll use the VIN number to track it."

A moment later he said, "It's in Nevada. Clark County."

"A breakthrough," said Ronnie. "When we die our cars go to Las Vegas for the afterlife."

Sid said, "Can you print the new owner's name and address and then go back to the Los Angeles map?"

"Sure," said Fuentes. He printed the Nevada registration, and then the Los Angeles map reappeared on his screen.

"Did you see something?" Ronnie asked.

Sid said, "Can you print that too?"

Fuentes clicked Print and Sid reached to the tray and picked up the two printed pages. He handed Ronnie the map of Los Angeles County and pointed at a spot in the northern end of the San Fernando Valley.

"What is it?" asked Fuentes.

"A license plate reader picked up the Lexus about a block from one of the housing developments last March, shortly before Ballantine died," said Ronnie.

"What does that tell you?"

"Nothing conclusive," Sid said. "But I think it strengthens our theory as to where the crime scene might be."

Ronnie said, "It's an opening in the ground that's been gone for a year and paved over."

"Thanks, Miguel," said Sid. "We'll be in touch."

"Where are you going?" Fuentes asked.

"I think we'd like to take a look at some of the other places where license plate readers spotted Ballantine's car."

When they were outside, Ronnie said, "Are we really going to do that?"

"Not me," said Sid. "But there's no reason to tell him that the only lead we have right now is what he just gave us."

# 20

It was morning. Nicole knew that much. She lay in the hotel room with the opaque curtains pulled shut where they met in the center of the big window and were pressed against the wall by two chairs so that no sliver of sunlight would penetrate their dark room.

Nicole heard the sound of the maid's cart being pushed along the carpeted hallway, and then a loud rap on the door of a room not far enough from theirs. "Housekeeping," the maid called. "Housekeeping." It was the third time Nicole had heard the cart rattling along, and then the voice. She thought dark, angry thoughts about people who didn't bother to hang DO NOT DISTURB signs on their doors. Then she realized that she and Ed could easily be the only ones still in a room. Maybe the doors didn't have signs up because the people had checked out. She devoted a few seconds to hating them anyway, and then rolled over and closed her eyes again.

She lay there on her side for three or four minutes. She heard the sound of the cart rattling again, another door opening, and then a couple of sets of heavy footsteps and the rumble of two wheeled suitcases going down the hall-way. There was the mumbled conversation of two men. Untroubled, unthinking men. That was a reassuring sound.

Nicole opened an eye to see the hotel's alarm clock on the bedside table. The red digits said 10:43. It was late, but she hadn't had enough sleep. She and Ed had been up all night.

Nicole had once worked as a hotel maid, and she had hated it. She didn't want to pick on this woman, who was living through the hard, irritating, and occasionally humiliating experience that she'd had to endure. She was tempted to swing open the door and get a look at her, but she wouldn't.

She looked over at Ed. He was a big animal lying there sleeping through the sounds because they meant nothing to his brain. The noises didn't include a sound of another animal trying to do him serious harm, so his brain discounted them.

Nicole rolled onto her back and faced the rough white ceiling, but she could see nothing except the red eye of the smoke detector. By now the gang of men who had attacked her house would know that the three who had stayed to search the house were dead. Would they be afraid? No. They were not the kind to be afraid, but they had terrified her. When she'd picked up the guns the three dead men carried, she had seen they were identical Czech Scorpion subma-chine guns. Who carried those?

They had been weirdly disciplined and interchangeable, as though they had no selves. Insects were like that. People tended to act together in a mob that would fall apart as soon as the numbers weren't needed anymore. These men had arrived and taken their positions as though they'd assaulted similar houses a hundred times before. And when they had determined that the Hoyts weren't in the house waiting for them, they had moved off together without making a noise or drawing any attention to themselves. The last three had already entered the house and taken a look around, so the most efficient way of searching the house was to leave them and let them finish the search while the others did what— returned to the hive?

"How come you're awake?" asked Ed.

"Nerves."

"Oh." He sat up in the bed and rubbed his eyes.

"Those guys last night knew who we were. They were sent to kill us."

"I get that," Ed said. "We were afraid all along that Boylan might have told the client who we were, and now we know he did. Feel like going back and killing him again?"

"I do," said Nicole. "I wish we could. Or that we could undo it."

"We're better off than we were before, because we used the time we had to prepare for shooters. We didn't just sit there in front of the TV hoping everything was going to be okay. We now know it isn't, but we got out in time."

"You call that better off?"

"We're not dead," he said. "That's pretty good. And come to think of it, I didn't bother to count, but just from eyeballing the money we stashed and put in our bugout kits, I think we got more money out of Boylan in one night than we ever would have gotten."

"We stole that money," said Nicole.

"So what? Where do you think the client got it? Milking cows?"

"I don't mean I care about that. I just mean that we didn't make a clever business deal. We committed a murder and robbery."

"A self-defense and robbery," said Ed. "Killing Boylan wasn't even a murder."

She said, "Legal details don't matter. We're in a very bad position. What are we going to do?"

"I don't have my wily master plan just yet," he said. "For the moment we try to make ourselves hard to find. Then we learn who the client is, so we can kill him."

Nicole sat up and folded her arms while she thought. The more she thought about the two parts of Ed's proposal, the less fault she could find with them. Of course they would try not to be found by the insect squad. That was practically a reflex, like ducking your head when you saw a rock flying your way. The other part, finding the client and killing him, was not inevitable. She had, until now, assumed that she and Ed would be leaving today on the first of a series of interstate highways. Ed's plan would prevent them from running away just yet, but it did seem to promise a solution that would last.

"I guess that's what we'll do, then," she said. She scooted off the bed and turned on a lamp beside it. "If you want to pee before I take my shower, now's the time."

He swept the covers off his legs. "Thanks. I'll take you up on that."

He went into the bathroom, and as he came out, she side-stepped into the doorway at the same time. She gave him a quick kiss on the cheek. "I'm glad you're such a badass," she said. "I feel better now."

"Me too," he said. "I don't have to take a piss anymore."

She went inside and closed the door, and in a moment Ed heard the shower running. He opened his bag and started laying out his clothes. He would want something dark, with a loose shirt that would hide a gun.

# 21

"What are you looking up?" Sid asked.

"Girlfriends." Ronnie didn't look up from the computer screen on the table in their hotel room. "I'm chasing the money idea. I want to see if any of Ballantine's girlfriends had enough money to buy him a house. I'm starting with Emily Prosser."

He went to the desk and opened the other laptop. "I can see what building permits have been taken out with her name as the architect since the decorating job at Intercelleron."

"Good," said Ronnie. "I'm running a credit check on her. If anybody asks you, she applied for a loan from Abels agency."

"I'll also see if there's any real estate in her name on the tax rolls."

They were long practiced at using easily accessible information bases to find out about people, and they set the forces in motion quickly. There would be waiting time for some of the information, and Sid used the time to study the police license plate reader data on James Ballantine's car. After Sid had plotted Ballantine's route from his apartment to Intercelleron and his likely route to the nearest and most convenient supermarket, about half the sightings were explained. The rest appeared almost random at first. When Ronnie called him over to the table, he spread the maps and notes out on the bed and joined her.

"Here it is," she said. "Emily Prosser's stuff. Let's start with the Building and Safety permits." She opened the file.

Sid ran his eyes down the list. "Not much. I see the permit for the Intercelleron project. After that, all I see is two jobs, both remodeling of single-family homes, about a year apart. Let's see her credit check."

Ronnie closed the Building and Safety report, and opened the credit check. "Oops, not so good. Four credit cards canceled, two open. Lots of late payments, and one of the two open cards is the kind where you deposit money to lend back to yourself and repair your credit rating."

"Let's see if she owns any real estate."

Ronnie opened the reply from the county clerk's office. "None found. None in Orange County either."

"So Emily wasn't going to be the one to buy him his dream house," said Sid. "I guess it was true love."

Ronnie craned her neck to look at him. "That doesn't deserve an answer. Go back to figuring out what the license plate sightings mean."

Sid returned to the desk and looked at the maps again. After about twenty minutes, he looked up. "Veronica?"

"What?"

"Where is that list of girlfriends?"

"In the electronic device of your choice. I typed it into my notes on this case, and also sent the list to you in an e-mail. Sorry to hide it under your nose like that."

"Did you include the addresses?"

"Yes."

He went into his e-mail, found one from Ronnie, and opened it. Then he marked an address on the Los Angeles street map, and picked up the map of the license plate sightings.

"Mira Cepic."

"Yes. I didn't forget the name. She's the last one on the list."

"Mira Cepic lives really close to the place where Ballantine got stuffed into the sewer. About three blocks."

Ronnie went to look over his shoulder at the street map, and he pointed at the mark he'd made for Mira Cepic's address. "She lives on Wintergarden." Then he pointed at a mark three blocks north of there. "And here's Clovermeadow Lane."

She walked back toward the table where she'd left her laptop. "Let's get some background before we get into this. I'll run a credit check on her too. You do the search for assets in Mira Cepic's name."

"I'll make it anybody with the same surname. It might turn up a husband or a parent, if she's got one."

"Good. In fact, I think we should buy complete background checks from the skip-trace company."

"Might as well get some use out of the fee we pay just to be on their client list."

They were silent as they set more forces into motion. After a few minutes of work, Sid said, "I'm getting the sense that Mira Cepic wasn't born here. I'm not seeing anything about schools, or the names of employers."

"Why don't we jerk the government around a little?"

"Okay. I'm adding a request for a criminal background check on her through the skip-trace company. The criminal ones usually come back with a Social Security number."

"Good," said Ronnie. "If we get the number, I'll be Mira for a while and fill out a request for my immigration status with the US Citizenship and Immigration Services."

"It could take a day or so. Just make sure our lawyer is on speed dial."

"Always," she said.

Ed Hoyt had placed the three cell phones in a row. He turned them all on and pressed the little picture of a telephone on the display of the first one, the second, the third. He looked from one to the next.

"Ready." Nicole had the hotel room's pen and note pad.

"I see a couple of numbers all three Russians had calls from." He read them off with the dates, and Nicole wrote them down.

Ed studied the phone lists and found six more numbers that had called or been called on all three phones. He found twelve that were on two phones. Then he turned off the three phones. "Might as well save the batteries," he muttered.

Nicole looked at her list and pointed. "All three of these guys got calls from this number on the day they came to get us at our house. The others all seem to be a bit more random. One or two of them called in a day, and then the other a week later or something."

"Okay. Then the number that called them all could be the head of the group," said Ed. "He must have been organizing these guys to go bother us."

"You know what else is interesting?" said Nicole. "These three don't seem to have called each other. Hardly ever, anyway."

"What do you think that means?"

"That they talked without phones," she said. "I'll bet they were roommates."

"Could be."

"So what do you want to do?" Nicole asked.

"Let's start by getting the billing addresses connected with all these numbers. I'll call Ron at the phone sales service and tell him to get started on it."

He took out his own cell phone and dialed the number of his friend Ron at the telemarketing company.

Sid and Ronnie Abel drove east from their hotel to Ventura Boulevard and north on Laurel Canyon, then to Victory Boulevard, and made their way to a rental lot at Burbank airport, where they rented a new car, and transferred the equipment they had brought to the back of it. They drove north and west toward the group of housing developments they visited when they had taken the James Ballantine case.

They headed directly to the streets of new houses surrounding the building site where the person in the car had shot out their windshield.

Ronnie said, "It's different in the daylight."

Sid said, "Everything looks different in the daylight."

"I know. But when we were here before, it seemed desolate, empty. It looked as though there were no people and there never would be any."

"Not for much longer. Look at the construction site now. They put those houses up fast."

When they reached the intersection with the gravel road Sid slowed down and looked. The few skeletal frames of houses had all grown taller, and now they were clad in sheets of plywood. Roofing material sat in stacks on roofs, and two more foundations had been poured in the past few days.

They passed the spot along Renfrew Street where the dark sedan had been parked on the night when the driver saw the Abels and took off at high speed. Today Sid followed the route he had taken that night when he went in pursuit of the dark sedan. He made the right turn onto Clovermeadow Lane, the residential street where there had been an open storm sewer when Ballantine was killed. He let the car coast along. Then his eyes moved to the houses.

"Interesting," Sid said. "The place must have sold out quickly."

Every house appeared to be occupied. There were children, their mothers sitting on porches and patios to watch them, a young man jogging on the street.

"Those are big houses, too," said Ronnie. "They must be pretty expensive."

"Seen enough?"

"Yes."

Sid stopped and completed a three-point turn, and then drove back the way he came. He turned right at the corner.

Ronnie looked at her phone. "The address is 9-7-6-5 Wintergarden Way. The third street."

They went past two streets that were nearly identical to Clovermeadow, all two-story houses that were identical except for cosmetic variations. Wintergarden was a bit older, and slightly more varied, as though most of the lots had been occupied by houses before the contractor with the pattern took over.

They turned onto the street and drove along slowly, reading the house numbers until they found 9765. It looked like the others in the area, with two floors and an attached two-car garage, a tiny green lawn, and a flowerbed in front. Ronnie used her cell phone to take photographs of the house, and then of the whole block.

The Abels continued to the end of Wintergarden Way and then turned onto the next street, which was called Callalily Street. They cruised up the street, studying the houses that backed up to Mira Cepic's house. "It doesn't look as though there's an easy way from this side to get a look into her house," Ronnie said.

"Want to try having our talk with her while we're up here?" said Sid. "Her house looks occupied. She might be home now."

"Not yet," said Ronnie. "I think we should wait for our background checks to come through. Everything real we've learned about Ballantine has been from the women in his life. We're probably not going to get more than one chance at this woman, and she's the last one. I'd like to have every bit of information we can get ahead of time. We may need the leverage."

"Let's go get something to eat, and then we'll come back after dark and take another look."


Sid and Ronnie returned to the neighborhood at nine thirty, when the sky had already been dark for an hour. They parked their rented blue Accord on a street a block to the north of the gravel road. Ronnie took out her Glock pistol, rechecked the magazine, and pushed it back in, then returned the pistol to the shoulder holster under her jacket.

Sid did the same, and then returned his pistol to the holster on his belt under his sport coat.

She looked at him. "You don't usually do that. I do that. Are you nervous?"

"No more than usual," he said. "But I haven't forgotten that the last time we were out here after dark, we had people shooting at us." He took out his compact camera, made sure the flash was off and the battery was strong, and put it into his coat pocket.

Sid and Ronnie got out of the rental car and began to walk.

It was another warm evening. There had been a strong breeze just before sundown, but when the sun disappeared, the wind had stopped and the air became still, so it felt as though the world were a giant room. The last of the spring rains seemed to have ended for good, and the next rainy day would probably be in November, eight months away. The thought made Sid remember that last year was an El Niño year, and about this date the rainy season had been far from finished. After James Ballantine was found, it had rained every other day for a while.

As Sid and Ronnie walked, they looked at the houses they passed. This neighborhood was like a thousand others in the city. Some cars were parked in open garages, and others sat in the driveways, probably because the garages were being used to store the mountains of mostly useless stuff people accumulated. It made Sid remember that he and Ronnie didn't have to worry about belongings anymore. Their house had been burned to ashes and then bulldozed and hauled away in dump trucks.

Sid could see the lights on in the house windows, a couple of kids staring at computers, and in other parts of the house there were television sets throwing a fluctuating bluish light on white ceilings. A woman came out of a kitchen carrying a toddler in pajamas. Sid and Ronnie crossed the street in a dark zone to keep from drawing the attention of a man who was working on a car in his garage. The Abels went by unnoticed, like passing shadows.

They skirted Renfrew Street, passing outside the circles of light under the last few streetlamps so they would not be easy to see. In another minute they were in the margin of the broad, weedy, brush-choked field that was bisected by the gravel road. They moved more slowly now, choosing the places where they set their feet, stopping now and then in the clumps of bushes and saplings to survey the land for the next few hundred paces ahead. Beyond the gravel road they could see the lights of the streets they had visited this morning.

After a few minutes they were passing Clovermeadow, the first street of occupied houses. By ten they were on Callalily, the street behind Mira Cepic's house. They walked along like an older couple out for their evening stroll. By now, they were the only pedestrians on the street. Ronnie knew that their gray hair had helped them avoid suspicion many times, and it might again if anyone saw them tonight. A few years ago, their daughter, Janice, had told Ronnie she should start dyeing her hair instead of letting it go gray. Ronnie had said, "Do you have any idea what gray hair is worth in our business? Middle-aged women are invisible. Men can't even see us."

They walked along Callalily, past one house, and then another, until they came to the one right behind Mira Cepic's house. It looked perfect. There were no lights visible in the windows. The Abels didn't change their pace. They simply turned and walked up the front lawn and onto the strip of grass beside the house.

Moving ever more slowly, they made their way to the edge of the yard. There were no dog bowls or dog toys in the yard, and there was no fence, so they kept going until they found a spot between that house and its neighbor where they could take cover and observe. The house had a chimney that protruded from its side far enough to hide Ronnie, and directly across from it was a small metal shed meant to hold garden tools. Sid took a position behind it.

The back of Mira Cepic's house was only twenty feet ahead of them now. There were lights on in the kitchen window, and a softer light glowed from another back window that was probably a bedroom, with the curtains closed. A few feet from it was a small, textured glass window that was undoubtedly the bathroom of the master suite.

Ronnie watched the house while Sid took out his compact camera and turned it on. The camera had a zoom feature with a four-power capability, and he aimed the camera and adjusted it.

They waited for a few minutes, but there was no activity in the kitchen. Sid signaled Ronnie to stay where she was, and moved cautiously along the side of the house. He came to a window and moved his head close so he could bring one eye to the corner.

Mira Cepic was in the living room, sitting in front of a high-definition television set about five feet wide. She was around forty, with blond hair to her shoulders. Her cheekbones were prominent, and she had a thin, angular look, like a marathon runner or a retired model. The fact that she wore no makeup and her hair was not combed didn't disguise the fact that her face was pretty. Her arms were bare to the shoulder, and they looked thin and sinewy.

Sid was aware that the human eye was extremely sensitive to movement. If her eye caught motion, not only would the sensation reach her brain, but she would also not be able to resist looking. Sid took at least a minute to move the camera far enough into the corner of the window so the lens could see the woman. He took three photographs. He noticed that what she was watching was a television show about young women trying on wedding gowns. He slowly lowered the camera, and then just as slowly withdrew. He made his way back to join Ronnie at the rear of the house. She looked at him inquiringly, and he nodded.

Sid and Ronnie prepared to turn and go back out to Callalily Street. But they both sensed a change. There were faint sounds from inside Mira Cepic's house. Then the woman appeared in the kitchen. She moved past the window to the refrigerator, where she took out a bottle of beer. She reached up and opened a cupboard for a glass.

Sid began shooting pictures of Mira Cepic again. She faced the rear window as she opened her bottle with an opener, and then turned away. A moment later the kitchen light went out. Sid and Ronnie waited a few minutes and then stepped out onto Callalily Street, and turned south at Renfrew Street, heading for the place where they had left their rental car.

"We got a good look at her, anyway," said Ronnie. "And pictures. I also took a couple of shots with my phone while I was sitting there."

"What did you think of her?"

"I think I want to see whatever information our trace has come up with before I commit myself."

"You don't have a good feeling either, huh?"

"I think she probably cleans up really nicely when she wants to. But my first impression is that she looks a little bit hard."

"Maybe it's time to start cooperating with the official investigation," said Sid.

"Let's get these pictures to Miguel Fuentes at North Holly-wood, and see if he can find out anything."

Ed and Nicole Hoyt watched Renfrew Street for half an hour, but they never saw the Abels after they went up toward the far side of the field and turned down another street. Nicole said, "I guess they're gone for tonight. I wonder what they're doing around here. Do you think they found that Mira Cepic woman's house?"

Ed said, "How would they find the girlfriend of one of those dead Russians? They can't know about the Russians, let alone who they called on their cell phones. I think the Abels are still hung up on finding out where Ballantine went into the sewer. I really hated to pass up a shot at them, though. They were out in the open, without much to hide behind."

"So were we. Even if we weren't out here where people would get alarmed at the shots and come after us, what would be the point?" asked Nicole.

"We got two chances at them at their house, and nothing we did seemed to put them in front of a bullet," he said. "Then we planted a bomb and knocked over a robot. It's been frustrating."

"Boylan hired us to do that job, and he's dead. We got much more money from his house than he would have paid us for the Abels," she said. "I think we came out a mile ahead on them. If we find the guy who hired Boylan, we'll be even further ahead."

"We did okay, I guess," he said. "But you can't make a living killing the people who hire you."

"Why not?" she said.

"What do you mean?"

"Why is that money any worse?" she said. "Money is money."

Ed smiled. "It's a funny idea. You get people to hire you to kill somebody, and you kill them instead. You take the money they would have paid you, and any other money they had."

Nicole said, "That's what we ought to be doing. Seriously. When somebody hires you to do a killing, you know they're doing it because they aren't up to a wet job themselves. In other words, they're weak. You know they have at least as much money as they're promising to pay, because hiring a killer and not paying him is something not even a moron would do. And they also have other money, at least as much as they're offering you. So if you kill them instead of their enemy, you can double your money."

"Jesus, Nicole." He stared into the night. "But I have to admit, the biggest thing I worry about when we do a job is that somehow the client is going to get caught, because he's actually got some reason to hate the target—something to make the police suspect him. And when the police start talking about death penalties and stuff, he's going to give us up."

"Right," she said. "The client is definitely the biggest threat."

"We'll have to think about going into the client-killing business. But it's got to be after we get whoever is sending these people after us."

"Yeah," she said. "You have to wonder, if he had the insect people, why would he bother to hire Boylan?"

"Or us," said Ed.

# 22

When morning came, Sid and Ronnie came down from their room and had breakfast in a booth at the back corner of the hotel restaurant where they weren't as likely to be noticed, and then took the elevator to the parking garage.

As they walked to their car, Sid stopped. Ronnie said, "What's wrong? Why are you stopping?"

Sid muttered, "Oh, there it is. I forgot for a minute that we had another new rented car. It's the gray one." He clicked the key fob, and the car gave a little yip in response.

As they got into the car, he said, "I guess this case is starting to get to me."

"Me too," she said. "The company says they're interested just because they can't bear to give up on James Ballantine, but they hardly knew him. The ex-wife, who's probably had to deal with racists from time to time, thinks it's obvious he was killed by racists. As soon as the first girlfriend learns he had other girlfriends, she tries to plant the idea one of them must have killed him. The married girlfriend says he was blackmailing her to keep having sex, and that raises the likelihood that somebody killed him because he asked for it. And the girlfriend who says she knew him best, knew nothing about him after two years."

"And everything we got from the background checks on the next girlfriend is garbage. Mira Cepic might as well have arrived from the planet Neptune the day before yesterday. Jobs? Education? Marriages? Last address? Not found not found not found."

"There's still the criminal background check you requested, and then we'll get the immigration status from the government," Ronnie said. "She's got to have grown up in another country. We'll get it eventually."

"If we're forced to wait long enough, maybe the people trying to kill us will."

"Yes," she said. "Somehow those people never seem to slip my mind. Especially when I look forward to going home to sleep in our own bed, and remember that we don't have a home or our own bed."

"I guess we should check with Miguel Fuentes in North Hollywood, and see if he's gotten any new information since we sent him the pictures of Mira Cepic and the background stuff."

"Or the lack of background. We should call him first instead of dropping in," said Ronnie. "Maybe it'll give him time to look for her in the system."

"I'll do it," said Sid. He took out his phone and hit the number for the North Hollywood station. "Can you please connect me with Detective Miguel Fuentes? This is Sid Abel."

Fuentes's voice came on. "Sid?"

"Hi, Miguel. We're getting ready to go talk to Mira Cepic, and we were wondering if—"

"Great timing," said Fuentes. "I was just going to call you. Can you both meet me at First Street in an hour?"

"The police headquarters building?"

"Yes. Those pictures you sent me caught my eye, and I sent them to Major Crimes. One of the detectives there thought he recognized the face, and sent the pictures to Interpol. Their guy will be here in an hour."

"We'll be there," said Sid.

"And Sid?"

"Yes?"

"I probably don't have to say this, but stay away from Wintergarden Way," said Fuentes. "When Interpol in Washington got the pictures, it took them about two minutes to call back."

Captain Albright was a woman about fifty-five years old with blond hair that she wore in the police on-duty bun. Her suit jacket was unbuttoned, and the others could see she had a .45 in a shoulder holster. She raised an arm to indicate the man in a gray suit who had come into the conference room with her. "This is agent John Roche. He's from the US National Central Bureau of Interpol."

She surveyed the big conference table. "This is Detective Miguel Fuentes of North Hollywood Homicide. Lieutenant Dennis Cole, Major Crimes. Sergeant Daniel Trevolino, Major Crimes. And joining us today are Sidney and Veronica Abel. They're the private investigators who took the photographs. They're both retired Los Angeles police detectives, and you can talk freely in front of them." She looked around as though the room contained hiding places. "I don't see Detective Hebert. Anybody hear from him?"

Lieutenant Cole said, "He's in traffic."

"We'll fill him in later," she said. Her expression betrayed a slight irritation. "Agent Roche is here to brief us about those photographs." She nodded to Roche. "Agent Roche?"

"Thank you, Captain," said Roche. He said, "Sergeant Trevolino forwarded the photographs to our office in Washington last night, and immediately two of our agents recognized this lady." He paused and watched the people in the room. "Ladies and gentlemen, you've got a panther infestation."

He seemed pleased with his choice of words, and even more pleased that they meant nothing to the others, who merely looked at him expectantly. "It's what the police in Europe call them—pink panthers, after the old movie. They're diamond thieves. The London police caught a couple of them once with diamonds hidden in a lotion jar, which was a trick used in the movie, and the press picked it up. It's an unfortunate name, because it keeps people from taking them seriously."

"They're from London?" Lieutenant Cole said.

"No," said Roche. "They were mostly from parts of the former Yugoslavia. Over the years, various European police agencies have arrested a hundred and eighty-nine of them. They were Serbian, Montenegrin, Bosnian. A few were from other places in Eastern Europe."

"That's a huge number of men for a jewel theft ring," said Cole.

"That's another thing," said Roche. "They're never all men. There are always women too. Let me run you through the way the thefts work."

He reached into the briefcase he'd brought and took out a file. Ronnie and Sid could see it contained printed photographs. He said, "The first step is that a woman comes to the door of the jewelry store. She's vaguely foreign. She wears all designer clothes. She's attractive. Sometimes she wears a little bit of high-quality jewelry. It's not garish, but the jeweler who sees her will recognize that it's very expensive. Usually she's alone. If she's with a man, he dresses and acts like he's capable of buying her whatever she wants."

Roche opened the folder and took out a print of one of the photographs Sid had taken. He handed it to Captain Albright to his left, and she looked and passed it on. Roche said, "The lady in the picture is Mira Cepic, and she's one of these women. She's originally from Romania, a child of Serbian parents who we believe disappeared shortly after she was born. She was apparently raised in an orphanage in Bucharest. This is significant because the Ceausescu government used to take some of these children and train them to be members of the Securitate, the secret police. We don't know much about her history in Romania—education, foster parents, and so on are absent from the record, and this would be typical of the children that the government took. At some point after the Ceausescus fell in 1989 we think she lived in Serbia. She was arrested with a Serbian passport in Bern, Switzerland, in 2008 after a diamond theft, and then again in London in 2012, carrying a Serbian passport and a Canadian one. Both times she was charged as one of the thieves, but later released."

"Why did they let her go?" asked Lieutenant Cole.

"It was hard to prove she wasn't a bystander or victim, because her job is ambiguous. The woman cases the store on the first visit and then gets the door opened for her on the second. The first day, the woman comes to check display cases, window displays, guards, alarms, automatic locks, and so on. At the same time she's appraising the diamonds that she can see. When she can, she photographs everything with a cell phone or small camera. Then she's gone. The next day, or a week later, the woman shows up again. Because she's been there before, the clerks know her. They remember she's rich and interested in buying something. They can hardly get the door open fast enough. As she enters, a man comes in right behind her. He's armed. He takes care of the guard and opens the door. Three more men come in quickly. Instantly they're smashing glass cases and pouring diamonds into pouches as fast as they can. It's usually over within sixty seconds. Their record is under thirty seconds. Then they're all gone."

"Where have they done this before besides Bern and London?" asked Lieutenant Cole.

"They've done about two hundred robberies so far. Paris, Saint-Tropez, Tokyo, Dubai, Biarritz, Monte Carlo. Anyplace where high-quality diamonds are in the biggest numbers, which is usually high-end stores. They hit the places where they can walk out with at least three to five million in diamonds."

"Diamonds only?" Fuentes asked. "Nothing else?"

"So far, yes," said Agent Roche. "I think we're talking about two generations of thieves here. The original group appeared around 1993. They were all veterans of the Bosnian wars, mostly from the Serbian special forces. We believe the reason they took diamonds was that they had a connection with a man who could market them. There was one particular diamond wholesaler in Antwerp who took the stolen stones, recut them, and sold them along with forged papers saying they were found in Sierra Leone within the past year or two. They got dispersed among other dealers quickly. It's an old-fashioned crime that went out of style."

"Why is it back now?" asked Fuentes.

"It came back because governments and police agencies got much better at tracking electronic transfers of money, particularly the kind that goes across borders. That's great. But it means we're back to dealing with diamond thieves."

Captain Albright said, "How many people are we talking about? How many are there in the whole gang?"

"So far, using DNA, fingerprints, and photographs, Interpol has identified eight hundred individuals, if you include all of the robberies back to the nineties."

"We're dealing with eight *hundred* people?"

"No. The structure isn't the sort of hierarchical pyramid that mafias and drug cartels have. There's no command and control setup. They seem to be autonomous crews that pop in and out of existence. So at any given time there might be two hundred panthers or zero panthers. They all seem to use the same methods—in Dubai they got into the store by driving two Audi S8 cars through the front of it, and in Geneva they escaped in a speedboat, but otherwise it was the same general plan—and the same conduits for moving the diamonds. They're all from Eastern Europe, and they all still seem to have military backgrounds."

Lieutenant Cole said, "So what should we be preparing for?"

Roche said, "If Mira Cepic is here, I think we have to assume there's a crew. I would expect that the group here in Los Angeles will try to do what they do. They steal diamonds."

"But what does a crew look like?"

"Each team will include one woman and three or four men. That's the number who can sit comfortably in the average sedan. They will have the whole robbery planned impeccably, including the getaway. As soon as they're out of sight they'll split up immediately. The diamonds will be smuggled out of the country, probably into the regular channels the panthers have been using for over twenty years."

Sergeant Trevolino said, "What do you know about the route they'll use to enter the country or leave it?"

"We know nothing yet," said Roche. "Because they've never struck anywhere in the United States or Canada before. We're checking now on how Mira Cepic got here."

Miguel Fuentes said, "How dangerous are they?"

"That's an important question," said Roche. "Are the panthers capable of homicide? They're all trained for war, and the oldest ones almost certainly have done some killing. They were soldiers during an ugly war. But the record since then is much less clear. None of these robberies has included murder. What we're most worried about right now isn't a few jewel thieves. It's their customers. The people who want diamonds so they can move large amounts of money from country to country right now are a very scary bunch, and they're up to much worse things than robberies."

There was a brief silence as the officers around the table contemplated the possibilities.

"Are there any more questions for Mr. Roche?" asked Captain Albright. She looked around from one face to the next. "No? Then we'll meet again at four." She heard a noise behind her and turned. "Detective Hebert," she said. "It's a shame you missed the briefing. Sergeant Trevolino will fill you in when we're through here."

She turned to the others. "What we'll want to do is develop a plan to find out which other members of the group are here and what they're up to."

As an afterthought she added, "Mr. and Mrs. Abel, thank you very much for your assistance to the police department. We'll let you know in a few days how this works out."

# 23

For over an hour, Ed and Nicole Hoyt had been in the over-grown, weedy yard of an old house, sitting at the back of the garage, where a boat on a trailer gave them cover to watch the second address they'd found on the Russians' cell phones. From there they could see the houses on the 5900 block of Glenview Terrace. It was Ed's turn with the binoculars. He said, "The car is leaving the garage at 5-9-6-0."

Nicole said. "How many in the car?"

"Two," he said. "One man, one woman."

"That's seven houses empty so far. Everybody seems to go to work at about the same time around here."

"That should help a lot."

"You're not thinking of doing it right now, are you?"

"I'm thinking we're going to have to do it in daylight, when all the neighbors are at work. And this is the right place. All three cell phones called the landline number of this house, and got calls from it."

"Before we try anything, we've got to plan this really care-fully," she said. "We have to strike fast—in, out, and away before any of them gets a clue. We should know where each one of them is, and check ahead of time to be sure there aren't any traffic jams on the freeway to keep us from getting off clean. And we should choose a route that won't lead them back to us."

"Of course," said Ed. "We'll do all that." He moved his binoculars to study the house they had come to watch. His voice came out as a quiet, tense whisper. "There's another car pulling out at the house."

"Which house?"

"*The* house."

"Fifty-nine eighty," she said. "How many in the car?"

"Two. Both of them men," he said. "I wish I knew where they're going."

"They're probably out looking for us," she said. "They still want to kill us."

"Can you get on your phone and check the traffic apps?"

"It only tells how the traffic is right now."

"Yeah," he said.

"I thought we were going to take our time. We were going to plan every detail."

Ed handed her the binoculars. "Look at the house. The back window on the right."

"I see him. He's cooking something on the stove. It looks like soup."

"He's alone," said Ed. "That's my point. The others left that house already."

"Are you kidding?" she said. "We're not ready for this."

"By the time we get ready, this guy's friends will come home."

"I know, I know," she said. "It could be a long time before there's another one by himself. I just . . ."

"Come on," he said.

"Never mind. Nothing," she said. "You're right. We've got to do it. But we're not ready. Just take a minute and help me understand the plan."

"There is no plan," Ed said. "He's there, he's alone right now, and that means right now is when we have to do it. No choice." He got out from behind the boat on the trailer and began to move, staying as low as he could in the tallest vegetation—goldenrods, some relative of dandelions that had tall, woody stalks, thistles.

Nicole sat still for a moment, and then followed. They came to the fence and climbed over it. After that there was an apron of cleared land, a manicured strip of domesticated grass before the back garden began, and they moved laterally to stay off it until they reached the back of the house.

Ed pulled his MP5 rifle out of his shoulder bag, inserted a magazine, and racked the first round into the chamber. He left the telescoping stock collapsed to keep the weapon short. Nicole took out her MP5 too and loaded it, her eyes always on the rear window of the house, trying to find the man again from her new angle.

As Nicole looked, she noticed something surprising about her feelings. If she just had to step into the house and kill the man, it would have been much easier for her. What they were doing now seemed less impersonal. She would have to endure far more involvement.

Nicole's mind kept running in one direction after another. There was the immediate question of whether the man in the kitchen had already noticed them and called his friends on his phone, or maybe turned around and walked out his front door, or even taken one of those nasty little machine guns out of a closet and crouched down to wait. There was the question of what she and Ed would do afterward, during the next few minutes, if they got him. Their car was parked on the next street, too far to even run to if somebody chased them. And then there was the step after that. What in the world was that going to be? The seconds were passing, and her mind was like a person in a burning house, running to each door or window, looking for a way out, and finding one after another blocked.

And Ed was already beginning to move again. For a second, a part of her felt itself tugged in the other direction, wanting to run back to the fence before Ed brought death down on them both. But something—maybe only the fear of being alone—made her stand up and go after him. She knew that having her with him kept his survival from being impossible, but it didn't make it likely. He was betting on getting through this on sheer audacity.

Ed and Nicole trotted along the back of the house and stopped on either side of the kitchen steps. At the top was the kitchen door, a white wooden door with four small panes of glass on the upper half. Ed was tall enough so he could look in the lowest pane at the place in front of the stove where they had first seen the man.

Ed shook his head at her and moved on to the next window, and then the next, heading along the side of the house now. Finally he looked in and nodded, then came back along the house. When he reached her, he whispered, "He's in the living room. He's watching a soccer game on TV."

Nicole allowed herself to feel his hope. The television's sound would help cover any noise they would have to make. She followed him to the kitchen door and watched him flick open his knife and slip the blade into the slit between the door and the jamb to depress the plunger. He leaned into it, and shouldered the door open. Nicole came in and closed the door quietly so the change in the air and the miscellaneous sounds of the outdoors wouldn't reach the man.

She took in the house. She could smell the soup, a mixture of odors with onions, garlic, and chicken competing for her attention. She saw it simmering in a covered pot. It occurred to her that she didn't want the man to turn the boiling soup into a weapon, so she turned off the heat.

Ed was moving along the hallway to the other part of the house still half crouching with his rifle at his shoulder. He had reached the side of the stairway leading up to the second floor. He paused and stepped to the side to let her catch up with him.

They pivoted around the foot of the staircase together, their rifles trained on the man.

He was sallow-skinned and about thirty, his hair cut with an electric shaver that made his hair and beard the same length. He had a sloping forehead and a sharp nose, but his head protruded in the back, so it seemed to be in balance. He turned his head to face them, and Nicole saw the close-set black eyes widen in surprise, and then narrow again. The man raised his hands slowly, as though he had been trained to do it exactly this way, showing the palms of his hands right away, but otherwise moving slowly so he didn't alarm a nervous opponent into shooting him. She noticed that he didn't raise them too much, so he would still have a chance to use them if the opportunity came.

"Higher," she said, and the man raised them a bit higher. "Who are you—*polizei*?" He waited. "Cops?"

"You wish," Ed said.

The man's eyes were on Ed, and he looked as though he felt a bit more confident, as though Ed were a presence he had seen before. Ed was big and strong and violent, and for some reason, that made the man more comfortable. "What do you want?"

"What I want for now is that you keep your hands up and shut your mouth until I ask you a question. Are you alone in the house?"

"Yes. My friends are out, but they'll be back."

Ed said to Nicole, "Keep him in your sights for a minute." She aimed at the man, so he had to stare up the rifle barrel while Ed put his rifle into his shoulder bag and took out his .45 pistol with the silencer already attached.

The man in front of the television set didn't like the implication. "Hey," he said. "I'm not causing you any trouble. There's no reason to shoot me. Take what you want."

Ed made sure he didn't step in front of Nicole as he set his gun on the table behind the couch and moved closer to the man. He took a set of plastic restraints from his bag, pulled the man's right hand behind his back, and then the left, and tightened the restraint around his wrists. He knelt in front of him and put another restraint around his ankles. Then he stepped back, picked up his silenced pistol, and held it in front of the man, aiming it at his head. "Tell us who you're working for."

"Working for?" the man said. "Nobody."

Ed punched the man on the side of the head above the ear, and then backhanded him so his nose began to bleed, the blood streaming down from his nose around his mouth and dripping from his chin.

The man said, "Wait, stop the hitting. I didn't understand what you meant. Tell me what you want to know."

"Somebody hired a bunch of you people to drive to our house to kill us in the middle of the night. We killed three of you instead. Does that sound familiar to you?"

The man seemed to be calculating what would happen if he said no. He could see Ed squaring his body and clenching his fist. "Yes," he said. "I do know about that."

"Who hired you to do it?"

"Please listen to me," the man said. "I didn't understand what you want at first. A group of eight men went out to find you. Your name is White."

"Hoyt," Ed said.

"Yes. White. We hired you. We paid you to take care of some private detectives through a middleman named Boyland. Isn't that so?"

"Boylan. Yes."

"And you killed Mr. Boyland instead. Am I wrong?"

"No. We did kill him. He came to our house late at night with a gun, and shot at me. So I killed him."

"I'm sorry if I have a poor understanding. But didn't he get killed at his house? And his wife too? Was she at your house?"

"No," said Nicole. "We killed him at our house because he came after us. We took his body to his house in his car and left it in his garage. We didn't know he had a wife. I had to kill her because she came at me with a gun."

Ed stepped closer to the man, looming over him. "Time to quit stalling. We want to know who is trying to kill us. Who paid you? Who ordered you to do it?"

The man seemed to be struggling. "I don't know how to say. We all decided. When Boyland died we knew we should never have hired anybody to protect us. So we decided to do it ourselves."

"What the hell did you have to protect yourselves from?"

"First there was a man. He got involved with a woman. She's one of us. She didn't tell anybody at first, just started going out to meet him on dates. Then pretty soon she was staying at his apartment all night, and letting him stay at her house." He looked at Nicole, as though appealing to her. "You know how this goes."

"Who was this man?" she asked.

"He was a black man, named Ballantine. She said he was very nice to her at first. And she tried to be careful. Then he wasn't very nice to her anymore. But by then she couldn't just break up with him and hope he would never tell anybody about her. So she killed him. A few of us—her friends—came over and got rid of his body for her. There was an open storm sewer in a street a few blocks from the woman's house. It was a rainy night and water was rushing into that big pipe. We put him inside and let the water take him. That was a year ago."

"Then what?"

"A couple of weeks ago there was an offer of a reward for whoever had killed this man. It was from a private detective agency. One of our friends knew Boyland. He went to ask him what people do in such situations in this country. Boyland said he would take care of the detectives for a little money. A good deal. So he hired you, isn't that right?"

"Yes," said Ed. "Why are you the one asking questions?"

The man shrugged. "'Isn't that right' is a figure of speech. I know he hired you."

Ed said, "I'm going to ask you one more time. Who is the one who sent men after us when Boylan was dead?"

"We did. All of us."

"So we should kill all of you, right?"

"No," the man said. "You get nothing by killing any of us."

"Why not?" said Nicole, who was becoming indignant.

"We're—" and then he said two words that sounded like *"panda lopova."*

"What the hell is that?"

"Thieves. Just thieves. We came here to California about three years ago because we wanted to retire here. It's warm and sunny. We go to the beach, we play golf, and go to each other's houses to play cards. We haven't done anything bad here. We don't have anything you want."

"I'll tell you what," Nicole said. "I want not to be dead. I don't mind killing as many as it takes to keep from being dead. Starting with you right now."

"I can fix this," the man said. "I can!" He was sweating, and his breathing accelerated, but he was intent, not scared.

"How?"

"You have nothing to gain by killing us, but neither do we, by killing you. All we want is to be left alone. So do you."

"That's true. So?"

"So you haven't lost anything yet. You've already made your money. We've lost three men, and we've lost the money we spent just keeping people away from us." He leaned forward now, his eyes intense and unmoving. "But we don't need revenge or repayment."

"What do you want from us?" asked Nicole.

"Nothing. You go away right now, before somebody else shows up here. I tell my friends about our deal, and you go on with your life. You don't bother us. We don't bother you."

Nicole looked at Ed for a few seconds. Ed was one of those men who made thinking look like hard work. Finally, she saw him turn to glance at her. She shrugged, knowing that he would like the decision only if he thought he was the one to make it.

He said, "All right."

The man grinned, his teeth giving him a discomfortingly canine expression. Nicole wondered if she had made a mistake.

"You're being smart," he said, as though he'd read her mind. "You can go, and you won't have to worry about being dead next week, next month, next year. We won't come after you again." He seemed so happy that Nicole almost began to feel worse. She told herself it was just his teeth. He had come from some country where people didn't have a lot of use for dentists.

She took a step backward, and Ed took one too.

The man said, "Wait. Don't forget to free my hands."

Ed stepped toward the man, and flicked open his knife.

Nicole said, "No. Don't cut him loose. Leaving him will give us another few seconds to get going."

As they backed up toward the staircase, Nicole heard the sound of a car pulling into the driveway. She heard a car door slam, then another. She spun on her heel and ran toward the kitchen door at the back of the house. She felt rather than heard Ed's big, heavy feet running on the floor behind her, vibrating the boards and making them sink and spring upward as he came. She flung the door open and turned to aim her rifle back up the hallway in the direction of the front door while Ed got outside. She heard the front door swing open, and then the bound man's voice.

He shouted in some other language, calling out to his friends as they came in the door. She could tell it was at least two men, from their overlapping voices and the noise of their feet as they entered and ran to cut him loose. She stepped out, shut the kitchen door, leapt to the ground, and ran after Ed across the backyard to the fence.

She ran hard, sprinting to catch up with him and to maximize the distance between the back door of the house and the spot between her shoulder blades where they would aim.

After a few seconds she came close enough so Ed could hear her. "What if he tricked us?" she gasped. "What if he lied?"

"Give him time to tell his friends the deal," he said. "We just can't hang around while he does that."

They ran for a few more steps, and then there was a shot. She could tell from the sound that it went high and to the right, more at Ed than at her. Then there were three more in a rapid burst.

Ed and Nicole dropped to their bellies and rolled to face the house. Nicole aimed her MP5 at the back door while Ed took his rifle out of his shoulder bag and extended the buttstock to shoulder it. They lay there watching the doors and windows for a few seconds. "He had time," she said.

Ed said quietly, "What do you think he was saying when he was yelling to his friends?"

" 'The Hoyts are here. Kill them.' "

"You really think so?"

"Yeah," she said. "I really think so. No matter how crappy their language is, he could have said 'don't shoot' in a lot less time than that."

"They're waiting for us to get up and run," he said.

She looked at her watch. "It won't be dark for, like, six hours."

"If we try to stay here, there will be forty of them looking for us," he said.

"Are there that many?" she said.

"You know what I mean. There's only one way to do this," he said. "Let's go." He began to crawl toward the house, holding his rifle in front of him.

Nicole joined him, keeping her eyes trained on the back of the house. They slithered along, staying in the weeds and moving as quickly as they could. She tried to make peace with the idea that at any second the thieves could spot them and open fire. One second and she would be dead. But it wasn't this second. Or this one. Or this one. Each second made her think it had to be the next.

But here she was, right at the back of the house again. She was on one side of the steps, and Ed was on the other. Her knees and elbows ached, and she was a little winded. She sat still for a few seconds, recovering. She could see that Ed felt the same way. He rubbed his knees, and she could see his chest rising and falling.

Two minutes later, he seemed ready. She looked at him and raised her eyebrows in a mute question. He nodded.

Ed collapsed the stock of his MP5 rifle, took the sling out of his shoulder bag, attached the sling, and hung the rifle over his shoulder. He took out his silenced .45 pistol. Nicole completed the same operations. They climbed onto the back steps holding their pistols. Ed peered in the window, and found the kitchen was empty. They stayed low and slipped inside.

The man they had interrogated stepped into his kitchen. When he saw them, his eyes widened. Nicole fired her silenced pistol and hit him in the chest, aiming for the heart. He dropped to his knees, and then toppled forward, facedown.

Ed and Nicole stepped past his body, down the hall into the living room. As they came around the staircase, a man appeared. He seemed to be coming to investigate the thud his friend's body had made falling. Ed shot him twice before he could raise his short machine pistol. Ed and Nicole dashed past him around the foot of the stairs and saw the other man. He was engaged in fitting a magazine into one of the machine pistols. Ed put his next round into the man's head while Nicole shot him in the chest.

Nicole and Ed went to the bodies and patted their pockets. Nicole was the one who found the keys in one man's pocket. She held them up and shook them, and Ed locked the front door and headed through the hallway to the side entrance that led to the garage. They went out and got in the car that the two men had left in the garage, and Ed backed out. He fought the temptation to stomp on the gas pedal so the car would roar down the street, but he accelerated steadily.

Nicole held her MP5 aimed downward between her feet, and her pistol in her hand. She used the side mirror to see if people were coming out of the houses on the street. If they did, she knew, some of those people would realize that their friends weren't the ones driving off in this car. The corner was coming up, and as the car came closer to it, she waited. *Here it comes,* she thought. *Five seconds and we'll be out of sight and out of range. Four. Three. Here it is.*

# 24

Mira Cepic walked through the rooms of her house for the tenth time, making sure she had picked up everything she would be taking with her. She walked past the photographs of her family she had hung on the walls, ignoring most of them. She glanced at the one of her mother, a very pretty woman in a traditional peasant costume, her blond hair twisted into a rope-like arrangement on the top of her head, smiling at the camera with an old, forgotten festival in the background. Mira had picked her out of an old issue of German *Vogue* and adopted her as mother. For her father Mira had picked the man in the same magazine photo spread. Some photographer had undoubtedly selected the two, and they went well enough together. Mira had Photoshopped four pretty blond children into another shot of them in modern clothes, and always told visitors that she was the little girl second from the right—almost the youngest.

Mira didn't mind leaving the pictures where they were. She knew the magazine issue number, and could always find it again if she wanted to make herself new family portraits. She did mind leaving some of the other props she had accumulated during her three years in America. She had a kitchen that could have been a corner in a Williams-Sonoma store, with good, heavy French pots and pans, knives sharp enough to skin grapes, and lots of gadgets that buzzed and whirred to whip, froth, or mix.

She had never owned any real photographs of herself except the ones on licenses and passports. At the moment she had four of each, for the United States, Switzerland, Canada, and France. She considered France a necessity because the French wouldn't extradite anyone wanted for a capital crime in the United States.

She filled her pack with things she couldn't leave—money, her Scorpion Evo 3, her CZ .45 pistol, and ammunition. She always kept much of her wealth in diamonds, in case of an emergency like this one. She'd had a jeweler in Belgrade reset a few of them for her. She had a couple of big stones in cheap costume earring settings, an ugly necklace with ten real stones and twenty fakes so they all looked fake, a belt with a buckle made of a hollowed-out piece of silver with a few big diamonds hidden inside covered in lead. She also had a table-size cigarette lighter encrusted with identical diamonds that were real but looked fake because there were so many.

Mira had kept most of these things in her pack and ready to go. Most of her time had been spent cleaning the house as though it were the site of a burglary. She had shredded, burned, and flushed all of the pieces of paper she had accumulated. She had vacuumed everywhere to be sure of picking up hair and fibers, emptied the vacuum, and then thrown it away in a dumpster.

Mira stopped and looked out the rear window over the kitchen sink into her yard. She had shot Jimmy Ballantine in the back of the head out there one night with a little .22-caliber pistol with a silencer on it, and then fired a second round to be sure. That night, after her friends had taken away the body, the rain had begun again, harder than it had been, and the water had washed away the blood on the lawn. She had gone into the garage and disassembled the pistol, then sawed the parts with an electric hacksaw. Thinking about that night still made her sad. She had been in love with Jimmy. Even after she'd realized that he was not the way he had pretended to be, she had still loved looking at him and touching him and wishing he had been.

As she stepped in front of the big mirror on the bathroom door to push her blond hair up under her baseball cap, she wondered whether she should simply go on alone from her house right now. The others were sure to be feeling resentful. A few of them might even be ready to kill her. Each of them had taken risks, spent money, and finally come to believe he had succeeded in retiring to a safe, pleasant life in California.

She had ruined all of their plans, and gotten the three Russians killed. And then last night, Todor had sent a text message to tell her there was more trouble at Jovan's house. Right after that she had taken the battery out of her phone, but she knew that the others would be talking. Some would be saying all this trouble had come to them because Mira Cepic was incapable of keeping men out of her pants. And there was very little she could say to defend herself, because it was true.

Mira studied her reflection. It was all right. She slouched a little, pulled the cap down nearly to her eyebrows, and adjusted her stance to keep her feet a bit farther apart. The loose men's jeans she was wearing would help, and so would the big sweatshirt. She picked up her backpack by one strap, stepped out the back door, and locked it.

She concentrated on her walk as she went across the back-yard to the empty house she had bought a couple of years ago. She went in the back door and crossed the kitchen to go through the door into the attached garage. She got into the pickup truck, pressed the button on the garage door opener, started the engine, and drove out. The truck bed had three white plastic buckets of pool chemicals and a long-handled pool skimmer with a blue net, and a plastic hose. She had made the truck look as much like a pool man's vehicle as pos-sible. As she drove past her street she looked at her house. It had what the realtor had called curb appeal. She missed the house already. She let her eyes focus on the white van at the far end of the block, but detected no motion. The police officers inside doing surveillance on her house had only seen a pool man on his way from a customer's house on the next street.

Mira gave the surveillance van careful scrutiny until she couldn't see it any longer, and then concentrated on her driving. She knew she had succeeded because her truck looked like something that was self-explanatory. But she knew better than to spend time too close to another driver and hope he thought she was a boy. She had to keep her distance from other cars.

Mira drove the truck toward the Foothill Freeway entrance, timing the lights and adjusting her speed until she managed to coast onto the eastbound freeway entrance. She felt better after that, and it was easy to make sure nobody's eyes rested on her for too long. She got off near Gavrilo's house in La Cañada, where there were fewer other cars, and the corners had stop signs. When she drove up the long driveway to his house, and made it to the big, flat brick space at the back, she took a deep breath and let it out in relief. She took off her baseball cap and shook out her hair, and then walked to the side door carrying her backpack.

The door swung open and in the space was the tall, broad shape of Gavrilo. He had a wide face like a mastiff, and as he stepped forward he opened his arms, each as thick as one of her legs, and folded her into them. "Mira," he said. "Come in, come in. Why didn't you call? We've phoned, texted, and e-mailed, and nobody seemed to get an answer."

She freed herself from him gently. "I heard there was trouble, and I didn't know if it was safe to use my cell phone, so I killed it." She slipped past him into the house.

He closed the door and followed her as she moved across the shiny white marble floor into the vast living room. "You're probably right," he said. "It's hard to know what these American killers are able to do to find us all." There was a Persian carpet about twenty feet square, and he stepped onto it toward one of the big white couches.

"Find us all? That's what they're doing?" She set her pack by the wall where she could see it.

"You don't know?"

"I heard there was some trouble at Jovan's, but that's all."

Mira had known Gavrilo over twenty years. He had taken her in when she'd had no place to go in Belgrade and taught her to steal. They had been much younger then, and she had not minded that he had taken his repayment in sex. He was still a close friend after all these years. He sat on the couch and patted the seat beside him. She went and sat there.

"We found Jovan, Mihailo, and Bogdan in their house. It was afternoon, and the killers must have come in the kitchen door and shot them with silenced weapons. Jovan was alone in the kitchen, making soup when they got him. We found the other two in the living room. The television set was still turned on."

Mira put her head in her hands and rocked forward and back. "Oh, God," she said. "I'm so, so sorry."

Gavrilo lifted his big hand and patted her thigh. "I know, I know," he said. "These people are barbarians. Our friends will be gathering here for the next few hours. We have to talk about what to do."

Mira thought she sensed something in the tone of his voice that wasn't right. "What are the others saying?"

He shrugged. "Just what I said. What else can they say about the work of professional assassins?"

"Not about the killers. About me." She leaned forward a bit more so she could crane her neck and look at his eyes. "Do they want to blame me?"

He met her stare, his eyes tired and sad. "They're not happy about this. You brought trouble on us. It's true."

She said, "Thank you for telling me the truth, Gavrilo. I'll go right now, and I won't bring any more trouble. I'll leave the country by myself. You know that if I get caught, I'll never tell about anyone else."

"No, no, no," he said. "Nobody is going to harm you. All of us together made the decision to hire Vincent Boylan to take care of the detectives for us. And when his own killers killed and robbed him, all of us made the decision to send a squad to their house to get rid of them. We made the choice to do one stupid thing, and then to get out of it by doing the other stupid thing. Now we're in a fight. When you're in a fight you don't kill your own soldiers."

"Thank you, Gavrilo." She stood, leaned down, and kissed his cheek.

He looked at her critically. "Do you have guns with you?"

"My Scorpion and a .45 pistol. Why?"

"You look pretty with a gun. Kind of tough and sexy. And comb your hair and put on some makeup."

She understood. She turned, went to her backpack, and picked it up. He added, "Look confident. Make them remember you're somebody they'll want on their side if bad things happen."

"When do you expect them to start coming?"

He consulted his watch. "Ten minutes, maybe less."

She carried the pack to the small bathroom around the corner just past the entrance to the hallway, went inside, and locked the door. She took the pistol out and stuck it in the top of her jeans. She brushed her hair and put on makeup in the mirror, then stepped farther back and adjusted the angle of the pistol in the front of her jeans. It was hard and uncomfortable to carry it that way, but she knew Gavrilo was right about the look. And the way she looked was going to be important.

She had grown older now, and being beautiful was almost the same as being young. She had needed to be good at prolonging beauty and simulating youth for so long that she knew she could always look good with a little effort. And the men who were coming had all known her when she was young. Men who had known a woman for a long time could be counted on to see what used to be there, not what was there now.

She turned off the light, took her pack down the hallway and left it, then stepped back toward the living room. She saw

Todor, Srdan, and Tomislav come in the side entrance before she could get there. She had wanted to be seated, composed and feigning relaxation when they saw her, but she changed her plan. She hurried up to them as they stepped away from the door.

She called out, "I'm so glad you guys are here," as she approached, and then, "I've been so worried about you." She hugged each of them and planted a small kiss on each man's face. "Tomislav," she whispered. "Srdan . . . Todor." This put her face beside theirs one after another, and let them smell the subtle scent of her hair. "This is a nightmare."

"It is," muttered Tomislav. But the way he said it made Mira wary. Mihailo had been connected in some way to Tomislav's mother's family, at least by marriage.

She wept. "This whole mess is my fault. I thought we had all lived here long enough so I could have a foreign boyfriend. I thought it might even help us all to have connections with Americans who liked us. When it turned bad, you all helped me get rid of his body and everything. I think it was Mihailo who thought of the storm sewer."

Tomislav nodded his head. "I think it was. He was trying to help you, Mira. He had always wanted you to like him."

"I did," she said. "I really did." The truth was that she had never even thought of the possibility that he'd had romantic feelings about her. He had never made any overtures to her.

Tomislav brought himself to reach out and pat her shoulder. It wasn't comforting, but it made her feel she had passed his test. She was still uncertain about the others, so she forced her tears to flow a little by thinking about a bad moment she'd had as a child in Bucharest. She had found a stray kitten on the street, slipped it into her coat, and smuggled it back to the school. She had given it part of her food for two days, and then on the third came back to the room she shared with other girls and found it gone. Now she brought back in her mind the moment when the matron had taken her to the back of the building to show her the kitten's body on the trash heap. A boy named Cazimir had heard the kitten crying out for Mira, and then told on her.

Mira cried some more and then Todor put his arms around her, cradling her there. For a moment, her mind lingered on the kitten. Mira had already known she and the other children were being trained for the Securitate, and their job would be to inform on people—their teachers, friends, each other. Cazimir was simply a quicker student than she was.

Her mind was brought back to the present when she felt Todor's hands move down to her waist, and the hug becoming an embrace. She turned her head away from his shoulder so the top of her head was to his face, and brought her hands up to wipe her eyes, her elbows against his chest.

She stepped back into the bathroom for long enough to snatch a handful of tissues. During that time the men all moved into Gavrilo's living room and took seats on one of the white couches. The back door opened again. Mira watched the arrival of two couples, Anica and her husband, Dragan, and Anton and Sonja Karadzic.

Mira intercepted them and held out her arms to hug each of the women, carefully staying away from their husbands, but greeting them as she pulled their wives to her. The women all kissed the air beside each other's faces to preserve their makeup. The whole ritual was repeated when the sisters Marija and Jelena Arkadic arrived together.

Mira felt closer to the women than to most of the men. She had worked with each of the women dozens of times, going into some of the most well-guarded jewelry stores in the world and risking their lives to fool the clerks, managers, police, and security men. They had been rivals and friends and enemies. They had fought and schemed against each other, and cried real tears together that the men never saw. Now, in their midthirties to fifties, they were her cousins and sisters. If she had any long-lost relatives living in Romania, they might as well stay lost.

The women made their way into the living room and exchanged greetings with the others. This group had seen each other twice since the death of James Ballantine, after staying apart for most of the two years before that. Both gatherings had been held to deal with the crisis that Mira Cepic had caused.

Mira couldn't be sure how to interpret the warmth of the women's welcome. After twenty-year careers working on crews in the robbery circuit, they were all skilled at manipulating the men who were present today. Some of the men were relatives of theirs in the complicated and unknown reckonings of the Serbs, and others were former lovers or just sexual partners during drunken flings of a single night long ago. She'd had her own relationships with many of the men present, but it was impossible to be sure how strong any of these bonds with them would be now. She knew it would be dangerous to try to use them in the presence of the women.

"Today I'm sad," Gavrilo said, and the meeting began with the deep, resonant sound of his voice. "We've lost three more dear friends, Mihailo, Jovan, and Bogdan. These were smart, tough men in good health with very little to fear. It's a terrible thing. It pained me to lose our three Russian friends, Volkonsky, Gregorin, and Malikov. We all talked about that loss last time, and we still feel guilty for letting them stay to search that house alone that night. Now we've lost three who were even closer to us. Mihailo was like a little brother to me. When we were young and hungry we ate from the same dish. Bogdan was a great companion—fearless and quick. Jovan and I met in the army, and I liked him ever since because he was funny and sly. Where are their bodies?"

Todor said, "Zivko and I brought them. They're in the van outside."

Gavrilo said, "Thank you. We may as well bury them beside the others. I hate to bury any comrade so far from home, but we all knew when we came here that this is what would probably happen to all of us in time."

"We should never have come here," said Srdan. "We don't belong in this country."

"We had to try," said Anica. "At home, people were always curious about where the money came from."

Tomislav said, "My great-grandfather was a prince. Wasn't yours?"

The rest of the group gave a murmuring of appreciative laughter. They had all made up stories to account for the wealth they had built up. They were all too cunning to have let much of the money show in Belgrade, but none of them had been cautious enough to hold real jobs to explain how they were able to live. That had seemed to defeat the reason for having money. Instead they had come to California.

Mira was one of the first to think of it. She remembered saying, "We're in danger because we all have lots of money.

We don't need to keep pulling robberies anymore. We don't need more money. We just need to live in a place where other people spend money too."

Her first idea was that she and maybe two of the others would go to South America. There were plenty of countries where they could begin by impersonating tourists, and eventually buy residency papers. At first she had chosen Mihailo, who was quiet and reliable, and Dragan, who was handsome. When Dragan got together with Anica, Mira had invited her too. Four were a big enough party to handle most emergencies in a foreign place, and each of them had millions of euros. They could buy a piece of land together, and pretend to run a fruit plantation or a cattle ranch.

As their plans developed and their research broadened, more of the circle heard about them. When a new name was proposed, there was always a reason to add another person. Tomislav had once been apprenticed as a carpenter, and could supervise construction of their farm buildings. Jovan had received training as a medic, and saved lives in war. Marija was as beautiful as a movie star, and she spoke fluent Spanish. Of course, her older sister Jelena must come with her. The two had grown up on a farm and could repair machinery and cook. This had gone on until most of the members of the group were included. Eight crews had disbanded and left their homes in Europe.

Gavrilo said, "I think coming here was a good plan, but bad luck can defeat a good plan too. It's time to start thinking about doing something different."

Mira raised her hand high, like a schoolgirl.

"Yes, Mira?"

She stood up straight, as she had in the Securitate. "I have to tell you all that things are worse than you know. When I left my house today, it was for the last time. The police are parked in a van at the end of my street, watching my front door. I'm only able to be here because I went out the back way and made myself look like a pool boy."

The others looked at each other, their faces showing dismay.

"I don't know how anyone found me," she said. "I was watching in case the two private detectives came, or the two killers we hired to get rid of them. Instead, I know now the killers went to see Jovan, Mihailo, and Bogdan. I never expected police. Now I think the police must have come across my address among James Ballantine's papers or computer and decided it might mean something. I've cleaned my house and shredded and burned my papers. I've taken the drive out of my computer, broken and burned it too. Nobody should be endangered when I'm gone. I know that, from beginning to end, I'm the one who ruined everyone's chance to retire here. I'm sorry."

Srdan Zrinski said, "How did this happen? I never understood."

Mira stared at him for a moment. "I thought by now everyone knew." She looked around her in exaggerated surprise. "Are you all too pure for gossip?"

A few of the women appreciated the joke, but she noticed Anica and Marija were both suddenly interested in their feet. They felt sorry for her. She said, "A little gossip would have been kinder this time. Srdan, you're too young to have known me well in the old days, but I guess I've always been a little bit of a whore. I think that probably made me better at my job. When I was in a jewelry store batting my eyes at the guard, a part of me meant it. I think sometimes the guard felt the heat, and watched me instead of the door. After we came to California I stayed away from men for almost two years. I didn't want to be in a position where someone wanted to know all about me. Practically the only times I talked to Americans was when I was playing tennis at my country club. Then I took up golf too. If a group of three came, the starter would put me with them to make a foursome.

"One day I met a man I liked playing golf. He was a scientist at a company near the course. He had many qualities I liked. He was very intelligent, very well educated. He was handsome. The Americans I had met who seemed the most cool and sophisticated were black, and so was he. I fell for him. Things were fine for months. Most of the time we saw each other for dinner and then we'd go to his apartment or my house. We went away for a few weekends, but I told him I was afraid of airplanes, so we drove, and I didn't have to show identification or get on some list. Then one day he changed. He made it clear that he was the boss and I had to obey him. At first I kind of liked it, so I played along. Then I realized it wasn't a game, and he was serious. He had also figured out that there was something about me that I was hiding—something that had to do with where my money came from—and he thought that gave him his power over me. So I had to kill him. I shot him in my backyard with a .22—two shots to the head. Some of the guys helped me get rid of his body. For a year I felt lonely and sad, but I was sure I had avoided the trouble from him. Then that pair of private detectives started poking around."

Tomislav said to Srdan, "We tried to help, but instead we made it worse. That was the real problem."

Mira heard him, and it sounded to her like an investment paying off. She was glad she had rushed up to him when he had come in.

Gavrilo said, "We can talk about this forever. But I think Mira has made the right decision. It's time to move on. After the boys are buried, I'll start cleaning my house too."

Around the room, people nodded silently. Todor spoke up. "Where is everyone going—back to Belgrade?"

"Not me," Dragan said. "I swore I'd never go back, and I'll swear again now."

Marija said, "We started out with the idea of going to South America. Maybe there."

"We'll all have to split up," said Jelena. "Just the way we did to come here. We should agree on a few different countries, and when anyone gets settled in the right one, we can all slowly make our way there."

"I agree," said Gavrilo. "We'll need a contact man, someone any of us can call and leave a message for the others. How about Andrei Popovic? When you get where you're going, call him in Antwerp and tell him."

Mira hid her relief and delight. She had admitted her stupid mistake, and humiliated herself. Now nobody could ever accuse her of lying about it. What the others had said made it very unlikely that any of them could kill her. They had forfeited the chance to execute her without seeming cowardly.

The group began to break up into smaller conversations about places. Jelena and Marija were in favor of Argentina or Chile. Tomislav and Todor argued for Canada. Mira said nothing more. She had already decided to start in Belize. She had no Spanish, and the people there spoke English—some odd historical circumstance that she could learn about later when she was there. She turned and stepped off the big Persian rug to head for the bathroom to fix her tear-smudged makeup.

The shot went through her skull and she dropped to the floor, the pool of bright red blood growing around her head. Beyond her, the blood spatter had traveled about ten feet and made a pink triangle on the shiny white marble tiles.

Gavrilo looked over his shoulder, still holding the gun in his hand. "What?" he said to the others. "You knew it was time for her to go. Now she can be buried with the others. They were all good friends."

# 25

Sid and Ronnie Abel walked into the North Hollywood police station and saw Detective Miguel Fuentes already waiting for them near the front desk.

"This is urgent, right?" he said. "Because that was the word you used. 'Urgent.'"

Ronnie said, "I only said urgent because saying 'too late' seemed pessimistic."

"What is it?"

"Mira Cepic has split."

"Come to the back with me," said Fuentes. "I'm going to have to make some calls." He reached over the counter and took a couple of visitors' badges out of a drawer, and handed them to Sid and Ronnie, spun a clipboard around, signed them in, and took them to the bay where the homicide detectives worked.

As soon as they were in his cubicle, he indicated the two chairs facing his desk, and they sat. "How do you know she's gone?"

Sid said, "We drove back to her house."

"You knew you weren't supposed to do that."

"That's why we didn't need to ask. The first time we went there, we went through the yard of the house behind hers, that faces the next street. This time when we did that, it was daylight. We could see through a side window that the house was empty. No furniture on the whole first floor except a couple of lamps and some curtains. It occurred to us we might want to rent the place so we could keep an eye on her while we investigated her relationship with James Ballantine. We called the county clerk's office to have somebody look up who owned the house."

"Who?"

"Her," said Ronnie. "Mira Cepic."

Fuentes said, "So she had enough money for two expensive houses. Enough even to keep one empty. That's the upside of being a diamond thief. You think she did that to prevent anybody spying on her?"

Sid shrugged. "The place has a very good view of the windows of the house where she was living. It also provided a way to come and go without being seen. She could go from her back door across both yards to the other house's back door and into that house's garage, then drive out onto the next street."

"Do you think she did that?"

Ronnie said, "We looked at her house—both of them, in fact—and didn't see her. There was still a car in her garage, and none in the garage of the house behind hers. But that garage had tire marks and a few recent drips of a liquid, probably condensation from a car's air conditioner."

"So what convinced you that she hadn't just gone to buy groceries or something?"

"We went inside both houses," Sid said. "The one behind hers hadn't been occupied for a while. The heating and air-conditioning had been turned off. Upstairs there was no furniture either, just more lamps on timers. Nobody had done any dusting for at least a few months. I doubt that she ever had a reason to go up there."

Ronnie said, "We watched her main house for a while longer, and then went in. It has a two-car attached garage, but she used one side for storage—gardening equipment, pots, bags of soil and mulch, a lawn mower. The car is in perfect shape and has gas. It's a year-old Mercedes. The engine was cool, so we knew she hadn't used it in a few hours. She couldn't have gone out and returned without our seeing her. So we went into the house and found signs that she wasn't coming back."

"Like what?"

"For one thing, as of today, she has no paper," said Ronnie. "The woman no longer owns any. There's a thick carbon deposit on her otherwise-pristine fireplace where she probably burned some bills, receipts, and so on. And there's a blender on a kitchen counter drying, so she may have used that to destroy other papers. It does a better job than most shredders, and if you're never planning to use the blender again, it's fine."

Fuentes said, "Okay. I get that she did a major house-cleaning job, and that you didn't meet her while you were in her house. But if I were an international thief going away for even a day, I'd be careful I didn't leave anything incriminating lying around too. That's the downside of being an international thief. I mean would she just walk away from a house worth about three million? Make that two houses worth six million? And her car?"

Sid said, "There are no guns in the house, Miguel. She made her money pulling armed robberies. She's living alone, and the guy from Interpol told us all these people are ex-military. There's no one thing that proves she's gone for good. But there are a whole lot of little things that all point in that direction."

"Now you're making me nervous," said Fuentes. "If she hasn't left any guns, she's got them with her. Are you ready to go on the record with this little break-in?"

Ronnie said, "If we ever want to talk to Mira Cepic, I don't think we have a choice. She has to be found."

Fuentes picked up his phone and dialed. "Captain? This is Fuentes. Something just came to my attention. Sid and Ronnie Abel came to tell me our suspect Mira Cepic has packed up and left." He listened for a time, and then said, "Justification? I'm sure they'll be able to think of something. Okay, he's right here." He handed the phone to Sid. "Captain Albright wants a word."

Sid took the phone. "Hello, Captain."

Captain Albright said, "You broke into the woman's house, right?"

"In a manner of speaking."

"You're a retired cop, Sid. What were you thinking?"

"We were aware that Mira Cepic lived alone, and was suspected of living on the proceeds of armed robberies. That made her a likely victim for robbery, kidnapping, and extortion. She was especially vulnerable since the house behind hers was unoccupied. We noticed a door in the rear of her house that looked as though it might have been forced, so we knocked to see if she was all right. Since there was no answer, we went in. As soon as we had gone into every room in her house to be sure she wasn't lying on a floor dead or injured, we left. Then we came directly to the police to report what had happened."

"Very good for short notice, Sid," said the captain. "Is any of it true?"

"I would say that trained and experienced retirees like us had a responsibility to check on the woman. And because reliable reporting persons like us were alarmed at what we saw inside, your officers have probable cause to enter the house. It should be easy to get a warrant."

"Thank you, Sid. As soon as we've got it I'll tell our guys on surveillance to go in."

"I would," said Sid. "They're wasting their time outside in that van." Sid handed the phone back to Fuentes.

Fuentes put the phone to his ear for a second, and then hung up. He said, "Thanks, I think."

Ronnie said, "Have you got any more names yet? Any other panthers who have moved into the LA area?"

"I hear it's only three so far, from Mira Cepic's phone bill. They were cell phone numbers she had called. Major Crimes got the names and checked them against the list of panther suspects that Interpol had."

"Who are they?"

"They haven't told anybody the names yet. I do know that because of the phone company billing records Major Crimes thinks they're all living in one house. They're all Serbs, and they're here on doubtful visas."

"Doubtful?"

"Granted legally, but probably not factual. They're here on EB-5 visas. That's the kind where somebody brings in a certain amount of money and plans to use it to start a business that will employ people. I'm sure they brought the money, but they've had three years to start a business, but haven't. And at least two have arrests in Europe they didn't mention on their applications."

Ronnie said, "Has anybody gone to bring them in for questioning?"

"I don't think so," he said. "They're still using the list of panthers from Interpol and trying to see which ones entered the United States, so they can get them all at once."

"It's probably the best way," said Ronnie. "It's impossible to know what the game is until you know who's playing."

"I don't know," Fuentes said. "It would be great to stop a big robbery from happening, and obviously I'd love to keep anybody from being hurt. But we're getting nowhere on the crime that got you—and me—involved. This has less and less to do with the murder of James Ballantine."

"Maybe," said Ronnie. "But maybe this time we've just got to work our way through all the other things that have been happening and understand them before we can piece together the one thing that happened to Ballantine."

Sid said, "What do you think the department is going to do?"

"I'm not making the decisions," said Fuentes. "But I think the plan will be to watch the houses of the thieves we identify, and begin staking out all of the best places in the city for stealing diamonds."

# 26

Nicole and Ed sat on opposite sides of a wooden picnic table at the edge of a grassy park above the ocean along Cabrillo Boulevard in Santa Barbara. After they had checked into the hotel across the street from the ocean, they walked down to State Street and bought a takeout lunch of sandwiches and beer at a restaurant and brought it back here.

Their table was at the edge of the grass beneath the long row of tall coconut palm trees. The sandy beach began about six feet from Nicole's bare foot, and sloped gradually down to the blue water a hundred and fifty feet away. Nicole was watching a family from somewhere far away, where people's skin was still very white at this time of year, except on their necks, backs, and shoulders, where it had already been burned red by the sun. They were flying a box kite, and it had risen quickly into the blue sky, so now she could sight up the bright white string to the diminishing red spot of the kite.

The palm fronds above her made a fluttering, whispery sound in the steady breeze. As she glanced up at them, they reminded her of movies she had seen that were set on islands in the South Pacific. For all she knew, they were filmed somewhere near here. They were only a hundred miles from Hollywood. She noticed a couple of greenish lumps up where the fronds met the trunk, and it occurred to her that it would be a terrible irony to survive two shootouts with the insect people, and then get brained by a coconut at the beach.

She lowered her eyes again and rapidly scanned the park, the sidewalk, and the cars on Cabrillo Boulevard. She looked at the people walking along the beach where the surf washed up and subsided, leaving a firm, cool surface for their feet. Nobody she could see looked threatening. None of them stared in the direction of their table too long or too hard. None of the cars parked in the little lots along the ocean ahead of her had people sitting in them pretending to do nothing. That would have been a particularly ominous sight. This was a spectacular, sunny day with a faint breeze that smelled like a mixture of salt, air, and water. Parked cars were hot and cramped and smelled like plastic, and anybody preferring that would have been up to something.

She touched the bag she'd set on the bench beside her, and the hard, metallic lump of the collapsed MP5 comforted her. She returned her eyes to Ed. He was facing the pier and the harbor beyond, and he had a good view of the cars that turned at the foot of State Street. It would be very difficult for any enemy to surprise them.

"Well? What do you think?" she said.

"About what?" Ed went back to chewing his sandwich.

"What we should do," she said. "We've stayed out of sight for a couple of days, but what's next?"

"I'm open to ideas," said Ed.

She was getting frustrated. All he seemed to want to do was eat. "We can't go home. They know who we are and where our house is, and everything. Not to mention those three guys—the last ones."

"Right," said Ed.

"You say 'right,' but we're not moving. We're only a hundred miles from our house. We're not hauling ass across the continent."

"Right," said Ed. "They haven't come for us yet. So maybe this is far enough." He took another bite of his sandwich and another pull on the bottle of beer he had kept in the small paper bag from the restaurant. He swallowed. "If you think about this, it doesn't matter if we're a hundred miles away or ten thousand, if they don't know which it is. All they know is that we're gone, and they don't know which direction we took or how fast we went."

Nicole studied Ed for a few seconds. She wanted to stay frustrated and impatient with him. She had been prepared to be, but what he'd said made a certain kind of sense. She had even been planning to watch him eat while she was delivering her speech to him, and think about how gluttonous and gross he looked while he was gobbling his food. But even that wasn't true. He had to keep eating longer than she did, to sustain that big body, but he was always pretty polite. As she watched, he gave up on his sandwich, collected all of their trash—hers too—and carried it to a trash can. Then he sat down across from her and waited.

She said, "You don't think they're even bothering to search for us?"

"I wouldn't do it," he said. "And they've got to be smarter than I am."

"Why wouldn't they search?"

"That guy told us they're a bunch of thieves. We know they could afford to pay Vincent Boylan all that money to hire us. Like that guy said, we've got nothing they need. They obviously still have plenty of money. They just don't want more trouble from us. They failed to accomplish that by killing us, but having us on the run accomplishes the same thing. So why poke the snake?"

She turned away again and stared out at the ocean for a moment. "So we're going to leave it at that?"

"At some point, most people who live by stealing run into trouble and go to prison. A lot of the ones who carry guns meet other people who carry guns and die. That's just odds. Maybe if we wait awhile, this bunch will disappear. Then we can go home."

"I don't want to stay in Santa Barbara more than a couple of days. It's too close."

"How about Las Vegas?" he said. "That's more than twice as far from home, and it's a lot bigger."

"Okay," she said. "Las Vegas." Then she added, "For now."

"We should be all right there," said Ed. "They won't go looking for us."

Nicole shrugged. "Of course not. Why poke the snake?"

# 27

The people of the group had gathered in the far end of the yard three hundred feet behind Gavrilo's house. It was a quiet, peaceful place because it was separated from the house by the stand of old oaks that had been spared when the house was built. When they'd buried the three Russians, they had found that it was nearly impossible to dig a grave near the old oak trees because the roots had traveled outward a long way searching for water.

Gavrilo had left the trees there because they were big enough to provide shade. Southern California was a parched, hot place, and he had installed round wooden benches around the trunks of a few trees so he could sit there to drink his wine and listen to the warbling of the mocking-birds. These benches were where most people sat and waited their turns to dig.

They didn't dig four individual graves, because a row of man-sized mounds would be seen by police helicopters and arouse curiosity. The three Russians who had been killed during the raid at the killers' house had been buried in one grave, and these four would be buried together in another.

The grave was a single wide hole with a sloping path going down into it, so each shift of diggers could walk down into the pit and up again. Most of the digging was done by the men, but a couple of the women, Mira Cepic's old traveling companion Anica, and her closest friend, Marija, got into the grave and dug.

When the hole was about seven feet deep and eight on a side, three men were posted to watch to be sure the sky remained clear, and then several others brought the bodies down on stretchers.

Marija was forty-five, but still beautiful enough to make people stare at her when she walked on the streets of Beverly Hills. Today her wavy dark brown hair was tied back and her bright green eyes were hiding behind her sunglasses. She had changed into jeans and a sweatshirt to dig, and she had picked up a lot of dirt during the hard, sweaty work. She was aware that right now she looked like the peasant farmer she really was, but she was also aware that a little mud didn't keep the men's eyes off her. When she first became aware of herself as a child, the beauty was with her already, and it had never left her.

She looked down at the wrapped body of her friend Mira. About eight months ago she had done her best to help Mira. It was a huge favor, and part of the favor was that she'd decided not to tell her about it. She had read in the newspaper the name of Detective Kapp, the police detective who was in charge of the James Ballantine murder, and begun to search for him. When she found him, she stalked him from a distance. She observed that he was a drinker—not a typical social drinker, but a man who went to bars alone after work and bought a drink, and then another, and another, until he walked unsteadily. When he had drunk enough to quiet whatever his pain was, he went outside, got into his car, and drove home to a small apartment in a big stucco building in Van Nuys. If he had not been a police officer he would probably have been arrested by then and gone to jail, and maybe gotten cured. Marija was glad that wasn't what had happened, because another cop might not have been as easy for her.

Marija made preparations. When she was ready she made sure she was alone in the bar that he liked best, which was the worst and most out-of-the-way place he frequented. She didn't have to do anything to attract him. She'd never had to do anything except respond when men spoke to her. She smiled, talked with him, and drank with him, as she had with many other men over many years. With Kapp, instead of asking questions about jewelry stores and dissolving into the night, she had stayed long enough to put a dose of Rohypnol in his drink, and gone out to his car with him.

Dragan and one of the Russians had been outside waiting in Dragan's car, but the one who had known how it must be done was Marija, who had learned the method from her father. She had driven Kapp's car out of the city and stopped on the shoulder of a winding road in the hills. Then she wiped off her fingerprints, and the two men helped her prop Kapp in the driver's seat. She had used Kapp's shoe as the wedge to hold down the gas pedal. Her father had taught her that the man must be drunk before he was put in the car, and that the drug she used had to be a natural substance that was quickly metabolized, and therefore difficult to detect in the blood or tissues. There could be nothing out of place in the car, nothing that wouldn't have been there if the man had driven himself off the road and over the precipice. In automobile accidents, the victims often lost one or more shoes.

Marija looked down at Mira's body. *By now you know how I tried to help you,* she thought. *And I know you would have done the same for me. Rest now. I'll see you soon enough.*

Marija took her shovel and threw one shovelful of dirt on Mira, one on Jovan, one on Mihailo, one on Bogdan. Then she handed the shovel to her sister, Jelena. She walked up the sloping path to the grass and looked around her at the trees. It was going to be a shame to leave California. The air was warm like the breath of a baby. In most of Europe there was still snow on the ground.

At the grave, while others put their shovelfuls of earth over the bodies of the four, Anton Karadzic recited from memory an approximation of what his father, who had been an Eastern Orthodox priest, used to say. When he was a boy, Anton had often gone with him to keep track of his vestments and supply muscle if the pallbearers were old enough to have earned the honor but too old to carry the coffin by themselves. Anton could also still perform a passable wedding ceremony, but unlike his funeral, it wasn't binding.

He spoke with some feeling. He had inherited a good voice, and his friendships with the four dead thieves was sincere. He kept talking long enough for the mourners to cover the bodies with about four feet of earth. As he finished, five of the strongest men took the shovels and energetically threw in the rest. When the grave had been filled and the ground had been scraped and tamped down even, Todor took the four copper plates he had etched with the names of the four dead thieves, and set them at their heads. Then he shoveled dirt on top so they would not be found easily.

There was some talk that they would eventually be able to bring the bodies back to be reburied in Europe, but nobody believed the talk. It was hard enough to smuggle one live thief across a national border. In most cases it didn't matter. Whoever Mira's relatives in Romania had been, they had never known her. And Jovan's, Mihailo's, and Bogdan's closest relatives were probably the ones standing around their grave right now.

After the grave markers had been covered, a few of the men walked across the lawn, lifted bags of gravel from the bed of a van, and poured gravel over the site. Todor and Tomislav leveled the site with rakes. Then the men who had carried the gravel lifted the prefabricated wooden gazebo they had assembled and set it over the grave.

When all the work was done, the group gathered in the shade of the oaks and sat on the round benches. They opened bottles of wine and beer and drank a few toasts to their dead friends.

Gavrilo, who seemed to be the obvious one to speak, stood up. "Thank you, friends. I hope that somebody has taken care of the belongings the four had set aside for their futures." His half-lidded eyes drifted across the crowd and noted who reacted. Tomislav, Todor, Srdan, and Jelena all nodded and waved a hand to signify that they, as close relatives, had salvaged the money and valuables of the dead.

Gavrilo knew that the others all assumed one of them had taken all the valuables Mira had left—possibly Marija or Anica. But yesterday while some of the younger men had carried Mira's body out of his living room and some of the others had cleaned the blood off his marble floor, he'd had five minutes alone, and had rifled the backpack she had left in his hallway. He had taken most of the money and diamonds before anyone else could think to ask. Marija had come by later and picked up Mira's pack and taken it with her without looking inside it. Gavrilo felt no guilt about the theft. Everyone was a thief—Mira, Marija, Tomislav, and all the others. And taking Mira's money was like picking up a fallen soldier's ammunition on a battlefield. She had no further need of it, but because of it, he could go on.

Gavrilo said, "Now that we've done what we could for our friends, we have to think hard about the future. Who has a plan? What about simply walking across the border into Mexico?"

Todor snorted. "I'm not sneaking into a country that's on the verge of anarchy. We wouldn't last a year."

Sonja said, "And I'm not interested in going back to Serbia. Where would I go, my old village? I hated it then, and I'd hate it now."

"We should decide on one place," said Anica. "I don't want to be separated from all the people I care about."

Dragan, who had been sitting with his arm around her, pulled back theatrically. "You'd still be with me. Doesn't your husband count?"

"I meant my girlfriends. I can get bad sex anywhere."

The others chuckled to thank her for trying to lighten the mood, but the pervading sadness was too strong to overcome. When they arrived three years ago, they had been so optimistic. They had planned to stay in California for the rest of their lives. Now they were going to have to move again—probably scatter in all directions. This wasn't a new exploit. It was a retreat.

Jelena said, "The reason we're alive and rich is that we're careful planners. We've never done anything without making a detailed plan and executing it with precision. So let's make a plan."

Gavrilo said, "I'm willing to talk all night if that's what it takes. Who has an idea to start us off? It doesn't have to be a detailed plan, just an idea. Just tell us a country where you'd like to go." He looked around at the group, and watched four, then five men and women stand up from their seats among the trees.

# 28

"They're all gone," said Fuentes.

"What?" Sid said. He punched the speaker button on the phone so Ronnie could hear.

"The panthers. Mira Cepic isn't the only one. We checked the names and billing addresses of the people who recently talked to Mira Cepic on their phones. We checked their names against the Interpol lists, and we've found five more that matched. We sent officers to their addresses with warrants. And now all of them are gone."

"Gone how?" said Ronnie.

"The same way as Mira Cepic. Their beds weren't slept in. The garbage is gone, the vacuum cleaner has been heavily used and then removed, and every scrap of paper is gone. Each house has been left so it looks occupied until you start to search the place. The lights and televisions and things are on timers. The ones that have alarm systems have them turned on."

"How do you know all this?"

"I talked to one of the officers who went to serve the warrants."

"Have they dusted for prints?" Sid asked.

"He said they've called in the crime scene people, but there hasn't been anything useful yet."

Ronnie said, "What's the department's theory about what's going on?"

Fuentes said, "The people downtown all think this means the panthers are about to pull the robbery they've been planning. They think it must be today."

"The panthers have been planning a robbery for three years?" said Sid. "One robbery?"

"Captain Albright says the bosses are convinced of it. Once the panthers moved out, they started the clock ticking. They can't stand around on a street corner for the next week waiting for the right moment to pull their robbery. That's the thinking, anyway."

"So what's the department doing about it that they weren't doing before?" asked Ronnie.

"They're sending lots of officers to the obvious places—major jewelry stores, the jewelry district. You can hardly walk down Hill Street without getting run over by a plain unit. Every parking lot must be full of cars with government plates."

"How about Beverly Hills?"

"Beverly Hills has a hundred and twenty-seven cops on its force, spread over three shifts. There's too much for them to cover alone, so we're helping. The three hundred block of North Rodeo Drive has Van Cleef and Arpels at 300, Harry Winston at 310, and Cartier at 370. A crew of thieves could pick up the GDP of some countries without crossing a street. By now there are LAPD officers inside, outside, and on all the surrounding streets."

THOMAS PERRY

"What are they trying to do—catch them in the act, or scare them away?" asked Ronnie.

Fuentes said, "The reason for all the officers is to keep the thieves from shooting somebody or taking hostages. The thinking is that it's too late to be subtle. They're already on the move."

Sid said, "How about keeping them from getting away?"

"That's a whole separate operation. The TSA and airport police have been reinforced by a whole lot of LAPD officers with lists of names, mug shots of the people we know are here, and so on. They're even in the short-term parking lots and in the shuttle stations for the long-term lots. The sheriff's deputies have been quadrupled in Union Station on the theory that Europeans are used to trains, and there are more deputies in every subway station in case they have to shut down the subways. The CHP is ready to close a freeway or two if they get the call."

"If they pick up Mira Cepic, we'd love to hear what she has to say about James Ballantine," said Sid.

"Me too," said Fuentes. "I'm hoping if we get her I'll be able to get her aside by herself and ask what she knows about him. I'll let you know as soon as anything happens."

"Thanks. We'll be waiting." Sid cut the connection and looked at Ronnie.

"I know," she said. "It's frustrating."

"She's the only one we've found, male or female, who strikes me as a possible suspect," Sid said. "None of the people we've talked to had the right edge to them."

"We don't know if Mira Cepic does either."

"No. If not, it could have been one of her male friends, who saw Ballantine as a rival for her. Or the killer could have been an enemy of hers. But for the first time, we're talking about the sort of person who might shoot somebody in the head a couple of times and put his body in a storm sewer."

The men and women of the group of thieves had no real name for their organization, or for the larger, older syndicate of diamond thieves the international police called the pink panthers. Most often in Europe they had spoken of their group by indirection, calling the others their friends, their circle, or just some people they knew. Going away from their home city of Belgrade to commit a robbery had been referred to as going on a vacation, or visiting a relative. Since they moved to Los Angeles, they had decided that it was safest not to see each other often, but each time there was trouble, they instinctively flocked together.

As Gavrilo finished the work of preparing to leave, the members of the group began gathering at his house again. There had been times when Gavrilo wished he had not quit his life of robbery so soon. He had saved plenty of money, but if he had gone on for another year or two, he would certainly have had more, and more was better. He thought about these things while people arrived at his door, each of them carrying a pack or a valise or a shoulder bag.

They had all gone to their secret hiding places and taken out their valuables, preparing to leave the country. He knew from experience and observation that people who were extremely careful for years would often panic in an emergency. He had also learned that pickpockets would sometimes intentionally startle a victim to see which place on his body he touched to check for his wallet. When Gavrilo was a young man working alone in a village he had started a fire in a small hotel to see where the owner went to save his hoard of money.

But this was just a passing thought, like a reflex. He was not thinking seriously about robbing his friends, not forming a plan, anyway. He had already inherited most of the money and diamonds that Mira had brought with her in her pack, and he was pleased with that. He was good enough at appraising diamonds to know they were excellent stones. He was not good enough to assign prices to them, but he could count, and he'd counted two hundred stones in the five-to-ten-carat range, and seen lots of smaller stones. She'd also had quite a bit of American money with her, all in hundred-dollar bills, and some big stones set in cheap costume jewelry.

Gavrilo was distracted because he was a thief. He had not stopped being a thief just because he had left Europe, so he hadn't stopped seeing ways to take things. The sound of the doorbell reminded him that he couldn't stay upstairs packing while he had guests downstairs. As he descended the stairs, he thought about all of the members of the group. They were leaving the country, so they had gone to their banks to empty safe-deposit boxes, then gone to the most secret hiding places in their homes—pieces of hollowed-out furniture, the bodies of sculptures or toys, kitchen appliances, the bottoms of large potted plants. All of that wealth was now stuffed in shoulder bags and backpacks, being carried into his house.

When he reached the entry he was surprised at the number of people who were here. He didn't feel up to the hugs and handshakes, so he simply waved at everyone and skirted the group to get into the living room.

The others followed in his wake, giving him little chance to breathe. They were all chattering at once, but he caught a few sentences.

"They have hundreds of police out searching for us. The airport is full of them!"

"They're watching the trains and buses!"

"When I drove past my place there were police cars parked in front. They're searching my house."

When Gavrilo saw the alarm and worry in their eyes, he knew that the universe was presenting him with a test. "Come in, come in," he called. "Don't stand out there in the foyer, come and sit down. We'll find a way to handle this. We can't panic, or everything will be lost. They'll search some houses and they'll stand around in the airports. But they won't find anything in our houses and they won't find us in the airports. We just have to stay in a safe place to wait until they give up, and after a few days we'll leave. Don't worry. It's a matter of simple patience."

Tomislav said, "They showed pictures on television of the police breaking into my house. They had body armor and helmets, like soldiers. It didn't look like America."

"I'm sorry, Tomislav," said Gavrilo. "They'll be in everybody's houses soon. Here too." He raised his voice. "Everybody stay calm. We've done this before. We just have to wait long enough so the police think we already got away. Then we'll split up and go quietly, one at a time."

"But how can we do that in Los Angeles?" Jelena said. "And where? They're already at our houses, and they'll be here soon. So where can we all wait this out? Some of us have had our faces on television."

"We've all been hunted before," Todor said. "We just got used to living like rich people for a few years. We got soft. And I hope we will again. But for now, we have to go back to thinking like thieves—lean and smart. Is there anybody who knows a place where we can be safe for at least a few days?"

"We've got to get away from this house right away. That's for sure," Sonja said. "If the police come here and find those graves, they'll think we killed our own people."

There was an uncomfortable silence as men and women began to look at Gavrilo, holding him in the corners of their eyes. He wasn't sure how to interpret their stares, but he knew he'd better get them thinking about something else. "Come on, everyone. Doesn't anybody know a place where we can wait this out?"

Near the back of the group, Srdan's hand came halfway up, and then drooped down by his side.

But Gavrilo was desperate for a distraction. "Srdan. I saw your hand. What are you thinking?"

"I have an idea, sort of."

# 29

Ed Hoyt leaned back in his lounge chair and stared at his copy of the *Los Angeles Times*. As he read, his big hairy feet moved, and his toes clenched and unclenched. Nicole's eyes were hidden behind her dark sunglasses, studying him.

She had been lying peacefully beside this small pool at the end of a line of pools at the Bellagio hotel, savoring the pleasant feel of the dry desert air. She had gone in to swim a couple of lengths, a feat only possible at this time of the morning, before other people got up and stood in the pool like posts. Then she had come back and lay here on her chaise longue beside Ed, feeling the hot, parched air drinking the water off her skin. The faint breeze seemed to her to carry microscopic particles of sand that buffed her skin and made it feel tight and clean and new.

Nicole had repeated the process three times, and when she had come back to lie down beside Ed for the third time, he'd had the newspaper. She loved that about Las Vegas—if you looked like a reasonably good tipper, people would bring you what you wanted. She looked him over again. She had mixed feelings about lying next to Ed in bathing suits.

Ed was big, about six foot four. He was hairy, with tufts of black hair on his chest that tapered into a streak of hair going down his belly past his navel. He was also very muscular. That was a good thing, really. Her husband was in great shape, especially for a man in his forties. But he made her feel a little bit déclassé when he was this visible. Here they were at a fancy hotel—one of the few in Las Vegas that was still fancy, now that Las Vegas had become so eager for young people and their children—but Ed didn't look like a high-class man. Rich lawyers, the CEOs of big companies, men of hereditary wealth didn't look like Ed. They didn't have all that body hair. They had it waxed or shaven, so they were smooth as girls. And they were in good shape, but not the same way as Ed Hoyt. He looked like a cage fighter, a martial arts teacher, maybe even like what he was. He was very male, very virile, but maybe a little bit too flashy and obvious.

He was a bit like a male version of some of the women she had seen around the pools in Las Vegas. They had wonderful perky round breasts and tiny waists, and asses like a pair of bubbles. Nature had been good to them, but maybe a bit too generous. They might be utterly blameless, and many of them hadn't paid to have anything enhanced. But when the eye settled on them, the brain didn't say "science major." Ed was like them. There was nothing subtle about him, and he was no more self-conscious than a dog.

She closed her eyes and lay there, and reminded herself to take him as he was. She was with him, and they were alive and healthy. They'd had to rent a two-bedroom suite at the hotel so they would have two safes instead of one to hide all the cash they'd brought with them.

Ed said, "You know what it says in the paper?"

"I have my eyes closed. I haven't seen a paper in four days. No."

"The weird people who hired us aren't just thieves like that one guy said. They're from a famous gang of jewel thieves. The police are looking for them. They were in this country getting ready to rob the jewelry stores on Rodeo Drive, and a bunch of jewelry businesses in the jewelry district downtown."

"It can't have been entirely successful if the *LA Times* knows who they are."

"The cops recognized one of them, and then figured out a whole bunch of them were here, so they flooded those places with cops before the thieves could do it," said Ed. "The police sat there for two or three days waiting for the thieves to show up, but they never did."

Nicole still didn't open her eyes, determined to devote most of her mind to feeling the treatment her body was receiving from the warmth, the breeze, and the relaxation of her muscles. "How many were there to start?"

"The cops think maybe forty."

Now she had to open her eyes to be sure nobody was too close to them. "You killed a couple, remember." She had shot at least three, but that was irrelevant.

"The police say they each stole millions of dollars all over the world for years. All they take is diamonds."

"Oh, you know how that is," said Nicole. "Some store gets robbed of two dollars. They tell the cops and the insurance company it was twenty. The clerks let the thieves get away before they report it so they can take eighteen themselves before the cops get there."

"This isn't some liquor store in Bakersfield," Ed said. "It's places like the Harry Winston store in London. Other places in Paris, and Tokyo. They just come in and rake off the diamonds."

"When, exactly, did you get so interested in diamonds? I practically had to beg you to buy me a pair of earrings."

"It's not the diamonds," Ed said. "It's the fact that it's these people. We worked for them, even if we didn't know it right away. We went after the Abels and kept them fully occupied while these people planned—and maybe even carried out—the theft of the century. For all we know, they pulled it off and it hasn't been reported to the cops yet. After we risked our lives for them, they turned on us. We got screwed."

Nicole shook her head. "I don't see how you can twist what happened to them into anything about us. We weren't their partners or something. Vince Boylan hired us to do a job for them. And we paid ourselves very well with Boylan's money. The end."

"They shot at us."

"We shot at them, and we're not dead."

"Want to know who identified the members of their gang? It was Mr. and Mrs. Abel. If that bunch of freaks had kept us on and treated us decently, they wouldn't have lost anything. They could have stolen twice as much money by now, and the cops wouldn't be searching all their houses and showing their pictures in all the train and plane terminals."

"Okay," said Nicole. "They would have been better off with us than without us. No argument."

"I'm saying more than that," said Ed.

"What more is there to say?"

"They owe us damages."

Nicole coughed out a big "hah!" laugh before she'd had time to stifle it. Then, because the laugh was so big and unexpected, and because Ed looked so shocked, she laughed even harder, the regular way. She held one hand up and clapped the other over her mouth. After a few seconds she pushed the laughter back down. "Sorry, sorry. It just caught me by surprise. You sounded like you were planning to sue them."

"Obviously not," said Ed.

"Sure you don't want me to call a lawyer?"

He folded the paper and tossed it onto her stomach. "If you read it, you'll see that about forty of them are now on the loose with all those diamonds from their old jobs. They were planning to get out of the country with them, but that didn't pan out. They can't have made it."

Nicole opened the paper, found the start of the article, and began to read. After a few minutes she glanced over at Ed again. He was lying there with his eyes closed, his face turned peacefully to the blue sky. "Why can't they have made it?"

"The cops were warned ahead of time—by the Abels, but that's not the point. The cops threw everything they had into keeping the thieves from getting on a plane or a ship or a train or a bus, and they had enough time to transmit all of their pictures to every foreign customs service. So far, not one of them has turned up."

"You believe they let themselves get trapped in this country?"

"Let themselves or planned to."

"Planned to? Really?"

"You saw that house where the three guys lived," Ed said. "They funneled money here for months in advance—maybe years—and moved in."

"The paper says that was so they could spend a lot of time casing the jewelry places and planning their robberies down to the last detail."

"Right," he said. "I'm sure they did that. They had figured out that the safest place to live in this country is on a quiet street in an outer suburb. Did they do all that for one job, or even a day of jobs?"

She put down the newspaper. "Oh my God," she said. "What if you're right?"

"Don't make it sound like a fluke."

"I didn't mean it that way," she said. She sat in silence, staring across the palm-lined row of pools and baroque fountains planted in the long fake piazza. Her mind was working its way through all of the details she knew about this gang of thieves. Now and then she would say something.

"When those idiots killed that man and dumped him in the sewer, most people would have just called the whole operation off, and moved on. When the Abels started looking for the idiots, offering rewards and things, they'd certainly leave."

Ed didn't open his eyes or move. "Mm-hmm."

"They stayed, and hired somebody to get rid of the detectives. Us—no, Vincent Boylan, who hired us. They were committed to staying awhile, and to keeping it a secret."

She didn't detect a reaction from Ed, but she went on. "They spent time planning robberies at what's got to be some of the hardest places in California to rob. We always assume that what happens after something like that is a quick getaway that very minute. But these people know a lot. Running away is usually the part that gets you caught. Getting away is a second whole job. It takes time to plan, time to arrange.

And there's no reason you have to do it right away, or all at once."

Ed still didn't say anything, but she saw a little tremor at the corners of his mouth.

Nicole got up and walked off across the sun-warmed, smooth pavement, past the fountain pool with the four-sided bearded face blowing streams of water onto the bathers, to the long rectangular pool beyond. It was getting to be past breakfast time now, and already there were people sitting on the submerged benches that ran the length of the pool on both sides. She swam to the far end and back, and then did it three more times. She stood, leaned back at the edge to catch her breath, and returned to the chaise beside Ed.

She lay still, feeling the water baking off her, the gentle abrasion of the desert breeze, and the looseness of her arm and leg muscles. She said, "So where do you think they are now?"

He said, "Their houses are out. The cops have already been watching those places. So they must have found somewhere else. They're foreigners. There are a bunch of them. They don't have a lot of options."

"Name one."

"A house they know for sure is empty and the owners aren't coming back. Vincent Boylan's house, or our house."

"Jesus," she whispered to herself.

She turned to look at him again. He lay there looking like some big dumb guy who'd been in a lot of fights. And he was that. But he was something else. She sat up, leaned over, and kissed his cheek. "Come on," she said.

"What for?"

"I want to show you something."

He opened his eyes. "Where is it?"

She stood up, threw her cover-up over her head, and stepped into her sandals. "It's going to be upstairs in the room." She began to walk toward the rounded arch leading into the hotel. In a few seconds she heard him catching up with her.

# 30

It was late afternoon as Ronnie Abel stood in line at the post office on Tujunga Canyon Boulevard. She was wearing a blond wig. It was uncomfortable, but it was a good match for the color and cut of Mira Cepic's hair on the pictures she and Sid had taken of her. The handout from the meeting with Agent Roche from Interpol had included the first two pages of her passport, including the picture. Her California driver's license picture was even better, because the terrible digital camera in the Department of Motor Vehicles office had taken Mira Cepic by surprise, and the lighting had made the wear on her skin show. She and Ronnie could easily be the same age. They both had bright blue eyes, and were about the same weight and height.

Ronnie couldn't be sure this would work. But she and Sid had spent a lot of their lives looking for people who had not wanted to leave anything around that might tell the police where to find them. Mira Cepic wasn't the first to leave a house so clean it was difficult even to find a clear fingerprint, let alone paper. It was easy to throw away paper. The hard part was to make sure no new paper appeared—new credit card bills charged for plane tickets, new charges for stores in different cities, monthly reports for bank accounts. The simplest way to keep that from happening was to stop the mail.

Ronnie waited patiently while the three people in front of her in line took their turns at the counter. The bored postal workers worked methodically and politely to fulfill the requests of the patrons, weighing things, selling stamps, taking the money and credit cards. She was afraid that she would get the woman on the right, but hoped for the man on the left. He seemed to be thinking about other things, the kind of person who worked automatically, letting his hands do the thinking. The woman seemed sharper to Ronnie, not daydreaming, but studying customers to keep her mind occupied. In Ronnie's experience women tended to be better at picking out small flaws in a person's appearance. Men glanced and moved on.

The two workers were moving through their backlog of patrons at roughly equal speed, and then the woman drew a man who only wanted to buy a roll of stamps with a credit card. She took care of him quickly, and then it was Ronnie's turn. Ronnie looked behind her and saw that the customer after her was a young woman with two toddlers. She was holding a stack of boxes in her left arm and letting her two toddlers each hold a finger of her right. She looked miserable. Ronnie said, "Come on. Go ahead of me," with a slight accent.

The girl smiled and frowned at once. "Really?"

"Sure." She ushered the woman up to the counter. As they arrived, the bored postal woman met Ronnie's eyes, as though to say, "We've been there, haven't we?" She and Ronnie both smiled.

The man in the other position sent his customer away with a receipt for his certified mail envelope, and Ronnie stepped up to him. She said, "I have a hold on my mail, and I'd like to pick it up, please." She was careful not to overdo the accent, but she had practiced it in case she needed to pretend she didn't understand the rules. She used it so it wouldn't suddenly appear if she needed it.

"I'll need ID."

Ronnie took from her purse the copy of the California license and the copy of the first two pages of Mira Cepic's passport and put them on the counter. "My wallet was stolen while I was away in Europe, so all I have is the copies."

The man looked at Ronnie and then at the copies, and then at Ronnie again. His mind seemed to stall. "Hold on." He took the papers and left his station. Ronnie began to hope.

The man went to the woman's station. He showed her the papers and said, "This lady had her wallet stolen. Is this okay? Can we take this so she can get her mail?"

When the woman looked at the copies, her face seemed stern. Then she looked over at Ronnie, smiled again, and nodded. "Sure. This will be fine."

In a moment, Ronnie was signing a yellow receipt and taking a bundle of Mira Cepic's mail, held together by rubber bands.


A half hour later, Ronnie took off the blond wig and brushed out her hair. The hot, tight wig had been awful, and taking it off was a relief. She watched as Sid went through Mira Cepic's mail on the table in their hotel room. There were a few bills, a lot of ads and catalogs, a number of solicitations for charities of all sorts, a couple of women's magazines. He kept setting things aside, and then he stopped.

"Veronica," he said.

"What, Sidney?"

"It looks as though she got a card from a friend." He held up a square white envelope. He began to open it with the knife on his keychain, careful not to cut the return address. He pulled out a birthday card.

Ronnie stepped up behind him and looked over his shoulder. "Of course. I was just staring at a copy of her driver's license. Her birthday is two days from now." She picked up the envelope. "Alexei Malikov. That address is north and west of here. Can you get the directions and send them to my cell phone while I put on some comfortable shoes?"

"Sure."

He cut and pasted the address into the map site, and watched the directions appear.

Ronnie said, "We'll have to stop for surgical gloves and stuff on the way. Maybe we should pick up a pry bar too."

"The stuff we used on Mira Cepic's place is in the car," Sid said. "I'm hoping this place is like Mira Cepic's."

In another few minutes they were in their latest rental car, heading west toward the address of Alexei Malikov. As Sid drove, Ronnie looked at the traffic map on her phone.

"The freeway looks pretty clear. All you have to do is get on the 101 and stay on it until the Topanga exit. Then turn north, and I'll tell you what's next. Malikov. That name sounds Russian, doesn't it?"

"It does to me," said Sid. "But I don't speak Serbian or Russian, so I'm not the one to ask."

"You're all I've got. Agent Roche did mention that the thieves are from a lot of different countries, so I guess it fits."

"We'll just have to see what we can find out," Sid said. "Maybe this guy will be at home, waiting to tell us where Mira Cepic is."

They arrived at the house in a half hour. The neighborhood was relatively new, composed of two-story houses that all filled their lots, barely leaving enough space for a wheelbarrow to pass between them. Sid and Ronnie parked a distance away and watched the house as evening came on. No lights went on in the house, and no vehicle entered or left the garage. Ronnie looked at her watch.

"What do you think?"

Sid looked at his. "I guess so. Mr. Malikov is clearly not home. And there are no police watching the place." He opened his door and got out of the car, and Ronnie got out on her side.

They walked around the block to the next street, and took advantage of the darkness to walk between two of the houses to approach Malikov's house from the rear.

When they reached the back door, they both put on their latex gloves. Sid took out the powerful magnet he'd bought at the hardware store, knelt beside the door, and moved it slowly along the bottom of the door until he felt a bit of resistance. He located the small magnet that had been embedded in the door by the alarm company. Its purpose was to hold the switch beneath it in an open position until the door opened. Once the magnet was moved out of position the switch would close and the alarm would go off. Sid carefully positioned his magnet so it attracted rather than repelled the alarm magnet in the door, and then stood up. He opened his pocketknife, pushed the blade in by the doorknob so it depressed the lock bolt, and then stopped.

Sid nodded to Ronnie. She grasped the knife handle and kept the bolt out of the way while Sid knelt again. He pushed the door open slowly. As the door moved, he slid his magnet inward a fraction of an inch to be certain it was holding the alarm switch up. Then he and Ronnie stepped inside and closed the door until it was still open only a crack.

Sid and Ronnie closed curtains and blinds as they moved from room to room in the dark. When they were satisfied they had made it difficult to see inside from any angle, Ronnie turned on a lamp.

They searched the house thoroughly, but efficiently. They were aware that once they'd broken into the house, each moment increased the chance that they would be caught.

It was apparent immediately that this house had not been cleaned out the way Mira Cepic's had. There was dust, there were cans in the recycling basket in the kitchen, and there were male clothes lying on the floor of the first bedroom. Then they found a second bedroom, and a third, but they had been neither occupied nor cleaned.

Ronnie went back into the kitchen and opened the refrigerator, then quickly closed it again. "He's gone, but he left in a hurry," Ronnie said. "And it was a few days ago. There's old food in there."

In the first of the bedrooms there was a desk, with old receipts and a calendar. Sid sat down in the desk chair and began examining the papers. "Half these things are in the Cyrillic alphabet."

"Take everything that might be personal, or isn't a power and water bill. We'll try to figure out what all of it is later."

When Sid had cleared all of the paper from the top of the desk he looked at the calendar. "The twenty-third," he said.

"What about it?"

"That's the last day on the calendar. The one he hasn't torn out. And the check register shows that as the last day he wrote a check." He opened the next drawer. "Ammo. All of it 9mm." He opened the next drawer. "This one's got nothing but supplies—file folders, envelopes."

"Okay," Ronnie said. "I'll get started on the other rooms."

A half hour later, Sid found her in the last spare bedroom. When she saw him come in she said, "It's all about the same—9mm ammo, a gun-cleaning kit, but no guns. A small amount of cash, but nothing special."

"Ready to give up?"

"More than ready," Ronnie said. "We're pushing our luck."

They went downstairs and slipped out the door, set the lock on the knob, and closed it. Sid took his magnet away, holding his breath, but the alarm didn't sound.

On the way home, Ronnie said, "Do you think we should tell Miguel Fuentes what we found?"

"We don't know if we found anything, or just helped the guy clean his house."

"You know what I mean. Should we tell Miguel we went to the house and took a look around?"

"I don't see how we can," said Sid. "He and Brenda Albright let us slide on breaking into Mira Cepic's house. They're not going to do it again. Anyway, the whole department is in on this now. They've been keeping people on long shifts for three days waiting for the panthers to do something or try to leave town. If anybody finds out we were in there, we're going to jail."

"I guess we'd better go back to the hotel and see if we can find out what we were taking that risk for."

# 31

The drive from Las Vegas to Los Angeles was 270 miles, and it always made Nicole a little bit nervous. It was at least four hours of driving with the least risk-averse group of travelers ever to be on a public highway. The fact that most of them had just had a lesson in the folly of optimism only made them impatient, and a few of them mean.

She had read once that a long stretch in the middle had no local ambulances, or hospitals to drive them to, so if you were in an accident on Interstate 15, the people who would eventually come to pick you up were inmates from a nearby prison. The idea had not made her less nervous, but it had suggested to her that if she ended up in prison, that sort of volunteer work might be a worthwhile way to pass the time.

Nicole leaned back in her seat and let Ed do the driving. She and Ed had spent a whole extra day in Las Vegas before they had managed to pull themselves together and get out on the road.

When Ed had told her that those jewel thieves must be hiding in somebody's house, she was so impressed with him that she had spent most of the afternoon fussing over him and fooling around with him in their suite. And then, before she thought much about it, she realized that they should not have been drinking in the middle of the day, because they were now both too far under the influence to drive back to Los Angeles that day. One thing Nicole really had not wanted to do was to get them pulled over along Interstate 15 by the Highway Patrol.

She knew if that happened, Ed was certain to do his best to kill the cop and drive away. She also knew that Ed would be too slowed down and sloppy to do the job well. He might get the two of them killed. Even if he managed to accomplish the simple task of bringing his pistol up to the window and squeezing the trigger, and then kept his thinking from getting stupid on the long trip past the other cops looking for them, what would it be for? He wouldn't have arrived home in any shape to rob a bunch of foreign jewel thieves that night. There was no point.

Instead, Nicole decided to spend the rest of the afternoon and evening keeping Ed occupied and amused. That had turned out to be quite a project. Ed was a man with big appetites, and he was in a manic mood. He'd had a couple of drinks in the room, a couple more during the enormous lunch he'd ordered in the restaurant at the Aria hotel, sitting under the colorful hanging butterflies with their four-foot wingspans. He seemed to be inspired by a gang of Chinese men at the big round table beside them, who appeared to have ordered everything on the menu, and were eating their way through it.

Ed had looked over his shoulder at their table and said, "That looks good." Of course it looked good. They were eating lobster with one hand and steak with the other, and eyeing the chicken and fish on the next plate. Ed had ordered as though he wanted to outdo them, and certainly had vanquished at least a couple of them—individually, not as a group.

Ed had gotten them a taxi to Mandalay Bay. The early evening was a blur of casinos and bars, and then a return to the pool at the Bellagio, where Ed decided that the best way to sober up was to swim laps.

Nicole had put on her wrap and walked along the patio stones above him and a few paces behind, keeping an eye on him to be sure he didn't drunkenly hit his head and drown, or get into some dumb altercation with one of the men who stood still in the water like fashion models.

Watching him swim had probably been a mistake for her. Even when he was drunk he was a surprisingly strong, graceful swimmer. He looked great with those big shoulder muscles flexing to pull him along. And now that he'd spent a few days in Las Vegas lying around in the sun he was tanned and healthy looking. He had strong, even teeth like a horse, and they were bright white because he didn't like coffee and had never smoked. When he saw her on a turn and grinned, she felt her knees weaken and she was smitten again.

That led to the next set of distractions for Ed, chief among them Nicole's body. Then there were more drinks, more food, and more Nicole before they both collapsed and slept for about twelve hours.

Today she had gotten him into the car and they headed back toward Los Angeles. Nicole was exhausted anyway, and slept another hour or more on the trip home, but Ed showed no sign of wear today. When Ed drove he didn't listen to the radio and he didn't talk much. He just kept the car aimed between the lines and stared off at the vanishing point, moving ahead like a coyote trotting across a desert at midday.

As they came into the semicivilized margins of San Bernardino around Glen Helen park, more and more cars flowed into the channel of traffic on both sides of them. She broke the silence. "At least at this time of day the traffic into the city won't be as bad as the traffic going out."

"No," he said. "We'll be there in good time. We can get some dinner and maybe take a little nap before we go to work."

She reached up and rubbed the thick knot of muscle beside his neck. "You getting tired, baby? I'll be happy to take a turn driving."

"I'm fine," he said.

"Just keep it in mind."

He said nothing, but she knew it didn't require an answer. She always felt a little bit bad when she reached this part of the trip. The desert was so immense and clean and empty, and from here on the world was a stew of crowds and brand names and ugly buildings and moving steel.

Nicole began to think about what they were going to do tonight. In most ways, it wasn't smart. She and Ed already had plenty of money in their duffel bags, and they had a few safe-deposit boxes in other cities and a few bank accounts. It wasn't anything like the amount a gang of jewel thieves probably had in diamonds, but it was a lot, considering what she'd started with.

She and Ed hadn't done some of the talking that they should have by now. They still had a house. It wasn't a very valuable house, because it was in a sort of crappy area that was half rural and half not, and it wasn't fancy. But they should do something with it—sell it, or rent it out, or walk away—only they hadn't discussed the house yet. Most of it still belonged to the bank, and it was in a pair of false names, so she supposed it wasn't such a big deal if they chose to walk away.

A bigger issue was when they took their fair share of the diamonds from the Euro gangsters, meaning whatever they could take from them, where were they going to go? Since she had met Ed Hoyt, she had always accepted the likelihood that they were going to be on the run someday. It had been such a constant possibility that she had sometimes formed fantasies about it. The problem was that her fantasies had always taken place in Europe. She and Ed would hit a big score, and the scene would change to their hotel room in Paris or Barcelona or Prague or Amsterdam, depending on which was the city she'd last seen in a magazine layout or an online travel ad. But now that they were about to rob members of a huge European crime network, Europe was not going to be a good place to start a new life. If they were recognized, they'd be dead.

She could anticipate that this was not going to be an easy conversation. Ed would just shrug and say, "We'll go over the border to Mexico." But she really didn't want to go to Mexico. The whole country was full of drug cartels with armies of killers, and the extra killers who were temporarily out of work made a living kidnapping people. Everybody else in the country was willing to swim rivers, climb steel walls, and crawl through deserts to get out of it. She would have to offer Ed an alternative right away, before he got too attached to Mexico. What was it going to be—Canada? She needed to think.

And then there was the problem of the diamonds, which were the whole point of this job. She had read in the papers, just as Ed had, that diamonds were a good way to move big money. They could be recut or broken up to seem like new diamonds, moved from one country to another, reset in different ways. But she and Ed didn't have any connections for selling diamonds in any other country. And even in America, the few times she and Ed had taken anything in the course of a hit and sold it, the price they could get for it was about a quarter of what it was worth. Diamonds had to be a whole lot harder to sell, and dealing in some foreign country with strange foreigners had to be worse than risky. She sighed, and then looked at Ed.

He seemed to be fully occupied by the act of driving, still staring ahead, moving the car along. As she had many times, she envied him. He seemed to be able to turn off whole sections of his brain for periods of time, and think about one simple thing. He seemed to live in the present just doing whatever task he'd been presented with just then, and not fretting about something else three spots down the list.

When they reached Glendale they stopped at a parking lot near the Alex Theatre and walked to a restaurant on Brand Boulevard. Even without the antique theater, this part of Glendale had always struck her as something out of another time—family-run restaurants with small pink-and-green neon signs in the front windows, streets with cars parked nose in to the curb. She remembered blocks like this from when she was a teenager in small-town Arizona. Evening in Glendale was a bit of relief to the senses, and she began to feel revived almost immediately.

They got back on the freeway, drove to Universal City, and checked in at a motel where they could back their car up beside their room and Ed could swing their duffel bags from the trunk to the room without moving his feet. They slept for a time and woke at midnight.

They dressed in dark clothes and shoes, loaded and hid their pistols under their jackets, and moved their MP5 rifles and extra ammunition to the tops of their duffels, where they could reach them easily. They moved the duffels back to the car and cleaned the room, but didn't check out. They got into the car and drove.

Ed drove along Ventura Boulevard to the west, through Studio City and Sherman Oaks. When he turned left at Dixie Canyon toward Valley Vista, Nicole said, "So you think they're hiding in Vince Boylan's house?"

"I don't know," Ed said. "There's a lot to be said for the place. It's away from the main streets, but not far away. It's upscale, it's private, and it's in an area with lots of trees and stuff, so it doesn't stand out much. And there are a few places where the panthers could park cars around there."

"Do you think there's enough room for that many people to sleep?"

"Upstairs there were at least four bedrooms, right? And there's a den downstairs, and at least two couches in the living room. And they probably don't all sleep at the same time. I wouldn't. I'd have people up on three shifts waiting for something like us to come along."

Nicole was resigned to letting Ed decide. No matter what, they were probably going to have to check both places, because the jewel thieves could be somewhere else, maybe out of the country already. But Ed had a right to give his theory a chance.

Ed parked their car around the last bend before they reached the house, so that if the panthers had posted lookouts, they wouldn't see the Hoyts arrive. Even driving past the place before they parked might alert them.

Ed and Nicole opened their duffels, took out their MP5 rifles, and hung their slings around their necks to hold them, then covered them with their Windbreakers. In the event that some ordinary person saw them, he might think they were just a nice couple walking home from a neighborhood party. They moved off the road just before the curve and walked upward into the steep sloping yard of a neighbor. When they were in the backyard above the house on the hillside, they began to alter their course again toward Boylan's, still climbing a bit so they would have a better view of the second-floor windows.

Ed and Nicole crossed behind four houses before they had a sight of Boylan's. They found a spot behind a thick old sycamore tree that had small shrubs planted in a circle around it, and sat down.

There were no lights showing in any window at Boylan's. The only lights were from a fixture above the garage door and another set into the overhang above the front door. Both fixtures were controlled by light sensors that switched them on at dusk and off at dawn. Ed and Nicole watched and waited for any movement inside the house, any kind of silhouette at a window. After about twenty minutes there had been none.

At the hotel Nicole had installed the night scope on her rifle. She turned it on and raised the rifle to her shoulder. She looked down the scope at each window in turn, trying to make out anything resembling the shape of a body through the white wispy curtains that Boylan's wife had hung on the second floor. The view she had at this angle didn't reveal anybody.

"See anything?" Ed whispered.

"Not from here. We've got to get in closer. How about up that way?"

Ed stood and began to move farther up the hillside, angling a bit toward the house. Nicole scanned the yard around Boylan's in case a lookout appeared, but nobody was visible to her. She followed Ed. When they reached a spot where she could use her scope to look downward into all of the rear and side windows of the second floor, she stopped and braced her rifle on her knee and looked again. The beds were visible in two bedrooms. "Nobody's in there," she whispered.

"Let's get closer."

They stepped closer and closer to the house, and as they went, Nicole was more convinced that the panthers were not using the house as a hideout. Nothing moved, nothing looked human, nothing seemed to be in use, and nothing had changed since she'd been here before.

As they walked along the side of the house, Nicole identified her feeling. Boylan was dead, his wife was dead, the house was dead. She whispered. "They're not here. I'm ready to go."

Ed whispered, "I want to see if they've been here and left, or never came at all."

Nicole knew that mattered. If they'd been here and gone, it would mean they'd recovered already, split up, and initiated whatever their plan B was. They would have left Southern

California already, and by now they would be on their way to some other country. But if they hadn't come here to hide, then they had gone somewhere else to hide.

Ed went to the back door, stared in the window at the kitchen, and spotted the alarm keypad. "It looks like nobody turned on the alarm."

"That's because they're dead."

"I meant the cops." He flipped open his knife and jimmied the door.

As he did, some part of Nicole's brain waited for a shot or a ringing alarm. There was nothing. He stepped inside and she followed.

She looked into the refrigerator to see if there was fresh food, but found only some gray meat, a couple of unopened cartons of almond milk that probably wouldn't spoil until the end of time, some things that were hard to date, like beer and frozen food, and some tomatoes that looked like the skin of a mummy. She felt the oven, but it was cold. There were no dishes in the dishwasher, and none of the lingering dampness that would have indicated a recent use.

Nicole and Ed went upstairs. There were no signs that anyone had been here. When Nicole looked up the hallway through the night scope, she saw the floor was still marked with tape, and that the blood from Boylan's wife had not been cleaned up. It was still visible as a dark blotch on the wall-to-wall carpet.

She spoke in a normal voice. "Nobody has been here since the cops left. Let's go."

"Yeah, you're right." Ed lowered his MP5 rifle and covered it with his jacket again. "Maybe I overestimated those people. This would have been a great place to hide while they cooled down and everybody convinced themselves that they were already back in some crummy country."

Ed pretended to look around. "I'll bet this place will sell cheap, because somebody died here."

"I don't care if it's a dollar, I'm not interested."

He shrugged. "You did your best to avoid killing her. She practically insisted." He looked at his watch. "Well, we've got another stop to make tonight."

# 32

"Here's an address," said Sid. "Malikov was using the back of this real estate ad as a scratch paper. It's 2-9-9-5 Quillivray Way, Chatsworth." He looked at Ronnie. "Where's Quillivray Way?"

Ronnie opened her laptop and typed in the address. "It's way out in the northwest of Chatsworth." She looked at the paper Sid held in his hand. "What does that say, in the corner?"

"I don't know. It's either Russian or initials. Looks like an *M*, backward *N*, small *p*, small *a*."

"Let's try Google Translate. Russian to English." She typed *M-N-p-a* into the box on Google Translate, and then watched. "Nothing. Maybe the program doesn't recognize it unless the *N* is backwards. Let's try this another way." She typed on the English side. "*M-I-R-A*." On the Russian side appeared *M*, backward *N*, small *p*, small *a*.

"What does it say?" asked Sid.

She clicked on the audio symbol, and a Russian voice said, "Mira."

Sid set the paper down. "Maybe that's where she is. I guess we'd better get out there and take a look."

As Sid and Ronnie Abel drove into the northwest part of the San Fernando Valley around 1:00 a.m., there were fewer and fewer cars on their route. The long, straight roads made it possible to see a few solitary sets of headlights, and even an occasional flash of colored paint under a distant streetlamp, but they were nearly alone. In this part of the Valley the streets had become dark and quiet.

They drove to Moliere Road, and stopped just before it intersected with the 2400 block of Quillivray Way. They parked their rental car, got out of it, and walked into the covering darkness. They moved up Moliere to Quillivray. There were no streetlamps or sidewalks. After a few hundred feet they passed a wooden sign beside the road. Sid let the glow of his cell phone illuminate it for a second: QUILLIVRAY. AN EQUESTRIAN NEIGHBORHOOD. PLEASE USE CAUTION.

Ronnie said, "It just means watch what you step on."

Sid said, "It is pretty rural. It would make a good place to sit tight and wait for the police manhunt to run out of steam."

"Quit it. Every time you say something like that, I feel like ducking. The last time it was 'this would be a good place to kill somebody.'"

"This wouldn't be a bad place for that either."

"Thanks, Sid."

They became silent and watchful as they moved on to Quillivray Way. The houses were far apart on large pieces of land, but the houses themselves weren't either pretty or very large. A few had outbuildings of the sort that might be stables or studios or workshops.

Many of the houses had the same 1920s style, a brick or clapboard one-story ranch house with a long concrete porch along the front shaded by an overhanging roof. The fences were nearly all chain link, perhaps made to keep a dog or a few chickens behind it in the dusty yard. Many of the houses had been expanded at some point with boxlike additions.

As Sid and Ronnie walked along the street toward the 2900 block the houses got newer and bigger, and the edge of the street was no longer sloping earth like the banks of a river. There were stretches of curb, and some sidewalks. But the lots were still large, relics from the era when it had still been a reasonable idea to move out of the crowded city and buy a house with an orchard on it or space for a truck garden.

Sid and Ronnie studied each house as they came to it, looking for signs their years of experience as police officers had taught them that a group had moved into a house and hidden there.

None of the houses had lights on at this hour, and there were no modifications done to make the windows opaque. There were no houses with heavily reinforced doors, no bulky barriers piled against the front of a house to make it bullet resistant. When abnormal numbers of people were living in a house, it often showed in the quantity of garbage that was produced. There was nothing like that here.

A couple of times they ventured into backyards to sight along the row of houses to see if there was anything not visible from the front—hidden vehicles, light leaks in windows, sentries posted to watch the street.

They kept moving, making their way from block to block, trying not to present a silhouette or make noise. This was a quiet neighborhood surrounded by other quiet neighborhoods, and beyond them, foothills and then a wall of jagged mountains that showed uninterrupted gray except along the crest where three red lights mounted on a radio tower blinked to warn off low-flying planes.

The house at 2995 was a bit away from the others, and there was an extra space around it because the building on the oversized lot to the left of it had been torn down at some point, and the home to the right side still had a swath of old orchard beyond its chain link fence, and then two hundred feet of empty space before the tiny garage at the end of a driveway that consisted of two parallel strips of concrete.

The house at 2995 had several of the qualities that Sid and Ronnie had been watching for. The façade was brick and mortar, but it seemed to be an add-on that didn't fit the original style. The windows had a matching set of curtains, but six inches behind each one appeared to be an opaque layer like blackout curtains.

There was a big black pickup truck with tall tires parked nose outward in the driveway. It reminded Ronnie of a watchdog—a pit bull, maybe, with a big blunt muzzle. It occurred to her that a truck like that wasn't a likely sign that the Europeans were here. The big truck would probably look ridiculous to a European, and it wouldn't help a robber keep a low profile. But she knew it was possible that the house's occupants had been murdered by the panthers, and this truck belonged to a dead man. And maybe the truck had been kept as an escape vehicle. It gave the place the look of being occupied, but it was also the sort of truck that somebody could use to make an off-road run through the desert to the Mexican border.

Sid and Ronnie paused near the house to exchange silent signals and then split apart to enter the property. Sid went to the right side up the driveway, where the neighbor's orchard would complicate his silhouette, and Ronnie went to the left near the edge of the lawn where the empty lot began.

They each found a vantage where they were difficult to see, sat down, and waited. For the agreed-upon fifteen minutes, they stayed absolutely still and listened for any sounds, observing everything they could see. At the end of fifteen minutes they moved again, this time close enough to touch the house.

On Ronnie's side, all of the windows had been blocked by blackout curtains, and when she put her ear to the glass, she heard nothing. She continued beside the house to the back corner, and looked into the two-acre backyard. Parked on the back lawn behind the house were four vehicles. She held her position.

Sid moved to the big black pickup truck in front of the garage and looked inside. The truck's interior looked pristine from the driver's side window. Even in moonlight he could see that there was nothing on the seats or the floor. He moved around to the truck bed, but it had a hard-shell cover that was locked, so he kept going until he reached the passenger side. Something looked odd from that side. The seal along the bottom of the window on the right door seemed to have been scraped. He felt it with his finger, and it was rough. Maybe somebody had used a slim-jim to open the lock without a key. He cupped his hands around his eyes and pressed his face to the window. He could see from this side that the cylindrical ignition lock had been pried out of the steering column, leaving the wires protruding a couple of inches. The truck had been hot-wired.

He thought for a moment. Trying to communicate with Ronnie now could give away her position. The fact that someone had hot-wired the truck would give the police probable cause for a search, but it didn't prove anybody was in the house, and telling Ronnie wouldn't contribute to her safety. Right now she should already be crouching somewhere near the back of the house, as alert to all of the dangers as she could be.

Sid moved on. The windows on his side of the house were all blacked out. The garage was closed and it had no windows, so he moved around it toward the back of the house. In a moment he and Ronnie would meet, and they'd determine then whether they should try to enter the house.

As he took his next step he heard an unexpected sound in the distance. It began to grow gradually—car engines and the hiss of tires on the empty street. He pivoted and backtracked around the garage to the front corner, hid, and watched.

There were three SUVs. All of them came around a corner far down the street moving toward the 2900 block. As soon as they'd cleared the corner, they turned off their headlights, and moved along the center of the street in single file. The cars went slowly to keep their noise low, almost coasting for the last few hundred feet. The only illumination came from their red brake lights when the drivers stopped in front of 2995. Sid could only hope that Ronnie had heard them coming too and taken cover in time to keep from being seen.

Each SUV had only a driver inside. When the drivers opened their doors to get out, Sid could see that they had all turned off the dome lights so the interiors would remain dark. They got out and walked to the front steps, but only one man climbed to the door. He knocked.

As soon as he did, the door swung open and people began to come out of the house. There was a dim light on somewhere deeper inside the house, and now Sid was able to make out a few of the faces when they turned back to look behind them toward the light or whisper to a companion. First there were a couple of younger men, and then three women, and then three more men. Then there was another woman, then several more men. Each of the people carried a large shoulder bag, a pack, or a small airline carry-on.

There was a long pause, while shadows cast by the light inside seemed to be moving rapidly about. The light went off, and the final dozen men came outside, and the last one closed the door.

Sid stared. There was no question these were the panthers, but they were about to leave. In a minute they'd be in the cars and heading off, and he knew that meant they had reason to think they'd never be caught. If he was going to do anything, it had to be now.

Sid backed away from the front of the house, taking out his phone, and dialed 9-1-1. When the operator answered, he said in a low voice, "My name is Sid Abel, and I'm a former LAPD homicide detective. I'm at 2-9-9-5 Quillivray Way in Chatsworth. The crew of jewel thieves the LAPD is looking for are here, getting into cars and preparing to move out. There are at least thirty. This is urgent. Please get this call to all police agencies in the northwest part of the Valley."

He cut the call and pocketed the phone, but he sensed that something had already gone wrong. A moment ago there had been a low sound of whispered and muttered conversation as the panthers moved toward their cars, but it had stopped. The world had gone silent, as though all movement had halted and every person was listening, trying to determine exactly where he was. He took out his pistol and stood still, hoping he was wrong.

There was a harsh whisper, and then footsteps coming from the front of the house. Sid couldn't run around the house to the back, and lead them straight to Ronnie. He took a couple of steps and hoisted himself over the chain link fence into the next yard.

The first two panthers appeared at the front corner of the garage, where he had been a moment ago. They had heard him rattle the fence as he had gone over it. One of them switched on a flashlight and aimed the beam in Sid's direction, but Sid had anticipated something of the sort, and lay flat a few yards into the orchard in a depression between two rows of trees. When the beam of light didn't find him instantly, it began to move. It swept along the fence, searching hungrily for a sight of him. After it had passed him, he remained flat on the ground with his face down.

Suddenly the beam flicked back to his hiding place, stayed there for about three seconds, and then began to move away again. The silence was shattered by a loud burst of automatic weapon fire, and the muzzle flashes illuminated the trees around him. The air in the orchard was full of flying bark chips and splinters as the bullets tore into the trees.

A moment later the silence returned, and Sid sensed the shooter had paused to replace his spent magazine. Sid looked, aimed, and fired his pistol twice at the torso of the human shape beside the man with the flashlight. Then he moved his aim to the flashlight just as the man switched it off. Sid fired three times, but he was not sure whether any of his bullets had found the man.

Next Sid heard a sound he had been dreading—the familiar pop of a Glock pistol. He knew it must be Ronnie firing from the far end of the house. There were three more rapid shots, then two. Sid got up and ran along the grove of fruit trees toward the sound, but then the air around him exploded again with flying bark and chips as shots came at him from the front corner of the garage. He dropped to the ground and flattened himself while the bullets pounded into the trees above him.

At the far end of the house, Ronnie pressed her back against the bricks as she aimed her pistol toward the backyard. That was almost certainly where the next panthers would be coming from. She had already stopped a group going out the back door toward her to reach the hidden cars, then turned back an incursion from the front of the house, and now it was time for them to try to trap her in a cross fire.

The first two stepped out from the back corner, as she had expected. She fired four shots rapidly, and they dived or fell back out of sight.

She began to turn her head to check the front again, when there was a burst of automatic weapon fire from the empty lot beside the property. At first Ronnie thought the person was firing at her, but then she saw splinters and chips of brick flying from the front corner of the house. Someone in that vicinity returned fire for a moment, and then the person in the empty lot fired again and the shots stopped.

Ronnie caught movement and strained her eyes to see a small person running toward the house carrying a short rifle with a long magazine protruding from the underside.

The woman dashed out of the field to where Ronnie crouched, and knelt beside her. She was small and blond, had an H&K MP5 in her hands. Over her shoulder was some kind of bag, which Ronnie assumed must contain ammunition. The woman said, "We can't stay here. They'll just keep coming. Come on."

The woman trotted along the side of the house, her rifle raised to her shoulder. She stopped beside a small rectangular opening in the foundation with a metal screen over it. She glanced at Ronnie to be sure she was covering her, unlatched the metal screen, and tugged it off. She slid her body into the opening, feet first, and beckoned to Ronnie to follow, then grabbed her rifle and pulled it in with her. Nicole waited inside the opening. She had seen that Veronica Abel was trapped, and known she would die in a minute. She needed to keep her alive, for now. "Hurry," she whispered.

When the woman disappeared, Ronnie hesitated. Out here she was exposed, but in there she would be protected from fire by the foundation of the house. She took a deep breath, crouched, went to her belly, then slithered into the dark rectangle.

The woman edged close to her, reached out, and pulled the metal screen back into place so it covered the opening. Then she rolled once and began to crawl away.

They were under the floor of the house on a dirt surface. Ronnie could see three other screened openings, because they were all slightly lighter than the crawl space where Ronnie was now. In the near darkness, she could make out a plank surface above her with thick joists holding it to the foundation and to the planks running under the floor. There were copper water pipes running along above her, and a couple of thick ceramic drainpipes coming down from above to join the main drains that ran underground to the sewers.

The woman was crawling away from the foundation now, and Ronnie followed. They kept going until they reached a spot where the ground seemed to drop off. Ronnie peered over the edge, not quite able to make out much until the woman lowered herself into a small room, like a concrete box about ten feet on a side.

Ronnie lowered herself down beside her. There were a hot-water heater, a nest of telephone wires and cables, and a set of wooden steps leading up to a door. The woman whispered, "I'm Nicole."

"Ronnie." She held out her hand, but the woman ignored it.

"What we've got to do is go up there, step out, and clear the house to be sure they're all outside. I'll go right out the door, and you go left. Then we'll move together toward the front door to clear the house. You know how to do that, don't you?"

"Yes," said Ronnie. She had been feeling dazed at the sudden appearance of this woman—or sudden reappearance. Nicole was definitely the woman who had been on the video recordings planting the bomb in the house in Burbank. She was carrying an MP5, roughly the kind of rifle that had been fired at Ronnie and Sid in the night attacks. It occurred to Ronnie that she could put her Glock to the woman's head and handcuff her right now. But this Nicole had just pulled Ronnie out of a cross fire. And there were dozens of people upstairs who wanted them both dead.

The woman patted Ronnie's shoulder. "Ready?"

"Ready."

Nicole went up first and stood with her feet on the top step while Ronnie climbed up beside her. Nicole slowly turned the knob, and then, in one motion, pushed the door out and sprang out after it. She dashed to the right and Ronnie went to the left. Ronnie saw no targets—no movement, no human shapes. She waited, her weapon aimed up the hall toward the front of the house while Nicole checked the kitchen behind her.

When Nicole came up beside her, they stepped forward together, moving from room to room, making sure nobody was left in the house. They returned to the living room. It was a large, open space with windows at intervals. Nicole crouched at the nearest window, reached around the black-out curtain and unlatched it, then slid it open. She knelt to the side of the window and moved the curtain a half inch to look out along the barrel of her weapon.

Ronnie opened the window across the room from the woman's, so she could see the driveway and the orchard, the last spots where Sid had been.

There was another burst of automatic fire outside the house, and a moment later, five shots from a pistol. Ronnie swept the curtain aside and looked for a target, but saw nothing. She held her pistol ready, looking from side to side for a target.

Another burst of fire came from somewhere near the cars parked in front of the house. Nicole leaned out with her rifle and fired a burst out the front window toward the cars, and then ducked back in. Shots pounded against the front of the house, and others punched the curtains on Nicole's window inward.

Ronnie ran for the next side window, looked out, but still saw nothing. There was automatic fire, and she fired five shots at the muzzle flash, and then ducked back. Shots exploded through the window, and pounded the bricks outside.

Nicole said, "Try not to shoot my husband. He's big— taller and heavier than the thieves. He's wearing a black outfit like mine. Okay?"

"I know what he looks like," said Ronnie.

Nicole froze, staring at her.

"I know you too," said Ronnie. "You missed some of the cameras in that house in Burbank."

"What are you planning to do?"

"Same as you—try to keep my husband alive." Ronnie peered out the window at the dark yard.

Outside, at the rear of the house, Gavrilo kept low and hurried along behind the row of parked cars. He had his Scorpion strapped to his back because his hands were full. One of the intruders had shot Srdan and Tomislav from the orchard next door, and he had come upon them near the front corner of the garage. Gavrilo had taken Srdan's pack and stripped off the vest Tomislav had on. The vest had about fifteen pockets, and each was filled with money or diamonds. The vest was a bit tight for Gavrilo and constricted his movements, especially with one backpack over each shoulder. When he had come upon the body of Jelena, he had taken her shoulder bag too. He tried the door of the first car, but it was locked. He tried the next, and it was unlocked, but he couldn't find the keys.

The plan had been to leave each of the cars with its keys on the seat, so where were the keys? He bent low, felt around on the floor in front of the seat, and ran his hand between the seats, but the keys were not there. He moved a few steps farther, burdened by the bulk of his own backpack and the extra packs and bags he had taken from his fallen friends. At least one of the cars had to have keys in it. The next car had to be the one.

He stepped to the passenger side to keep away from the line of fire, and he could see the car keys in the ignition. He slipped the first pack off one shoulder, the next off the other shoulder, and he felt lighter. Then he slipped off Jelena's shoulder bag, opened the back door, and set them all on the backseat. He had gotten used to Tomislav's vest, but if he was going to try to drive anywhere, he knew it wasn't a good idea to wear it. He straightened to take it off. As he got the vest off, he heard something behind him. He turned and saw a tall man he didn't recognize. He pulled the sling of his Scorpion submachine to bring it down from his back to his hands, but before he could aim it, the man's shot hit him in the chest.

As he fell against the car, he looked up at the tall, muscular American. For a second he wondered about the man. Did American police officers use silencers? And then he died, leaning against the car.

Ronnie and Nicole crouched in the living room. There were more shots, all of them high, just above the level of the bricks, piercing the wall and peppering the opposite wall above their heads.

Ronnie said, "You know this house, don't you? Is it yours?"

Nicole said nothing.

Ronnie said, "Just answer one question. Why did James Ballantine die?"

"Who's that?"

"The black guy in the storm sewer. You were hired to keep us away from that case."

"I don't know everything. I heard that he was dating one of the women. He figured out that she was somebody who had a lot of money and a lot of secrets. Maybe he knew what she was—that she was a jewel thief. He tried to boss her around and make her give him money. She didn't like it, so she killed him."

"Where is she? Do you know?"

"No. I don't know any of them," Nicole said.

"That will have to be good enough. I've got to get out there now and help my husband."

Ronnie rose to her feet and stepped through the back door, off the steps to the ground. She dashed in the direction where Sid had been, along the side of the orchard. She saw him break from cover. She felt relief and fear in the same instant. He was alive, but what was he doing?

As Sid came over the fence, he saw her, stopped with his gun in both hands, and aimed ahead to cover her. When she caught up they ran around to the front of the house.

At the front of the house was chaos. There were bodies on the ground, and people running to get into the waiting cars. In the distance they could hear sirens. Sid sensed motion behind him and turned his head, but what he saw didn't make sense. A large man was carrying five bundles—three backpacks and a couple of shoulder bags slung over his shoulders. He climbed into the big pickup truck. A second later a blond woman dashed up from the other side and threw herself into the passenger seat. Sid raised his weapon to aim, but Ronnie held his arm and said, "Not them. I promised."

There was a wail and then the whoop of a siren at the far end of Quillivray Way. The two people in the pickup truck ducked their heads below the windows. Two of the panthers' SUVs at the curb pulled out, swung around, and roared off. The first three police cars to reach 2995 kept going, speeding after them.

When he'd ducked down, the man in the black pickup truck seemed to have noticed the popped lock and loose wires on the steering column. The starter motor kicked in, the engine started, and he sat up and pulled out of the driveway. He turned the first corner as though he were trying to chase the police cars, and disappeared.

Sid and Ronnie hurried toward the first of the men lying on the front lawn. Sid knelt beside him to see if he was alive while Ronnie stepped to the next person. Another group of police cars arrived, lighting up the houses along the street with flashing red and blue lights and glaring white spotlights.

It was in that second that the explosives in the house went off. Even as Ronnie was thrown off her feet to the ground, she knew that Nicole had done this. Nicole had come out of the basement first so she would have a moment while Ronnie could not see her. She had turned right toward the kitchen.

As Ronnie sat up, she saw that a fire had begun behind the open windows, and watched it rapidly flare up and begin to devour the house. The kitchen, Ronnie reminded herself. Nicole had probably pulled a pipe bomb out of her ammo bag and placed it behind the stove, where the gas would catch and help the fire spread quickly. This had been Nicole's house, and she'd known exactly how to obliterate it.

"Are you okay?" It was Sid.

She nodded and got up on one knee. Sid waved his arm at the paramedics, pointed, and called out, "This man is alive."

He said to Ronnie, "Come on. We should give the paramedics room to work." He helped Ronnie up and began to guide her toward the street.

Ronnie said, "I know what happened to him."

"Who?"

"Ballantine. Mira killed him. Tomorrow we can write our report and get paid. Then I want to go and see Janice, and then Mitch. When that's done, I don't know. I guess we can go rent a house while we rebuild ours. I'm sick of hotels."

# 33

Outside the suite at Many Glacier Hotel in Glacier National Park in Montana, Nicole Hoyt sat on the balcony and looked at Swiftcurrent Lake and beyond it, at the jagged mountain peaks and pine forests. It all looked to her like a picture puzzle, the thousand-piece kind she had loved as a kid. It occurred to her it was possible that she'd seen exactly what she was looking at now in one of the puzzles. Just north of here was Waterton Lakes National Park, and that was in Canada, but looking out at a stretch of woods in a bunch of mountains didn't tell her where the line was. She supposed that was the point of being here.

Ed came out of the shower and tromped around the room with his towel hanging from his neck.

"I might remind you that the drapes are open."

"I don't mind," he said. "I'm not shy."

"Walking around naked like that, people might think you're a bear and take a shot at you."

"Wouldn't be the first time, and won't be the last."

"If they hit your fat ass, that would be a first," she said.

Ed went back into the bathroom.

Nicole came inside and slid the curtains across the window, then followed him in. She watched him unscrew the top of her lotion bottle and pour a pile of loose diamonds out onto the counter.

"Stop playing with those things," she said. "You lose one in the room, and we'll have FBI agents following us forever."

"I keep looking at them because I still can't believe we did it. If we got this many, just think how many there must have been," he said. "And these are good ones, the big kind, the best."

"Right," said Nicole. "We're really, really rich. Before, we were just rich."

"It's not like I'm having one made into a diamond pinky ring."

"No," she said. "We're going to put them all in safe-deposit boxes for the next few years, remember?"

"Right," he said.

"Maybe the next hundred years."

"Nice to know we have them, though."

She nodded. "And I'm done."

"What?" He looked at her in the mirror.

"I'm giving you notice, Ed. I quit."

"Quit what? Me?"

Nicole stared into the mirror at him. "No, dumbhead. I want to have babies, and I need you for that. We've pushed our luck way beyond the limit. I don't want to do this stuff anymore. From now on if I hear a sound in the night, I want to be pretty sure it's not somebody coming to kill me because of something I did. It'll take me years, but I'll wait it out."

Ed's brow furrowed. He stared into the bathroom mirror into her eyes, but he didn't speak. She waited, thinking of all of the possible things that could happen in another second, feeling the time going by, bringing something hurtling toward her that was now beyond her control.

"Spit it out," she said.

"Where do you think we should live?"

"Anyplace where I'll never run into Ronnie Abel again."

Todor stood beside Anica and Dragan at the rail of the cruise ship *Empress of the Waves* while crew members in crisp white uniforms scurried along the walkways preparing the ship to dock at the port of Cartagena. He looked past them at the other passengers along the railing staring down at the dock or gazing out at the city. He could see Marija, Anton, Sonja, and at least twenty members of their circle without even trying. He said in Serbian, "Well, now we'll have another try in a new country. It's amazing that so many made it out of that place. I'm never going back there. The whole country is inhabited by criminals." Anica and Dragan looked at each other for a second, but said nothing to contradict him.

Read on for an excerpt
from Thomas Perry's next thriller
*The Old Man*

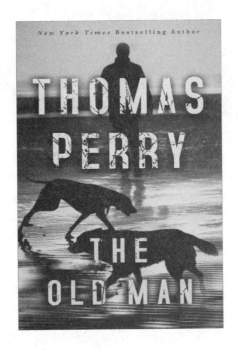

Available January 2017 in hardcover and ebook

# 1

"An old man should have a dog." Dan Chase's daughter had told him that ten years ago, after his wife died. The part that surprised him was the term "old man." He had just turned fifty then. But he supposed she was only giving him advance notice, time to get used to the idea and find a suitable dog. After a man's wife died, he had to do something not to die too.

After decades taking responsibility for a wife, then a daughter, then her husband and sons too, he woke up one morning and realized that the conditions he had been accustomed to seeing as permanent had changed. He was no longer at the center of things. After his wife died the house had gone silent. It wasn't the hearth where the clan gathered for warmth and sustenance anymore. It was just a solitary man's place.

The dogs were looking at him expectantly right now. He opened the door and the two big mutts, Dave and Carol, slipped out ahead of him into the yard, already galloping, a pair of black streaks. They always charged across the five hundred feet of yard to the back fence, their bodies elongated as they bounded along. When they reached the fence they stopped and trotted around the perimeter, patrolling. When they'd made one circuit and found nothing to pursue, they made one more circuit sniffing the ground before they returned to Dan Chase, hoping for an assignment.

After he had taken his daughter's advice he found there was much he remembered about dogs from when he was a boy. All dogs wanted to be good dogs, no matter how unpromising they seemed. You just had to help them find a way. And they were sunshine creatures. When their master opened his eyes in the morning it was their signal that the day had begun, and a day was to be greeted with joy and intense interest. They were a good example for an old man.

Chase started to walk and the two big dogs fell in beside him to skirt the side of the house to get to the gate. The two dogs were on his right at the moment, but they constantly changed positions, maintaining an orbit around him as he went. He opened the gate and, as always, they squeezed their sleek, muscular bodies through the opening ahead of him.

Dan Chase wore a pair of short leashes hanging from his neck, so if he saw a stranger walking toward him he could snap the leashes on Dave and Carol's collars. Even a person who loved dogs didn't necessarily want to meet two hairy, black eighty-pound beasts running free before he'd been introduced to them. Dave and Carol didn't mind. The big thing was to be out and going somewhere with Dan Chase.

Every day the three walked four or five miles, and did their errands on the way. About once a week Chase would take the car out, just to be sure the battery was charged and the oil got on the parts, but the rest of the time they walked. The walk was usually silent, except when they ran into somebody that Chase wanted to talk to, and there were some occasions when he spoke to the dogs. He had never believed in telling them what to do unless he had to, so the dogs generally got along by doing what Chase did. But when he did speak to them they stopped, their ears perked up, their heads turned, and their sharp, intent eyes focused on him.

Dave and Carol had been from the same litter, acquired together by animal control. The volunteer told him their mother had been a cross between a black Labrador and a standard poodle, but the father was something unknown. Nobody knew what he was except that he must have been bigger and hairier. Chase couldn't bear to split them up, so he didn't. When his daughter came to visit after he'd brought them home from the pound, she said, "Oh, Jesus. That's not the kind of dog I meant. Look at their feet. They're going to grow up big."

"I like big dogs," he said. "They're calmer and quieter. It's scared dogs that bite."

"I don't know," she said. "You really want to have two animals that could kill you? You're—"

"An old man. A stiff breeze could kill me."

"You know what I mean."

"I do," he said. "It's just another reason to make sure they never want to."

His relationship with Dave and Carol had worked that way, over time. This morning the three made their way along Norwich's Main Street past a succession of white clapboard houses and a couple of restaurants and hotels to the bridge over the Connecticut River that led to Hanover, New Hampshire. They were having a gentle early spring this year, after a winter that had hit early and held on, and kept most inhabitants of northern New England defending small areas of warmth for days at a time and going out only because there was somebody paying them to do it.

As Chase and his dogs stepped onto the bridge, Chase looked out over the river. Today the dark water was higher than yesterday, swelled by the early spring melt. The sun had been shining fairly steadily for a few days, and he judged that the big pockets of snow in the high places had begun to yield.

The first sign that something was wrong came just beyond the end of the bridge on the New Hampshire side. Chase's ears were attuned to the sounds of his world, and one of the sounds was the movement of cars. He had gotten used to the steady passage of cars across the long, narrow concrete bridge, about one every five seconds, going between twenty-five and thirty-five miles an hour, the sound approaching first from over his left shoulder, and then turning to a *whish* as it came abreast of him, and then fading far ahead. This vehicle came off the bridge just after he did and was moving much more slowly than cars usually did. Chase looked up the slight incline in the road ahead of him to detect a reason for a car to slow. The road ahead was clear, but the car drifted along on his left side, hanging behind him as he walked.

Chase pivoted to the right and walked up between the riverbank and the first house. The two dogs seemed to hesitate behind him, but he said quietly, "Come on." So they did. He didn't look back, but took out his cell phone and touched the camera symbol, held up the phone as though to take a shot of the river, but aimed it over his shoulder toward the car. He took a shot, and then hit the video symbol and kept the phone in his hand with his arm down at his side, pointing the lens behind him as he went.

Dave and Carol were happy enough to resume their walk, and in a moment the rhythm of car sounds was restored, with cars going up the incline toward Wheelock Street at the usual rate.

He looked at the picture he had taken. The shot was badly framed and at an angle, but the car was clear. It was a silver compact car, something like a Subaru Impreza. For the past few years those things had become as common as pigeons all over New England because they were cheap and had good traction on snow and ice.

His view of the driver's face was blocked by the car's roof. The one thing Chase could see from his high angle was the passenger seat, which had a lone object lying on it. Was that what it looked like? He squinted and stared, but he could think of nothing else it could be. It had to be a toy, a replica, or the real thing.

A part of his mind that he had kept dormant for a long time awakened. He changed his plan. The best time to walk back across the bridge was now, while the driver was still headed in the other direction and would have to turn around on a side street to follow. When that happened Chase wanted to be on the right side of the car where the driver couldn't shoot him easily. He muttered, "Come." Then he swung both arms to signal the dogs, trotted quickly across road, and headed back across the bridge.

When they returned to the Vermont side of the river, he moved off Main Street. If this person knew Chase was in Norwich, he or she would certainly know where he lived. He would be much safer if he got there first. He picked up his pace and cut across a couple of unfenced backyards and down an alley that led to the gravel parking lot behind the Norwich Inn.

Chase had not been ready. He had stayed here in this peaceful corner of the country for too long. When he came to the area he had bought guns and ammunition and hidden them in his house, his car, and his garage. But he hadn't carried one in ten years. There had been no sign of danger, and he had been out of sight for so long by then. He admitted to himself that what had ended the habit had been Anna's death. She had always been the one to remind him to stick a pistol into his coat before he went out. After she died he had not been very interested in protecting what was left of his life.

Chase's eyes and ears were now alert and sensitive, evaluating every sight and sound, trying to pick up anything that didn't belong, anything that had changed. He reminded himself that he couldn't be sure that there was anything to detect. A car had followed him across a bridge, its driver apparently slowing to look at him or the dogs. This might be nothing.

As Chase and the dogs moved along the paths and shortcuts toward his house, he checked the streets for the silver car. He was careful to check the parking lot in front of Dan and Whit's Country Store. The Congregational Church's lot was visible across the green, and it was empty.

He reached the final block before his house and headed along the fence to the side opening near the back door. The dogs surged ahead of him and sniffed the ground, zigzagging as they did when following an invisible trail. Chase left them at it and stepped into his garage. He had placed a .45 Colt

Commander under the seat of the car the day he bought it, and a second one in the spare tire bay under the floor of the trunk. The gun weighed thirty-six ounces and held only seven rounds, but there had been times when he'd bet his life that it would fire them all smoothly and accurately, and he was still aboveground. He took the pistol from under the seat and hid it beneath his coat.

When he emerged from the garage he saw that Dave and Carol were agitated, rushing to the distant fence and running back across the yard to the steps. Maybe someone had been here in their absence, and they resented the incursion. He stood with his back to the clapboards of the house and the gun in his belt under his jacket, waiting to see. After a short time, the dogs settled down. Whoever they had sensed must be gone. He put his hand on the gun and walked to the front steps. He looked in the window, and then opened the back door without stepping into the opening. There was no sound of feet sidestepping for a better angle. No shot. "Okay," he said, and the dogs leapt up on the porch and moved inside.

When Dave and Carol trotted across the floor, stopped on opposite sides of their big water bowl, and began to lap up the water, he let go of the gun. If anybody had been in the house, the dogs would have sniffed the air and gone to hunt for him.

Chase walked through the house, verifying that nothing had been changed or touched. He was almost certain this was unnecessary, but he had gotten lazy and irresponsible lately, so he made the extra effort. When he first moved to town he had taken lots of precautions, but over the years he had not bothered to stay ready.

Apparently today had been a false alarm, possibly even his subconscious producing a chimera to startle him into doing what he should. But he knew the real thing would seem just about as subtle and innocuous. Someone he didn't know would show an interest in him. But once the attack started, it would be loud and fast. Maybe today had been a blessing, a harmless event reminding him to make some corrections.

He patted the two dogs, gave them each a biscuit, and went to check on his preparations. He walked to the closet in one of the spare bedrooms where he kept his escape kit, opened the backpack, and looked inside. The money was there—ten thousand in US hundreds, another five thousand in Canadian hundreds, and ten thousand euros. The two guns were Beretta Nanos, and each was accompanied by four spare magazines full of 9mm rounds.

The three wallets contained the necessary credit cards and licenses for three different identities—Henry Dixon of Los Angeles, Peter Caldwell of Chicago, and Alan Spencer of Toronto. He had American passports for Dixon and Caldwell, and a Canadian passport for Spencer. The expiration dates on the cards were well spread out, and he checked and verified that he had not been inattentive enough to let any of the credit cards expire. He had known he could count on the companies to keep sending new cards. The companies paid themselves from bank accounts he'd held in those names for twenty-five years or more.

He went to the next hiding place in the small attic at the peak of the house, opened a box of Christmas ornaments, and pulled out the second kit, which included more money and female identities with the same surnames as the men.

The photographs on the cards were of Anna. He took this second kit down to the spare bedroom with him.

He had three prepaid burner cell phones in his kit with the batteries removed. He plugged one of them into the surge suppressor under the bed to recharge the battery and stowed the others. He started to take the kit he'd made for Anna out of the room to throw it away, but then changed his mind. He took the contents of Anna's pack and added it to his pack. If he ever needed a kit at all it would be dangerous to leave anything here that revealed his next surnames. He and Anna used to call the packs bugout kits, because they were only to be used if they ever had to bug out—abandon their home and escape. The kit contained everything either of them would need to start over again somewhere else.

He let Dave and Carol out into the backyard again. Usually around this time they liked to have him throw a ball so they could race after it, but today none of them felt like playing. Instead, the dogs followed him as he walked around the yard looking for footprints, signs that the fence had been scuffed when someone had climbed it, or other indications that anyone had been there. The dogs could still be funny and puppyish when they felt like it, but today they were serious, even solemn. They stayed close, staring up at him now and then with their big, liquid eyes, as though to read his thoughts.

Chase spent the rest of the day watching for signs that never came, and making up for his neglected preparations. He checked and engaged all the locks on doors and windows and tested the alarm system. He spent a few minutes in the garage tying a piece of monofilament fishing line to a pair of tin cans from his recycling bin, and then tying another piece to the necks of two bottles.

They all had dinner at the usual time, and then the dogs went out while Chase did the dishes and cleaned up. After they came in he engaged the alarm and watched television for a while, keeping the volume very low so he or the dogs would hear any unusual sounds. At 11:30 p.m. after the weather report he took the dogs to bed. As usual, Dave and Carol jumped up and lay on the left side of the bed, nearest to the door.

When they were settled, Chase went to the end of the hallway that led from the kitchen and set up the two cans connected by the transparent fishing line. Then he did the same with the bottles at the beginning of the bedroom hall-way. He was fairly sure the electronic alarm system would function well enough, but he knew making his own would help him sleep better.

It was nearly 3:00 a.m. when the clatter of tin cans broke the silence. He opened his eyes, and the dogs both lifted their heads from the bedcovers. Chase could see in silhou-ette that their heads were both turned toward the doorway, and their ears were pointed forward.

Dave launched himself off the bed. There was a heavy thud as his forepaws hit the hardwood, and then rapid scratching sounds as he accelerated down the hallway. Carol leapt after him, adding to the *scrit-scrit* of toenails down the hall.

Dan Chase was on his feet in a second, stepping into his pants. He picked up the Colt Commander and the flashlight from his nightstand and followed. He paused at the end of the hallway, leaned forward to let one eye show at the corner, but saw only dark shapes in motion. He turned on his flashlight in time to see Dave barrel into a man at the far end of the room and begin to growl.

The man went down, but he punched and kicked at Dave, trying to get the dog's jaw to open and release his arm.

"Lie still!" Chase shouted, and switched on the overhead lights. "Don't fight them."

Then the man had a gun in his hand, and Chase could see it had a long silencer attached to the barrel. The silencer was the man's enemy, because the extra eight inches made it too long for him to turn it around to fire into the dog. He managed to get it close, but the twisted arm gave Carol her opening. She ducked in beside Dave and bit.

This time the man was in trouble. Soon Carol was tearing at his shoulder, working her way up toward his throat. He knew it, and he struggled harder, using the unwieldy pistol to hammer at the dogs.

"*Lasst ihn los*," said Chase. He aimed his gun at the man's torso.

The dogs released their jaws. The man hesitated.

"One chance," Chase called. "How are you going to use it?"

The man rolled to his side and got off a shot that went past Chase's ear. Within a half second Chase's shot pounded into the man's chest and he dropped the gun and lay still.

Chase had to do many things in a short time, so his movements were fast and efficient. He kicked the man's pistol a few feet away in case the man was alive. He patted each of the dogs while he ran his hand over them to see if they were hurt, and he spoke to them softly. "Dave, Carol. You're very, very good dogs. Thank you, my friends." They would probably be bruised, but there was no blood, and neither of them flinched at his touch. They licked his face as he knelt to check on the man.

The man on the floor had dark hair and olive skin. He was about thirty years old, with a widow's peak that showed he would have been bald in a few years if he had not come here tonight. Chase had never seen him before, unless he was the one in the silver Subaru.

There was no pulse at the man's carotid artery. The bullet hole in the chest was in the right position to go through the heart. The blood was draining under him from the exit wound, not being pumped out. Chase felt for a wallet, but found nothing in the man's pockets except a spare magazine for the pistol and a knife with a four-inch blade—not even a set of car keys. The lack of identification wasn't entirely a surprise. A man they'd send after Dan Chase would be one who could only succeed or die, because if he were caught he'd be more dangerous than Chase. Of course he had no phone, but Chase wasted a few seconds searching again for one.

Chase went to the upstairs closet for his escape kit, added the phones, took the pack outside, and hung it on a nail in the shed so it would be hard to distinguish from his fishing gear and the oars and motor for the aluminum boat turned over in the yard. On the way back he searched for the silver Subaru, but he didn't see it.

He went inside through the kitchen door, took the cans and bottles outside, disconnected the fishing line, and threw them in the recycling bin, picked up the phone, and dialed 9-1-1.

"Nine one one. What's your emergency?"

"This is Dan Chase at Ninety-two Neville Street in Norwich. A man just broke into my house with a gun, and woke up my dogs. He fired at me, so I shot him. He hasn't got a pulse."

"Please stay on the line, Mr. Chase. Help will be there in a few minutes."

"All right. Tell them there's no need for sirens. No use waking everybody in town." He stood in the kitchen with the phone to his ear for a moment until the dogs came in and sat on their haunches staring at him.

He cradled the phone on his shoulder while he opened the cookie jar and took out two dog treats and let their big jaws take them. He pulled out two more and bestowed those too, so the dogs would know that he appreciated them. All dogs wanted to do a good job.

Through the window he saw the flash of red and blue lights on the trees beside the house. Chase prepared himself for the next part. There would be a lot of talk. Then he and his dogs would go.

# 2

The police were about the way he'd expected them to be in this situation. A man who had owned a home in town for nineteen years, paid taxes, and lived without afflicting his neighbors was awakened by his dogs when an armed man broke into his house tonight. The armed man fired a round at the home owner, who shot him through the heart. The cops took the victim's statement, dusted the house for fingerprints, took photographs, and bagged the obvious stuff—both weapons, the ejected brass casings, and the bullet the attacker fired into the woodwork. Before the body was removed, they expressed the opinion that what had happened was unfortunate, but not very far out of the ordinary as home robberies went.

The only part that Chase regretted a little was not removing the silencer from the shooter's pistol. Having a silencer seemed unburglar-like to him, and sure as hell would make some cop scratch his head. The saving fact was that although silencers were illegal in Vermont, the house was half a mile from New Hampshire, where anybody who wanted a silencer could pay two hundred bucks for the federal transfer tax and have one.

The police had been sympathetic, and they hadn't even told him not to leave town. They would probably think of that in a day or two, but they wouldn't call him before midday tomorrow because he was a local man who'd had a shock and lost half a night's sleep. They would not be too far wrong, but right now the crime victim was driving at seventy-five miles an hour southbound down Interstate 89.

He took out the first of the prepaid cell phones and dialed his daughter Emily's number.

"Hello?" Her voice was raspy. She must be in bed stretching to reach the phone.

"Hi, kid. It's me. I'm really sorry to call at this hour. But it's finally happened. One of them found me at the house, so I'm on the road."

"Are you bringing the dogs to me?"

"Maybe eventually. Right now, no. Dave and Carol have been through a lot tonight. I think they need time with me before I do anything like that. Come to think of it, so do I."

"Jesus, Dad."

"I know, honey. I only called so you wouldn't think they got me or something. I can't help what's already happened. You'll be all right. There's nothing in the house that links me to you. No papers, no pictures, and to the extent I can accomplish it no prints of yours or DNA. I always clean the place after you leave. I'm going to be able to hold on to this phone a few more days, but no more than a week. If you need me, call it. Here's the number."

"I can see it on my screen."

"Oh, yeah."

"I hate this," she said. "I hate it, and it never had to happen."

"We're not sure yet if anything did happen."

"You just said it happened. I assume there's a dead man in your house?"

"They moved him pretty quickly. This happened in Vermont, honey. It was a slow night."

"Right. But it happened," she said.

"I'm sorry. But you're out of this mess and free from it. I'm glad."

"What bullshit. Nobody who loves anybody is ever free from anything."

"I meant you to be."

"I know you did. So now I have more money than a princess, only I'm still afraid to spend it, and my father is on a cell phone on a highway bullshitting me because he thinks he might not get to talk to me again."

"It probably won't be that bad."

"I hope not. But don't take any chances. If you have to, you can rent a motel room and leave the dogs in it, and I'll be there to pick them up as soon as a human being can take a plane there. If you're with them, I'll take all three of you."

"I've never doubted it," he said. He drove in silence for a few seconds.

"You're awfully quiet," she said.

"I'm really sorry."

"I get that," she said. "I've always gotten that."

"It doesn't hurt to repeat it."

"Yes it does. It all hurts."

"I guess you've got to get ready for work, don't you?"

"Yes."

"I love you."

"Obviously. And I love you. Call when you can."

He slipped the phone into his pocket and kept driving. As he drove, he listened to the deep, nasal snores of Dave and Carol, who were asleep together on the backseat.